DEATH OF A RANCHER'S DAUGHTER

#2 IN THE LADY LAWYER MYSTERIES

SUSAN P. BAKER

WWW.SUSANPBAKER.COM

DEATH OF A RANCHER'S DAUGHTER

NO. 2 IN THE LADY LAWYER MYSTERIES

Copyright © 2020 by Susan P. Baker

ISBN-13: 978-0-9980390-1-5

ISBN-10 0-9980390-1-2

Interior formatting & design and cover design by Laurie Barboza (Design Stash Books) DesignStashBooks@gmail.com

Produced in the United States of America.

For information and/or permission to use excerpts, contact:

Refugio Press
P.O. Box 3937
Galveston, TX 77552.

Books by Susan P. Baker

Novels:

My First Murder, No. 1 in the Mavis Davis Mystery Series
P.I. Mavis uncovers corruption deep in the heart of Texas while searching for the murderer of a mysterious woman.

The Sweet Scent of Murder, No. 2 in the Mavis Davis Mystery Series
When her search for a missing teenager turns to murder, Mavis discovers disgusting details about a Houston River Oaks' family.

Murder and Madness, No. 3 in the Mavis Davis Mystery Series
To fulfill a dying woman's wish, Mavis plunges headfirst into the Galveston island investigation of a grisly ax murder.

Death of a Prince, No. 1 in the Lady Lawyer Series
Mother & daughter criminal defense lawyers defend the alleged murderer of a millionaire plaintiffs' attorney in Galveston, Texas.

Death of a Rancher's Daughter, No. 2 in the Lady Lawyer Series

Ledbetter Street, A Novel of Second Chances
With the deck stacked against her, a Galveston mother fights the court system for guardianship of her autistic son.

Suggestion of Death
A father who can't pay his child support investigates the mysterious deaths of deadbeat dads in the Texas Hill Country.

Texas Style Justice
Faced with life altering decisions, an ambitious Texas Hill Country judge must determine what price she is willing to pay to reach her ultimate goal of being appointed to the Supreme Court.

UNAWARE, A Suspense Novel
Galveston, Texas Attorney Dena Armstrong is about to break out from under the two controlling men in her life, unaware that a stranger has other plans for her.

Nonfiction:

Heart of Divorce Advice from a Judge
Divorce advice especially for those who are considering representing themselves.

Murdered Judges of the 20th Century
True stories of judges killed in America.

www.susanpbaker.com

DEDICATION

For Zoe, our science lover

CONTENTS

ACKNOWLEDGMENTS

Without going into lengthy particulars about all the assistance I've received with this novel over the long years it's been in the works, through fits and starts, before, during, and after other novels I've published, I would like to express my appreciation for/to the following people:

Irene Amiet, Laurie Barboza, Paul Heinrich, Mike Hennen, Gary Hoffman, Lou MacBeth, Dan McKeithan, Phyllis Moore, Richard Peake, Megan Reyna, Saralyn J. Richard, Kathy Sanford, Lynne Streeter, Lisa Windsor.

Additionally, there are folks, whose names I don't even remember, who provided insight when I first began this novel years ago. If you ever read this and you remember it, thank you, too!

If I've left anyone off, I beg your forgiveness.

CHAPTER ONE

THE TIME HAD come to break the news.

Sandra had waited for the perfect time to tell her law partner-mother she was quitting, but her plans had gone awry. On her way to the office, she had worked up the courage, but just as she arrived, Erma drove off and didn't return until after lunch. Then, Erma had an appointment with a new client. Now, finally, Sandra just had to wait for Erma to finish a phone call.

Ever since the appalling Stuart-thing had happened, Sandra had been depressed. She'd been wallowing in self-pity for too long. She'd made the decision to move away from Galveston, make a clean break. She'd been offered a job in Houston at an insurance firm, where they promised she'd never have to litigate.

She could buy a place midway between the two cities so she would be within thirty-minutes of her job in downtown Houston and thirty-minutes from her daughter, Melinda. Exercising her periods of possession would be fairly easy. Now, she just needed to get past a showdown with her mother. Sandra might be a forty-something, but the anticipation of a battle with Erma still created a great deal of angst.

While she waited, Sandra went into the kitchen for more coffee, hoping the caffeine would keep her wits sharp. She pulled her suit jacket tight and buttoned it against the draft. On the south side, the kitchen opened onto the back porch that led to the parking area and was often colder than the other rooms in their house-office, even when a north wind blew.

Erma, dressed in her standard black pantsuit but in her stockinged feet, sped around the corner from the sunroom. She all but skidded to a stop next to the dinette table.

"You're off the phone," Sandra said. "Good. There's something I need to talk to you about."

"I need to talk to you, too, and right now." Erma's hands hung by her sides, her stance a familiar one, as if she were about to engage in gun battle.

Did Erma know about the job in Houston? No. She would have come in yelling. Erma could have her say, but Sandra was still going to break the news about her job prospect. "Damn, let me finish pouring my coffee, will you?"

"Just hurry up and come into my office." Erma stalked back the way she'd come.

As soon as she filled her cup, Sandra stepped into their legal secretary's office. "Hey, Patricia, I'll be with Erma."

Patricia looked up from her computer. "Raining pretty hard out there. Hope Mel will be okay."

"I'm sure she'll be fine. She's pretty good at taking care of herself." Sandra shivered, still feeling a bit of a chill. "Everything going okay here?"

Patricia's eyes grew wide, as if she knew Sandra was procrastinating. "Yeah. Everything okay with you?" Not waiting for an answer, Patricia turned back to her computer.

Sandra drew a deep breath, her heart palpitating, and strode into Erma's office, where she dropped into one of the client chairs. Erma stared into space. "I'm here," Sandra said. "What's so important?"

A box of tissues sat at Erma's elbow, some of them in a clump on her desk. "Katy Jo Schindler is dead."

Sandra racked her brain. The name was familiar.

"She was murdered."

"Oh," Sandra said. "Sorry to hear that." She still couldn't place the name. She sipped her coffee and waited for Erma's next words.

"BJ called." Erma tapped her fingers on her desktop.

Another familiar name. Sandra had been so focused on herself, so out of it some days, her thinking was foggy. That was one of the reasons she wanted to make a change. She had turned a corner and was coming out of the doldrums.

"Are you listening to me? Rufina Barboza, BJ's best friend, has been charged with Katy Jo's murder."

"Oh, BJ Schindler." Sandra hadn't thought about the Schindlers in a long time. "Your friend BJ in Fredericksburg, right? And Katy Jo is one of the twins?"

"Goddamn, Sandra. Took you long enough. Yes, my good friend's daughter, Katy Jo, has been murdered."

Sandra nodded, wondering why Erma was telling her this.

"Don't you want to know how Katy Jo died?"

"If you want to tell me."

The front door squeaked, and Mel hollered, her voice reverberating in the tall ceilings. "It's only me."

"Hey, kid," Erma called.

A minute later, Mel tiptoed into Erma's office. "Hey, Grandma. Hey, Mom." She wore a pink sweater over a gray turtleneck, black skinny jeans, and a pair of black socks. Her hair, the same dark shade of brown as her mother's and what had been the color of Erma's before she'd gone gray, was pasted to her head like a rubber-swimming cap. "Before you ask, I left my shoes on the front porch with my umbrella. They're soaked. And I already dumped everything else on my desk." She kissed Erma on the cheek. "How are you today, Grandma?"

"Erma," Erma said. "How many times do I hafta tell you? At fifteen, you're old enough to call me Erma."

Mel scooted over to Sandra and kissed her cheek, too. "I need to dry my hair."

"How's your day been?" Sandra asked, glad to have a distraction from the conversation she and Erma had been having.

"It may be a rainy day, but it's a good day. I got an A on my essay." Mel flashed a smile.

"You're so brilliant, baby girl." Sandra pulled Mel to her for a hug.

"Get this," Sandra said while she still had the gumption to make her announcement. "I've been offered a job in Houston at an insurance defense firm. I'm pretty sure I'm going to take it."

Erma's face paled as she slammed her hand on her desk. "What the hell? Like you would work for any insurance firm—those mean, hateful, greedy bastards. What the hell are you talking about?"

"OMG, Mom." Eyes wide, Mel stared from Erma to Sandra. "You're going to Houston? What about us here?"

"Kid, dry off and go file away the folders on your mother's credenza," Erma said. "Afterward, you can answer the phone for Patricia so she can get some stuff done."

"Wait, I want in on this." Mel glanced at Sandra.

Sandra said, "Go on. We'll talk later." She closed both doors to the office behind Mel and sat back down. "After your heart attack and my fiasco with Stuart, I put some feelers out."

"What in the hell?" Erma said again. She put both hands on her desk and rose. "Are you out of your mind?"

Sandra picked up her cup and took another sip, giving herself time to consider her response. "Erma, you don't need me. You're loaded. You can retire and take it easy."

Erma pounded her desk. "Goddamnit, how many times do I need to tell you, I'm all right? The doctor's given me a clean bill of health."

"What he said was, if you'd stop drinking and smoking—or vaping—whatever you're doing these days, you could live a lot longer. But you're not quitting, and we both know it." She set her cup on the desk and strode around to the other side, sticking her face right up next to Erma's. "I smelled bourbon on your breath as soon as I came in here. I know you've got a stash somewhere. You think no one knows about your drinking?"

Erma pushed her away. "Get out of my face. Just had one little swallow. Was going to take a bit of a nap, if you must know. I thought it would help me doze off."

"Sure you were. We both know you're not taking care of yourself, but that's only half of it. You don't need me even if you want to continue doing a bit of estate work, but I think you should retire, take up painting or something."

"You don't want to work for an insurance firm. You're still depressed, that's all. This winter weather isn't helping any."

"I'm not depressed. I'm over it. I want a change. I don't want to do criminal law anymore."

"Yes, you do. You're great at it. You just gotta get over Stuart. He was an asshole. You're well rid of him." Erma bounded from her chair and started pacing. "Get ahold of yourself. There's no reason to go to work for a blood-sucking insurance firm, especially in Houston. You'd drive up there every day?"

Sandra's neck grew hot. She hated people telling her what to do, especially her mother. "They're going to pay me really well, and I'll have benefits. And, I'm going to move to Clear Lake."

Erma trotted to Sandra's chair and stood over her. "You're out of your effing mind."

If Erma got any closer, Sandra would be tasting the bourbon. In fact, the smell overwhelmed the breathable air. She pushed her away. "I won't have to litigate, and some days I'll even work from home."

Erma heaved a big sigh. She went to the glass-paned doors and peered into the backyard where the cars were parked off the alley. Sandra's eyes followed. The rain had eased up a bit, but deep cloud cover enveloped the island. Drab days certainly didn't help anyone's spirits, much less hers.

"Daughter, you know I've never been good at telling you how I feel, but if you take that job, you'll be making a big mistake."

5

Sandra pressed a knuckle to her lips. Neither of them was great at communicating with the other. Discovering Stuart's double life had taken a toll on Sandra, and Erma knew it. Sandra had renounced men, and she didn't want to do any more criminal defense work. End of story.

"Well, let me ask you this," Erma said. "Have you given them a firm answer?"

Sandra shook her head. "Not yet. Told them I'd get back to them."

"You know what the trouble with you is?" Erma shook her finger at Sandra. "Other than the everyday stuff? I've got it all figured out."

"Oh, great, amateur psychologist."

"Every good lawyer is one, you know." Erma sat down again. "You've lost faith in yourself, in your ability to judge character."

Sandra stared at her mother. A fight was not what she wanted. Fatigue dogged her every day. If she hadn't had Mel, she might have done something drastic, like cut her throat. At least that's what she had thought some days. "It's not that. I'm sick of going to the jail, sick of representing the dregs of society, sick of fighting with the district attorney's office."

"No," Erma said. "That's not your problem."

"I think I know my own mind."

"No, you don't. What would cure you, Sandra, my dear, would be a good, juicy case." Erma smacked her lips. "You've been doing nothing but crappy little cases, pleas of guilty in misdemeanor and felony court, a bit of divorce work. What you need is something you can really sink your teeth into."

"Last week you said what I really needed was to get away from Galveston for a while. If you're such an expert, which is it?"

"How would you like to spend some time in a sweet little historical town in the Texas Hill Country?"

"Uh-oh. I see an ambush coming. You're not suggesting I take a sabbatical from practicing law and spend time in Fredericksburg with BJ, are you?" Sandra stood. "I'm going back to my office. I've got work to do." She gave her mother a dark look. "Loose ends to tie up."

"Sit down, Sandra."

Sandra wanted only to get out of there. She shouldn't have mentioned the job offer. "Why? What now?"

"Just sit down and hear me out about BJ."

Sandra sat back down, her patience thin. "BJ called and told you about Katy Jo dying." Sandra started to get up again.

"Now wait just a minute. About Katy Jo..."

"My recollection of them is coming back. Katy Jo is—was the nice twin, if I recall correctly."

"Right." Erma covered her mouth for a couple of seconds. Her eyes welled up. "BJ wants to hire you to defend Rufina Barboza, because they don't trust the lawyers up there."

"Yeah. No. What? I'm confused." Erma was trying to manipulate her again. Her tears probably weren't sincere. "Rufina is that little Mexican woman BJ grew up with? BJ wants to hire me to defend her?" Not only had she sworn off murder cases, but she'd never liked defending guilty people, even though she knew everyone had a right to representation and all that.

Erma came from behind her desk, comporting herself as she would at the beginning of a jury argument. "She didn't do it. Rufina has been BJ's best friend for about a hundred years. She's been like a second mother to those kids." She clasped her hands behind her back. "Her parents worked on the ranch until they grew old and retired to Mexico. As a favor to BJ and Roy, Rufina left her job at the courthouse and took over running the house and supervising the household workers."

Sandra resisted a variety of negative responses that crossed her mind. "Why me?"

"The thing is, Rufina's scared. She's a little Mexican-American woman raised on a ranch, accused of the death of a rancher's daughter." Erma's lined face grew grimmer. "You can see how it is, can't you? She would be easy prey for the district attorney. She wants someone she can trust."

7

"You need to get your story straight. If she worked in the courthouse, she knows how the courts operate, unless she was a cleaning lady or something like that."

"She was a clerk, and that doesn't mean the DA can't railroad her."

"I haven't seen Rufina since God knows when. She doesn't even know me. Besides, I don't know anyone in the Hill Country. I don't know how they do things up there."

"It's still Texas, isn't it? The same law applies."

"This doesn't make any sense. Why would BJ call down here and ask me to defend her housekeeper or manager or whatever they call her?" She looked cockeyed at Erma. "Oh—wait a minute. Wait just a minute. I see what's going on."

"No, you don't. You don't understand."

"BJ called you for a referral, and you suggested me." Sandra jabbed her finger at Erma. "She doesn't want me at all. BJ called you to get a recommendation for a criminal defense lawyer, and you thought if you could get her to hire me, somehow it would change how I've been feeling."

Erma's face blanched. "No, that's not it. Not at all."

Sandra took her coffee cup and headed for the door. "No way. Your little scheme isn't going to work. You tell her to get someone else and keep me out of it."

"Didn't you hear me? They're looking for someone they can trust." Erma's voice rose two octaves. "That's why she called me."

"No." Sandra flung open the door, sending Patricia scrambling. "I'm not going way up there so you can feel like you've done something to make me feel better." She stalked across the hall to her office.

"Okay, so I haven't been completely honest with you," Erma hollered. She hurried after Sandra. "I'm not trying to make you feel better. BJ is one of my oldest and dearest friends. She called me to defend Rufina, okay? Me." She gripped her jacket's lapels, her chin jutting out. "And when I said I don't try those kinds of cases anymore, she said she'd settle for you—if you were any good."

The room turned a shade of red as Sandra threw herself into her executive chair. Anger burned in her chest. "Settle? She said she'd settle for me? Well, you just call her back—"

"I quoted her a fifty K retainer plus expenses." Erma barricaded herself behind one of Sandra's client chairs.

"I don't care what you quoted her," Sandra said, not looking up from her desk. "You call her back and tell her no. Not now, not ever. Never. And get out of my office."

"But Sandra—"

"End of discussion. I'm never taking another murder case, and you can't make me."

"Okay then, just listen a minute. I told BJ you might not take the case, but here's the thing. The arraignment is on Monday. Rufina at least needs an attorney for the arraignment."

Sandra crossed her arms and shook her head. "I'm not doing it. I'm sure BJ can find a decent enough attorney in the Hill Country. I'll bet there are over a dozen lawyers in San Antonio alone who are certified to try cap murder cases. One of them can run up there for the arraignment. It's only an hour away."

"Did I say cap murder? We don't know if the DA is charging her with capital murder yet, Sandra." The sudden edge in Erma's voice was as sharp as a filet knife. "We won't know that until Monday."

"What is this we? I know you're not talking about me. Anyway, Rufina has to know what she's charged with. They have to serve her with the indictment two days before the arraignment, so she should have gotten it yesterday." Erma couldn't have forgotten a thing like that. She wasn't that old.

"I know that." Erma cleared her throat.

"I'm sure if BJ hires someone up there, they won't let Rufina plead to anything without formal service of the indictment."

Erma stood still and stared at Sandra for a moment. "Well, okay then." She turned back toward her own office.

Sandra had never known her mother to give up that easily. "What does that mean?"

Erma tossed words over her shoulder. "I'll just have to do it myself."

"Are you crazy? You're too old and your heart is too weak for you to drive five or six hours to the Hill Country, much less take on the Fredericksburg County—"

"Gillespie County. Fredericksburg is the town."

"Whatever—DA's office," Sandra finished.

"Actually, I don't think Gillespie County has its own district attorney. I think the district has several counties in it. And anyway, I'm only sixty-eight. I expect to be driving until I'm at least ninety."

"I don't give a shit how old you are, Erma Townley, you're not going up there."

"But I promised—"

"The arraignment is not a crucial event in the grand scheme of things. Rufina can answer not guilty for herself, and the judge will ask her if she can afford to hire a lawyer, and she'll say no, and the judge will probably appoint one right then and there." Sandra's face grew hotter. She needed to calm down, or she'd end up with a heart condition like Erma. "You hear what I'm saying? She doesn't need you."

Erma stormed back to Sandra. "How are you going to stop me?" Her jaw looked like it was set in stone. "I promised my friend, so I'm going, and that's final. I don't care what you say."

"No, you're not." Sandra towered over her mother. Teeth clenched, she stared down into Erma's red face. "And if you have a heart attack right here and now, you'll just prove my point."

Erma tossed her head. "I can get angry without having a heart attack. That's all I am, angry. Stop treating me like an invalid." She stormed toward her office again.

"When was the last time you drove on the Gulf Freeway?" Sandra followed Erma into her office and stood at her back, fists clenched every bit as tight as her teeth. "Traffic has gotten worse than terrible." How did one reason with a determined old broad like her mother? "In fact, when's the last time you had your Lincoln serviced? What are you going to do if your car breaks down on the freeway? You have no emergency assistance set up for your car. Who are you going to call for help?"

"It's not up for discussion." Erma turned and smirked at Sandra again. "Now, as you succinctly told me a few minutes ago, get out."

At a loss for what else to do, Sandra went into her own office and called Erma's doctor. When he came on the line, she said, "Doc, this is Sandra Salinsky. I'm at my wits' end. Erma is determined to drive herself to Fredericksburg and take on a murder case. I can't get her to listen to reason."

A laugh came from the other end of the phone. "She's really going to do it?"

"You knew? You already knew about this?" She couldn't believe her ears. "How did you find out? Did she call you? What's the deal? Why didn't you call me?"

"You know how stubborn Erma can be. She called and asked what I thought as her physician, not as her friend. She said if she couldn't get you to take the case, she'd do it herself."

"You've been her doctor and her friend for over thirty years, and you didn't tell her she couldn't do it?"

"No one can tell Erma anything. I said she could have a heart attack at any time, driving on the highway, walking across the street, or arguing in a courtroom."

"Why is she going? You told her it could kill her, and she's still going."

"Oh, I didn't tell her it could kill her. I simply said any of us could die at any time, that her odds were worse than those of other people. She said she'd rather die doing something she liked than sitting around with her thumb up her—"

"I understand." Sandra wanted to scream. "Couldn't you have told her she couldn't do it? Couldn't you have advised against it?"

"If you're concerned with your mother's health, why not go up there with her? At least drive her, even if you aren't going to take the case."

Sandra sighed. "She's really got me where she wants me, doesn't she?"

No response came from the other end of the phone.

"If I put her on the phone, Doc, will you try to talk her out of it?"

"About five-minutes after she became my patient, I gave up trying to talk her into, or out of, anything."

"Shit." Tears of anger pushed at the back of Sandra's eyes.

"What's the harm in you taking this case?"

"She thinks she can manipulate me with this behavior."

"When it comes down to it, which is more important? Doing what you can to stop her from killing herself? Or winning a battle with your mother?"

"Oh, shut up, Doc," Sandra said.

His laugh wasn't harsh.

"Thanks anyway. Goodbye." Still shaking her head, Sandra stomped back into Erma's office. "All right, you."

"Why are you back?" Erma's lips quivered.

"Here's the deal. We'll both drive up on Sunday evening for the arraignment on Monday. We'll take my Volvo. Any questions?"

"Who's lead counsel?"

"I didn't say I'm representing Rufina in a trial, but I'll announce for her at the arraignment and see what I can do about bail. Afterward, we'll find someone up there BJ can settle for."

Sandra headed back to her office for what she hoped would be the last time that day. When she glanced over her shoulder, Erma had a shit-eating grin on her face. Sandra might have lost the first round, but she still had no intention of taking a murder case in what was tantamount to foreign territory.

CHAPTER TWO

THE SUN HAD long set by the time they arrived at the Dairy Queen in Fredericksburg, where they'd agreed to meet BJ. She sat outside, behind the steering wheel of a monster red pickup. A man sat shotgun.

BJ opened the door to the truck and eased herself down. A willowy woman in her sixties, she had wavy, gray hair barely covering her ears. She wore a black Adirondack barn coat over a black turtleneck sweater and wool pants and thick, brown leather ranch gloves. In the outside fluorescent lighting, her puffy blue eyes sparkled with tears. Her shoulders drooped as she ambled, heavy-footed, toward Sandra's car.

Erma swung out of the Volvo as fast as her little legs could carry her. She wrapped her arms around BJ. They hugged for a good long while, BJ's tall torso swamping Erma's short, chunky one.

The man, who was tall and husky and about BJ's age, judging by his gray sideburns and balding head, walked around the cab and stood by, arms dangling. He wore boots, jeans, a thigh-length tan Sherpa coat buttoned up to his neck, and black gloves. He shrugged when he and Sandra exchanged glances.

Having left her coat in the car, Sandra shivered with cold. They needed to go, get to the jail, and see if the jailer would let her in. Though tired from the long drive, she wanted to at least touch base with Rufina.

After a few moments, Sandra put her hand on Erma's shoulder. "Okay, break it up, ladies." When Erma stepped aside, Sandra gave BJ a brief hug. In spite of BJ's jacket, Sandra could feel how thin BJ was and wondered whether she was eating regularly.

BJ released her and held her at arm's length. "You've grown up to be a beautiful woman, Sandra." She wiped her eyes and nose with a wad of tissues.

"Thanks." Sandra subjected BJ's face to scrutiny. She wouldn't remind her she'd seen her at least a couple of times in the last few decades. "How're you holding up? You've had a traumatic couple of weeks." BJ looked a lot older and grayer than Erma, and they were about the same age. Katy Jo's death had clearly taken its toll. Sandra knew if she lost Mel, she might not ever recover. BJ must feel the same. She had to simply be presenting the best front she knew how.

BJ shook her head and blew her nose. "It's been tough. You don't know how much I appreciate y'all being here."

A flush crept up Sandra's neck. She was glad the dim light concealed the pink overtaking her face. No way she'd look at Erma, in case Erma wore an I-told-you-so sneer. "Glad to do it. But we'd better get going to the jail. I want to see Rufina."

"I'm sorry. I called, and they said it's too late. I even phoned the sheriff—tried to call in a favor—but no dice." Her chin trembled. "You—you can meet with her early in the morning, before they serve breakfast, if you want. The sheriff said he'd tell the jailer."

Sandra glanced at Erma. Small towns.

The man who'd been in the truck with BJ stepped forward and cleared his throat.

"Oh, hell." BJ sighed. "I forgot to introduce you to Elgin Burgess." Her shoulders slumped more, as if to say she couldn't do anything right. "He's an old friend and owns the ranch next over. Elgin, this is Erma Townley and Sandra Salinsky, the lawyers I've been boring you about all day."

Elgin pulled off his glove and shook both their hands. "Delighted to meet you, ladies. BJ didn't bore me a bit. Glad you could come up and help her and Rufina out."

BJ said, "Elgin and Roy were best friends since high school. He's been quite a help to me since Roy passed."

"I'm glad my sweet BJ has had your support, Elgin." Erma's grin spread all the way to her eyes.

"Nice to meet you," Sandra said. She'd been wondering who he was.

"Well, we might as well head out to the ranch," Erma said. "You're going to feed us, right? All I've eaten is a kolache when we stopped for gas in La Grange."

"Oh, sure. The girls have dinner waiting in the kitchen." BJ walked back to her truck. "By the way, watch out for deer in the road."

Elgin opened the driver's side door and gave BJ a hand up. "Follow us. You'll never find it in the dark."

Sandra yawned as she and Erma climbed back inside the Volvo. Six hours was a long time in a car with not much of a break. She really wanted some rest.

"Damn. She looks like shit." Erma pulled a tissue from the glove box and blew her nose. "I don't think she's taking care of herself."

"The stress of a murdered child and a best friend being the accused would make anyone look like shit. I'm surprised she can climb out of bed."

Erma buckled her seat belt. "She's got a ranch to run. Let's go. I'm hoping for a juicy steak."

"You aren't supposed to be eating a lot of beef." Sandra didn't need to see Erma's face to know she wore that smirk again. "You're just messing with me, I know." Sandra buckled up and backed out of the lot and onto the pavement behind BJ.

In a hoarse voice, Erma said, "I am hungry, though."

"Me, too. And I'm tired. And a little anxious about going into a strange courtroom tomorrow."

"Yeah, Sandra. Been a long day."

All Sandra wanted to do was eat and sleep. Soft lighting illuminated the closed shops on Main Street. Another time, she might want to investigate them, find out what they carried that was different from the tourist shops in Galveston. She followed the truck out of town. The streetlights grew dim in the rear-view mirror. Soon cedar brush and a few oaks lined each side of the street. The only lights were the twinkling of a star or two and the lights on the back of BJ's truck. Sandra focused her attention on the winding, hilly, two-lane road.

Her last visit to the ranch had been when she was in high school. The twins, Katy Jo and Kathy Lynn, had been toddlers. The little wispy-haired blondes, who babbled constantly, had to be watched every minute. She especially remembered, because she'd been stuck with them several times when she wanted to go out to the stables.

BJ's son, Rex, had been a babe in arms, no more than a few months old.

Roy, BJ's husband, had seemed like a giant. With muddy boots and worn jeans, he looked like a cowboy right off a television show.

What else did she remember? The horses. A mare Roy let her ride. The house. Enough rooms to get lost in. Some people speaking Spanish. A kitchen with a tall bar where she ate lunch every day, usually by herself.

She had vague memories of an older Latina woman, possibly Rufina's mother.

Now, when they arrived at the ranch, the parts she could make out in the dark looked the same. Two white vehicles sat in the circular drive, one an Expedition and behind it, a truck, an F-150. Sandra parked behind BJ's truck and took out her rolling duffle and their clothing bags. Elgin grabbed Erma's bag. "I'll take this in and head for home, BJ. He dragged Erma's roller bag into the house, while Erma took BJ's arm and walked her inside.

BJ trudged down a long hallway, past a couple of closed doors, and left them at their respective rooms. "You can wash up and meet me in the kitchen. I'll find what the girls fixed."

No sophisticated decorations in the guest room BJ had assigned Sandra. A red and green holiday quilt still covered the bed though the holidays were behind them. Another quilt lay folded at the foot of the bed. Four fluffy pillows rested against the wooden headboard, which had the Texas star in the center. A slipper chair covered with a western print stood in one corner next to a wooden table with a small lamp on it. An aged room-sized Oriental rug covered the dark wood floor. The pictures on the walls all bore a western or country motif.

When Sandra went to put her makeup pouch in the bathroom, she found Erma doing the same. Apparently, they'd be sharing.

"What's up with you?" Erma asked. "You're not saying much."

Sandra shook her head. "Just want to get this over with." She grimaced at the determined set to her mother's mouth, knowing Erma hoped she'd change her mind and take the case. "You want to clear out so I can use the facilities? And I'm too tired to hear any quips about how you used to change my diaper."

A few minutes later, Sandra found her way to the kitchen. Elgin was nowhere to be seen, but a thirty-something, blond guy perched at the oversized, pink-granite island. The kitchen was exactly as she remembered, large enough to prepare meals for a slew of ranch hands.

BJ came in right behind her. "Rex, stand up when a lady enters the room. Come over here and meet attorney Sandra Salinsky."

Rex slid off the bar stool. Taller than he appeared when slumped on the stool, he towered over her and his mother. He held out his hand.

"Pleasure to meet you, Sandy." Deep dimples speared his cheeks when he flashed a smile about a mile wide. His topaz blue eyes were the same shade as BJ's.

17

"Sandra." Sandra shook his hand, his grip strong but not bone-crushing. "You, too." He smelled of a woodsy fragrance, but his breath, like bourbon.

Rex's blond hair had begun to recede. His heart-shaped face bore only a few creases. Sandra tried to remember how old he was. Maybe thirty-five. He was definitely someone women would be drawn to, though his hair might be a bit too yellow to be natural.

Erma pushed Sandra aside. "Come here to your Aunt Erma and give her a big hug." She reached for his hand and pulled him down to her.

Sandra was in no mood for any kind of family reunion. She wanted nothing more than to eat and go to bed. She hoped any mention of the case would be reserved until the next day. She was too tired, and it was too sad. Erma chattered away about how she'd known Rex since he was knee-high to a grasshopper.

"Where's Kathy Lynn?" BJ asked.

Rex wrestled away from Erma and climbed back onto his stool. "Right after you left, she left." He glanced at Erma and Sandra and shrugged. "Sorry, Miss Erma. Guess you'll have to wait until another day."

BJ rubbed her chest. "I'm sorry, y'all. I told her to be here." She made a little grunting noise. "Some other time."

"Yes, some other time." Since Sandra didn't intend to take the case, some other time would be a long time coming.

A highball glass with melting ice cubes and the dregs of amber liquid in the bottom sat on the counter in front of Rex.

"Y'all pull up a stool." BJ opened a huge Sub-Zero refrigerator. She pulled out two plastic-wrapped plates of salad and set them in front of the women. "The girls fixed a little steak salad with raspberry vinaigrette. What do you want to drink?"

"What's he having?" Erma cocked her head at Rex as she wiggled her way up on a stool.

Before Sandra could say anything, BJ laid a hand on Erma's arm. "With your heart condition, you supposed to be drinking?"

"I'm not the one standing there rubbing my chest," Erma said. "Are you okay?"

BJ gave Erma a fake smile. "I'm okay, and you haven't answered my question."

"Two fingers is all, to help me sleep." Erma grabbed a napkin and unrolled it.

Sandra wanted the same but said, "Milk?" She could have said something to Erma but knew it was useless and didn't have the energy for a scene. She reached for a knife and fork from a crock of utensils standing in the center of the island. "Milk will help me sleep." She unwrapped her salad and cut into the strip of beef that lay across a pile of spring greens.

"So which one of you ladies will represent our sweet little housekeeper?" Rex eye-balled first Erma, then Sandra, and tossed back a swallow.

"Rex," BJ's voice sounded like someone reprimanding a little child, "mind your own business." She splashed some bourbon over a couple of ice cubes and pushed it across the bar toward Erma.

"What?" Rex flashed another smile. "Is something wrong with me asking who's going to be Rufina's lawyer?"

"I'll be handling the arraignment tomorrow morning," Sandra said after swallowing her first mouthful of salad, not too bad under the tart raspberry dressing. Did the baby boy intend to try to entertain them? Or would she be able to eat in peace and go to bed?

"You met with her already, right?" Rex asked.

BJ whacked at his arm with the back of her hand. She put a glass down in front of Sandra and turned to her son. "Why don't you go to bed?"

"It's okay, BJ," Sandra said, looking at Rex. "The jail didn't want to let us in, but I'm sure Rufina is a very sweet lady if she's been your mother's best friend for the last sixty years. I'm pretty sure I met her a long time ago. Is that what you're asking?"

"Yeah, but—"

BJ slapped the granite counter. "Enough, Rex. Enough. There's no reason they need to discuss Rufina's case with you."

Sandra cut off a piece of steak and forked some greens with it into her mouth. What was Rex doing at his mother's home, anyway? Why hadn't he flown the nest? Or was he there to visit for the Christmas holidays and hadn't left yet? Long visit. She glanced at Erma again, but Erma sipped from the glass of bourbon and wore a blissful expression, as though the booze had smoothed out her wrinkles. "Erma, eat."

"Want me to drive you to the courthouse tomorrow, Sandra?" Rex sounded eager. "We need to be sure you don't lose your way."

Sandra shook her head. "You're very generous, but I like to drive my own car. I need to go early to meet with Rufina, too." She took another bite, trying to eat enough to be satisfied, so she could leave. "BJ, you're going to come and bring Erma later?"

"The jail is across the parking lot from the courthouse," BJ said. "You won't have trouble finding it. We'll be there before the hearing starts. I can't stand the idea of Rufina facing the judge alone."

"She won't be alone, Mama," Rex said. "There are these ladies. And me. I'll be there, too."

"Shouldn't you be going to work tomorrow?" BJ rubbed her arms like she felt a chill.

Erma said, with a sidelong glance at Sandra, "You really needn't bother yourself, Rex. You go on to work. We'll take care of everything."

Rex threw back the dregs of his drink. "Oh, that's okay. I want to be supportive. After all, Rufina's been a part of our family since I was a little kid."

"She'll have her own cheering gallery." Sandra took her last bite of salad and pushed the remainder away. "I'm going to hit the hay. Exhausted after the long drive." Sliding off the bar stool, she said, "Goodnight," and strode toward their rooms, eager to distance herself from them, particularly Rex.

20

CHAPTER THREE

EARLY MONDAY MORNING, Sandra donned a hooded sweatsuit and jogged around the ranch grounds, careful to avoid mishaps in the dark. Cedar and other earthy scents filled the crisp, cold air. The lack of humidity, so different from Galveston, opened her lungs. She understood why people liked to live in the hills.

After her run, Sandra ventured into the kitchen for breakfast. A Latina, in her late teens or early twenties, nodded and averted her eyes. She wore jeans and a black Mexican peasant blouse and had a flowered apron tied around her waist. *"Café y desayuno?"*

"Coffee and breakfast? *Sí.*" Happy she comprehended at least a bit of Spanish, Sandra slid onto a stool and accepted a cup of coffee. Her stomach roared as she breathed in the aroma of bacon and eggs.

"My name...is Lucia," the younger woman said, pronouncing the word is as *es.* She laid a plate of scrambled eggs and toast in front of Sandra. *"Tocino?"*

"Gracias," Sandra said. "You got me on that last word. If that's bacon or ham, no thanks. *Y mi nombre es* Sandra." She began forking food down fast, hoping she didn't appear ill-mannered. She

wanted to shower and change, before anyone else turned up, and leave in time to have a good conversation with Rufina.

Lucia turned back to the stove, which held enough food for a platoon, including a pot of oatmeal and some grits. Sandra took her plate to Lucia, and the girl smiled her thanks. "*Adios*," Sandra said.

She showered and dressed in a pantsuit and pumps and did her makeup and hair, all with no sign from Erma. Grabbing her coat and briefcase, she thought she was going to escape without seeing anyone. On her way to the door, though, she ran into BJ, who didn't look a bit more rested than she had the night before.

"Good morning," BJ said. "Ready for some coffee?" She wore jeans and a blue work shirt with the sleeves rolled up.

"Already had mine and some eggs, thanks."

"How'd you sleep?" BJ asked as they walked toward the front of the house.

"Fine, and you?" Impatience had a hold on Sandra. She struggled to be polite.

"Oh, I'm one of those rare women who can sleep like a log, even after menopause—not that I can remember that far back," BJ said, her voice monotone.

Sandra didn't want to be rude but also didn't want the time to get away from her. "BJ, court's at nine. Have you heard my mother stirring?"

"Not yet. You can't sit for a spell?" Her eyebrows drew together. "There's something I want to talk to you about."

Sandra shook her head. "I can't right now. I need plenty of time to talk to Rufina. Let's have coffee after the arraignment." She hurried outside and into her car, feeling like she'd temporarily dodged a bullet.

From the house to the highway was more of a trail than a road but easy to follow. The ranch wasn't as far from town as she had thought the night before. A little more than ten-minutes after leaving the ranch, Sandra arrived at the jail. She parked in the small lot between the jail and the courthouse. The Gillespie

County Jail, though a modern facility, looked tiny. That boded well for a county of little towns, assuming it wasn't over-crowded, but she wasn't so sure how good that would be for Rufina. Small town Texans could be small-minded.

After showing her bar card to the deputy behind the bullet-proof glass, she passed through the clanking doors. An inmate mopped the concrete floor, and ammonia pierced her sinuses. The white tiled walls were like all other criminal justice institutions, depressing and dull. A deputy led her to a glassed-in conference room where she waited what felt like an excessively long time for such a small facility.

Rufina, it turned out, wasn't the stereotypical Latina housekeeper Sandra had pictured. Her face—Rufina's face—was difficult to look at. No question she'd been the victim of a fire. If Sandra had known, she'd forgotten. Her stomach compressed like a lemon being squeezed. She struggled not to show her shock, but her lawyer brain immediately logged it. With that face, Rufina would be easy to scapegoat. Studies had shown that jurors generally liked good-looking people better than those who weren't so pretty. Dressed in too-large, drab, blue jail scrubs with the hems rolled up, the tiny woman came only to Sandra's shoulder. Her straight black-and-gray streaked hair, woven into a braid, extended down her back all the way to her waist.

Clearly Rufina'd had some reconstructive surgery but not enough to make her easy on the eyes. Reddish brown waves of skin surrounded one of her black-brown eyes and stretched across one side of her face. Her nose must have been repaired. Though it wasn't beautiful, her nose was far better than scarred holes would have been. Her lips had been worked on as well, though again, they'd never be like the lips she'd been born with. Rather than hair, scarred and exposed skin sprawled across one side of her head up to a reconstructed ear.

Were she to become better acquainted with Rufina, and if Rufina was as sweet as BJ said she was, the injuries would not be a distraction for Sandra. A jury of twelve would be a different story. If they didn't know Rufina, jurors wouldn't be able to look at her. If they couldn't look at her, they wouldn't be able to see her as a person. If they did know her, they'd be struck from the jury *venire*. The defense lawyer's job would be to make Rufina as likable as possible. That would be quite a task even if she were to testify in her own defense.

Sandra steeled herself. "I'm Sandra Salinsky." She shook Rufina's small, damaged hand, thankful she would not be the one who would take the murder case to trial.

"I am so grateful you will take my case, Ms. Salinsky," Rufina said with just a trace of an accent. Full, throaty, and melodious, her voice ran counter to her appearance. She settled her scarred arm on the small table, smiling as best she could, and leaned toward Sandra as if she were afraid someone would overhear them. "I've heard you're a good attorney."

Sandra's cheeks grew warm. "I'm here for the arraignment this morning." She couldn't bring herself to tell Rufina anything more. She wrote *Rufina Barboza* at the top of a yellow legal pad. The overwhelming ammonia vapor caused her eyes to tear up, and she drew a shallow breath. "I only need a few facts for now, okay? What are they charging you with?"

"They say I killed Billie J's daughter, Katy Jo." Her eyes studied Sandra. She clasped her hands in front of her on the table as though she might bow her head to pray.

"Yes, but exactly what are the charges? Better yet, did they serve you with the indictment?" She stopped herself from tapping her pen on the note pad.

"Yes, ma'am. The indictment said I 'intentionally or knowingly caused Katy Jo's death by shooting her with a pistol, to wit: a forty-five-caliber automatic.'"

Sandra reared back, surprised Rufina could quote the indictment so succinctly. "Uh-huh." She made some notes. "Anything else? Was there a second paragraph?"

"No, ma'am. The normal legalese and nothing else. I have never even been arrested before, much less convicted of a crime. There is nothing to enhance the charge with."

"Well, that's something anyway." Erma had said Rufina had worked in the courthouse. She might have said as a clerk. "How is it you're so familiar with the law?"

There was that smile again. Rufina's eyes crinkled.

"I was a deputy clerk in the District Clerk's Office for many years."

Sandra whacked the table. "I knew that. Here in Fredericksburg?"

"No, ma'am. Mason County."

"Before we go any further, Rufina, would you mind, please, dropping the ma'am? You're older than I am. Call me Sandra."

Rufina glanced briefly into her lap. "Yes. Okay."

"So you were saying where you worked?"

"In the next county over, about forty minutes north. I'm friends with the clerks here. We used to sit together at conferences, and I went to high school with one of them."

"Excuse me, but you left a job in the District Clerk's Office to become a housekeeper? I mean, didn't Mason County provide you with insurance and retirement and other benefits?" Sandra reined in her bouncing knee. She caught herself rapping her pen on the paper. Though eager to get into the courthouse, she had to observe some formalities, not to mention common courtesy.

"Do you really want to know all this?" Rufina's eyes roved over Sandra's face as if she could read what was going on in Sandra's mind.

"I need to know a bit about you if I'm going to argue for bail after the arraignment."

"I understand, Ms.—Sandra. If you are going to defend me, you will need to know all about me."

Again, Sandra couldn't meet Rufina's eyes. She could kill Erma for putting her in this position. "Just a brief overview for now." She licked her lips and swallowed, her mouth and throat dry.

"I went to work for the district clerk in Mason County right out of high school. I worked there almost thirty years."

"How old are you?"

"Sixty-eight, same as Billie J. We grew up together. My father and mother worked on the ranch. She gave birth to me there. My mother became housekeeper when Consuela, the housekeeper before her, died. My parents worked on the ranch all their lives." Rufina's hands clasped and unclasped and twisted and turned as she spoke. "When my mother and father got to a certain age, they moved back to *San Miguel de Allende* where they came from. Billie J tried several women, but none worked out. They stole from her. They could not handle the job. She asked me to come and manage the house. She's my friend, so I agreed."

Sandra scribbled a summary of Rufina's story on her legal pad. "Very helpful, thanks. So I can tell the judge you've lived on the ranch for several years?"

"I grew up on the ranch. My husband, he worked on the ranch. We lived in one of the cottages. When my husband died in the fire that caused all this," her hand swept her face and body, "Billie J built me another cottage to live in."

The back of Sandra's neck tingled. She gritted her teeth and swallowed. Curiosity about the fire threatened to take over the conversation, but she glanced at her watch. Not enough time to delve into it, not that it was relevant to the allegations. She cleared her throat. "All right. I think I know how close you are to BJ."

"And the children. I would never hurt the children."

Their eyes met. Sandra's heart pounded. She felt sorry for Rufina but couldn't let herself get involved. Determined to give up criminal defense work, Sandra was going home to Galveston the next day to pack up her office and move to Houston. "You don't have any idea what the police say your motive was, do you?"

Rufina shook her head. "I don't know of any reason they might think I would hurt Katy Jo."

"Okay. That's enough information for now. The arraignment's at nine, right?"

"Yes. The courthouse is right across the street from the parking lot. You had to drive past it to park."

Sandra stood. "I'll find it." She held out her hand. "*Mucho gusto.*"

Rufina took Sandra's hand. "You speak Spanish?"

"Enough to say nice to meet you and ask where the bathroom is. And to order *cerveza*, oh, and breakfast. But I'm learning."

"*Mucho gusto*, Sandra." Rufina pointed to the conference room door. "You must go back out the way you came, so they can buzz you through. *Hasta luego.*"

"See you later." Sandra nodded and with a couple of strides, exited the little room and arrived at the control booth. She looked back through the small window in the conference room door. Rufina sat as she had earlier, with her hands clasped on the table in front of her, but this time she had bowed her head.

CHAPTER FOUR

THE DEPUTY HIT the switches that let Sandra out into the lobby, where she found Erma and BJ huddled on a wooden bench like two schoolgirls, deep in conversation. Both of them wore dark pantsuits, coats, scarves, gloves, and sensible lace-up shoes. "What are y'all doing here?" Sandra put on her coat and glanced through the control booth window and into the conference room. Rufina still sat at the table, her head bowed, and her hands clasped.

"How is she?" Worry lines creased BJ's leathered face. She took Sandra's elbow, escorting her across the lobby and out the door into the chilled air.

"She's fine. Very nice lady." Sandra glanced back at Erma, who followed as fast as her short legs could carry her. Had Erma deliberately not told Sandra about Rufina's injuries? Or had Sandra known and forgotten? They had plenty to talk about on the drive back to Galveston.

"You don't remember Rufina from when you were a child, do you?" BJ asked when they reached the sidewalk. The bare branches of an enormous pecan tree threw shadows on the ground.

Sandra shook her head. "Should I?" Pecan shells littered the sidewalk from the fall crop and cracked as they walked over them to the parking lot.

"Yeah, I guess not. You weren't practicing law with your mother when Rufina and I went down to see her about Roy's estate. I believe you were with the district attorney's office." They reached their vehicles. "Anyway, did you figure out what they've charged her with?"

"Murder, not capital murder. You could have asked her. Not that it matters for today, but do you know what the basis is for the charge?" Rufina had seemed harmless.

"They say they found the gun outside her cottage, like she dropped it when she was running away." BJ shook her head. "I don't believe it, but they don't care what I think."

"There's got to be more than that. Why didn't you tell me she'd worked in the courts for so many years?" And why hadn't she told her about the burns? Sandra pressed the remote on her key fob and unlocked the Volvo. She retrieved her briefcase and relocked the car.

"I told you she worked at the courthouse," Erma said.

Sandra slid her legal pad into her briefcase and started for the limestone building, which held the court and clerk's office. "I didn't realize she worked as a court clerk."

Erma shrugged. "It just didn't sink in the other day when we discussed things."

"Everything's happened so fast." BJ turned to Erma who was breathing hard. "I thought you told Sandra all about the family."

"Nah. She may be my daughter and law partner, but we're not glued at the hip." Erma hooked BJ's arm in hers. "Let's go to court and see what's cookin'."

"Over there's the library." BJ pointed to a historical building. "Supposed to become the courthouse but never did."

They entered the back door of an ugly building and climbed two sets of Texas pink granite stairs. The air inside wasn't much warmer than outside. Sandra slipped her unencumbered hand into her coat pocket. BJ led them to the courtroom. Outside in the hallway, a few people milled about.

BJ said, "It's still early. Let's wait on the bench at the far end across from the Ladies Room."

They headed away from the courtroom. Erma said, "I'm going to the john. Be right back."

BJ sat down and pointed to the bench next to her. "I want to talk to you." She removed her gloves and loosened her scarf.

"Has Erma been talking about me?" First chance she got, Sandra was going to kill Mrs. Bigmouth. She set her briefcase down and buttoned her coat. "Isn't there any heat in this building?"

BJ laid her warm hand on Sandra's. "She tells me you only came up here to do the arraignment, that you won't represent Rufina. Mind telling me why? Is it the money?" BJ's general demeanor, her watery eyes and soft voice, made her plea appealing.

Sandra recognized the emotions behind BJ's words. This wasn't the first time she'd been faced with this response to rejecting a case. She would have preferred telling BJ on her way out of town or even calling her after they returned to Galveston. That might have been the chicken way out, but it would have been the easiest. Looking into BJ's bloodshot eyes and feeling the slight pressure of her hand made Sandra want to please this motherly woman. "I don't know what all Erma told you."

"I'd like to hear it from you."

Sandra squared her shoulders. There was no avoiding BJ's eyes, glinting from welled-up tears one moment, filled with determination the next. "Well—it's lots of things. Not the money, but to preempt my cases in Galveston with this one—who would take care of things down there while I'm up here for motion hearings and all? And if Rufina isn't going to plead out, there'll be a trial. Erma can't handle the office by herself in spite of what she thinks."

BJ withdrew her hand. "Rufina is definitely not pleading guilty." She crossed her arms. "She didn't shoot my daughter.

30

She never would have done that. Erma says you have friends, and y'all cover for each other all the time."

"It would be an awful lot to ask of someone, especially if the trial is a long one." Sandra sighed. "Besides, I have a daughter. I've been trying to spend more time with her lately. I won't bore you with the details, but I've been trying to improve our relationship."

"You could bring her up here if you have to come on weekends." BJ's face lit up. "Or, say, how about over her spring break? She could swim and ride. And next summer, same, same. I mean the trial wouldn't be for a while, right?"

The muscles in Sandra's neck tightened. She rolled her shoulders back. "I don't know. I don't know how they do things up here. Probably not." She shifted on the bench and glanced over BJ's shoulder at the door to the ladies' room. Why didn't Erma keep her fat mouth shut?

BJ grabbed Sandra's forearm. "I would work with you, Sandra, provide you with whatever you need, an investigator, staff."

Sandra brushed her hair off her forehead. Saying no was so hard. "Why can't you just hire someone local?"

"You don't understand. Roy, well he was a great man, but he made a lot of enemies."

"What's Roy got to do with Rufina?"

"Let me be blunt with you, Sandra."

"Please do." Where was Erma?

"I don't know who I can trust in this town. This is how it is." Her eyes ventured toward the other end of the hall. "Besides Roy making enemies when he was on the Commissioners' Court for so long, there are people here who don't like, and have never liked, the fact that Rufina is my best friend."

"Because . . ."

"I'm white, and she's not."

"You're shitting me."

"I kid you not. You've got to understand these small-town people. There's only been one Latino elected to office here, and that was recently, not that a lot have run for office, but still . . ."

"So you think that would make a difference—you think if you hired a local attorney to represent Rufina that would make a difference in the kind of representation she got?"

BJ nodded. "I'm convinced a local lawyer wouldn't do as good a job as someone who doesn't live here."

"Aren't there any Latino lawyers here?"

"Criminal lawyers? You're kidding. They'd starve to death. The whites wouldn't hire them. Most Latinos don't make a lot of money, so they couldn't pay a lawyer much."

Erma may have been right when she called it Podunk Junction. "Still, BJ, what about the surrounding counties?"

"Same. Did Rufina tell you she ran for district clerk in Mason County and was soundly defeated? You can be an employee, but you can't be the boss."

"What about San Antonio or Kerrville or Austin?" Sandra rubbed her forehead and glanced at the ladies' room door again.

"But why not you, Sandra? You can do it and not knowing anyone here would work to your advantage." BJ inched a little closer.

"Well, to be perfectly honest—a phrase which I abhor—I'm quitting criminal defense work."

"Erma said you're not serious. She said you'd get over it. Said you're too good a lawyer to throw it all away, and that insurance companies are blood-suckers." She raised her eyebrows. "Did I get that right?"

Sandra clenched her jaw. "To put it in the vernacular." She could see she needed to make at least a temporary concession just to get out of the conversation. "I'll think about it, but I'm not promising anything. I'll just think about it."

"Think about what?" Erma's voice rang out like a mission bell.

BJ glanced at Sandra who had stood up. "Representing Rufina."

"Oh, that," Erma said.

"We need to go down there," Sandra said. "We'll talk about this later." She gave Erma the stink eye.

A number of people sat on benches outside the courtroom or stood in twos and threes. The lawyers were easy to pick out by their apparel—suits—and their race—Caucasian.

Erma and BJ followed Sandra into the courtroom where there were a few more people. The temperature, if anything, was even lower. "Y'all have a seat." Sandra left her briefcase on the counsel table and walked to the front of the courtroom, which was traditional, but outdated. A wall furnace rattled and smelled like something dead was burning. Two wide counsel tables with thin, wiry microphones centered in them and a couple of chairs each, crowded the area in front of the bar. The jury box sat under windows overlooking the parking lot. Worn spots in the tile floor showed where lawyers traditionally did their posturing.

The court reporter didn't really have a station, not even a shelf for her materials between herself and the public. She sat in front of, and to the right of, the bench. Sandra handed her a business card. "I'm Sandra Salinsky, appearing for Rufina Barboza at the arraignment."

They shook hands and the reporter said, "LuAnn Steadman." She was so short that when she stood, Sandra thought she had not yet gotten up.

"What's the routine?"

"This week there's a visiting judge. He calls the docket first and disposes of the easy cases," LuAnn said. "You may as well take a seat. It'll be awhile. Unless you want to go back there and meet the judge."

"Sure." Couldn't hurt to be introduced before the hearing. Sandra pulled another card from her shoulder bag and followed the reporter not twenty steps to the judge's tiny chambers, where a white man in a black robe sat at a small metal desk. He slipped a pen between the pages of a file and stood.

"Judge, this is Mrs. Salinsky, an attorney from Galveston."

Sandra didn't bother to correct LuAnn about her marital status. She held out her hand. "Good morning, Judge."

"Jay Jefferson." He shook her hand with his massive warm one. "Galveston. Not been there in years. What brings you to these parts?" He had cheeks like a cherub, white-blond hair, and bushy white eyebrows and mustache. He stood only a bit taller than Sandra but had a broad body.

"Arraignment on Rufina Barboza."

He nodded. "Nasty business. Have you conferred with the district attorney yet?"

"No, Your Honor. Haven't met him."

"LuAnn, take her out in the hall, and find Mr. Holt."

"Yes, sir." LuAnn stepped outside.

"Thank you, sir," Sandra said.

"Be with you in a little while, Mrs. Salinsky. Pleasure meeting you." He sat back down, dismissing her.

As Sandra passed back through the courtroom, she shrugged at BJ and Erma and followed LuAnn into the hallway, through double doors to the right of the District Clerk's Office and into a large break room. People had gathered around a coffee pot, which filled the air with an aroma far more pleasing than what the courtroom furnace spewed. LuAnn approached a medium-tall white man dressed in a patterned, long-sleeved shirt under suspenders, dark gray slacks, and black western boots. He was speaking with a uniformed Texas Ranger with a gray Stetson under his arm.

"Excuse me, Mr. Holt." LuAnn touched his elbow. "The judge asked me to introduce you to someone."

Holt turned to Sandra. While not as grim looking as her nemesis in Galveston, the glint in Holt's dark brown eyes set her on edge when he flashed a smile and held out his hand. "You are?"

"Sandra Salinsky." She didn't hesitate to put her hand in his. Shaking hands with one's opponent was customary.

Holt cupped Sandra's hand with both of his, as though she were a long-lost friend. "Samuel Holt. Pleased to meet you."

Sandra pulled her hand away. "Could we step into the hall, Mr. Holt?" She nodded at the ranger and turned toward the door.

34

Before scooting back through the doors leading to the hall, LuAnn's eyes met Sandra's and flared for no more than a millisecond. What was behind LuAnn's almost imperceptible bit of body language?

Once outside in the hall, Sandra said, "I'm here for Rufina Barboza's arraignment."

He stepped back and crossed his arms. "The Mexican maid who killed the Schindler twin."

Sandra blinked twice and maintained her composure. Did he really say that? Like most prosecutors she knew, and she'd known a fair number having worked in a DA's office, he'd already tried, convicted, and sentenced Rufina. "Allegedly, Mr. Holt. Allegedly killed Katy Jo Schindler."

"Yes, of course." He rocked on the balls of his feet and ran his thumbs up and down his suspenders like he was nothing but a good old country boy. His breath was like the inside of a coffee urn in need of a scrubbing. He wore his dark brown hair a bit long with a lock dangling almost down to his left eye. His glasses were oversized square black frames. He had a dark stubble beard and a heavier mustache. "So you're a lawyer?"

"Yes. I'm representing Mrs. Barboza in the arraignment and wondered if we could talk about bail."

"No bail, Mrs.—"

"Ms. Salinsky. Bail is standard in any given murder case, so what's the problem?"

"Flight risk. Don't want to lose her to Mexico."

Sandra cocked an eyebrow. "She's an American citizen. As the prosecutor, you already know that."

He shrugged. "I'm not agreeing to any bail. You don't like it, go to the judge."

"That's exactly what I'll do today." Her neck had heated up. Why did all district attorneys desire to achieve perfect assholedom?

"We'll see about that," Holt said.

"What do you mean?" Sandra tried to think of happier times. Pleasant thoughts were the only way to contain herself when she got pissed off, like sipping wine while sitting on her balcony, enjoying the view of the Gulf.

"Nothing, Mrs. Salinsky." He slurped from his coffee cup, his eyes never leaving her face.

She mentally shook herself to get back to the present. "Ms. And I don't understand why you won't agree to a reasonable amount of bail. All defendants are entitled to bail. In Galveston, a murder defendant can easily get a couple of hundred thousand."

"Well this ain't Galveston, Houston, or even San Antonio. You're in Gillespie County, and in Gillespie County, we don't let our capital murder defendants make bail."

Sandra gritted her teeth and made her best effort to retain her cool. "What are you talking about? The indictment says murder."

"We're fixin' to re-indict her. The Grand Jury's meeting now."

"I don't get it. How is it cap murder? It was a shooting, right?"

Holt laughed. "You've been talking to the defendant. Should have come to me first. Retaliation, my dear. Retaliation makes it capital murder."

Her heart lurched. This was the first she'd heard of a retaliation charge. "No one has said anything about retaliation. You want to clue me in?"

"You met your client this morning, I hear. Surely you saw her face."

Sandra frowned, her eyebrows drawing together. What did Rufina's looks have to do with anything?

"Obviously, no one's told you. Guess you don't know Katy Jo Schindler was responsible for the fire that killed Mrs. Barboza's husband and scarred her for life. She finally got her revenge."

Now it was Sandra's turn to step back. She couldn't believe her ears. "You'll never get a conviction on that, Holt."

"If you think so, little lady, you'd better go back to the big city where you came from and let a real attorney handle this case." He wadded up his cardboard coffee cup and sank it into a trash can across from where they stood.

So, the cocky district attorney thought the case would be a slam dunk? Sandra's face burned with anger as she headed back into the courtroom. The circumstances of the murder, the interview with Rufina, and BJ's plea had all left her with mixed feelings. Now, as much as she'd never intended to involve herself in Rufina's case, after everything she'd seen and heard since they'd arrived the night before, she changed her mind. The insurance firm that had offered her the job in Houston would just have to wait. She was all in for Rufina Barboza.

CHAPTER FIVE

❝THIS IS ONE of the ugliest goddamn courtrooms I have ever seen," Erma said when she and BJ approached the first row of benches behind the bar. "See that filthy wall furnace. I didn't know anyplace used those things anymore." She'd have been all over the County Commissioners to get off some money for a new one had that been a courtroom in Galveston.

BJ shrugged. "You gotta understand. They don't want to waste resources on a room that's not occupied that often. There are four counties in this district. There's not a judge here every week."

"You're defending it because Roy was one of those tight-fisted County Commissioners." Erma swiped her hand over the place on the bench where she intended to sit.

"Remember you're in Fredericksburg, Erma." Rex slid across the seat behind them. "This ain't the big city." He hung his elbows over the back of their bench.

Erma had an urge to tell Rex to go jump in the Pedernales River. He'd been annoying ever since the evening before. BJ shook her head and ignored him.

"Uh oh, here comes trouble." Sandra looked fired-up enough to launch a rocket.

"What is it? What's wrong?" BJ's eyes followed Erma's.

"Somebody's pissed Sandra off. Steam is practically coming out of her ears."

Sandra stalked to the counsel table and opened her briefcase. Several other lawyers sat there.

"How can you tell?" BJ asked. "She looks just like she did when she left a few minutes ago."

"Her walk. You can tell by her stride and that fixed smile. She's fit to be tied about something."

Sandra slammed her pen and legal pad onto the table.

"All rise," the court reporter said.

The judge entered the courtroom and positioned himself in his chair. "Be seated."

A man and a woman came from the same doorway as Sandra. Erma scrutinized them. Which of them had set her off? The two of them sat at the other table.

"That's not the regular judge," BJ whispered. "I don't know this one."

"Appears agreeable enough. At least he's smiling under that mustache," Erma said. "But with judges, you sure as hell can't go on appearances."

"Listen up while I call the docket." The judge began to recite cause numbers and names, just like in any other courtroom in the State. Lawyers stood and answered for their clients, proving up uncontested divorces as the judge reached them.

Sandra sat, back rigid, arms crossed. Erma wanted to find out what had happened, but she couldn't talk to Sandra until the judge called a recess.

"Keller v. Keller," the judge said.

An attractive young woman, wearing a flowered dress and carrying a black wool coat, stood. She'd been sitting down the pew from Erma. "I'm Mrs. Keller, Judge, but my uh—attorney hasn't shown up yet."

"We'll hold on that. Go see if your lawyer called the clerk."

"Yes, sir." She scooted in front of Erma and BJ to get to the aisle.

After the civil cases, the judge said, "We'll take ten-minutes while the deputies bring in the defendants." He stepped off the bench.

As soon as the judge exited and several attorneys left, Sandra bounded out of her chair to get to Erma and BJ.

"What's up with you?" Erma asked when Sandra opened her mouth to speak.

"BJ," Sandra said, "you didn't tell me how Rufina got burned."

BJ's forehead crinkled, and she stood. "What's that got to do with anything? It was a long time ago."

"The district attorney, a man named Sam Holt, is saying Rufina killed Katy Jo in retaliation for setting the fire."

"Oh, shit." Erma craned her neck to watch the two women's faces. She stood and stretched, so she could be in on the conversation.

"So they—whoever they are—are saying she wanted revenge? Oh, my God." BJ's voice echoed.

"Keep your voice down," Sandra whispered. "See that ruddy-looking fellow in the gray wool suit? That's the DA, Holt, a real sexist pig."

"You know him?" Erma asked BJ, thinking it might help if BJ spoke to the man.

BJ shook her head. "I think he lives in Kerrville. He's got all four counties in the district to take care of."

"Yeah." Rex leaned about as far forward as anyone could over the back of the bench seat in front of him. "He lives in Kerrville."

BJ shot Rex a look that said you-keep-out-of-this and turned her back on him.

"Shit," Erma said again. "What a mess."

Sandra whispered, "BJ, he's going to charge her with capital murder."

40

"Murder plus retaliation?" Erma closed her eyes and shook her head.

"Equals cap murder." Sandra tapped her pen on the bar that separated them.

Tears overflowed BJ's eyes. "My poor friend." She sank down on the bench.

The side door to the courtroom opened, and Rufina entered, hands cuffed in front of her. A deputy sheriff with a shotgun and a string of male prisoners followed Rufina into the room. Dressed in identical shapeless blue jumpsuits and shackled together by chains on their ankles, they shuffled forward. A second deputy, his hand resting on the butt of his unstrapped, holstered pistol, brought up the rear. They hadn't linked Rufina's chains to the men's. With her facial scarring and still wearing the over-sized drab blue jumpsuit, she was pitiful. Large slides engulfed her tiny feet. She lifted her hands in acknowledgment. A wan smile passed over her face like a shadow.

"Just look at the guns those deputies have. They don't mess around in this part of the country," Erma said.

After the inmates sat in the jury box, Rufina glanced their way again. BJ dug in her purse and brought out some tissues, which she used to mop her eyes. Erma wrapped an arm around BJ's shoulders. She held back her own tears. She didn't know what the hell had come over her in the last few days, tearing up several times like she had. "Try to hold yourself together."

Sandra spoke to the nearest deputy. A moment later, she rounded the jury box and whispered behind her hand to Rufina for several minutes. Rufina's eyes darted from Sandra to BJ and Erma and back again. Erma thought she would die if she didn't find out what they were talking about. She wanted to ignore courtroom decorum and run across the room, but BJ needed her to stay by her side. Rufina's head bobbed up and down in response to something. She took Sandra's hand between her own cuffed ones and smiled up into her face.

Erma said, "Whatever Sandra just said must be good. Rufina smiled."

Sandra remained by Rufina's side until the judge returned.

"Are there any other civil matters ready before I call the criminal docket?" the judge asked.

An old bald man stood. "I have another divorce case."

The young woman, Mrs. Keller, who had left the courtroom to call her lawyer, sat on the back row. She raised her hand.

"Y'all come forward."

The judge conferred with both people for a few moments. The old lawyer beckoned to someone in the audience. Mrs. Keller, whose face had turned a dark pink, stepped aside. A short, gray-haired woman went up front where she and the old bald man began her divorce proceedings.

Erma sighed. Behind her hand she whispered to BJ. "This is the worst goddamned part of going to court, waiting for other cases to get over."

BJ nodded. Erma clasped her hand.

After the judge granted the divorce and the lawyer and his client departed, Mrs. Keller stepped up. She raised her hand for the oath. He began asking her questions. Did she have a copy of her petition? Did she bring a document to read from to prove up her divorce? He handed the court's file to her and crossed his arms, leaning back in the huge, brown, cracked-leather chair. With shaking hands, the woman thumbed through the pages and glanced at the door as if she expected the cavalry to arrive. Finally, she began reading but not from the correct paper. The judge never said a word. Erma had an inclination to help the girl and rose to her feet, prepared to approach the bench, when Sandra sprang out of her chair.

"Your Honor, I could speed things up if you'll allow me to assist the petitioner." Sandra gave the lawyers at the other table a withering glance.

"Certainly, Mrs. Salinsky."

"That's my girl," Erma muttered. "She may not always show it, but she's got a heart in her chest someplace."

Sandra took the file from the woman and directed her to sit in the witness box. "Let the record show that respondent signed a waiver, which was filed on or about October fifteenth."

Sandra ran through the formalities and proved up the case in a matter of minutes. She conferred with the young woman, went back to her briefcase and retrieved a card, which she handed to her, and gave the file back to the judge.

"You may step down, Mrs. Keller," the judge said. "Tell your lawyer to bring in your decree by Friday."

"Yes, sir. Thank you," Mrs. Keller replied.

The judge pronounced the divorce, and the young woman left the courtroom. He handed the file to the clerk and took up the criminal docket. Sandra twisted in her chair and shook her head at Erma, who wasn't sure what Sandra meant by that. The deputies unlocked the chains around the defendants' ankles. The judge began calling names from a list. The prisoner would climb out of the jury box to stand before the bench with his lawyer. The judge would recite a litany of legalese. If there wasn't an attorney representing the defendant, the judge would go through a routine of appointing an attorney.

When he came to the end of the men, he called Rufina's name. Erma elbowed BJ.

The deputy took Rufina by the arm and escorted her to stand in front of the judge. The man Sandra had pointed out as the DA stood. "State's ready."

Sandra positioned herself between Sam Holt and Rufina. "Sandra Salinsky for Mrs. Barboza, Your Honor."

Erma whispered to BJ, "Rufina resembles a Lilliputian next to Sandra, especially with Sandra wearing those three-inch heels."

The judge said, "Mrs. Barboza, the State of Texas has charged you with murder. How do you plead to that, guilty or not guilty?"

Before Rufina could speak, Holt said, "Judge, if I may, we're re-indicting her for capital murder."

"By that you mean—"

"Your Honor, right now my client is only indicted for murder." Sandra's voice echoed throughout the bare-walled courtroom. "She's entitled to be arraigned on that charge."

Holt stepped toward the bench. "Your Honor, we have new evidence that we're taking before the Grand Jury this week. I'd like to postpone the arraignment until the indictment is handed down."

Erma could tell from Sandra's stiff posture and clenched fists that her temper was barely in check.

Rex leaned forward again and whispered in Erma's ear. "She's really pissed, huh?"

BJ shushed him and waved him back.

Not to be outdone, Sandra took a giant step forward. "Your Honor, she's not indicted on capital murder yet. We're ready to enter a plea."

The judge turned to Holt. "When do you think the Grand Jury will have the new indictment, Mr. Holt?"

"Any day, Judge. Perhaps even today." He rocked on the balls of his feet and clicked his ballpoint pen.

"Judge?" Sandra flexed her hands by her side. "We still stand ready to enter our plea."

The judge glanced from Sandra to Holt. "You can't know for sure what the Grand Jury will do, Mr. Holt."

"No, Your Honor. But my case is straightforward. The defendant shot a young girl to death out of revenge."

"Your Honor," Sandra said. "Are we litigating this case today? Is this Mr. Holt's opening statement? I was under the impression we were here for the arraignment."

Erma cringed. No judge liked to hear that tone in an attorney. She hoped Sandra wouldn't piss off the judge before things barely got started.

"I can do without your sarcasm, Mrs. Salinsky."

"Sorry, Judge. We'd like to enter a plea and get bail set."

"I understand. How do you plead, Mrs. Barboza, to murder?"

Rufina glanced up at Sandra who nodded. "Not guilty, sir."

"Your Honor, the State requests no bail be set for fear this woman will flee to Mexico." Holt wore a smug expression.

"Judge, my client has lived in Gillespie County all her life. She's not going anywhere. She's entitled to a fair bail. Also, could you set the trial date today?"

BJ drew a sharp breath and grabbed Erma's arm. Erma sprang up and sat back down. Had Sandra really asked the judge to set the case for trial? What the hell had gotten into her? When had she changed her mind?

"Shit," Rex spit out and slammed his hand on the wooden frame.

The judge's face screwed up, and he shook his head in Rex's direction.

Feeling like she'd been shot with adrenaline, Erma scooted past BJ, pushed through the swinging door that divided the courtroom, and hurried to Sandra's side.

The judge's face turned sour. "Who are you?"

"She's my co-counsel in this case, Judge Jefferson." Sandra rested her hand on Erma's shoulder. "Erma Townley. She'll be second chair at the trial."

Erma took a deep breath and puffed out her chest. When the DA leaned forward to get a glimpse of her, she cocked an eyebrow at him. She wanted to slap his smirk to the wall but would settle for one of her darkest looks, usually reserved for hostile witnesses.

"Well, I'm not prepared to set this case. You have to go through the court administrator in Kerrville. The clerk will give you ladies that number. Get yourselves a copy of the local rules while you're here."

Holt cleared his throat and spread his feet apart like a soldier at ease. "Judge, we can be ready quickly on this one. Just need the new indictment—"

"Mr. Holt, you know how things work around here. Don't do any grandstanding for my benefit."

"What about bail, Judge Jefferson?" Sandra asked.

"We oppose it, Judge," Holt said.

The judge shook his head and huffed out a breath. "I'm assigned here all week." He thumbed through several sheets of paper stapled together. "We'll have a hearing at nine a.m. tomorrow morning."

"What about today, Your Honor?" Sandra asked. "Could you squeeze it in this afternoon after lunch?"

"Tomorrow at nine or call the administrator. Which would you prefer, Mrs. Salinsky?"

Erma tapped her lips. Sandra would bust a gusset if she didn't calm down. Erma put a hand on the small of Sandra's back. "Thank you, Judge. We'll be back tomorrow morning."

Sandra glared at her, but Erma turned on her heel and winked at BJ. She didn't know what had gotten into Sandra, but she loved it. Now they could go back to the ranch and celebrate at least a small win. The first major hurdle of the case was over. Sandra was in, and that was all that mattered for now.

CHAPTER SIX

SANDRA CROSSED THE hall to the District Clerk's Office, Erma close on her heels. Two ladies glanced at them from their desks. One of them stood, an apple-cheeked brunette. "May I help you?"

"We've been hired to defend a murder case and wanted to meet y'all while we're here today," Erma said, barely able to rest her arms on the tall counter.

"Excuse us a moment." Sandra tugged on Erma's arm and led her out into the hall far from anyone who might overhear them.

"What? What?" Erma asked, jerking her arm away.

Sandra's stomach hadn't settled down from the churning she'd felt in the courtroom. She held a ballpoint in her hand and clicked it like Holt had done and stared down at her mother. "Let's agree on one thing. I'm lead counsel. You're second chair."

Erma sucked in air like she was drawing on a cigarette. "Did I do something to upset you?" She sank her hands into her pockets and did a little sidestep.

"You know what you're doing. Are we in agreement or not?" Sandra expelled a ragged breath. She needed some time alone.

Erma shrugged. "Yes. You're first chair. What's the big deal if I do the talking sometimes?"

"Sometimes it isn't. In this instance, though, I want people to understand I'm lead counsel." Sandra dropped her shoulders. Fatigue replaced her anger. She needed some time to digest everything that had taken place that morning. "Here's what we can do. We'll go back and meet those ladies, then you can return to the ranch with BJ. I'll hang around town so I can have some time by myself." She clicked the pen some more, waiting for a reply.

"Whatever you say, Mrs. Salinsky." A devilish gleam danced in Erma's eyes. "You're the boss."

Sandra did an eye roll. Erma never quit. "Please don't give me a hard time. We definitely need some space." She strode back into the District Clerk's Office. Erma followed, her shoes slapping on the floor. The same apple-cheeked brunette came up to the counter.

"I'm Sandra Salinsky from Galveston. I want to apologize. Already been a long day, and it's not noon yet." Sandra stuck out her hand. "This is my law partner, Erma Townley."

"I'm Annie Gretsky, Chief Deputy District Clerk." She shook Sandra's hand first, then Erma's. "The clerk's in with the judge. Her name's Bonnie Miller."

The other woman in the office approached them. "Velma Schultz. Y'all are from Galveston? An aunt and uncle of mine live down there."

In her experience, Sandra had found in small towns, some folks were wary of strangers while others were often chatty. "I wonder if we might know them. By the way, we're handling the Schindler murder case."

"Oh." Annie nodded, deadpan.

Sandra looked from Annie to Velma. They probably already knew that. Probably everyone in the courthouse knew exactly who they were.

Erma said, "Y'all know my good friend, BJ Schindler?"

"I knew Commissioner Schindler," Annie said.

"Roy. He was a doll," Erma said.

They chatted for a few minutes before Annie said, "What can we help you with this morning?"

Sandra looked at Erma who said, "I'll be moseying on back inside the courtroom. See you later, Sandra. Enjoyed meeting you ladies."

Sandra touched Erma's shoulder. "I'll grab my coat when I'm through here. Y'all eat lunch without me. Think I'll nose around the shops afterward, might even stay for dinner."

Erma said, "Okey-dokey."

"Annie, is the file on Rufina Barboza fully set up yet?" Sandra rubbed her tight neck muscles. She could use a massage, but that would have to wait until they returned home.

"About to finish with it."

"May I have a copy of the indictment and y'all's local rules? I was also wondering if you would point me in the direction of the law library." The two women exchanged glances. Velma left the counter. Annie said, "The judge has some law books across the hall."

"I saw a few in his chambers on a shelf behind that little desk. Does he use another office when he's here?"

"No, ma'am. What you saw is it. Pitiful, huh?" Her eyes crinkled in a smile. "The commissioners, they hate to spend money on the courts." Annie glanced back at Velma. "Even Commissioner Schindler."

Velma said, "There's a room—almost a closet—behind the judge's chambers that has some other books in it. What were you looking for?"

"Black Statutes?" What Sandra truly wanted was to check out the courthouse setup for when they returned. She was beginning to realize there was no place in a law library for them to utilize during trial, for breaks or otherwise. "What about an attorneys' conference room?" Lack of a conference area would pose a problem. She wanted to see what else the county had to offer in the way of amenities for lawyers, if anything. Annie shook her head. "No to the conference room, but there is a set of Black Statutes. Want me to ask him if you can have access to them after the Grand Jury leaves?" She leaned toward Sandra.

Was she kidding? "The Grand Jury meets in the judge's chambers?"

"It's not really his chambers, though there's a connecting door."

"I'm not sure I understand." The Gillespie County Courthouse seemed to shrink by the minute. "Out of curiosity, where does the regular jury deliberate?"

Annie rubbed a knuckle across her lips. "Same room?"

"So what if the Grand Jury is meeting when a jury is deliberating?"

Velma, who was dealing with papers on her desk, said, "That can cause a problem sometimes."

"And the judge can't check the law then either," Sandra said.

Annie shook her head. "I guess not."

"He's online with Westlaw though, right?" Did they have the Internet?

"I'm not aware of what he does or what the visiting judges do. Bonnie would know." Her eyes went to Velma again. "Maybe wait for them to take a break?"

"Now that I think of it, I remember hearing our judge discussing how much Westlaw cost with one of the County Commissioners," Velma said.

"So the Internet's available here in the courthouse, right? I could do my own research? What about Wi-Fi?"

"Oh, sure. We got the Internet a long time ago." Annie smiled with pride. "And Wi-Fi. I can give you access if you want."

"Not today, but I'll want it when we're in trial." What would she do then? Erma had steadfastly refused to learn how to use the Internet.

"Here's a copy of the indictment and the rules for you, Mrs. Salinsky." Velma handed her the paper. "I'm going to lunch now, Annie."

"Thank you," Sandra said. "Good to meet you, Velma." The indictment and the rules were each only one page long.

"Do you need anything else, Mrs. Salinsky?" Annie asked.

Sandra let out a little chuckle. "I'm divorced, Annie. So Ms. Salinsky, but please, Sandra is my first name."

"I apologize." She grinned and shrugged.

"So, Annie, I understand your judge presides over several counties. In the part of the state I come from, each judge has only one county, so how does—what does he—"

"The judge today isn't our regular judge. He's a visiting judge."

"I got that, but your regular judge—"

"He has four counties. Each county gets a week unless something huge is going on."

Sandra had the distinct feeling her questions were beginning to annoy Annie. "So visiting judges substitute for him a lot?"

"Not every month, ma'am, but if he has to be in another county, yes. Depends..."

"How does he handle everyday stuff in this county when he's in another county and no visiting judge is here?" She needed that information for when she returned for motion hearings and other pretrial matters.

"The lawyer goes to the county where the judge is that week."

"How far are the other county seats from here?"

"Varies. Forty-five-minutes to an hour."

"So people actually drive all the way to another county instead of waiting for a judge to be here? How does that work?"

"They pick up their file and take it over there. Like if someone is in a hurry or something. If they want a TRO or Protective Order, they'll definitely drive the file to the judge."

"What if the party doesn't have a lawyer?"

"They pick up the file themselves."

Things were different in Galveston. Only clerks, judges, or other court officials handled the files. With most everything being online now, it wasn't as much of a problem as in times past.

"Do you have e-filing here?"

"Yes, and, of course, fax filing."

"Thanks, Annie. You've been a great help. Please tell your boss I hope to meet her next time I'm up here." Sandra walked back to the courtroom, which had emptied. She perched on a bench and read through the indictment, which said Rufina was charged with murder, "to-wit: with a handgun." Sandra grabbed her coat and went to the District Clerk's Office again where Annie was eating a sandwich at her desk. "I don't want to bother you when you're eating. I can come back later."

Annie jumped up. "No problem." Muffled voice. "What do you need?"

"I'd like to use the library this afternoon if I may. I didn't bring my computer and using my cell phone to do research is a pain since everything is so small." She hated to lie, but she needed to check out the setup before Erma and she went back home. "Also, could you please write down the court coordinator's phone number for me?"

"Sure." Annie left her desk and went out a side door. After a few minutes, she returned. "The judge says go to lunch. You can use the room after the Grand Jury recesses, most likely after two."

"I'll be back then. And that phone number?"

"Listed on the local rules at the bottom with the coordinator's name."

"Oh, sorry. Didn't see it. Thanks so much. I'm out of here and headed—which direction should I go?"

"Out the front door, turn right, and you'll find most of the shops and restaurants on Main Street."

"Thanks again, Annie, you've been wonderful. See you later." Sandra pulled on her coat and took the stairs down to the first floor. She looked forward to the distraction of a new town and new shops. Heck, she looked forward to focusing on something other than murder. While she was nosing around, she hoped to find a place that would deliver an edible arrangement to the clerk's office as a thank you for being so patient.

CHAPTER SEVEN

ERMA AND BJ headed back to the ranch. The sun hid behind cottony clouds. A slight breeze moved the cedar, but the oaks stood firm.

BJ had grown quiet. Erma wanted a siesta and wagered BJ could use a rest, too. All the court business had clearly overwhelmed her. While there was time, Erma wanted to nose around the house, particularly the master bedroom where Katy Jo had been killed. "BJ, do you mind me examining your bedroom?"

BJ slumped over the steering wheel. "I can't get my head around everything, especially Sandra's agreeing to take this case. She didn't really want it, did she?"

"I told you that last night, but I was right, wasn't I? She's changed her mind. That's all that matters. So do you have a problem with me checking out your bedroom?"

"I hate to make her do something she doesn't want to do." Her listless eyes never wavered from the road.

Clearly BJ needed a nap. She acted like she was on drugs, unable to focus on what Erma was saying. "Are you worried she can't do the job?" Erma didn't drag Sandra all the way up there just so BJ could be fickle and change her mind.

BJ's eyes darted to Erma's and back to the road. "Rex thinks we should hire a San Antonio lawyer."

The little runt. What was his problem? "When did this come about?"

"He thinks y'all not being anywhere near local might affect Rufina's case."

On her return to the courtroom from the clerk's office, Erma had found Rex still there. He hung across the bench and whispered to BJ. Rufina and the other prisoners were gone. "What's going on with your son? I'm not convinced he gives a shit about Rufina," Erma said. He'd been unbelievably charming the night before, but Erma wasn't convinced he had Rufina's best interest at heart.

"You're wrong." BJ took one hand from the steering wheel and patted Erma's arm. "Rex is like a son to her, and she's like another mother to him."

That cleared up any question in Erma's mind about whether BJ could listen objectively to what Rex said. Annoyance churned inside her. "I don't know what to say, BJ. We're either in or we're out. If you want Rex to run this case, tell us now, and we're out."

"Erma—"

"You're not going to jerk us around like a couple of marionettes. If we're to handle Rufina's defense, it'll be start to finish or not at all."

"I didn't mean to hurt your feelings. God."

"Just practicalities. We've begun working on Rufina's case, but barely, so we can quit now and refund your retainer, minus our time for coming up here for the arraignment, and y'all can hire another lawyer." Erma gritted her teeth. She knew she shouldn't get riled up, but BJ even mentioning what Rex had said rubbed her the wrong way. "We're not going to put a lot of time in and then you give the case to someone else."

"Rufina's brother, Carlos, wants a San Antonio lawyer, too."

Erma cut her eyes at BJ. Was something going on she was unaware of? "If Carlos cares so much, why wasn't he in court this morning? What's his story?" Could it be that Rex didn't think a woman was as competent as a man and Rufina's brother thought so, too?

"Carlos thinks a Latino would do a better job for his sister."

"What's an attorney being Hispanic/Latino/whatever have to do with anything?"

BJ shrugged. "I don't know. Carlos seems to think it makes a difference though."

"BJ, people are weird. I know a black attorney who keeps a white attorney on her staff because clients come in who want a white attorney. I'd kick their ass to the curb, but she takes their money and doesn't worry about it. Everybody is prejudiced in some form or fashion. Sounds like Carlos is no exception. That doesn't make what he thinks any truer than what Rex thinks. Don't y'all know it's a defense attorney's job to wade through all that? And to piss off the judge sometimes?"

BJ's snort sounded like a piglet's squeal. Erma laughed, too. "I'm so confused."

"I know it. You recently lost one of your daughters and your best friend is in jail. Now are we in or out? If we're in, I need to see the inside of your bedroom."

They pulled into the circular driveway, and BJ switched off the ignition. "I don't know why I listen to Rex. He doesn't know what he's talking about half the time anyway."

Erma wasn't about to weigh in on that. She unbuckled her seat belt and reached across the console to hug BJ. "It's going to be fine. Sandra will do a bang-up job for Rufina. So will I."

BJ wiped away a tear. "Do you mind if I don't go into my bedroom? I had the girls move my things to one of the guest rooms after—after—I haven't been inside the room since the night of the—"

"Why don't you go get us a cup of coffee and rustle up some lunch. After that, I think we both could use a nap." Erma climbed down from the truck. "I need a few minutes to—uh—see the room." She had started to say the murder scene but caught herself. BJ got out and went inside. Erma followed her

"You'll have to excuse the room's appearance. No one's been inside except the sheriff's deputies and all those official police-type people, except for the girls to get my things." BJ turned toward the kitchen. "I haven't let them clean it."

"Make my coffee decaf," Erma said to BJ's back.

Erma flipped on the lights and eyeballed the huge bedroom. Even from as far away as the door, which she estimated was twenty feet, the bloodstained mattress drew her attention like a magnet. After a few minutes of staring, of thinking what the night of the murder must have been like for BJ, Erma focused on the rest of the room. Thick padded rugs in a deep blue and burnt orange covered the floor. Rafters made of four-by-eight beams ran across the ceiling. Heavily draped windows kept out natural light. The air smelled stale. One side of the room was a sitting area with a small, round oak table and two hardback oak chairs. The opposite side was the sleeping area. Matching night tables with tooled leather lamps stood on each side of the king-sized bed. Identical dressers lined the opposite wall with about a sixty-inch television on a stand between them. The door to the bathroom was not far from the right side of the bed.

The Schindlers had significantly come up in the world since Erma had become friends with them. She remembered their tiny four room house that had not much more furniture in the bedroom than a double bed and a nightstand. If BJ and Erma had wanted any privacy for girl talk, they'd go out on the porch or take a walk. Erma extended her arm toward the bed as though she held a handgun. Though the room was quite large, there would be no problem for a shooter to hit someone from that distance if circumstances were right.

She paced at the foot of the bed and stared down at the stains. A deep sadness tugged at her heart. To lose someone so dear would be almost unbearable.

The death of Erma's friend Phillip the year before had devastated her. Now she realized how she would feel if she ever lost Sandra, her only child. She would lie down and never get up. Shaking her head, Erma walked over to the bathroom and peered in. At least BJ had the other two kids, not that the two of them combined would equal one Katy Jo, who had always been the nice child, the obedient child, the most loving child.

Satisfied she'd seen enough, Erma went to her room to wash up. A few minutes later, following the aroma of bacon and coffee, she found BJ in the kitchen assembling BLTs with one of the Latina workers.

Erma pulled a mug out of the cabinet and poured herself a cup of coffee. "BJ," Erma said and took a sip, "where were you when Katy Jo was shot?"

Grief marred BJ's face like it had been carved into her skin with a dull knife. "Bathroom. Like we all do at our age, I'm up several times a night, especially if I've been entertaining and had a few drinks. Everyone had more than a few that night."

From the bar stool she'd climbed up on, Erma looked at BJ, who towered over her. "That must have been a humdinger of a family get together. Why was Katy Jo in your bed?"

BJ swiped at her hair. "Ever since she was a little girl, she'd climb into bed with us. Well, after Roy died, just me. We'd cuddle when she was little. When she got older, we'd talk sometimes way into the night, like best friends." She mopped her face on a dishtowel. "Earlier that night, she said she wanted to discuss something with me, but not around all the others."

Erma sipped her coffee. "And Kathy Lynn? What about her?"

BJ shook her head. "Sometimes when she was little she'd cuddle, but after she reached her teenage years—puberty, I guess—never. We didn't have the same kind of relationship."

Erma had a couple more questions she hoped wouldn't up-set BJ too much. She didn't want to cause her friend any more angst, but if they were going to try Rufina's case, they would be delving into intimate matters. She took BJ's arm and pulled her closer. "Tell me honestly, BJ, is it possible Kathy Lynn was jealous of her sister?"

BJ huffed out a sigh. "Kathy Lynn has always been a hand-ful. She might have been jealous of my relationship with her sister, but you'll never convince me she would harm Katy Jo." She plopped down on the stool next to Erma and put her face in a dishtowel, a sob escaping. The young Latina who'd been helping fix lunch turned her attention on the kitchen counter.

"Aww, now." Erma rubbed her friend's back. "I didn't mean to upset you, hon, but you've gotta know this whole business is going to be tough. Sandra and I will be asking a lot of hard questions."

BJ lifted her head. "I understand. Next you'll be asking about Rex."

Erma held her hands and shrugged. "Well..."

"I can't believe that of Rex either. Katy Jo was devoted to him." She dried her face. "I can't believe it of either of my other children."

"Well, let me ask you this." Erma bit her lip and waited for BJ to look her way. "Has it occurred to you that maybe Katy Jo wasn't the target?"

CHAPTER EIGHT

"HEY," SANDRA SAID into her cell as she climbed into her car, shutting the door behind her to keep out the cold. She was chilled from walking the couple of blocks from the last place she'd shopped. She dropped her packages on the passenger seat and started the engine.

"Hey back," Erma said. "Where are you?"

"Still in town. I knew you'd hang with BJ and find out what you could so thought I'd do a little shopping." She'd splurged on a pair of tall black leather boots she could wear to court with her skirt suits and a black alpaca jacket. "Find out anything interesting?"

"Hold on." After a moment of background noise, Erma said in a loud voice, "BJ, I'm going to take this in my room. Be back in a few minutes." In a muffled voice, she said into the phone, "I was surrounded. BJ and I had a nice visit. Kathy Lynn was here for a while, though she resisted speaking with me alone. I looked over the crime scene, but that's about it. What about the courthouse? Any place we can use for home base?"

"It didn't take me long after I went back to figure out Gillespie County has no amenities for lawyers." Sandra punched a button on the dashboard so the heater would run full blast.

"Nothing? No conference room?"

"*Nada. Nilch. Nicht.* And the law library is minuscule—a small room with few books. The judges and local lawyers have to be on Westlaw."

"Saves the commissioners a lot of money if they don't have to buy updates for law books. Not much help for the regular person, though, if they can't afford a lawyer." What Sandra had said just affirmed Erma's impression of commissioners everywhere.

"I doubt that would worry the commissioners. Anyway, that little room can't double as an attorney-client conference room either, since jurors will be in and out. There's no space available to us."

"Humph. I'll talk to BJ," Erma said, "tell her we'll need a room in town."

"Tell her close to the courthouse and with some kind of kitchen, so we'll have a table to spread our stuff out on and at least be able to have some semblance of breakfast. There might be an extended stay hotel. I'll drive down Main and see if I spot one."

"Anything else we might need to think about?" Erma would prefer to hit up BJ for everything at one time.

"We'll bring my laptop and our own printer unless we want to use the business office if the hotel has one, which is not my preference." Sandra scanned the parking lot. When she didn't see anyone, she backed out.

"Mine either. So when you get here, we can both talk to BJ about the kind of space we want."

"Is Kathy Lynn still there? I'd like to speak to her."

"She left mighty fast after lunch. She's pretty skittish. Rex's here if you want to talk to him."

"Yeah. No. I'll leave that to you."

Erma groaned. "Thanks a lot. So I'll see you in a little while?"

Sandra grimaced. No way. "I don't see why I shouldn't have dinner here in town. I saw a cowboy bar-restaurant not far from here where I could eat." And be sure to avoid Rex.

"Sandra—"

"Erma—"

"Don't you think you should spend more time with the family?"

"Uh—no. I need some time by myself to digest all this, plus there are a couple of clients whose calls I need to return. I want to touch base with Mel, too. And call Patricia in a minute and fill her in about us spending another night here, unless you've done that."

"No, I haven't. All right, I'll see you later, but be careful driving out here tonight."

Sandra laughed as she hung up. Erma would always be her mother and act like it. Sandra would always be the daughter and act like it, too.

She drove around the courthouse to the place across the street, Will's Bar & Grill, in a two-story limestone building with oak tree roots erupting out of the sidewalk. They had blocked off the original entryway, so she walked through a white picket fence, past outdoor picnic tables, and down a narrow walkway to enter. The aroma of cooked beef and onions floated out to greet her.

Inside, a low-to-the-ground stage and a faded red velvet curtain were in the front of the room. Next to the stage, a short-order kitchen looked like it had been carved out of a wall. A few people sat at wooden tables with worn, oak chairs and rolls of paper towels mounted on sticks in the center. Sandra skirted around them to the back of the room, to the table in front of the locked-off, glassed-in former front door. Through the window, she had a view of the pecan trees across the street and traffic flowing back and forth. She threw her coat on the back of a chair and glanced around to see what the drill was.

A long, dark dance-hall bar, with numerous beer bottles and cans lined up across it, ran in front of the west wall on which a huge mirror hung. Behind the bar stood two no-nonsense-look-ing middle-aged women in long-sleeved western shirts and jeans. They were taking orders from the people who had formed a line. No music played, but talk and laughter reverberated from the tall ceilings to the plank floor. If she'd wanted a change of atmosphere, Sandra had come to the right place.

Beer bottles clinked as a woman cleared the two-person table next to Sandra's, reminding her of the wind chimes hanging on her balcony back in Galveston. One more day and she could return home. She crossed the room to the bar, stopping at the end of the short line. When she got to the front, she asked, "Can y'all recommend a German beer?"

The woman was all business. "*Spaten Oktoberfest* is pretty good. You want some food, too, before we get busy with the after-five crowd?"

How big could the after-five crowd be? "You have a grilled chicken salad?"

"Yup."

Sandra handed over her credit card. "Italian dressing, please."

The second woman pulled a bottle out of an old beer box. "Here's your beer."

The first woman said, "Pick up your salad at the window behind you—the one next to the stage." She gave Sandra a square plastic contraption and returned the credit card. "When the lights flash on this thing, it'll be ready."

"Thanks a bunch." Sandra smiled and the woman inclined her head in acknowledgment. Sandra scooted back to her table and sat down, putting her feet on the rung of the chair across from her. The beer tasted cold and strong. Just what she wanted. After punching the office number into her cell, she heard, "Law Offices of Townley and Salinsky."

"Hey, Patricia. It's me. Wanted to tell you we're still in Gillespie County."

"Things didn't go well?"

"Reasonably well—I'll fill you in when we get home—but the judge wouldn't set bail without a hearing tomorrow morning at nine. We should get out of here before lunch."

"So cancel your appointments? And hey, remember you said you'd do the Cutler divorce tomorrow on the uncontested docket? Want me to call her and tell her you'll meet her on Friday morning?"

Sandra sat back, heaving a huge sigh. The past two days had worn her out. She still had the bail hearing the next morning, but it shouldn't take long. And then the five-to-six-hour drive back to Galveston. Closed inside a car with Erma. "Yes, please, Patricia. Friday would be great. I know we'll be tired when we get back and have some catching up to do."

They chatted for a few more minutes and disconnected. Sandra took another swallow of the *Spaten Oktoberfest.* Ordinarily, she didn't drink beer, but something about the German cowboy atmosphere had made her want to stray from wine. She scrolled through the texts on her phone, responded to some, and then the emails. When she glanced up, what a few minutes earlier had been an almost empty room was filling fast. Most of the people looked like white-collar workers stopping off for a drink after work, but several of the men could have just come in off a tractor. They wore heavy coats and work boots. She sat back and watched. When the lights on the contraption flashed, she trekked to the kitchen where the only thing on the serving bar was a salad in a washtub-sized stainless-steel bowl. She glanced at the cook, who grinned. "You haven't been here before. You're going to need a to-go box."

"I think you're right." She picked up the bowl, plastic utensils, a packet of dressing, and crossed the old dance hall floor where her heels sounded clunky in conjunction with the chatter. Someone had laid and lit a fire in a limestone fireplace, which looked like something out of a medieval castle. Long tongues of flame licked the blackened stone. The wood smell brought holiday memories. Christmas was about the only time they lit a fire in Galveston at Erma's house, the climate being so mild.

As she started to call Mel before she tackled the salad, her eyes met those of a tall blond man. His hand rested on the chair on which she'd propped her feet. "May I help you?" She peered into glimmering green eyes. Or were they hazel?

"Mind if I borrow this? There are five of us." He indicated an adjacent table that only had four chairs. He, as well as the others—some of whom were women—wore office attire.

She looked him over. Broad-shouldered, small-waisted. One of those country-boy types who could single-handedly lift a bale of hay. She shrugged and dropped her feet. "Be my guest."

"Thanks." He looked her over in return and took the chair. Sandra punched in Mel's number.

Mel's voice mail answered, "Hi. I can't talk now. Leave me a message and I'll call you back."

Sandra disconnected. She texted:

> *Erma and I are stuck in Gillespie County for another night for a hearing in the a.m. If we don't get home tomorrow in time to see you, guess we'll see you on Wednesday after school.* ♥ *Mom*

Though she'd had lunch at the brewery on Main Street, for some reason Sandra felt extremely hungry. Later, when she had eaten her fill of the salad and returned some more messages, the country boy dragged the chair he'd borrowed next to her and sat down. What could he possibly want?

Recorded country music played so loud that when he spoke his words were lost. He smelled of beer and something fried. When Sandra asked him to repeat himself, the man leaned toward her and cupped his hands next to her ear. His breath made the tendrils of her hair tickle her cheek. "I said you look like you're from out of town." He'd removed his jacket and tie and rolled up his sleeves.

His delicious manly aroma rang alarms inside Sandra. No way. After the fiasco with her former partner, Stuart, she was through with men. Some guy she didn't even know was not going to arouse her by breathing into her ear. Ridiculous. She would nip that in the bud right then. She nodded but didn't reply. If she was unresponsive, maybe he'd go back to the farm.

"I'm Jared Longley," he said when the music stopped.

The waitress came, and Jared ordered himself another beer. "Bring this stranger what she's drinking, too, Libby."

"No need for that. I'm fine."

"One more won't kill you. So what's your name?"

"Attorney Sandra Salinsky." She hoped he would be put off, since some men didn't like professional women. They shook. His hand was warm and, though hers was large, his was massive. She hadn't gone there to get picked up, even by someone as interesting-looking as him. His closely-cropped blond hair was white at his temples, belying a first impression that he was quite young. He had a smallish nose for someone his size; a scar ran across it to his right cheekbone. He was quite huge. Farm boy for sure.

"The beer's to thank you for the chair. Besides, I'm curious about you. Would you, by any chance, be the attorney who helped out my little sister with her divorce this morning?"

"Yeah, that would be me." So maybe he didn't intend to pick her up. Still, she needed to be careful. "Your sister seemed eager to get it done, and her lawyer didn't show."

"That would've been me. I was running really late."

Baling hay, no doubt. "Well, it wasn't fatal."

"Thanks for doing that. You made her day."

"You're welcome."

"So what are you doing here?"

"In Will's or in Fredericksburg?"

"Clearly you're hiding out in Will's, because if you wanted a good meal there are some wonderful restaurants around town."

The waitress had returned and slapped him on the arm. "Don't let Bob hear you say that, Jared." She set their beers down and took the empties. "He thinks he's a pretty good chef." She shook her head as she walked off.

"So why are you here?"

"You don't know? I thought in small towns everyone knew everything about everybody. And, actually, my salad wasn't bad."

He took a swig of beer and glanced at his friends, who were scooting out their chairs. "See you guys later," he called. They yelled their goodbyes.

"So what kind of lawyer are you?" Sandra asked, raising an eyebrow. "Besides the tardy kind."

"Usually real estate. And you're not answering my question. Should I guess?"

Sandra didn't want to like the guy but talking with him wouldn't hurt anything. The fact the waitress knew him by name, and he'd arrived with a bunch of other businesspeople, told her he was local and known in town. She and Erma would be going home on Tuesday after the bail hearing and, she hoped, not returning for several months unless they had to come back for some pre-trial motions. Since he practiced real estate law, they'd probably never run into each other again. She toyed with the label on her beer bottle.

"Okay, I'll guess." He drummed his fingers on the table. "The Schindler murder case."

"I knew you'd know about it. Billie Jo Schindler hired my mother, who is my law partner, and me to defend Rufina Barboza."

"Whew. Mrs. Schindler wants you to represent the murderer of her daughter? Isn't that extraordinary?"

"Alleged murderer. And she's innocent."

"Of course you'd say that." He took another swallow of beer and tipped back in his chair, waiting for her reaction.

Sandra's stomach clenched. Was he a redneck? A bigot? Did he hate Latinos? And was he reflective of most of the people in town? "I don't even know you, and you're trying to aggravate me?"

He laughed. "Just giving you a hard time. I did a little criminal defense when I first got my law license. I have an idea of what you're up against."

"Then you know more than I do. I'm worried about the kind of people who'll be in the jury pool."

"When's the trial? Got a date yet?"

She shook her head. "Hope to get one tomorrow at the bail bond hearing." She studied him a moment. Since he was a local attorney, she might be able to get some useful information out of him.

The music started up again, so loud Sandra wanted to cover her ears.

Jared cupped his hands around his mouth and said, "Hey, do you want to go somewhere for dinner? My treat to thank you for taking care of my sister."

Sandra glanced at the half-empty salad tub. "Ate already."

"Oh. I guess I ate too. What about another beer? There's a brew pub a few blocks from here. Why don't we go there? Might be a little quieter."

"I know where it is. I had lunch there."

"Believe it or not, on weeknights this place heats up, and the brewery is, I guess you could say, more conducive to conversation."

Sandra glanced at her watch. She could either submit to a boring evening at BJ's with Erma, BJ, and her obnoxious son, if Rex hadn't gone back wherever he crawled out of. Or she could have another beer and pick this lawyer's brain. Not a difficult choice. She could drive down the street to the brew pub, so she'd have her car. She just needed to limit what she drank. Boy, would District Attorney Holt love it if she got arrested for driving while intoxicated.

CHAPTER NINE

E RMA CLICKED OFF the phone and left the bedroom. "We can go ahead and eat, BJ, because Sandra's not returning until later." She finished the one bourbon on the rocks BJ allowed her and set the glass on the bar before sitting down at the dining room table. Over lunch, they'd settled into a discussion about the girls. Thankfully, Rex didn't return from town until hours later. Kathy Lynn came and went before Erma had a chance to spend any significant time with her, like a private interview. She was hoping Kathy Lynn might have dinner with them.

Now, Rex and Elgin Burgess were deep in conversation. Each held a Mexican blown, blue-rimmed shot glass. Elgin appeared right at home. Earlier, she had noticed when Elgin entered the house, he knew his way around. Roy and Elgin had been friends for a while, but did his familiarity with the Schindler home mean anything more?

"Not interrupting anything, boys, are we?" BJ rounded the table and started to pull out her chair at the table's head.

"Not a thing, Ma." Rex wore what must be his customary, rosy-cheeked smile.

Elgin jumped up and held BJ's chair. Erma could understand if he was interested in the widow Schindler but didn't see how BJ could be attracted to him, even given the fact that decent, eligible older men were few and far between. His face resembled a bull frog's. Maybe he had a quality that wasn't apparent on the surface. Elgin sat to BJ's left and shook out his napkin while keeping his eyes on BJ. Erma was at BJ's right, while Rex took the seat opposite his mother, the position of the man of the house.

"Hey, Erma." Rex held up his glass. "You want some mezcal? This is some fine stuff."

Erma took the shot glass from Rex and sniffed it. Smoky. No surprise that Rex bought the good stuff. He looked like he'd had a bit too much already. She handed the mezcal back. "I've been given my ration of booze tonight, son, but thanks for asking." She winked at BJ, hoping BJ understood she was forgiven for rationing out the booze. "So tell me, Elgin, how'd you happen to come by at dinner time?"

"He manages to drop by for dinner several times a week." Rex snickered like a horse. He threw the amber liquid down his throat and grimaced.

Elgin tossed his mezcal down as well. "Billie Jo tells me that after the arraignment, she went ahead and hired you and your daughter to represent Rufina in the trial. Isn't that an awful lot of trouble for someone from so far away?"

Elgin stopped speaking when Lucia, one of the Hispanic women Erma had met earlier, laid the serving dishes on the table.

"Don't worry about us." Erma reached for the bowl nearest her, dished out some squash, and handed it to BJ. "We practice law all over the State. Elgin, you want to hand me the roast, or you keeping it all for yourself?"

Elgin took a couple of slices of meat and started the platter circulating. "You think she did it?"

"Everyone's entitled to the best defense they can afford, regardless," Erma said. "Don't you know that?"

"Elgin, I wish you'd stop." BJ's voice was strident, like she was at the end of her rope. "Ever since they arrested Rufina you've been like a broken record. I won't have it."

"Darlin'," Elgin said, patting BJ's arm. "I don't mean anything by it. I guess I'm wondering whether Miz Townley has some idea of who might have done it if it wasn't Rufina."

"Goddamn, Elgin, I only got here last night. And the name's Erma." She took a slice of pork. "This sure smells good, BJ." She held out the platter to Rex. "Are you going to pass that rice?" She hoped Elgin wasn't one of those people who had a sense of morbid curiosity—who liked to discuss cases ad nauseam when they didn't know what the hell they were talking about.

Rex laughed. "I guess she told you, huh, Elgin."

"I tell you what, as soon as I figure out who really killed Katy Jo, you'll be the first person I tell." Erma spooned some gravy over the rice. She cut into the roast and took a healthy bite. Perfect, tender and moist.

Elgin ate heartily, which was no surprise for a man his size. He was physically enough of a man for BJ, if that's what his dropping by was about, but he was ugly as homemade soap. How long had he had designs on her? BJ had said he owned the spread next door. She hadn't mentioned Elgin to her, ever. Not that they talked that frequently. When they did, often it was about matters having to do with the estate since Erma was the estate's attorney. Lucia returned to the room with a bowl of applesauce. She kept her eyes down the whole time she was there.

Elgin cut each piece of pork into large pieces and scraped the squash, rice, and gravy on top of it. He closed one eye and studied Erma with the other. When he seemed to have arranged everything on his plate to his satisfaction, he forked an enormous bite into his mouth.

"Let's talk about something else." BJ took a bite of food herself.

Erma should probably abide by BJ's desires, but there might not be another opportunity this good to ask questions. Rex appeared to focus on the plate in front of him. "Where were you, Rex, when your sister died?"

Rex shook his head like he wasn't believing she asked him that. "Ma—"

BJ's knife clattered onto her plate. "Erma, please."

Erma put a spoonful of applesauce next to the pork. Why did people related to a victim always think they shouldn't have to answer for themselves? She'd found families amusing on more than one occasion.

"My question is simple enough, Rex. I'm sure the police or sheriff or whoever must have asked you the same thing."

Rex poured Elgin another shot of mezcal, then filled his own glass.

"You're not the cops, Miz Townley." Elgin swallowed about half a glass of water and stared at her.

"If I'm—we're—to defend Rufina, we have to investigate. I thought you understood that, BJ." Erma hated to put her on the spot. "By the way, were y'all drinking mezcal the night Katy Jo died?"

Rex grinned before shooting a look at his mother that asked her to shut Erma down.

"I guess I knew you'd have to quiz us," BJ said, "but can we wait until after dinner?"

Erma wanted to hear Elgin's story, too. He acted like the man of the house except he hadn't yet achieved the place of honor at the other end of the dining table.

"I told the sheriff's office where I was." Rex raised an eyebrow. "After we ate, I put Elgin in his truck and went to bed."

"Okay. All right. No sense getting your bowels in an uproar." Since they hadn't answered her mezcal question, she would assume the answer was in the affirmative. With their pink cheeks and veined noses, though Rex's face paled in comparison to Elgin's, they could easily be a couple of alcoholics. She would know since she had a long history of heavy drinking herself.

These days she powdered her nose heavily every morning to cover the evidence.

"Aren't you going to ask me where I was?" Elgin's eyes met Erma's as he piled more vegetables and meat on his fork.

Interesting he would volunteer. "If you want to say."

He chewed and swallowed his mouthful. "I'd gone home. Alone." His eyes shifted to BJ like he regretted he'd been alone.

"All righty." Erma cut another bite of the pork. "That's what I like, the spirit of cooperation."

"Could we eat our dinner in peace now?" BJ asked.

Erma nodded and smiled at each of them. They all relaxed and started eating again. She swallowed a mouthful. "Where would Rufina get a gun?"

Elgin slapped his fork on the table. "Come on, woman. Give us a break."

"Up here in this part of Texas, everyone has a gun," Rex said. "Most people have more than one."

"You have one BJ?" Erma knew the answer. She'd prepared the estate's inventory when BJ's husband died. Roy owned a shitload of guns. She wiped her mouth and set her napkin down. The food was so good she didn't want to stop eating. There was probably a whole stick of butter in that steamed yellow squash.

"You know, I do. We have a cabinet full of guns—rifles, shotguns, handguns—Roy loved weapons." BJ cut her eyes at Erma like she wondered what Erma was getting at.

"Do you keep the cabinet locked?" Erma glanced at each of their faces, in turn. Even Rex was suitably serious.

BJ nodded. "Every cabinet is kept locked. If anyone wants to open the cabinet, they have to ask me for the key. Almost everyone is aware of where I keep the keys, though."

"Like Rex, here?" Erma maintained a solemn face, though when Rex reacted, she found it difficult.

"Now wait a minute. Are you saying I killed my own sister?" His boyish smile had long disappeared. His face grew red, and a vein angling down his forehead bulged.

72

"I didn't mean to imply that, Rex boy. I just wondered whether everyone in the family knew where your mother kept the keys. Calm down."

BJ's eyes darted from Erma to Rex. "Erma . . ." She apparently thought better of what she was going to say.

"So Kathy Lynn would know about them? What about the staff? And old Elgin here, did he know, too?" Erma plucked another piece of meat from her plate.

"Yes, Kathy Lynn knows. I suppose the staff knows. They've all been with us a long time," BJ said.

"Rufina sure as hell knew. She was in charge of those girls." Rex pointed his fork in the direction of the kitchen. "They had to dust those cases inside and out." He beamed at Erma over his shot glass before he took a sip.

"But Rufina always asked me for the keys," BJ said.

"And old Elgin here?" Erma peered through her glasses at Elgin.

Elgin shook his head. "BJ has never told me about the keys."

Erma nodded. "Of course, I'm making an assumption the murder weapon came from the gun case. What kind of gun did the authorities say was used?"

Rex cleared his throat. "1917 forty-five."

"Did Roy own such a weapon?" Erma asked.

BJ nodded. "It was his father's from the war."

"So the forty-five was missing? Has the sheriff determined that particular weapon to be the only possibility or was something else missing?"

BJ glanced at Elgin and Rex. "No. Just that gun. The cabinet was found locked. The keys were where I always kept them. And yes, it was a forty-five. We're waiting for the sheriff to tell us whether the gun used was that particular one. When the sheriff conducted the inventory, everything else was there." Tears spilled down BJ's cheeks. "But, Erma, anyone who knew where I stored the keys could have taken the gun, shot K-K-Katy Jo, and put it in front of Rufina's house." She mopped her face with her napkin.

Erma felt a twinge of pity for her friend. "BJ, you're absolutely correct. What's odd though," she looked at Rex and then at Elgin, "is that a tiny woman like Rufina would have chosen a forty-five. I bet its kick would feel like a donkey's and would leave a bruise on her the size of a dinner plate."

"If she didn't hold it right, the recoil could have left a mark on her." Rex shrugged.

"Here's something else I've been wondering." Erma focused on BJ then Elgin then Rex. "I don't see any real security around here, at least I haven't so far. People traipse in and out without setting the alarm. I wonder, what's the possibility of someone's having waltzed right into this house, taken that gun or brought their own forty-five, and fired the shot?"

Three perplexed faces were turned toward Erma as she swallowed from her water glass and scooted back her chair. "I think I'll retire to my room now. Goodnight all."

CHAPTER TEN

WHEN SANDRA OPENED her eyes, she lay naked in an empty king-sized bed. Daylight streamed from above the black-out drapes. An unmistakable musky aroma surrounded her in the blue and green plaid sheets. The antique-looking furniture and cutesy decorations led her to think she must have checked into a country-style bed and breakfast. Then memories flooded her brain. She had checked into a bed and breakfast but not alone.

Holy crap. Court was at nine, and the clock read eight-fifteen. Head pounding as a result of all the beer she'd drunk, she wrapped herself in the sheet in case Jared was still around and went in search of her clothes. She found them hanging in the steamy bathroom. How had she slept so deeply she hadn't heard Jared's comings and goings? In the front part of the little cottage, her purse and coat lay on the buffet with a note, an apple, and a still-hot cardboard cup of coffee next to two aspirin. The note read:

> *Thank you for an enjoyable evening. I'll call you.*
> *Jared*

She could cut her throat. She ran for the shower. Not sure where in town the B & B was located, she didn't know how long it would take her to drive to the courthouse. Not that anything was that long a distance in Fredericksburg.

Her face grew hot at the memories from the night before. She had never felt particularly pretty when she was a young girl. She'd had no father to flatter her. Her mother had no inclination to do so. One summer when she was high school age, Sandra had used her earnings to have her hair styled and a lesson in applying makeup. She remembered the day she unfolded herself from the stylist's chair and heard the murmurs of approval around the salon. "A gazelle," a woman had said. She'd also taken dancing lessons on the sly, which her mother had always denied her, saying they were a frivolous waste of money. By the end of the summer, she had gained more confidence.

Whether her early history of feeling unattractive or from some other pathology, she knew her weakness. She was unavoidably attracted to handsome men who flattered her, who made her feel appealing. She knew how she responded, and yet the day before, what had she done? Gone to a beer pub ostensibly to pick Jared's brain. Now, she needed to push thoughts about the events following their departure from the brewery out of her mind. She had to hurry, shower, and dress to be at court on time.

If Erma found out, Sandra would have trouble ever living it down. She'd never tell Erma, but her mother wasn't stupid. Eventually, something would clue her in, and Erma would never let it go. Anyway, she wasn't planning on sharing the information with anyone. Jared had been one of the best lays she'd ever had, including both husbands. She wanted to be able to take the memory out and play with it like a child with a new toy. She didn't want Erma besmirching the recollection—making it something dirty, when Sandra didn't regard it that way. She wanted to remember that night only through her own eyes. She had needed Jared at that moment. They'd had a wonderful time.

He'd said it was as good for him as she'd known it was for her. But, their encounter was now history.

After showering, she scrambled into her clothes, tied up her hair, and set out for the courthouse. When she went outside, her Volvo, with the keys in the ignition, sat in front of the B & B. She'd love to tell Jared she appreciated his consideration, but she didn't intend to see him again, so she wouldn't be telling him anything.

At the courthouse, Sandra climbed the stairs and hurried down the hall, entering the courtroom as the judge finished calling the civil docket. Her mother sat at the counsel table. When Erma spotted Sandra, she subtly shook her head. Sandra nodded at BJ, who perched on the end of the front row bench. Rex, thankfully, was nowhere to be seen. And Kathy Lynn, well, again there'd be no meeting with her, since she wasn't present either. Kathy Lynn's name would go to the top of the list of witnesses they would have to talk with before trial.

Leaning over her mother, Sandra said, "Sorry I'm late." She dumped her things on the table, avoiding Erma's eyes. When the judge finished the civil docket, he called their case.

"State's ready," Samuel Holt announced, waltzing in from the hallway.

"Defense is ready." Sandra stood.

"We'll be in recess until the deputy brings the defendant." The judge went into chambers.

Erma swiveled in her chair and hissed, "Where in the hell were you last night?"

Sandra grimaced. Her head throbbed. She glanced over her shoulder to see if anyone was paying attention, but no one was. She muttered, "I drank too much, so I got a room. Didn't want to drive all the way out there."

"I was scared shitless this morning." Frowning, Erma turned away.

"I apologize. Didn't mean to frighten you. What did you think I meant when I called and said I was staying in town?"

Erma cut her eyes back at Sandra. "Thought you'd be back after dinner."

"Again, I'm sorry. I had planned on it, but..." She shrugged one shoulder and turned to BJ. "Are you going to testify if we need you?"

"Yes." BJ's eyes swept past Sandra. "Here comes Rufina."

Erma muttered, "We have a lot to talk about on the way home."

Sandra met Rufina at the far side of the counsel table. The deputy unlocked her handcuffs and shackles. "You doing all right today, Rufina?"

"Yes. You? You're a little pale."

"Sweet of you to ask about me when we're here about you." Probably everyone had noticed Sandra wore the same clothes as the day before. She might look rough, but she didn't care. She just wanted the judge to set bail so she could go back home.

"The judge will set my bail today, right?"

"Hopefully. And we'll get a trial date as well." If the judge would cooperate. Sandra touched her queasy midsection. She needed something more solid than coffee and a few bites of an apple to offset the alcohol.

"Thank you. I know you'll do your best for me."

Sandra nodded and stood as the judge returned to the bench.

"State versus Barboza," the judge announced. "Bail bond hearing."

"Judge," Holt said, "I don't believe defense counsel filed a writ—"

"Sure I did, Your Honor." Sandra opened her file. "I hand wrote it. The paperwork should be in the court's file. I filed it yesterday afternoon." Sandra put her hands behind her back and rolled up on the balls of her feet as Holt had done the day before.

"Well, the State didn't receive a copy as required by the rules." Holt clicked his ball point pen behind his back.

"I dropped off a photocopy, Judge." Sandra held up a document. "I have an extra if Mr. Holt wants it." She handed him a barely readable photocopy. Not her fault the copy machine she'd been able to find made such lousy copies.

"Let's move along," the judge said. "You have any witnesses Mrs. Salinsky?"

"Yes, sir. My client and Mrs. Roy Schindler." Normally Sandra wouldn't call a woman by her married name—her husband's name—but she wanted everyone, including the record, to recognize who BJ's husband had been, hoping his having been a county commissioner would have some influence.

Holt pivoted and keyed in on BJ as though he'd seen her for the first time. Surely he knew who she was already. BJ's eyes never wavered from his.

"Will the witnesses please rise and raise their right hands?"

Rufina and BJ both stood. The judge gave them the oath and said to Rufina, "*Habla Inglés?*"

"Yes, sir. I'm an American citizen."

The judge nodded. "Would you be so kind as to take the witness stand then, Mrs. Barboza? You may be seated Mrs. Schindler." The judge kicked back in his chair, rocking a couple of times before settling in.

Rufina approached the witness stand. She glanced back at Sandra and climbed into the box. Her hand trembled as she pushed the chair close to the microphone before sitting down. When she slipped into the chair she looked like a child—a horribly scarred, shriveled-up child.

"State your name for the court and the record," Sandra said.

"Rufina Lucia Morales Zavala Cortez Barboza." She looked at the judge and raised her hands in a what-can-I-do gesture.

The judge sniffed and busied himself with writing.

"Now, Mrs. Barboza, would you please tell the court your age and address?"

Rufina visibly relaxed as she replied to Sandra's questions. Her answers came readily as Sandra laid the foundation for bail to be set. After a few minutes, Sandra flipped to a clean page on her notepad. "Now we're here asking the court to set bail in the matter of this murder you're charged with, do you understand?"

"Yes, ma'am." Rufina's eyes darted toward the court-room door.

A Latino male, who appeared to be a number of years younger than Rufina but still middle-aged, had come in. He wore jeans, a buff-colored wool jacket, and a black felt cowboy hat he pulled from his head. He slid onto the back bench.

"How much money do you have in the bank, Mrs. Barboza?"

"If you are not counting my retirement, somewhere around fifty-five thousand dollars."

Sandra swallowed her next question and leaned over to Erma. "Where'd she get that kind of money?"

"Beats the hell out of me," Erma said. "I talked to BJ about how much bail she could make, but BJ never mentioned whether she thought Rufina could make it herself."

"And you have access to those funds, Mrs. Barboza?"

"I would have to cash a certificate of deposit for the fifty. The five thousand is in my checking account."

"I see," Sandra said. "Do you own any property you could put up to secure your bond?"

"Yes, ma'am." Rufina leaned close to the microphone. "A hundred acres on the way to Del Rio."

Sandra held in the urge to giggle. She didn't dare look at Holt. She had been so concerned with her mother's and BJ's tricking her into representing Rufina, Holt's attitude, and her own mental state, that she'd stereotyped Rufina. She had simply assumed Rufina had a little retirement from Mason County and nothing else. Sandra hadn't meant to be prejudiced. But she'd made assumptions about this little, old, damaged, Hispanic woman. She'd been out drinking beer and doing other things with Jared when she should have been conducting a thorough background of her client. She mentally kicked herself and vowed to do better with the remainder of the case.

She couldn't help but grin at Rufina. "And is your property free and clear of any liens?"

"Yes, ma'am, it is." Rufina's tiny eyes glittered.

Sandra stood. "Pass the witness."

Samuel Holt, sitting with his back ramrod straight, cleared his throat. "Rufina, you told the judge you're an American, correct?"

Rufina held his eyes. "That is correct."

Sandra jumped up. "Your Honor, I object to Mr. Holt addressing my client by her first name."

Holt threw his pen down in front of him.

The judge leaned forward and said into the microphone, "I'm sure you know better, Mr. Holt."

"Yes, Your Honor. Mrs. Barboza, your family is not American, right?"

"My parents came to this country from Mexico. They were legally here. When they retired, they went back to Mexico."

"Exactly where in Mexico?"

"In the mountains, *San Miguel de Allende,* sir."

"Your parents still living?"

"Yes, sir. They are in their nineties."

"Other relatives live in Mexico?"

"Yes, sir, and in Texas."

Holt nodded. "Now, this money you have stashed away, Rufina—"

"Objection, Your Honor." Sandra jumped up again. Holt was clearly trying to get her goat, so she kept her voice down but still assertive. "Characterization 'stashed away.' While I'm at it, I'm objecting again to him calling my client in such a familiar way."

"Sustained." The judge frowned toward Holt's side of the courtroom.

Head down, Holt's eyes cut sideways at Sandra. She smiled instead of giving him the middle finger, which she yearned to do.

"What's the source of this money you have in . . ." Holt looked at his notes, "a certificate of deposit?"

"Objection, Your Honor." Sandra stood again. "Where she got the money is immaterial."

"Sustained. Mr. Holt, stick to the issues. You can develop your case later. I only want to hear about bail today."

"Yes, Your Honor," Holt said, clicking his ballpoint pen. "Mrs. Barboza, when is the last time you visited your parents in Mexico?"

Sandra rose again, thinking she ought to just remain standing. "Objection, relevance. What has any visit she's made to her parents got to do with anything?"

"Judge, I'm trying to show she's a flight risk." Holt threw his legal pad on top of his pen on the table.

"Be my guest." The judge raised one eyebrow.

Holt rubbed his hands together as though they were cold, and he was standing in front of a fire. "Mrs. Barboza, isn't it true if the judge lets you out of jail on bond, you're going to run to Mexico?"

"That's being direct," Erma whispered to Sandra.

"No, sir. Why would I do that?"

"To be with your parents. To hide out?"

"Sir, my parents can come to see me whenever they want. I would buy them tickets." Rufina folded her hands on the counter as Sandra had seen her do in the jail. "I am not guilty, and I am not going anywhere. Why do you think I would hide in Mexico? Has someone been talking about me to you, sir?"

"Who would that be?" Sandra whispered behind her hand to Erma.

Holt stared at his legal pad and shook his head like he didn't know how to respond. After a moment, his head came up. "I'll ask the questions, if you don't mind. You answer them."

The judge jerked straight up. "Mr. Holt, in this courtroom, I instruct the witness as to what's proper, not you."

Holt snorted like a rode-hard horse. "Certainly, Your Honor."

Her face unreadable, Rufina kept her eyes on Holt.

"Have you any other assets to use as collateral for bail, Mrs. Barboza?" Holt asked.

"Not really, sir. But I think my acres would be worth a lot, is that not true?"

Holt shrugged. "Pass the witness."

Sandra shook her head when the judge raised his eyebrows at her. She stood again as he instructed Rufina to step down. "Mrs. Roy Schindler."

BJ and Rufina crossed paths. BJ brushed against Rufina's shoulder. Rufina's eyes on her friend were like watery black pools. When she sat next to Sandra at the end of the table, she emitted a long sigh. There was so much more to her Sandra needed to learn.

Erma took her friend on direct examination, while Sandra stroked Rufina's hand.

"You're Mrs. Roy Schindler, correct?" Erma asked.

"Yes. Billie Jo Schindler. My husband, Commissioner Schindler, is deceased." She raised the microphone's long neck to her mouth.

Sandra kept a straight face. BJ had responded as hoped.

"How are you related to Rufina Barboza?" Erma asked.

"We've been best friends since we were children."

"Since you were born, pretty much, right?"

Rufina took Sandra's hand and formed what Sandra had come to recognize as a smile.

"Her parents worked on our ranch. Mrs. Barboza—Rufina— and I were born the same year. We used to play together as tod- dlers, and we went to school together."

Erma nodded. "And now? Is there another facet to your relationship?"

BJ shrugged. "You could call it employer-employee, I guess. Rufina manages the household and has for the last fifteen years, give or take."

"Ever since—"

BJ glanced at the judge. "Kind of a long story, Judge." She straightened her shoulders. "She began managing the household staff when her parents retired, but there's some history you ought to know." She looked at Erma as though for permission to continue.

"Go on," Erma said. "You're fine."

"Before that, Rufina and her husband, who worked on the ranch, were taking care of my children at their cottage, while Roy and I were at a political affair. There was a fire. Rufina's husband died." Her eyes teared up when she frowned in Rufina's direction. Her voice grew high-pitched and broken. "And my friend was badly burned."

Rufina's head fell to her chest. A quiet sob poured out of her. She covered her mouth with her hand. Sandra dug in her shoulder bag for a tissue. She steeled herself to stop her own tears. She tried never to get worked up, but since the Stuart-thing and her depression, she hadn't always been able to control herself.

BJ continued, "When Rufina returned from the hospital and rehabilitation, I begged her forgiveness. I wanted her to come and live in my home." BJ's eyes were full of pain. "She wouldn't do it. She lives in one of the cottages, though. Real close by."

"When did she become household manager?" Erma checked something off on her legal pad.

BJ turned to the judge. "I wanted to give her money. The insurance paid some money, but I wanted to give her more. Rufina wouldn't take it, but when I needed her, she came to work for me. We're like sisters."

"Mrs. Schindler, you understand we're asking the judge to set bail today, so Rufina can get out of jail?"

"Yes, I want to pay the bail bond."

Rufina shook her head and said in a raspy voice, "I'll pay my own way."

The judge scowled at the defense table.

Sandra pressed Rufina's hand. "Shh. You can't talk now."

"Judge, I will make her bond. BJ's voice was hard as granite. She turned to him. "She's my friend. My family has been enough trouble to her. I'm paying." Her voice boomed from the microphone and bounced off the back walls.

"Okay," Erma said. "How much can you pay?"

"Whatever it takes." BJ cocked her head at Holt as though daring him to try for a figure out of her reach.

"Pass the witness."

Holt jumped up. "Mrs. Schindler, you understand if you make her bail and she escapes to Mexico, you'll lose your money."

"Son, she's not going anywhere. I don't know who put that idea into your head."

"Your boy named Rex?" His mouth formed a cruel line, as if he'd thrown a punch.

Erma elbowed Sandra and whispered, "Little shithead."

"Yes." BJ clenched her teeth.

"Why would Rex think Rufina would run to Mexico?"

Sandra sprang to her feet again. "Judge, I've asked for the court to instruct Mr. Holt not to call my client by her first name."

"I'm not, Judge. I wasn't addressing her client."

"It's the same thing, Your Honor. It's belittling. I hope you aren't going to tolerate this behavior at trial."

The judge came to attention again and jabbed his pen in her direction. "I'll tell you what I'm not going to tolerate, young lady, and that's you berating me for not doing my job as you define it."

Sandra drew a deep breath. She'd crossed the line without intending to. Had Holt set her up? He wore a sly smile, his face reminding her of a fox's. "May I approach the bench, Your Honor?"

The judge crossed his arms. "Come ahead."

"Judge, I want to apologize. I realize I overstepped my bounds and hope you'll forgive me." Sandra reached her hand out to him. "Sometimes I get carried away." Apologizing killed her, but Sandra knew the rules. She didn't want to be on the judge's shit list for the rest of her life and possibly into the next one. She might not see him in that court setting again, but no telling where visiting judges might pop up around the State.

He raised an eyebrow at her. "Don't let it happen again." He gave her hand a quick shake and directed his attention to Holt. "While you're both up here, Sam, I can't think of a reason not to set bail for this woman."

"I figured you were going to say that. How much?"

The judge's eyes flickered at Sandra. "Five hundred thousand."

"Five hundred thousand!" Sandra took a step back. "Dollars?" She shook her head. A litany of words tumbled through her brain, most of them would cause her to be thrown in jail for contempt if they spilled from her mouth.

The judge's forehead drew up. "Don't start with me, Mrs. Salinsky."

Sandra sighed. "No, sir. Since we're up here, would you be so kind as to set this case for trial?"

"Now, Mrs. Salinsky," the judge's tone of voice was like one someone would use to address a child, "I told you yesterday I can't do that. You and Mr. Holt go out in the hall and call the court coordinator for a trial setting."

"Yes, sir." Sandra welcomed the chance to breathe different air than the judge.

"You write all that down, LuAnn?" the judge asked.

"Yes, Your Honor."

"We're in recess then." The judge left the bench.

Sandra stalked back to counsel table, her teeth aching from clenching them so much. "You get all that, Erma?"

Erma backed her chair toward the bar. "Yep, five hundred thousand. Good job, daughter."

"What's that supposed to mean?" Was Erma being sarcastic or genuine? Sandra was in no mood for sarcastic.

"Hell, the ten-percent that will have to be paid out is chump-change for BJ."

Holding a set of handcuffs, a deputy approached their table.

"Just a minute, please, Deputy," BJ said as she stepped off the witness stand. "I just want to hug my friend for a moment. Any law against that?"

The deputy nodded. "Go ahead."

BJ wrapped her arms around Rufina and stooped over her in a hug. "I'll have you out in a jiff. And no arguments over money, you hear?"

Rufina nodded. Her long hair flowed around her like a veil.

Sandra headed for the hall where Samuel Holt stood with his cell phone to his ear. What was he up to now?

"The coordinator asked how soon you want the case set. I told her I could be ready quickly."

Sandra put her hand out for the phone. "Hello, this is Sandra Salinsky. Who am I speaking to?"

"Amber Chamberlain, Mrs. Salinsky. I told Mr. Holt I don't have any settings for a capital murder trial for quite a spell."

Sandra swallowed the lump in her throat. "It's not capital murder, Miss Chamberlain."

"Regardless. The soonest I could schedule you with no guarantees is next December."

"Holy crap." Sandra was glad the judge had set bail, no matter how high. At least Rufina would be out and about.

"What did you say?"

"Sorry, Miss Chamberlain, but are you telling me you have no judge who can try this murder case in less than almost a year? I'm going to file a speedy trial motion." She had trouble believing there wouldn't even be a visiting judge available. Could Holt have something to do with that?

"Listen, Mrs. Salinsky, you can file what you please, but suddenly I have no settings until March of next year. Get my drift?"

"Boy do I," Sandra said. "Thanks for your help." She clicked off the phone and tossed it toward Samuel Holt who fumbled but managed to catch it.

"Hey, Salinsky, what the hell?"

"I see what's going on." Sandra did an about-face.

"You ain't seen nothing yet."
Sandra looked back. "And neither have you."

CHAPTER ELEVEN

WORN OUT FROM the long trip home, not to mention the court hearing and her activities on Monday night, when Sandra arrived at her condo Tuesday night, she showered and fell into bed. For once, her monkey mind didn't disturb her sleep.

Rejuvenated on Wednesday morning, she donned some sweats and ran on the seawall for a few minutes. The cold, damp, salty air energized her even more.

She and Erma had engaged in their usual banter during the drive home, but also discussed their strategy for Rufina's case. Since Erma had raised Sandra, their thinking aligned on most everything, so it was easy, even fun, to come up with a game plan.

After taking a shower and having a protein smoothie for breakfast, Sandra headed to the office, wanting to arrive earlier than the others so she could have some quiet time. She wanted to pound out some motions to file in Rufina's case, not wanting to wait for Patricia to do the documents any more than she wanted to wait over a year for the trial. A hearing before the presiding judge, not some visiting judge, was her preference, though she'd take what she could get. If she could find out who would be trying the case, she'd see if her hearings could be scheduled before him—or her.

She was in the middle of drafting a speedy trial motion when her cell phone rang before nine a.m.

"Is this Sandra?" asked a vaguely familiar male voice.

"Who is this?" She was in no mood to be disturbed. After the work on Rufina's case, she needed to address the stack of files that had accumulated on her desk Monday and Tuesday.

"Jared. I looked for you at court yesterday, but you were gone."

Sandra didn't like the school-girl sensation in her chest. She didn't want anything to do with Jared. She'd sworn off men like an alcoholic swears off booze after joining AA. Yes, she'd had a slip, but it was a one-time thing. She didn't want complications in her life. His calling placed her in a position of having to deal with him. She'd scooted out of town and planned to avoid him when she went back. Now this. "How'd you get this number?"

"Is this a bad time? I thought we could go to breakfast."

Sandra pushed back her chair and picked up her coffee cup. "Are you in Galveston? Because I am."

"Oh. I wanted to see you before you left."

"Why?" She wanted to hang up and get to the work on her desk. She hadn't yet checked her calendar to see what her schedule looked like for the rest of the week. All she remembered was the divorce scheduled on Friday. Still . . .

His voice grew deeper. "Did I do something to offend you? I thought we had uh—fun the other night."

Sandra stared at the ceiling. Her feelings betrayed her, but she wasn't going to succumb to them. Involvement with another man was not what she wanted. "Look, Jared, I did have a good time. I enjoyed meeting you and our evening together. We live hours apart, and I'm not looking for a long-term relationship."

"Whoa. That about sums it up, I guess. You have a great life then, Attorney Salinsky."

The phone went dead. Sandra set aside the heaviness in her chest as she laid her cell phone next to the landline on her desk. That took care of Jared. She allowed herself a moment to remember how considerate he'd been in the sack and turned back to her computer.

"Hey, what's up?" Patricia was laden with the newspaper, her purse, and a large cardboard cup of coffee. She had her coat half off, looking like she was ready to start the day. "How was your trip?"

"I have a stack of motions I want to file on Rufina's case, so I thought I'd do them myself. Everything going okay around here?"

"Lots of messages for you, but otherwise, fine. Best time of year to leave town, since everyone is slow to restart after the holidays. Let me put my things down, and I'll make you some coffee."

"Already did. You go ahead and have yours, and we'll talk in a few minutes." Patricia had become addicted to chain-store coffee years earlier from the first moment she'd stepped foot over their threshold. She'd confessed to knowing she spent too much money on it, but claimed she didn't have a life, so why not spend her money on something she enjoyed? Sandra envied how Patricia put so much heavy cream in her coffee every day and never gained an ounce. Sandra had to work hard not to end up looking roly-poly like Erma.

Patricia shuffled off to her own office, leaving Sandra alone with her computer. Sandra had loaded the same software on her computer that Patricia's held, except the probate stuff. Erma did probate, not Sandra, and Erma wouldn't touch a computer with a ten-foot pole. Patricia did all Erma's paperwork as well as her email. Erma wouldn't even try to get her own email. At least she'd answer her own cell phone.

Sandra poured herself another cup of coffee while her speedy trial motion printed. She'd mail one of every motion to Holt's office, one to Rufina, and file one away. The clerk's, she'd fax. While she leaned against the counter, she watched through the glass-paned door as her mother maneuvered her Lincoln Continental between Patricia's little Toyota and the tree that dominated the backyard. Having arrived the earliest,

Sandra had parked her Volvo next to the back steps with plenty of room to spare.

When Erma came inside, she said, "One of these days, that tree is going to have to go."

"Morning, Erma." Sandra had heard the tree refrain often enough to ignore it.

Erma dropped her black leather handbag on the dinette table and shed her coat, hanging it on the coat rack in the hall. "What are you up to this brisk morning?"

Sandra sipped her coffee and smiled at her mother. "Barboza motions. Did you get some sleep?"

"Humph. Except for getting up three times." Erma picked up her purse and strutted into her office. A few moments later, she returned.

Sandra handed her a mug of coffee prepared with plenty of sugar and cream, the way she liked it.

Erma's eyes did a once-over of Sandra's face. "Sandra, I—"

"Don't start on me this morning. I'm not in the mood for it." She stalked from the kitchen, circled her desk, and landed back in her chair.

Erma stuck her head inside the door. "I want to say how grateful BJ is that you took Rufina's case."

"Fine. I've got work to do." She wasn't going to discuss her taking the criminal case or her taking another job.

"Well, and me, too." Erma stepped inside the doorway. "I'm thankful, also."

"Don't go maudlin on me." Sandra rummaged through her briefcase to find the Gillespie County District Clerk's card with the fax number on it.

"You know I'm not much for sentiment, daughter."

Sandra found the card. No fax number. She glanced at Erma and took a deep breath. That her mother rarely revealed her feelings was the understatement of the century. Perhaps she should stop and give the old girl some feedback, though she battled with the same issues herself. Growing up with a mother who worked night and day, giving her very little face time except at meals and when she tucked her in some nights, didn't give Sandra much to model after.

Erma stood in the doorway, mug cupped in her hands, a solemn expression on her face. She wore what had become her signature color, black, as though on her way to a funeral, and stared at Sandra.

"It's decent of you to say so," Sandra said. "I appreciate it. Just next time . . . " Sandra stopped herself. There wouldn't be a next time.

"I get you." Erma backed across the hall. "Well, let me see what's doing."

Picking up their landline, Sandra dialed the Gillespie County Clerk's office. "Morning, Annie? This is Sandra Salinsky. How are you today?"

"Fine, Mrs.—Sandra, and you?"

Sandra hated wasting time on pleasantries but forced herself to go through them. "Fine. Back at home."

"How was the drive?"

Sandra rolled her eyes. "Fine, thank you. Listen, Annie, I don't want to take up a lot of your time. I know how busy y'all are in the clerk's office. Your office card doesn't reflect the fax number. I need to send you some motions."

"Oh, I'm sorry, Sandra. I must have given you one of the old cards."

Sandra couldn't help but wonder whether that was intentional. Did they forget to give new cards to all the out of town attorneys? "May I have the number?"

"Well, of course. Got a pen?"

"Yes, go ahead." Sandra wrote down the number, repeating it back to be sure. "Let me ask you this, how do I procure a setting on my motions? Do I call the court coordinator for a setting and then record it on the fiat and mail it to you or what?"

"Fiat?"

"The Order Setting Hearing."

"Oh yes, you'll have to take that up with the coordinator."

Sandra blew out a gust of air. "Well, thanks so much for your help. Take care." She hung up and strode into Patricia's office where she found Erma. "I'm making progress with the clerk, I think."

Erma sat across from Patricia. They'd been deep in conversation. They both looked as though they'd been caught committing an illegal act. "What now?" Erma asked with a glance at Patricia.

"They gave me a card without the fax number on it, so I called and got the number. Seems it was inadvertent. They gave me an old card by mistake."

"Of course they did," Erma said.

"You'd think the edible arrangement I sent would have some effect."

"Maybe they didn't receive it yet," Patricia said. "What was in it?"

"Fruit and candy. Remember the one we sent you last year on Valentine's?"

Patricia nodded. "Yum. Yeah. Shame to waste it on them."

"On top of that," Sandra said, "the clerk won't tell me how to obtain a setting."

"Look at the local rules."

"I have the feeling I'm going to get awfully tired of small-town goings-on before this case is over."

"I gotta feeling you already are," Erma said.

"You're right about that." Shaking her head, Sandra backed to her office, her footfalls pounding like hammer strikes on the hardwood floor. Digging in her briefcase again, she found the Gillespie County rules. Erma was right. The rules were the best offense and defense in a case.

A while later, when she'd finished the discovery motion and printed it, Sandra checked her emails and found one from Rex. It read:

Hey, Sandra, did you hear? Your girl's been indicted for capital murder. Guess you'll have to come up here sooner than you planned. I thought you'd like to know. Rex

And a second one right below the first email:

By the way, if there's anything I can do to help you and Erma, don't hesitate to call. Remember I'm only an hour's drive away in San Antonio. Rex

A familiar burn rose in her face. Sandra slammed her hand on her desktop, a pen bouncing. She'd returned home with the definite impression Rex would love to help Rufina, and them, right off the highest hill in Fredericksburg. What was his motive in emailing her? What did he have in mind? If what he said was true, did Holt get the judge to raise Rufina's bail? Or had it remained the same? She picked up the phone and called the clerk again.

"Annie, this is Sandra Salinsky again. Got a moment?"

"Sure, Sandra. What can I do for you?"

"Has a new indictment on Rufina Barboza been handed down?"

"Hmm. I'm not at liberty to say."

"You would know, though, right?"

"Do you want me to tell you what the usual procedure is?" Voices came from her office background.

"All right, I'll bite."

"Grand jury meets once a week until they finish whatever Mr. Holt has scheduled for them. When they're finished, they go into court to return the indictments. Then they give them to us. We record them and open files. If there's a previous bail set, we gather up the paperwork. Usually the previous bail is continued."

"Usually?"

"Mr. Holt might ask for the bail to be raised."

"Judge Jefferson is there until the end of this week, right?"

"Yes, ma'am."

95

"Has Rufina Barboza's bail been raised?"

"I'm not at liberty to say. Do you want me to tell you the rest of the procedure?"

Sandra was sure steam spiraled from her ears. "Okay."

"If a higher bail is set and the defendant is not in jail, a warrant is issued for the defendant's arrest. The sheriff's deputy goes out and arrests the defendant and they have to start over."

Their procedures weren't much different from any place else, except Sandra often received some notice on her Galveston County cases. "You're saying Rufina Barboza could be arrested again? Like this week?" No doubt, without a courtesy call from the DA asking her to bring in her client.

"Could?"

"Yes. I know you're not going to tell me either way."

"Yes, she could. If the judge raised her bail or didn't set bail."

"So how soon before the indictments and all become public?"

"They try to make all the arrests first."

"Can you tell me, any new indictments been recorded yet?"

"I'm—"

"Not at liberty to say. I get it. Thanks again, Annie. I appreciate it."

The background voices stopped, and Annie's voice took on a confidential tone. "Sandra, for sure Mr. Holt took Mrs. Barboza's case before the Grand Jury again, but beyond that, I don't know. I hope that helps." In a louder voice she said, "Call anytime, Sandra."

As much as she hated dealing with people on the telephone, Sandra realized the Barboza case was going to be one of those where she would have to have a lot of phone contact. She punched in Rufina's number.

"Hey, this is Sandra. We may have a problem. The district attorney may have persuaded the Grand Jury to re-indict you. This time for capital murder."

"Wh—what does that mean?" Rufina's voice was raspy.

"It's not good. If Holt managed to do that, the visiting judge may have raised your bail. They could take you into custody again."

"Arrested? Why does Mr. Holt hate me so much?"

"I have no idea what his problem is. But if they come for you, go with them willingly and ask BJ to call me right away. I'll do everything I can to get you out of there as fast as possible."

"All right, Sandra. I hate to go back to jail, but *gracias* for warning me."

"I'm not sure what's going on, but I suspect that's what Holt is trying to do."

"I know you are doing all you can. I'll tell Billie J, too."

"One other thing before I hang up. Why does Rex not like you?"

"You mean hate me? Rex hates me ever since his mother sold me those acres. If there was something before, I don't know what it could be."

"How did her selling you that land affect him?"

"I think he wants to inherit as much as possible. He's been a problem since he was little."

"Well, stay out of his way. There's something going on with him, and I hope to learn what it is before everything is said and done."

"Thank you again, Sandra."

"Don't keep thanking me, Rufina. I'm just doing my job. I'll be in touch."

After they hung up, Sandra crossed the hall and peeked into her mother's office.

"What's up now?" Erma laid down a document she'd been reading.

"Possibly Rufina's bail." Sandra slid into the closest chair. "I think she's been indicted on capital murder charges."

"You think?"

"Got an email from Rex. He said so, but Annie in the clerk's office wouldn't confirm it. What's Rex's problem? He started out trying to charm us and now this..."

"Spoiled brat, if you ask me. BJ and Roy never denied him anything. What'd he say in the email?" Erma pushed back from the file she was working on.

"That Rufina had been re-indicted, and he offered to help us if we needed anything."

"Humph. Well, number one, how does he know about the indictment if the clerk won't tell you?"

She shrugged. "Holt, I guess. I'm sure there's something going on there."

"That smells."

"Yeah, it does." Sandra rubbed her chin. "Could be the small-town thing, like they went to school together?"

"Nah. Holt's gotta be way older. And number two," Erma scribbled something on a legal pad, "could Rex be of any help to us?"

"I don't know, but I wouldn't trust him on a dark country road. Or anywhere else, for that matter." Sandra brushed her hair back.

"Me, neither. There's just something..." Erma shook her head. "I wonder what he's up to?"

"Do you think he killed his sister?"

"Could have. He didn't appear to be too broken up about it."

"Sociopath." A chill ran across the back of her neck.

"My thoughts exactly. Unless he's a psychopath, which is even scarier." Erma sipped from her cup, and her nose scrunched up. "Cold. So what are you working on now?"

"I've got the motions done, but I'll file another writ if Rufina is re-arrested. Here's the thing, though, could you call the court coordinator for the settings? I think we got off on the wrong foot yesterday morning."

"No shit. Give me the number."

Sandra waited while Erma made the call. She had a million other things to do but wanted Rufina's case squared away.

"May I speak to Mrs. Chamberlain, please?" Erma spoke in a sweet, southern tone of voice way different from her normal gravelly one. "This is Erma Townley, calling from Galveston." She winked at Sandra.

"Yes, Mrs. Chamberlain—Amber—this is Erma Townley. I'm one of the attorneys in the Rufina Barboza murder case. How are you today? I'm doing fine, thank you for asking. The reason I'm calling is we've got some motions to file and wonder if you could assist us in obtaining settings. What's your procedure on motion hearings?"

Erma covered the phone with her hand and whispered, "She doesn't set cases over the phone." She moved her hand.

"Ah, I see. What about fax? Would I be able to fax the motions to you for the settings? A letter only? May I fax the letter?"

She shook her head. She wrote the address down. "Do I include the fiat with the letter?" Erma nodded.

"And you'll mail back the settings? All right. Thanks so much, Amber. You take care now, y'hear?" Erma slammed the phone down. "Son of a bitch."

Sandra laughed. "Now who's like a kettle about to boil over?"

"Yep. We've both got to get ahold of ourselves. This case is going to be one hell of a long haul."

☩   ☩   ☩

Thursday morning, Sandra placed another call, one she dreaded but forced herself to make. She got his number off her cell and when he answered, she made her voice as sweet as she could. "Jared, this is Sandra Salinsky. I want to apologize for yesterday." She'd never been much for eating crow.

"How did you get this number?" His deep voice held a caustic note.

"Jared, I'm really sorry. You caught me at a bad time."

"Who did you say you were?" His tone became slightly less abrasive.

"Okay. I deserve that. What can I say to make things right?"

He cleared his throat. "Go out with me the next time you're up here."

She hoped he didn't hear her deep exhale. A relationship with a man was the last thing she wanted, but she needed the help of a local attorney, and Jared was the only one she knew. "Well, it can't end up like the first time. I don't normally do things like that."

"I don't either. I don't know what got into us." His voice had changed and now sounded like it held a smile, a pitch higher.

"The beer perhaps?"

"I'm glad you called me back, even if it isn't because you want to see me."

"What do you mean?" Yeah, no. Jared was not dumb.

"You need local counsel, don't you?"

She was glad he wasn't there to see her response. This time her face reddened with something akin to shame. "Are you implying I have an ulterior motive?"

"I was at the clerk's office yesterday when you called Annie."

"Oh." Caught *flagrante delicto*.

"I don't mind. I don't do criminal law, but I have office space you can use."

Sandra wanted to hang up and never face him again, but she couldn't. "I don't know that I'll need anyone to help, really."

"Yes, you will. I happen to know Sam Holt is eager to get your client indicted for cap murder."

A spurt of anger rushed through Sandra. "Do you happen to know if he succeeded?"

"Nope. I mean, yes, I know, but no he hasn't succeeded yet. The Grand Jury is holding the case open. He wants to present more evidence if he can find any."

"How the hell do you know that when I can't get it out of the clerk?"

"I went to high school with Sam Holt."

She felt like she'd been gut-punched. "Shoulda known. Well, it was nice knowing you."

He hooted with laughter. "Hold on. That doesn't mean I won't help you out, and believe me, in this town you need a friend."

"I kinda figured that. I'm re-thinking even taking the case."

"No, that's a good thing. She needs outside counsel—trust me. Tell you what, if he manages to get her re-indicted, I'll handle the bond reduction hearing for you, but if you need anything complicated done, I'm not your man."

"Very sweet of you, Jared. I appreciate it. Can I pay you?" Life would be simpler if he'd say yes.

"Yeah, and I've stated the terms. Dinner the next time you're here."

She gritted her teeth. She really didn't want to get involved. She needed to keep telling herself that. "It's a deal. You'll stay in touch about my client?"

"Sure. I've got to go now. Got a closing this morning, and I'm standing here in my pajamas."

Sandra couldn't resist saying, "You wear pajamas?"

"Only in the winter and only if I'm sleeping alone."

"Good to know." She made an effort to muffle her laughter. "Take care."

Erma stood in her doorway. "You seem pleased with something, daughter. Care to share?"

"Nada," Sandra said with a rueful smile.

Erma crossed one leg over the other and leaned on the door-jamb like a jaunty elf. "I'll find out about it, you know. You might as well confess here and now."

Sandra turned her back on her mother and made with busy work until Erma returned to her own office. There would be no sharing of Jared. No way. No how. She still didn't intend to have a relationship, but she needed him now. No one could try a capital murder case in a strange town without at least one local ally. A stroke of luck had given Sandra hers, and she intended to hang on to him for the duration.

CHAPTER TWELVE

THE LAST WEEK of January, Sandra drove to Fredericks-burg alone for hearings on her motions. She spent the night in the same B & B she and Jared had shared. The next morning, she donned a long black skirt and long-sleeved, royal-blue blouse, and the new boots and jacket she'd purchased on the previous trip. When she went outside, she breathed deeply of the crisp, cold air, so different from Galveston's humid, but warmer air. As she climbed to the second floor of the courthouse a few minutes before her nine-a.m. setting, Sandra thought she looked her best.

Inside the courtroom, a different court reporter from the previous hearings had her face buried in a paperback book. Sandra dropped her small, red leather attaché' case on the counsel table and approached the court reporter, who put away her book.

"Sandra Salinsky for Rufina Barboza." She held out her hand.

The reporter, who had a cherub's face and curly short blonde hair, shook Sandra's hand with her soft, supple one. "Evelyn Koehn. The judge is in chambers."

Sandra handed her a card. "Should I go in?"

The reporter nodded, "Yes, ma'am," and typed something into her court reporting machine. "Mr. Holt's in there." She cocked one eyebrow reminiscent of what the last court reporter had done.

Sandra cocked an eyebrow back. "Something you want to tell me about Mr. Holt?"

Evelyn said, "I wouldn't have said, if you hadn't asked. He's not real popular with the defense bar."

Those few words told her what she needed to know. "Understood. Thanks." Sandra circled the bench and knocked on the chambers' door frame. The anxiety she felt at facing Holt again dissipated when her eyes landed on the judge. "Hello, Judge Olsen. Long time no see." She stepped closer and held out her hand.

"Ms. Salinsky. I trust you're doing well." A woman about Erma's age, Judge Olsen was a sturdy, tall brunette with gray-streaked hair and dark blue eyes. Sandra and Erma knew her from when Judge Olsen was on the bench in Galveston.

Sandra restrained herself from reaching for a hug. "I'd almost forgotten you retired up here and might be substituting."

The judge said, "Sit down and tell me what's been happening on the island." She glanced at Holt who sat up and pulled his chair close to the desk, which wasn't difficult in the small room. "I'm assuming you and Mr. Holt are acquainted."

Sandra nodded and shook Holt's hand, though she'd have preferred to keep her hands behind her back.

Holt's frown was almost imperceptible. "You two know each other, as well. Both from Galveston. I should've known." His eyes had lost their usual sparkle.

"Judge Olsen used to sit on the family district court bench. I do family law, too."

"Yes, we're old friends," Judge Olsen said. "Sandra tried her first child custody case in my court."

"So you're hearing criminal cases now, Judge? I mean other than juvenile." Sandra sat in the other plastic chair in front of the desk, her knees nearly brushing it. "I remember you did some criminal work before you took the bench."

"I hear everything. I go where they send me." She rocked in the worn, overstuffed chair.

"You're looking wonderful. Retirement agrees with you. Gosh, I'm so surprised you're here."

Judge Olsen smiled her thanks. "Mr. Holt tells me you've signed on to a murder case."

"Erma and the victim's family go way back."

"Well, I'm unlikely to see you again. I don't get many assignments." She picked up the court file and leaned back.

"So you won't be the trial judge?" Sandra asked.

"She doesn't do capital murder cases," Holt said.

Sandra glanced from Holt to the file to the judge. "So the Grand Jury has returned an indictment for capital murder? I haven't been officially notified."

Holt said, "Not yet, but they will."

The judge shot Holt a look of reprimand. "He's correct. If it's a capital murder, the regular judge will preside or else another judge who's experienced in cap murder. My limit is regular old murder." Her eyes crinkled. "But I've been assuming this case is cap murder." She thumbed through the file. "The indictment is for murder, Mr. Holt? What's this about?"

"Ahem. Our Grand Jury is holding the case open—we're waiting on some evidence, and then they'll hand down the cap murder indictment."

"Ms. Salinsky is expected to prepare for trial without knowing what her client is charged with?"

"I'm hoping the indictment will come down by the end of this week, Judge." Holt's eyes shifted from one woman to the other.

"He's been hoping for a while now."

A muscle flexed in the judge's cheek. Her eyebrows drew together. "This is highly unusual and not like you, Mr. Holt, not that you've appeared before me many times."

Sandra enjoyed watching Holt squirm.

Judge Olsen slapped the file closed. "Well, what we're proceeding on today is the assumption this is murder, not cap murder. What do I need to hear, and do we need a record?"

"Yes, Judge, if you don't mind. I'd like a record on everything." Sandra barely kept the note of glee out of her voice. Apparently, not every judge would put up with Holt's antics.

Holt stood. "I guess we'd better go into the courtroom."

The judge nodded. "Let me put on my robe."

Sandra followed Holt through the door. Settling at counsel table, she pulled out the Barboza file, which was beginning to thicken with pleadings. What was Holt trying to pull with that capital murder bit? Merely giving her a hard time, or was there some evidence which would bump the case up from murder? She didn't believe there was motive enough at the present time.

"You could have called. I would have agreed with most everything you're requesting," Holt said.

Sandra didn't want to argue with him. She had no intention of letting him set her up in an agreement on her motions or, for that matter, anything else.

When the judge came out, they took up the motions. The judge granted the Speedy Trial motion, which wasn't required but told Sandra she'd have to try to get an earlier setting from the court coordinator. Finally, they came to the discovery motion.

Holt preened like a red-breasted robin. "I think we can cut this hearing short, Judge. My office has an open file policy, so Mrs. Salinsky can come look at anything in the file."

Judge Olsen glanced at Sandra, her eyebrows raised. "What do you say, Ms. Salinsky?"

As a former prosecutor, Sandra wasn't going to fall for that old prosecutorial trick. If she didn't have a court order signed by a judge, and Holt produced something at trial she'd never seen, she wouldn't be able to keep it out of evidence. "I'd like a signed order, Your Honor. If you wouldn't mind ruling on each paragraph, I'd appreciate it."

Judge Olsen rubbed a knuckle across her lips and nodded.

"That's not necessary, Judge," Holt said. "She can have access to anything I've got."

"Is there a reason you don't want to take Mr. Holt up on his offer?"

Sandra glanced from the judge to Holt. "Is there a reason I can't have a signed court order?" That sounded prickly, but she didn't care. She had to protect her client.

Holt threw his hands up as though amazed. "I don't know what you're used to in the big city, Mrs. Salinsky, but we don't do things like that up here. We still do things on a handshake."

He clearly enjoyed putting her on the spot, but nothing she could do about it. "Judge Olsen, this is a murder case, if not a capital murder case. I don't mean to imply anything about this particular district attorney's office, but you used to do criminal defense work. In a murder case I've got to dot every *i* and cross every *t* to protect my case for appeal."

"Oh, now wait a minute—" Holt said.

"I'm afraid I must insist on having signed court orders for everything."

The judge consulted her watch. "It makes no difference to me. I get paid one way or the other."

"Judge, I'd like to be out of here soon," Holt said.

"Then I suggest you agree to everything she wants, or we can proceed with Ms. Salinsky's discovery motion."

Forty-five-minutes of arguing and posturing later, Sandra packed her briefcase with the signed court order and said goodbye to the judge. When she arrived at her Volvo, someone had taken a key or a knife and scratched a large *X* across her Texas Democrat bumper sticker, beginning with the paint above the bumper. A spike of adrenaline darted up her back. If she hadn't fully realized it before, Sandra could see now how far into enemy territory she was.

She walked around to the passenger side to see what else they'd done. Nothing, thank God. Her hands shook. She glanced around, but no one was near the few vehicles parked at the courthouse. People dotted the sidewalks. A woman came out of a shop. A couple pulled a newspaper out of a box on a corner. No one seemed like a culprit, but, really, what would the culprit look like?

She unlocked her car and threw her things into the passenger seat. A muscle in her neck ached. A vein throbbed at her temple. She shouldn't have taken Rufina's case, but if whoever had keyed her car had more in mind than insulting someone from the other political party, if they intended the damage to scare her away, they were in for a surprise. She never backed down.

Grabbing her phone, she called her office. She'd move the car to a different spot and get a bite to eat before she left town.

"Hey," she said when Patricia answered the phone. "Erma around?"

"Everything going okay?"

Sandra rubbed her lips together. "Mostly. Everything going okay in Galveston?"

"Sure. We've got it all under control." Patricia's voice held a lilt, so Sandra could tell Patricia was happy.

"Great. Let me talk to Erma, please."

"Okey, dokey. I'll put you through."

"Sandra." Erma's voice was so loud Sandra wondered if her mother had added a little something to her morning coffee. "How'd it go?"

"The judge was Judge Olsen from Galveston."

"No shit? Well, that must have been fun."

"Holt wasn't too happy, but WTH, we don't care, right? She granted everything in our motion. I'm headed to the B &B for my stuff. I'll eat lunch before I head back."

"Safe travels."

Sandra tossed her cell into the seat beside her. She could have told her mother a lot more about her day, about the keying of her car and how much she wished she hadn't agreed to take Rufina's case, but it was better to hang up and not go into it until she returned home. Working for an insurance firm had to be better than this. She hadn't given them a response either way yet, but she was leaning closer to working for the "sweatshop," as Erma called it.

When she slid out of the car at the B & B, a truck pulled in beside her.

A short Latino male, who smelled like he'd just come in off the ranch having been mixing with the livestock, practically threw himself out of the driver's door. He wore a brown work jacket, a dark blue, plaid, long-sleeved snap-down western shirt, jeans, and mud-caked western boots. He grabbed his straw western hat off his head, rushed up to Sandra, and started shouting in Spanish.

The words all ran together, too quick for her to understand with her limited Spanish, but they sounded like "*Yo no quiero que usted*" something "*mi hermana!*" Something "*abogado de* San Antonio."

Sandra stepped back and glared at the little man who, though short, was thick and strong-looking. With the heels on her boots, she was at least six inches taller. Her heart pumped fast.

"No *habla*," she said, though she knew *abogado* meant lawyer. She put her fists on her hips. Since it was broad daylight, she didn't think anyone would stand by and let the man assault her. "You want to say something to me, you gotta speak English."

He said something else in Spanish she knew was an insult, and then said in decent English, "I don't want you on my sister's case. I got a lawyer from San Antonio who is going to represent Rufina."

Sandra stood her ground. She recognized him as the same man who had come into the back of the courtroom the day of the bail hearing. There was no way of knowing whether he was the person who had damaged her car, but he could have been. He was worked up. Why was he so angry? All she had done was drive five-to-six hours to Fredericksburg, meet with his sister, appear in court with her and get bail set, go home, and then return to the Hill Country and go to bat for her. Why the hell was he so pissed?

"Hey, I didn't volunteer for this case. Billie Jo and Rufina wanted me."

"Now you can get off it. I got another lawyer. Go back where you came from. We don't want you here, you and your old mama."

The hair rose on Sandra's arms. They might not want her, but they had better not start in on her mother. "Wait a minute, *señor*," she said. "Who is we?"

"Me." He pointed at his chest with his thumb. "Me and Rufina and the rest of *mi familia.*"

Sandra's face burned like she'd been slapped. That was news to her. If Rufina didn't want her, all she had to do was say so. She'd had plenty of opportunity. Sandra sized up the little man. His weathered face could crack any moment. Still, Sandra was offended and defensive and didn't like to be verbally accosted on the public street. She didn't know what his problem was. She was a good lawyer and was taking care of business.

"*Como se llama?*" She asked his name.

He hesitated a moment before answering. "Carlos."

"Well, Carlos, I don't why you have an issue with me and my mother, but we—I—am taking this case very seriously. I'm working it hard. You don't know me, true, or anything about me, but if you ask around—call down to Galveston—you'll find I have a good reputation for being a damn fine criminal defense lawyer."

Though it seemed impossible, his angry face screwed up even more. "If you're so *maravillosa*, why is *mi hermana* so scared she won't come out of her *casa*?

CHAPTER THIRTEEN

EVEN IN THE middle of a weekday, Fredericksburg's Main Street was filled with tourists and townspeople. As a destination town, people came for the shopping and the restaurants and bars. Sandra moved her car again, this time to park in front of a bakery that offered ready-made sandwiches and coffee. The yeasty aroma of baking bread greeted her, causing her stomach to growl. Wending her way through the throng, she purchased a sandwich and hazelnut-flavored coffee.

She unbuttoned and loosened her jacket and picked a table facing the street. The sandwich was on locally baked, thick multigrain bread. She chewed while contemplating what should be done about Rufina. Whatever had happened to make Rufina afraid, Sandra needed to find out right away. Still cold from standing outside with Carlos, she shivered and sipped some coffee. BJ must be aware of the situation and should have called. Sandra scrolled to BJ's number and clicked on it.

"Sandra!" BJ said in a louder than normal voice. "I'm so glad you called. I need to talk to y'all about Rufina."

"That's why I'm calling. What is this about her wanting different lawyers?"

"Where'd you hear that?" Her tone hadn't lowered.

Sandra held the phone away from her ear. "Her brother, Carlos. He accosted me outside my car a few minutes ago." She pulled a small piece of crust off her sandwich.

"You mean y'all are here?"

"Calm down, BJ. You're yelling." Sandra popped the bit into her mouth while she gave BJ a moment to settle down. "Only me. Had hearings on some motions today. Rufina didn't tell you?"

"Rufina is—is I guess you could say hiding in her cottage."

"That's what Carlos said. Who or what is she hiding from?"

"Can you come out here? I mean, are you in a hurry to go back to Galveston?"

Sandra started to answer when someone stopped at her elbow. She raised her head. Jared stood with a sandwich in one hand and a cup of coffee in the other. Sandra's breath caught with the memory his cologne brought back to her. He wore no coat. His tie was askew. The top button of his long-sleeved light blue dress shirt was undone, but otherwise he was decked out in lawyer attire down to his shiny boots.

"What do we have here?" He raised an eyebrow. "Could it be Attorney Salinsky?"

She pointed to her phone and waved him to a chair. "Not in a huge hurry," she said into the phone. Jared dragged a wooden chair from under the table with the toe of his boot and sat down.

"I wish you would come out here and talk with her," BJ said. "Rufina hasn't told me what happened. She was okay the first few days after she got out of jail."

Sandra swallowed hard. She wasn't prepared to stay, didn't want to stay, but circumstances change. Avoiding Jared's eyes, she studied his hands as he unwrapped his sandwich.

"You could talk to Kathy Lynn while you're here." BJ was trying to sweeten the pot. "She's supposed to come over this evening for dinner. You could stay the night and head back early tomorrow morning."

"Hold on a minute while I check my calendar." Sandra tapped the calendar app. Nothing she probably couldn't rearrange. "All right. Let me contact my office. I'll be out there later today. Will you tell Rufina, or should we let it be a surprise?"

"I'll tell her. She'll let me in, and she'll talk on the phone, but she won't come out. See you later. Thanks."

Sandra put her phone on the table. "Mr. Jared Longley." Her eyes met his hazel ones, now a bit shy of brown. "I'd invite you to join me for lunch, but you've done that."

He stared at her, his brows raised, his lips compressed. He glanced at her sandwich and back up to her face.

"Turkey," Sandra said.

He laughed out of the side of his mouth.

Sandra snorted. "Not you. The sandwich."

He nodded and took a bite of his, chewing for a moment before swallowing, and said, "Chicken."

She studied his face, his eyes. "Me or the sandwich?"

He ate another bite. "You were supposed to call me, so we could go to dinner the next time you came to town."

She sipped her coffee, savoring the hazelnut and avoiding his eyes. "Arrived this morning."

"I didn't receive your message." He raised an eyebrow again.

Her eyes met his again. "Didn't leave a message."

"Didn't call?"

"I'm not going to lie."

"Don't want you to."

"I was planning on driving up and back in one day."

"What time was your hearing?"

"Nine."

"Nine." He took a small bite and chewed for a minute. "You left Galveston before sunup to get here for a hearing at nine?"

She blotted her lips and focused through the window at the people crowding the sidewalk. Time to fess up. "Well, okay, I did lie a little."

"You spent last night here."

She reared back. "You knew that?"

"My cousin owns the B & B."

She scooted back her chair and started to rise. "This isn't going well."

He put a hand on her arm. "Sit down, Sandra. Let's finish our sandwiches."

Even through her coat, her arm burned at his touch. She sat back down. Her stomach twisted. "How long were you going to let me go on with my story?"

His eyes slow danced. "Oh, I don't know." He took another bite, a huge one, as if knowing it would take him a while to chew it all and swallow, giving her time to make her excuses.

"I had planned on driving straight back after my hearing. I got in late, too late to do anything but fall into bed. But you probably know that as well. When I woke up this morning, I figured I'd run over to the courthouse and come back and get my stuff and check out." She swallowed some coffee. "The day hasn't been going the way I planned. And I have a hearing tomorrow in Galveston I don't think I'm going to make unless I drive late into the night, which I don't like to do, especially since I've been up a jillion hours in the past few days. And, BJ wants me to go out there and talk to Rufina and I said I would." She stopped to breathe.

He stared at her while she spoke. He finished his sandwich and brushed the crumbs into a little pile on the wrapper before tossing everything into a nearby trash can.

Sandra stopped herself from doing any more rambling and held her hands in her lap. Definitely the day wasn't going right. She'd lost her appetite. The coffee was no longer hot. She dumped her food in the trash, too, and waited for him to speak.

She needed to call her friend, Ray, to cover for her at the hearing on a protective order in the morning. If Ray couldn't do it, Sandra would need to call Erma, who hated protective orders and wasn't up on the law, either. As a last resort, she could try to get a reset, but the hearing really needed to go forward for the safety of the client.

"So what are your plans for the evening?"

"I guess you're pissed, but you shouldn't be. If I'd meant to stay longer, I would have called you." She pulled her hands into her lap to hide a small tremble.

"Now I know you're lying."

"No, honestly, I would have. We have a bargain. You did say we could use your office during the trial."

"Huh. That would have been the only reason. I get that. You wouldn't want to jeopardize our agreement, if not our relationship."

Sandra lowered her eyes. "I—I'm not sure." Where did those words come from? She had told herself she didn't want a relationship. Now she's implying she's not sure? What the hell was wrong with her?

His eyes widened. "You want to come across and look over my set-up since you're here? Don't think you're leaving tonight if you have to go out to BJ's."

She held up her palm and drew a deep breath. "You overheard my conversation. I could go see your office, but I have to make a few more calls." She gave him a business-like expression she hoped communicated she had no intention of sleeping with him again. "And I've got to check out of the B & B. I hope your cousin won't charge me for a second night since it's getting late."

"All right, I hear you. I'm going to my office. I had a meeting that took all morning and need to address some things on my desk. Why don't you come by after you've sorted everything out? We're in the bank building across and down the street." He pointed toward the east.

She had trouble believing he could be so nice after she'd confessed to lying. His lips turned up at the corners, revealing one dimple. She hadn't noticed that before. Why would someone like him be unattached in a world where there were so many more women than men?"

"Okay, Jared. But I want you to understand—"

His palms flew up in a hands-off gesture. "Just come see the space this afternoon, that's all. You'll have plenty of time to take care of business at BJ's and go to bed early so you'll be rested for your drive home tomorrow."

"Now you're sounding like my mother."

"Whoa. I take it that's not a compliment." He cocked his head.

She picked up her purse and slung it over her shoulder. "This is awkward."

"Sandra, I don't know what's going on with us—if there is an us—but I told you I'd help you out. I fully intend to do that." He pushed back. "We don't really know each other, though I'd like to get to know you. I mean aside from—well, you'll spend some time in my office when your trial starts—"

Sandra tried not to laugh. He felt as ill at ease about their personal situation as she did. She didn't want a relationship, that was true. But she liked this guy, this blond farm-boy-type who she could tell had a story of his own. The easiest thing for her would be to do nothing, to focus on the case, the trial, doing her best for Rufina, and to let things with Jared play out over the course of the coming months. She touched the back of his hand. "I'll come by after I get my things."

He put his chair under the table. "We're on the third floor." He indicated she should walk ahead of him.

When they went out the door, he said, "See you."

Sandra nodded. She buttoned up her jacket against the cold and watched him head toward the crosswalk. She liked that he was so big, so tall—even without his boots. She preferred taller men. And one in good shape, not too thin, not starting to get fat, muscular—what was she thinking about that for? She laughed at herself and hurried toward her car, looking back once more. Jared, too, glanced over his shoulder as he crossed the street.

⚕ ⚕ ⚕

Jared's cousin was understanding and didn't charge Sandra for an extra night. She packed her overnight bag with the few clothes she'd brought and threw them into the car. She called

Ray, the attorney-friend who would cover for her when Erma couldn't or wouldn't. He agreed to take care of the protective order hearing.

Pleased that for once everything was going well, Sandra parked beside the bank building that held Jared's law office. The sidewalks were as busy with shoppers as they had been earlier. The displays in the store windows had been changed since the last time she'd been there. Bunnies and pastel-colored eggs were now in place. Gone were the woolen coats and warm pantsuits. Spring fashions with a country flair hung on the mannequins.

Elation filled her as she drew in air all the way to the bottom of her lungs. The day had turned out much better than it had begun. She'd prevailed in getting what she wanted in her hearing. Holt learned things wouldn't always go his way. Judges wouldn't always favor him. And, if Sandra had anything to say about it, the jury in Rufina's case wouldn't go his way either.

She would talk with Rufina to get to the bottom of her fears and be able to interview Kathy Lynn. She even looked forward to spending some time with BJ, to learning more about the family.

Inside the bank building, she punched the elevator button and straightened her clothing while she waited. On a whim, she pulled out a tube of lipstick and swiped her lips. Wondering if the onions from her sandwich were still on her breath, she dug deep into her purse for anything that might alleviate the odor and found two paper-wrapped mints. Now if she only had a little spray bottle of cologne...

When the elevator came, she pressed the button for the third floor and drew another deep breath. She was there to see the office layout. That was all. Just to see the setup and how it would work during the trial. Nothing was going to happen between Jared and her. She had almost a year before trial, and she intended to use every opportunity when she was in the Hill Country to work on the case, only the case.

When she entered Jared's office, a familiar-looking youngish woman sitting at a gray, farmhouse-style front desk asked, "May I help you?"

Sandra glanced around the carpeted reception area and tapped her lips. "Looking for Jared. Is he in?" The walls bore framed country scenes. Though the colors in the furniture were subdued, bordering rustic and charming, the style was not outdated.

"He said you might be looking for him. He's a big tease, and I thought he was kidding."

Sandra gripped the strap of her bag which hung over her left shoulder. "I'm sorry. If we've met, I don't remember."

The woman nodded. "I'm his sister. Remember you helped me with my divorce?"

"Oh, yes." Sandra shook the young woman's hand. "I didn't recognize you."

"Well, of course you didn't." She flapped her fingers at Sandra. "I look a lot better than I did even a few weeks ago. I was stressed back then. I don't work here. I'm just subbing for the regular receptionist who is out having a baby. I thought the least I could do would be to work for my brother when he needed someone after he represented me for free. Except for the part of it you did, I mean."

Sandra stood in front of the receptionist's desk while the woman talked. "I'm embarrassed I don't even remember your name."

"Laura. Was Laura Keller. Now Laura Longley."

"That's enough talking her ear off," Jared interrupted from the long hallway.

Sandra's body responded to the sound of his voice, growing twitchy outside and jittery inside. "How are you, Mr. Longley?" As if she hadn't seen him an hour earlier.

Jared looked her up and down, his eyes stopping a couple of times. "To what do I owe the pleasure, Miss Salinsky?" As if he hadn't invited her there.

Sandra looked him up and down in return, her eyes stopping a couple of times as well. "Remember I said the next time I was in town I'd look over that office space you offered? Are you busy now?"

He hesitated like he was going to say something, then his lips parted in a grin. "No, a little paperwork to do. But it can wait."

"And the library, too. I'd love to see your library. I'm assuming you have a board table—a table we can spread our stuff out on if there's not enough room in your spare office?"

His eyes became a dark, shiny green. "Sure do. Laura, don't disturb us if I receive any calls."

Laura appeared to be studying the top of the computer keyboard. "Glad to see you again, Miss Salinsky." She turned to a document resting to her left and thumbed the space bar.

"You too, Laura." Sandra walked toward Jared. "How many offices do you have in this complex?"

"Head down that hallway." He touched her back in a light prod. "Several. I only have one associate right now. He's in a meeting with a surveyor."

Sandra rubbed at the goosebumps his touch raised on her skin, glad she wore long sleeves and a coat. She let him escort her past the first office on the left.

"That's his. This next one on the right is mine." His desk sat in front of large windows with a panoramic view into the distance. "Super view, right?"

"Super," Sandra said, mimicking him. She wasn't sure she was capable of saying much more. For someone who didn't want a relationship, she sure felt drawn to the man.

"The one right next to it is the empty one. The one you can use." He took her to a room about half the size of his office, which held a desk, executive chair, two chairs opposite, and a wide bookcase with files stacked on most of the shelves. "Laura can take those files out. But looking at it, I see what you're getting at. Not much room in this small office for people to spread out. I'm sure you'll need more space. Across the hall is the library."

He opened a door to a stereotypical attorney's law library, crowded with lawyer paraphernalia. The walls were lined with bookshelves filled with tan and black and various other colored law books, some of which looked like they dated back to at least the previous century, if not the one before. A commercial-sized copier sat at one end. A long, wide conference table stood in the middle with ten chairs surrounding it. An empty water pitcher, plastic cups, and the tray on which they sat were centered on the table. "We do depositions in here. Plenty of room for everyone."

Sandra's eyes roamed from Jared to the table and back to Jared. She might regret her actions later, but she doubled back to the door and closed it, locking it behind her. Her jacket fell to the floor and moments later, their clothes graced the backs of the chairs. The table was hard on her back, but she didn't care. There was a lot more room to spread out than on the carpet.

CHAPTER FOURTEEN

B J LOOKED LIKE hell. Her hair was stringy. The shirt and jeans she wore looked like they hadn't been changed in days. She hugged Sandra like she was some kind of long-lost relative. "So happy you came. Let me show you to your room." BJ didn't smell good either. She needed a bath in the worst way.

"If it's the same as last time, I think I can find it."

BJ snatched the overnight bag from Sandra's shoulder and headed toward the back of the house.

"Alrighty," BJ said, dropping Sandra's bag on the bed. "Here you go. Can I fix you something to eat? Want a drink? I've got most anything you'd like."

Sandra set her purse down on the night table and stepped out of her shoes. A drink would be wonderful, something strong, but she would pass. "A cup of decaf? I appreciate you putting me up."

"Nonsense. If you had told me you were going to be here last night, you could have stayed then, too."

"I arrived rather late." She took off her jacket. "Go ahead, and I'll join you in a few minutes. By the way, what time will Kathy Lynn be here?"

BJ stopped in the doorway. "Uh, she won't."

"I don't suppose she was the one who passed me on the way in. Does she drive a ruby red Mustang?" She had suspected Kathy Lynn wasn't going to be there in the first place and had been surprised when a young blonde woman raced past her going in the other direction. "What happened?"

BJ's leathered face whitened. "I stupidly told Rex when he called that you'd be here, and Kathy Lynn was coming for dinner. She showed up, but when I told her Rex would be here, she didn't stay five-minutes."

What was it between Kathy Lynn and Rex? Sandra would like to get to the bottom of that eventually. "I'm going to have to talk to her sooner or later. Good thing there's a year to prepare for trial." She didn't want to go to Kerrville to see Kathy Lynn, so she'd been glad to hear they'd be able to meet that night. Still, there was plenty of time.

"Sorry. But even so, Rufina is still locked in her house. She's the one I'm hoping you can help with right now."

"Okay. I'll be in there in a few minutes. I want to talk to you before I see Rufina." She rubbed her feet. They were complaining from wearing high heels all day. Well, most of the day. She pushed thoughts of Jared out of her head. She pulled on a pair of flats and used the restroom. Her cell pinged. A quick look told her Erma had called five times. Sandra had ignored the pings when she'd been with Jared. She tapped in her mother's number.

"Goddamn, about time," Erma said when she picked up. "Where the hell are you? Patricia said you called and said you were going to be gone another night."

"I'm at BJ's now." Sandra explained she needed to talk to Rufina. "And I wanted to talk to Kathy Lynn, but she didn't want to talk to me." She pushed the door closed and sat on the bed.

"What do you mean? What happened?"

Erma's breath sounded labored. Sandra hoped Erma had just climbed the stairs and not that she'd started smoking or vaping or whatever addiction she was into now. "I think Rex has intimidated Kathy Lynn into not talking to us. Something's going on there. I can't help feeling it has to do with Katy Jo's being shot."

"You think he did it?" Erma's voice rose an octave. "He's a little worm, but I can't believe he'd deliberately kill his sister."

"From everything you've always told me about the girls, if someone needed killing, Kathy Lynn would be dead, not Katy Jo, but I haven't a clue who the shooter would be."

"Yeah. Katy Jo was the sweetest baby, always content in her carrier, cooing like a little dove. Kathy Lynn was colicky and gave BJ fits. And nothing changed in all those years...."

Sandra let her eyes wander while Erma recited the oft spoken refrain Sandra had heard since they'd decided to take the case. The room decor still hadn't changed from the holidays. Maybe BJ didn't have the energy to do it.

Erma coughed into the phone. "Katy Jo grew up to be the sweetest and most helpful young woman to her mother. But Kathy Lynn...what a bitch."

"Well, I've got to interview her sometime, but there's plenty of time. Hey, I need to go. BJ's waiting for me in the kitchen." She started out the door.

"So you don't even want me to tell you why I called you so many times?"

"Because you love me and miss me, Mommy Dearest?"

"No, that's not the reason."

"So you want me to guess?"

"That goddamned court coordinator called the office this afternoon. The Kerrville court coordinator. If we want it, we can have a trial setting in March. Otherwise, we'll keep the one she gave us for next year. How do you like them apples?"

Sandra stopped dead in the hall. Her blood ran hot. She'd never had high blood pressure, but this murder case might trigger it. Another reason to quit practicing criminal law and switch to civil. Civil was only about money. "Son of a bitch. I wonder what prompted the change of heart."

"Said they had a cancellation. Somebody decided to plead out. Said she knew it wasn't much notice. Take it or leave it."

"This doesn't pass the smell test. I think Holt is fucking with us."

"And I'm not enjoying it one bit. It'll be almost impossible to be ready in a month."

Sandra's mind raced with all that would need doing if they took the earlier setting. BJ entered the hall with a mug in her hand. Sandra held up one finger to stall her for a minute. They were being jerked around by Holt and God knows who else, but that didn't mean they couldn't deal with it. She was sure Rufina would be agreeable. For a client, the sooner matters were resolved, the better. They'd take the setting.

Erma coughed again. "I suppose we can wait until the setting we already have rolls around. Remember, delay can be the defense lawyer's best friend."

"Not in this case. Call back and tell her we'll take it. Rufina can't stay locked in her house forever."

"What are you talking about?"

"Rufina won't come out of her house. She thinks she's safer inside than out. That was why I initially agreed to spend the night. I need to talk to her and find out what's going on with her."

"Shit. Okay, we'll talk more about that when you're home. You'd better haul ass back here as fast as possible. If we're going to take that earlier setting, we've got a trial to prepare for."

"Then *hasta mañana, Mamacita.*" Sandra clicked off and turned her phone to silent.

"Was that Erma?" BJ handed the steaming mug to Sandra. The scent of coffee dominated the air. "I fixed us a snack. What's going on with her?" She wiped her hands on a dishtowel tucked into her waistband. BJ wore the same fake grin she often pasted on her face, but her red, puffy eyes told a different story. She was barely holding herself together.

Sandra followed her back to the kitchen and slid onto a bar stool. All the food on the counter left little room for her elbows. BJ or one of her employees had set out a spread of olives, green and black, and hummus and crackers and cheese and some stuff Sandra didn't recognize, together with bottles of fizzy water. If this was a snack, she couldn't wait for dinner. She took a sip of coffee and a bite out of a chunk of cheese on a cracker. She'd like nothing more than to take the mug to the sofa and put her feet up. But she had a lot of questions for BJ, and she'd better get started, so there would be time for Rufina before Rex showed up.

"Why don't you first tell me what's up with you, BJ? Why are you always wearing that fake grin?" Tears burst from BJ's eyes. She pulled the dishtowel from her waist and covered her face.

Though she wasn't the sentimental type, something about seeing that big woman cry tweaked Sandra's heart. BJ stood in her jeans and snapped down western shirt and boots, all toughness drained out of her, and bawled her eyes out. Sandra wasn't equipped to handle emotional people—at least not the sad stuff. After all, with Erma the emotions were aggressive, blasts of curse words together with lots of demonstrative gestures—except when performing for a jury. Sandra had seen plenty of acting there. She slid off the stool and went to BJ and rubbed her back. "Would you like a glass of water?"

BJ wrapped her arms around Sandra, almost squashing the stuffing out of her. Sandra continued to pat BJ's back, hoping the episode wouldn't last very long, so she could breathe something other than BJ's body odor. Too, she was tired and wanted to talk to Rufina, then eat dinner and go to bed early. As soon as she thought that, she felt another twinge—a twinge of guilt. After all the money BJ had paid them, the least Sandra could do was provide a shoulder. She tightened her arms around BJ and murmured, "You're okay. Everything will be okay." That sounded right.

After several minutes, BJ raised her head. Her blotchy face was swollen, her bangs smashed against her forehead. "I'm s-so s-sorry."

Sandra led her to the sofa and table in the alcove in front of the front window that overlooked the driveway and sat her down. The sun had about set, the sky a maroon and gray. After retrieving a box of tissues from the guest bathroom, she said, "You sit here. I'll bring you a glass of water."

BJ blew her nose long and hard and then sniffed and blew again. Sandra found a large glass and drew water from the dispenser in the refrigerator door. She sure would like a drink about now. And not water. She slurped from her coffee before setting the water glass in front of BJ, who swallowed most of it in one gulp.

Sandra sat adjacent to BJ. The multi-paned window gave a perfect view of part of the circular approach to the house. Lights would come in if someone drove up. "Are you ready to tell me what's going on?"

BJ made a little noise like a puppy's yelp. She blew her nose again. "I don't know how my life turned to shit."

Sandra pulled one leg up under her and turned toward BJ, waiting until BJ was ready to talk.

"Something happened between Kathy Lynn and Rex, and I'm not privy to it. I've asked both of them outright, separately, and neither of them will say."

Sandra kept eye contact as much as possible. After BJ wiped her eyes with one of the fresh tissues, she continued, "Don't know if it has to do with Rufina or not. Rex comes around like a gunfighter looking for trouble, and Kathy Lynn makes herself scarce when he's here. I don't think they've been in the same room together since...since..." She broke down and sobbed some more.

Sandra continued to be uncomfortable and fought to be patient. She wasn't used to crying clients. Seldom when visiting them in jail did they break down. Of course, life had hardened many of them. When she'd been in the DA's office, victim advocates took care of most of the victims and witnesses.

Sandra waited until BJ got ahold of herself before asking, "When did all this start?"

BJ breathed deeply several times and wiped her nose. "I'm all right now. I think. "Since...since the night Katy Jo died. Everyone was here. We had dinner together."

"By everyone, you mean the kids and you?"

She sat back. "Yeah, well, here's how it is at Christmastime. Roy started this tradition years ago when he got the ranch. Unless his family did it, I don't remember. Maybe they did."

Sandra breathed deeply and clenched her hands together to help herself be patient while BJ told her story.

"Anyway, when it gets close to Christmas, we always have an early afternoon dinner for everyone who works on the ranch. A real spread. A buffet. They all come and bring their families, and I hand out the bonuses. Roy used to, of course, but now I do it. I've never been real crazy about it. To me, it seems kind of demeaning."

Sandra telegraphed her a discouraging look, so she wouldn't go off on a tangent.

"So anyway, everyone was there."

"Everyone being..."

"Rufina, her brother Carlos and his family—though Carlos was acting rude. I don't know what caused that. The other hands and families came. We had quite a crowd. Then afterward, we had the family dinner, me and the kids and Elgin and Katy Jo's boyfriend, Doug. It was a kind of pre-Christmas dinner for us."

"Katy Jo's boyfriend, Doug?" That was the first anyone said Katy Jo had a boyfriend. "Where does he live?"

"Dallas. You've heard of bigger'n Dallas? Doug was being scouted to play pro football till a bad knee injury changed his life. He's a giant redhead, but gentle as they come."

"Kathy Lynn have a boyfriend?"

"She's between boyfriends right now."

Sandra chewed on her upper lip for a moment. "Anything happen at that dinner that was out of the ordinary?"

"No. I gave out the bonus checks to the employees who were there, in envelopes, of course. The newer hands don't receive as much, but everyone gets something. No one ever seems to be distressed about that."

"So the family pre-Christmas dinner was after that? Rex, how was he that night?"

BJ's eyes rose to the ceiling. "He was Rex, though a little more obnoxious than normal because he'd had a few shots of mezcal." She shook her head. "He hasn't been real manageable since his daddy died."

If ever, Sandra wanted to add. "Let's go back to Kathy Lynn and Rex not being in the same room since that night. What about at the funeral?"

"Kathy Lynn sat on one side of me and Rex on the other. At the viewing, Kathy Lynn stayed as far away from Rex as possible. She wouldn't even look at him." Her eyes welled up again.

Sandra and Erma were going to have to figure that out, and fast, now that they were taking the March setting. A shiver ran down her neck. "You have no idea what's happened between them?"

BJ shook her head. She sat straighter and rolled her shoulders back and glanced out the window into the pitch dark. "I guess you need to go to Rufina's before Rex gets here."

Sandra glanced at her phone. It was nigh onto dinnertime. "Who would Rufina be afraid of, BJ?"

"I guess whoever really fired that shot. I can't think of anyone else. Do you think Rufina knows something she doesn't want to tell us? We've always confided in each other before this. It's crazy. If she's scared to come out now, when she's freed after the trial won't she still think she's in danger then?" BJ's face screwed up again. "I'm so confused."

"Don't—" Sandra said, holding up her hand. "No more tears. We've got to figure this out. We've got a million things to do, people to talk to—including Kathy Lynn."

BJ dried her cheeks. "What was Erma calling about? Is something wrong?"

"We have a new trial setting."

BJ's face didn't give any indication that she already knew. "That's good, isn't it? When will it be?"

"End of next month, March, which is too soon. We're wondering whether the district attorney obtained the setting, so we wouldn't have time to prepare. I wouldn't put it past him."

"Won't they give you another date?"

"Nope. It's either this one or the one so far in the future, calendars aren't even out yet."

Light came through the alcove window, headlights.

"Rex," BJ said. "Do you want to talk to him or head to Rufina's?"

"If you'll show me a side door and point me toward Rufina's cottage, I'm outta here."

CHAPTER FIFTEEN

   "WHY ARE YOU here?" Rufina had opened the door a crack. "Billie J send you?"

"No one sent me, but I understand you're refusing to leave the house."

One eye appeared through the crack, the good one. "*Sí, es verdad.*"

"*Por qué?*"

"Safer inside. I would have stayed in jail, but they wouldn't let me."

Sandra nodded. "I would think you wouldn't want to stay in that depressing place. Didn't I hear someone committed suicide in there?"

"It wasn't me." Rufina stepped back to let Sandra inside. "I guess since you're my *abogado* I can trust you." She waved Sandra into the cottage.

"Ha. Ha. I'm glad you have a sense of humor." Sandra glanced around the entry hall. The place was quite sweet with what looked like recently painted sheetrock and wood trim, several pieces of art, and good lighting. She kept walking into a dining room-living area combination. A rustic table, with a place-setting for one, and six chairs, stood to the side. A heavy smell of spice filled the air. Cumin, maybe? Sandra's stomach reminded her lunch in the bakery had been more than a few hours ago.

"An inmate tried to hang himself a few days ago." Rufina followed her. "That's what they say."

"You don't seem too distressed over that." A dark-orange sofa sat in the center of the living area and faced a lit fireplace. Sandra stepped between the sofa and a yellow and orange print fabric-covered rocker and held her hands over the fire to warm them. The had been relatively warm, but the night had grown cold. She'd left her jacket lying on the bed in the guest room.

"Sandra, I grew up here. The news might not make the weekly paper, but inmates in our jail do die every once in a while, especially Mexicans."

"Yeah? Yet you would have preferred to stay in jail? May I sit down?"

Rufina took a ball of yarn and a crochet hook from the sofa cushion and gestured for Sandra to have a seat.

Rufina sat in the rocker, her toes scraping the floor as she scooched back. She held the yarn and hook in her lap and stared at Sandra.

"I take it for some reason you think you're in danger and that you'd be safer in the jail than in your house?"

"Your questions are like every other *abogado's*." Rufina rocked back and forth.

"That's because I am one." She smiled at her own weak attempt at humor. "I could use your help in preparing for trial. We have a lot to do and not much time. Our court date is now the end of next month."

Rufina exhaled. "Mother of God. That's not much time."

"Yup. They gave us the date, and we didn't want to pass on it, though it'll be a scramble." She stared at the little woman for a moment. Would Rufina be open and honest with her or hold things back like so many defendants. "So why are you afraid to come out of your house?"

Rufina rocked some more and stared into space as though deciding what to say.

"Someone threaten you?"

"Did you know someone is telling people BJ and I are lesbians?"

"No shit?" Sandra mulled that over. Should she ask if it's true? If it was true, then so what? What did it mean to Rufina? She cocked an eyebrow. "That's why you're afraid to come out of your house?"

Rufina rocked faster. "My brother, Carlos, he came to the jail and started yelling at me, his face all red, the veins sticking out of his neck. He said I brought shame on the family."

"Uh, yeah. I saw him like that late this morning."

"You did? *Dónde?*"

"On Main. He said you want to fire me, and he would hire you a San Antonio lawyer, which is what you wanted."

"*Nunca!* No way. His lawyer would make me plead guilty so the family would not be embarrassed if it came out in trial that Billie J and I are lesbians."

"So you are lovers? You and BJ? Not that it matters."

"No, we're not." She shook her head. "We are close like sisters, but ugh, no. She looked at Sandra. "I mean no offense if you are, but me? Us? No."

"I'm not either."

They both laughed.

"Carlos hasn't threatened you, has he? Other than with another lawyer?"

"Not exactly, but he was mad. His temper is bad sometimes. And he's prejudiced."

"Against gay people?"

"Against gay people, black people, white people, almost everyone."

"So you wouldn't invite him in for coffee to discuss the matter?"

"He wouldn't believe me when I told him it wasn't true."

"So you think he might hurt you? Like an honor killing?"

Rufina's face screwed up. "No. Mexicans don't do honor killings, at least as far as I know, and never in our family. I can't explain why he thinks that of us. He's known Billie J and Roy since he was a *niño*."

"I must ask, would he hurt me? He got up in my face, plus someone keyed my car. Would he do that?"

Rufina considered it and shook her head. "He's never been that way before. He just gets angry. I don't think he would hurt you."

"Do you think if he catches you outside, he would do something to you?"

"Or someone else would."

Sandra tilted her head and closed one eye. "Like who?"

"Sandra, I worked in the courts for many years. I have seen many things. I don't trust people. What if someone wanted me dead, so they could blame me for Katy Jo's murder and close the case?"

Sandra's head pounded with the beginning of a headache. She put her head in her hands and rubbed her scalp. "Yeah, what if. These days, it could happen." She couldn't very well tell Rufina not to worry, because something like that was always possible. She peeked through her fingers. "I'm thinking here." She smiled out of one side of her mouth. "I really do need your help in preparing for trial. Particularly if you think you know who might have shot Katy Jo."

"I don't. And I don't know how I would be of help."

"For starters, I want to interview the ladies who work with you in the house, at least briefly. Am I correct when I assume they aren't fluent in English? You could interpret."

"Billie J's Spanish is like a native's."

"BJ's the boss. Would they answer honestly if she were interpreting?"

Rufina shifted her eyes. "How are you going to feel when someone kills me?"

"Rufina, be reasonable. We'll do whatever we can to protect you. BJ will do whatever she can."

"She can't do anything. People come and go on the ranch."

"What if we got her to give you a different cottage and changed the locks on it and put locks on all the windows and got you a dog—a big dog?"

"A German shepherd?" Her eyes lit up.

"Whatever you want. In fact, I'll do you one better. How about if we switch cottages with you when we're up here? BJ wants us to stay in the house, but we have news for her. Ain't gonna happen." Sandra wanted to be more than one room away from Rex if he came for the trial. "Erma said BJ has a vacant cottage, a two bedroom. We're going to insist we stay there during the trial, rather than in the house. You can stay in that cottage, and we'll take yours." She watched Rufina's face—the undamaged side of her face, which was the only readable side. Rufina was thinking hard, her forehead drawn together.

"And in the meantime? What about over the next month? If I go to a different cottage in the next month, people will figure it out." She leaned down to the same level as Sandra who still had her head lowered. "This is a two bedroom, too." She jerked her head to the right, which plainly led to the bedroom side of the cottage. "When my husband was alive, it was ours to live in or use for whatever, like a *casita* down in Mexico. Often the *patrón*, the boss, will give the workers a place to live. After the fire, Billie J rebuilt it, only better. This is the best cottage on the ranch, but you can stay here during the trial. *Está bien.*"

Sandra acknowledged that last bit with a nod. "Why do I get the impression you're not telling me something?"

Rufina took a deep breath. "I know something no one else knows."

"About the murder?" Pain persisted in Sandra's head. "You have to tell me everything, Rufina. Everything whether you think it matters or not."

Rufina bit her lip. "You won't tell anyone? You won't tell Billie J?"

"You're the client. I won't reveal anything you don't want me to." She rubbed her temples.

Rufina blurted, "Katy Jo and Doug met in my second bedroom."

"You are kidding me. And no one knows?"

Her eyes flared. "Just me. No one else did. They only met here after dark or if no one else would be around."

"Why? Why keep it a secret?"

"For privacy. I spent a lot of time at the house in the evenings when just me and Billie J were home. They were going to be married someday but didn't want anyone rushing them. Plus Billie J, she can be old-fashioned sometimes." She shrugged one shoulder. "She wanted Katy Jo to go to school for her PhD first. She said someday Doug would need to go back to school. You can't work construction forever. Your body gets worn out. Katy Jo would need a good job to support them. And Rex—"

"I suppose he would have harassed them."

"*Sí.*" Her eyes rested on a spot over Sandra's head. "He hated her. He would do anything to make her unhappy."

"No one's told me why he hated Katy Jo. Had she done something to him?"

Rufina shook her head and shrugged.

Sandra sat up and rubbed her temples again. So much to figure out. Did it all fit together somehow to make a picture that would save Rufina? "Were Doug and Katy Jo in your cottage the night of the murder?"

"I think so. I heard voices."

"But you didn't see them? And they didn't see you?"

"I didn't see them. I don't know if they knew I was there, I was in my bedroom. They probably thought I was there asleep."

"Boy, it would be so helpful if Doug could testify you were in your cottage at the time of the shooting. I'm going to have to talk to him."

Rufina said, "*Sí lo haría.*"

Sandra wasn't sure what that meant, but Rufina's face had lit up, so it had to be good. "Back to getting you out of this house. You think my idea about switching cottages is workable?"

"*No sé.* It will take time to set up the cottage. And the locks— and you still haven't told me, what do I do in the meantime?"

"I've got an idea."

Rufina sat back. "What are you thinking?"

"You can come to Galveston with me while BJ gets someone out here to do the lock thing—she'll put locks put on every window and door of where we're supposedly staying. Hell, on both places if she can do it unobtrusively, but for sure the one where we're supposed to be staying, making everyone aware of it—and she can get someone to switch the necessities from one cottage to the other, so no one will suspect. Someone trustworthy. You trust the other ladies who work for her?"

Rufina gripped the rocker's arms. "Go to Galveston with you? Would the judge let me do that? Where would I stay? How would I be safer there if anyone knew where I was?"

"With Erma. She's got a beautiful guest room. You'd be safe in her house. During the days you'd be at the office with us. I know there is more stuff for you to tell me—us—about what went on at the ranch. So much we aren't aware of. Remember, it's only a little over a month now instead of a year. There's no time to waste."

Rufina stared at Sandra for a long while.

"Tomorrow we could talk to some of the ladies, and the rest over the phone. I'm sure BJ would provide a private part of her house for them to use the phone. Erma or I would pose the questions and you could interpret both ways. That is..."

"What?"

"If you think you can translate accurately, without, uh, putting in your two cents, your spin on it. Some interpreters have a hard time being strictly a mechanism for translation."

"I could do that. I could, if it means my freedom—maybe my life."

Sandra stared into the fire. Would the judge agree to let Rufina go to Galveston with her? Why not? The judge knew both Erma and her. Holt sure as hell wouldn't like it. He'd be objecting, groaning and moaning. She didn't want to spend a lot of time thinking about what his reaction would be. She'd try to make it happen in the morning. "I think we may be able to pull this off, Rufina."

"*Bien*, Sandra. If you think Erma won't mind."

"I'll call her. By the way, may I have a drink of water and some aspirin if you have any?" The aspirin wouldn't sit well on her empty stomach, but in a few minutes, she would go back to BJ's for dinner.

She placed the call to Erma.

Afterward, she explained to Rufina what would happen the next day and to pack a big bag, one large enough for a month's stay. Sandra was confident Rufina would be going to Galveston.

⚐ ⚐ ⚐

Rex stood just inside the ranch house door Sandra had used to go to Rufina's cottage, though how he knew when she would be back, she had no clue. He invited her in with a sweep of his hand. Weird. Definitely weird. He smelled like he'd been hitting the mezcal again.

"Hey, Sandra," he said. "Welcome back."

Sandra rubbed her arms to warm them as she scooted past him. "Hello Rex," she said in a formal tone, hoping he'd realize she wasn't in the mood for his antics.

"We're having pulled pork. Do you like pulled pork, Sandra?" He walked too close behind her after she strode past him toward her room.

From what Erma had told her, BJ had served pork when Erma had eaten there. "Whatever." She could almost feel Rex's breath on her neck. For some odd reason, she remembered an old joke her mother used to tell when she'd had one too many. She'd tell of being hired by a client arrested for sodomy, back when sodomy was an oft-charged crime. Erma would grin, having trouble containing herself when she told what a great lawyer she was, because she got the charge reduced to following too close. She'd slap her knee and laugh and laugh, and since her belly laugh was contagious, others would join in, whether they'd heard her tell that story more than once.

Sandra stopped, causing Rex to bump into her, and turned on him. "What the hell are you doing?"

"Aren't you going in to supper?" He stepped back, but not before she was practically suffocated by the whiff of alcohol.

"I'll be in the dining room in a minute." She put her palm within centimeters of his chest. "Now get away from me."

He shrugged. "Well, all right, if you want to be that way about it."

God, he was one strange dude. She continued to her room. When she closed the door, she had the sense that someone had been there during her absence and rummaged through her things. There wasn't much to find in her overnight bag and her purse. She dumped out everything to see if anything was missing, to make sure no one—namely her number one suspect, Rex—had planted something. The thought of his hands in her things caused her to shiver. She didn't know what he could be up to, but what she did know was she couldn't trust him. He could be a patron of one of those spy shops, fancying himself a spy for the district attorney. That would be easy to picture.

Not finding anything unusual, after returning everything to its respective pockets, she washed up in the bathroom, scrubbing her hands. The thought of him was just icky. No telling where those hands had been. She left the bedroom, but fortunately he wasn't lurking in the hallway. She didn't see him until she arrived in the dining room.

Billie Jo glanced at her. "Ready for a meal? I put the earlier stuff away. Hope you didn't want any of it. Thought we could eat buffet-style." Her eyes shifted to Rex who sat at the far end of the table, a leer pasted on his baby-face.

So much for discussing what she was free to discuss about the case with BJ. Or even the accommodations, or rather, the change in the accommodations. The aroma of the roasted pork lured her to the counter where she filled her plate with vegetables and a lump of meat. She took a chair on the far end from Rex and tried to pretend he wasn't present. Billie Jo sat opposite him so that she and Sandra were adjacent to each other.

Sandra's mouth watered as she bit into the pork. Tasty and tender. "Nice meal, BJ. Thanks."

Rex made several attempts to engage her in conversation, but Sandra didn't reply.

BJ said, "I guess you can't discuss anything Rufina said, can you?"

Sandra shook her head. "Attorney-client privilege. BJ, even though it's still fairly early, I hope you don't mind if when I finish dinner, I go to my room. I need to make some calls, and I'm tired."

"Not at all." She stared down at her dinner. "I understand."

"Hey, Sandra," Rex said, "we have some cognac if you want to come into the den for an after-dinner drink."

He was about as subtle as, who, no one ever? "No, but thank you for asking."

"So what did Rufina say about not wanting to come out of her house?" He took a swig of whatever he was currently drinking.

"Rex, I know you're trying to have fun, but I'm not going to play." She glanced at her plate. After two more bites, she pushed back her chair. "Excuse me." She picked up her plate and headed toward the kitchen where she handed it to one of the women who worked in the house. "I'm off to my room. BJ, will I see you in the morning?"

Rex said, "You won't see me, I'll be going back to work in San Antonio."

"I'll be up. I don't sleep late." BJ walked with Sandra to the hallway.

"Goodnight," Sandra said and strode down the hall. As soon as she arrived at the guest room, she went inside and locked the door behind her, thankful it was en suite, and she wouldn't need to go out to the bathroom. She also locked the bathroom door that led to the adjoining room where Erma had stayed the last time.

Someone had left a folded nightgown and fluffy towel on the bathroom cabinet, so Sandra stripped down and showered. After brushing her teeth and her hair and turning down the bed, she went to the door to switch off the light. Was she imagining a light knock at the door? Thinking it might be BJ, she unlocked and opened the door.

Rex stood there, the odor of booze on him stronger than ever. "Hey, Sandra."

Sandra pushed the door, but he put the toe of his boot in the way.

"What do you want, Rex?"

"You haven't been answering my emails." He ogled her, his hand on the outside doorknob.

The little shithead thought he could frighten her. She'd like to knee him right in the groin. "You don't want to do this. Pull your foot away, and we'll both forget about it." She gave the door another little push, but it wouldn't budge.

"Oh, I don't mean no harm, Sandra. I wanted to tell you something."

Sandra gritted her teeth. "What is it that can't wait until you send me another email?"

He ran his eyes up and down her body. "You sure you don't want that drink?"

"So are you going to tell me what you want?" Had BJ gone to bed? She couldn't know what Rex was up to. And probably not what he might be capable of.

"I wanted to tell you that I look forward to seeing you next month when you come back up here for trial." A look of little boy innocence climbed on his face.

Sandra shivered. Why did she think Rex had known about the trial setting before he ever arrived at the ranch? She didn't respond.

His face grew dark.

She steeled herself, holding her hand steady on the knob, prepared with her right knee to defend herself. "I'm going to bed now, Rex. Take your hand off the doorknob and your foot out of the doorway, or I'm going to scream bloody-murder, and your mother isn't going to be real happy with you."

"I want to help you out, Sandra, that's all." His watery eyes flared, and he blinked twice like he was trying to focus.

His words piqued her interest. "What do you mean?"

"I told the DA the Schindler family would be real appreciative, real appreciative, the next time he stood for election if he could help us get to trial earlier for that murdering bitch, Rufina. I told him the family wants to put all our sorrow and grief behind us as soon as possible." He stared at Sandra as if hoping to be rewarded with some kind of reaction, relaxing his grip on the doorknob. His foot twitched.

Sandra's reaction was to throw all her weight against the door, slamming it and twisting the lock. She wouldn't give the little motherfucker the pleasure of seeing how pissed she was, at least not that night. She wouldn't forget what he'd done, though, and neither would Erma. If the right opportunity presented itself . . . they'd get him back one way or the other.

CHAPTER SIXTEEN

THE NEXT MORNING, Sandra left Rufina in a bakery on Main Street before going to the courthouse. She thought she'd find Holt and explain what she wanted while she waited for the judge to take a break from her hearing. On her way to Holt's office, she spotted him waltzing down the hall with a cup of coffee. When he saw her, he practically skidded to a stop. His previously placid face turned into one huge scowl.

"Ah, Miss Salinsky, what brings you here again today?"

"I hope you don't mind, Mr. Holt, but there is one little matter I wanted to take up with the judge before I head back to Galveston. Let's see if she'll talk to us when she takes a break." She glanced at her watch. "Which, if I know Judge Olsen, will be any minute."

"What's this about?" Holt led her to his office. "After you."

"I don't want to miss her," Sandra said. "You want to meet me in there?"

"Gotta get my jacket." He swallowed some coffee and straightened his tie. Sandra stood just inside the door. He pulled a blue pinstriped jacket that matched his pants from a hook on a hat rack. "Let's go." He crooked a finger at her.

When they reached the little chambers office, the judge was returning from the direction of the ladies' room. Sandra said, "Good morning, Judge."

"Good morning, counsel." She looked from one to the other of them. "What can I do for the two of you?"

"Judge, I wanted to let you know, since you're assigned to hear matters on the Barboza case this week, I'm taking my client to Galveston to stay with us until the trial. I wanted to give notice and make sure I'm not stepping on anyone's toes." She cocked her head at Mr. Holt, waiting for his objection. "For her protection."

Holt's face grew red, and he drew himself up like a red-breasted robin he often reminded her of. Before he could say anything, the judge said, "Don't bust a gusset, Mr. Holt. I know what you're probably thinking, that Miss Salinsky's client will be out from under the jurisdiction of the court."

"But, but—"

"Last time I checked," Sandra said, "Galveston was still within the confines of the great State of Texas."

Holt said, "Our regional presiding judge would never allow it. Never. The defendant is charged with capital murder."

Sandra snorted with disgust. "I think we've already established Mrs. Barboza is not charged with capital murder, Judge Olsen, and Mr. Holt needs to quit saying that."

"Well, she will be as soon as the Grand Jury hands down the indictment," Holt said.

"Mr. Holt," the judge said with a tone of ire in her voice. "I agree with Ms. Salinsky. It doesn't serve you well to keep alleging cap murder when the defendant is only charged with first degree murder."

Holt grunted and clenched his jaw.

Sandra stood silent for a moment. First degree was still nothing to sneeze at. "My client doesn't feel safe in Fredericksburg, Judge. She thinks someone is out to get her. Certainly, you would agree, it would be to the real killer's benefit to dispose of Mrs. Barboza since everyone is so convinced she committed the murder. If she died, even "accidentally," the case would be closed."

"No one is out to get your client, Miss Salinsky," Holt said.

"You don't know that. She feels how she feels, Mr. Holt. For one thing, her own brother is furious at her. Whether he'd try to harm her?" She shrugged.

"I know her brother," Holt said, "and he'd never harm a hair—"

Ignoring that statement while she really wanted to find out how he knew him, Sandra said, "Anyway, after she made bail, the only way she would leave her house was for me to promise to protect her. The only way for me to protect her is to take her to Galveston to stay with Erma until we return for the trial. Judge, she's so afraid, I'm the only person, besides Mrs. Schindler, she would even let inside her house since she got out of jail."

Holt's face had faded to pink. "What guarantees do we have that you'll return her to court?"

"Aw, come on. Mrs. Schindler trusts us, and she put up the half a million dollars."

"Well...sounds like a reasonable request to me," the judge said.

"Your Honor, really? Money is nothing to BJ Schindler," Holt said. "Half a mil—she'd never miss it."

"Judge, you know where Erma and I are located. In fact, though you moved up here, I know you'll be back in town sometimes. You could check on us. Or send someone. Would we risk our reputations if we thought there was any chance at all Rufina would flee?"

"Well—"

"It's not right," Holt said. "A defendant is not supposed to leave town after making bail."

"It's not like I won't know where she is," Judge Olsen said. "I know exactly where Erma Townley lives, as well as where their law office is. I don't see the harm."

Holt closed his eyes. The muscles in his jaw flexed.

Sandra bit her lip. She glanced again at Holt. He knew the game was over. Rufina was going to Galveston.

⚖ ⚖ ⚖

Sandra and Rufina pulled up in front of Erma's stately historical home after dark. The drive from the Hill Country to the Gulf Coast had been uneventful after they passed through a rainstorm, the gridlock on Interstate 10 into Houston being no worse than usual. Though focused on the perilous traffic, Sandra still managed to get Rufina to open up about her family's background and life growing up on the ranch. Background information like that could be helpful in trial.

Dark didn't necessarily mean late, since they were in the middle of winter. It was only dinnertime, but both women were drained. They'd driven from Fredericksburg to Kerrville, down to San Antonio, and caught the interstate. They'd only stopped briefly to pick up sandwiches.

Erma met them on the outside stairs under the bright porch light. "Hey, y'all come on in." She took the smaller of Rufina's two bags and curled an arm around the tiny woman's shoulders.

"Erma, you are too kind to let me stay here," Rufina said as they climbed up to the front door. "I'm very grateful."

"Nonsense," Erma said.

Sandra lugged Rufina's larger bag and dropped it in the entryway. She breathed heavily, another reminder to get back on her exercise schedule. The aroma of grilled beef floated out from the kitchen in the back of the house. Her mouth watered, but she wasn't going to stay for dinner.

"Take your coat off, Rufina, and hang it on the hall tree behind you next to the door," Erma said, toddling toward the stairs to the second floor. "Traffic bad?"

"We drove through a heavy rainstorm, but otherwise SOP for I-10, taking our lives in our hands all the way here," Sandra said. "I wish there was a different route, but what the hell?"

Rufina shrugged off her coat and draped it over one of the hall tree knobs. She gazed around the entry hall at the tall windows and ceiling and down at the original wood floors. "Bonita, Erma. This house looks like you."

"Thank you. Now let's take your things up to the bedroom and so you can settle in." Erma led the way up the stairs. "I have some dinner waiting in the kitchen. Once Sandra leaves, we can have a talk and you can get cozy. And don't worry. See the keypad next to the door? I have an alarm system. My house is safe."

"I'm not going to stay long." Sandra picked up the big suitcase and followed Rufina, who followed Erma up the stairs and into the guest room. Rufina had a bit of a spring in her step, as if she were already feeling at ease.

Sandra dropped the suitcase next to the four-poster bed. "I know you'll be comfortable in Erma's care."

"Sandra, you want some dinner?" Erma asked.

"No, I want to get home and take these clothes off and relax."

"Wait a few minutes," Erma said. "Rufina, I'll leave you to unpack. The bathroom is right next door. Plenty of linens in the cupboard. Come down when you're ready. If you want to rest for a while, there's no hurry about dinner. I can heat it up."

Rufina nodded and rubbed her lips together. She brushed her fingers under her eyes. "I'm very grateful. Sandra, I will see you mañana?"

"Absolutely," Sandra said on her way out the door. "Goodnight, *amiga*. Get some sleep. We have our work cut out for us."

Once downstairs, Sandra said, "She's a sweetheart. Like anyone else, she has two sides to her, a quiet demure side and a talkative, animated side. We had some interesting conversation on our way here."

"This was an inspired idea," Erma said. "What happened when you talked to the judge?"

Sandra wanted nothing more than to go home, but she beckoned Erma into the den where she gave her the blow-by-blow of the meeting with Holt.

Hearing the story, Erma laughed. "I bet he was about to stroke out."

"Yeah, he was. He'll survive." She stretched and yawned. "Let's talk more tomorrow. I'm hungry. I'm tired. I'm going home, check my messages and my calendar, and if there's nothing that can't wait, I'm going to eat and go to bed."

"Don't blame you." They walked together to the door.

"One more thing," Sandra said. "Rex. I gotta tell you, Erma. He's more than a little creepy." She related what had happened at her bedroom door the night before. "I had the feeling if he could have, he would have, if you know what I mean. He's way younger than I am, but he was looking me over like I was a cougar after him."

Erma wrinkled her nose. "Where was BJ during all this? You say it was only a matter of minutes after you went to your room?"

"I had showered, so a bit more than that. BJ had probably gone to bed." She stood with one hand on the doorknob.

"Should I call BJ about it tonight?"

"It can wait until tomorrow. I definitely want you to talk with her about giving us a cottage for the trial."

"Will do, first thing. Get some rest. We've got a lot to do."

"Don't I know it." Sandra pulled the door open. Cold wind blew in. "For now, I'm going to my condo where I can get warm and cozy."

⚓ ⚓ ⚓

Sandra dragged herself and her things up to her condo and laid down to close her eyes for a few minutes before fixing anything to eat and unpacking. She awoke to a blast of thunder and a crack of lightning. A moment later, a stuck car horn blared from the seawall. Glancing at the clock, she was incredulous. She'd slept until ten o'clock at night. Lethargy held her in its embrace and made her want to close her eyes and go right back to sleep. She had a few things to do, though. After washing her hands and splashing water on her face, she pulled a bathrobe over a nightgown and some slippers on her feet.

The refrigerator smelled stale and offered few choices. She grabbed a cup of yogurt and a spoon before opening the draperies to peek outside. If a balcony could flood, hers did. Water pooled where the tile was low. The plastic all-weather furniture had been blown about, one of the chairs caught in a corner, the other lying on its side. The little table was pushed up against the sliding glass door.

Out on the beachfront, the clouds parted for a moment and the half-moon lit up frothy, choppy waves. A few cars drove by, spraying water from each wheel well. An air leak at the bottom of the doors let a cold breeze spiral up her gown. She shivered and dropped the drapes. She walked back to the bedroom and sat on the bed with her back against the headboard. After eating a bit of strawberry-flavored yogurt, she scrolled through her emails, flagging the ones she wanted to read. Then she went back to the oldest ones.

The first was a message from a divorce client about a vitriolic email she'd received from her husband. Sandra advised her to print out the message and save it. The judge would love to see that.

The next two were from an assistant district attorney in Galveston asking whether she would agree to a continuance of two cases that were set the week of spring break, so she, the ADA, and her family, could go to the Bahamas. That reminded Sandra she needed to discuss spring break with Mel. Jack had always been good about switching days so there should be no problem, but they needed to talk soon. The fourth email was from Rex. She hated to open it but clicked anyway.

"HEY, SANDRA, JUST WANTED TO MAKE SURE YOU MADE IT HOME ALL IN ONE PIECE. BTW, I DIDN'T GET A CHANCE TO TELL YOU SOMETHING THAT I THINK YOU OUGHT TO KNOW IF YOU'RE GOING TO KEEP REPRESENTING RUFINA. DID YOU KNOW SHE'S A LESBIAN? JUST THOUGHT YOU'D WANT TO KNOW THAT. YOUR FRIEND, REX

Didn't he know proper email etiquette—that writing in all caps was the same as shouting? She wouldn't put it past him to know and do it intentionally to annoy her. What a buffoon. She'd print that email and put it in a folder with his name on it. In fact, she was going to ask Patricia to print out all the emails they'd received from him. They might come in handy. As to the allegations Rufina was a lesbian, who else might Rex have told? Carlos, maybe, otherwise why would Carlos think so? And how could Rex possibly think Rufina's sexuality had any relevance to a murder charge?

On the other hand, there had to be a reason behind the constant emails and the allegations against Rufina. Did they somehow tie into whomever killed Katy Jo? Was sending them supposed to be some kind of message within a message? Were she and Erma supposed to figure out something that for some reason he felt he couldn't tell them? Her gut told her she needed to follow up on everything Rex had said and done. But it would have to wait until the following day.

She read the rest of the emails, answering a couple, marking a couple more to print out and place in her clients' case files, before listening to her voicemail. She played those messages back, the first one was from Doug Christian, Katy Jo's boyfriend.

"Miss Salinsky, Mrs. S—Mrs. Schindler—gave me your phone number and said you want to talk to me about Katy Jo. I'm driving down to Houston this weekend. Call me back, and I'll meet you somewhere halfway between Houston and Galveston on Saturday." He left his number and hung up.

The next three calls were from Erma. Sandra finished the yogurt and put the container in the kitchen. Before she could turn out the light, her cell rang.

Jared's deep voice resonated. "Sandra, it's Jared. Did I wake you?"

An unbidden spurt of adrenaline warmed her chest. "I was just turning in." She sat up, pulling her feet under her, covering them with the bottom of her nighty. The rain's steady beat on the windows came more slowly than when she'd awakened. Good cuddling weather, but she'd have to make do with a phone call. And, she reminded herself, she wasn't sure about having a relationship.

"Wanted to make sure you arrived home safely. A cold front pushed through up here—had a small hailstorm."

Sandra had trouble picturing Jared, presumably at home, since she hadn't seen where he lived. Surely a real estate attorney wouldn't be at the office after ten o'clock at night. "Are you at your house? What kind of place do you live in? I don't even know that. A ranch? An apartment? A condo?"

"A house about a mile outside of town, with my mother."

Holy shit, a man who lives with his mother? No way. "Oh, I see."

Jared laughed, a deep, full-bodied guffaw that lasted about five seconds. "Kidding."

Sandra pulled a second pillow behind her and leaned back. "Very funny, though if your mother is anything like my mother, not so funny sometimes."

"I'm not sure what that means since I haven't met your mother—I look forward to the pleasure—"

"You say that now . . ."

He laughed again. "Isn't your mother a lawyer, too?"

"Oh, yeah," Sandra said, pulling her knees to her chest. "My mother's quite a character. Anyway, get back to where you live."

"I really do have a house about a mile outside of town."

"No mother?"

"My parents have a ranch between here and Bandera."

"So you live alone?"

"You're awfully curious for someone who has kept me mostly at arm's length."

"You evading my question, counselor?"

His voice held a smile. "Okay. I have a ten-year-old calico cat—a big, fat, spoiled, ornery girl who would make Garfield look like a saint."

"Hmmm, somehow I pictured you as a dog man."

"You pictured me?"

The conversation wasn't going in a direction she considered safe. "Not to change the subject, but do you know a man named Doug Christian?"

"Hmmm. Don't want to talk about us? When are you coming back up here?"

"Yeah, Jared, I don't know what to say. It's late. I'm still worn out from such a quick trip there and back. Let's see how things go."

"That works for me, Sandra. Doug Christian? Why? What's up with him? Never mind, for the murder case, right?"

"I guess you could say that." She hated to share information with him but could use any details he had about Christian.

"He was a hometown football hero some years back. Went to Baylor on a football scholarship, blew out his knee in the Baylor-Oklahoma State game. Had to drop out of school due to lack of funds. Never graduated. Last I heard, he worked construction in North Texas somewhere."

"Whoa, thanks for all that info. So you're a football freak?" Just what she needed. But, if a man liked football, a woman would have lots of time to do her own thing. Shit. Why was she even thinking like that? She didn't want a long-term relationship.

"Aww, not like I was. You're not?"

She shook her head, like he could see her. "Sports aren't my bag, but I do like to run."

"All right. So we've found mutual ground. Me, too."

"Good. Now I want to pick your brain a little, and then I'm going to hang up. By the way, I'll be back up there in three weeks or so to get ready for trial, which has been moved up. Way up."

"How far up?"

"Next month. Don't tell me you didn't know."

"You didn't tell me."

"I'm shocked. No one else did either?"

"I guess my spies were asleep at the wheel. When did that happen?"

"Yesterday."

"Humph. So that's good though, right?"

"Doesn't give us much time to prepare. But, anyway, a couple of things you might know or be able to find out easily. About Rex and this guy, Doug."

"Shoot. I'll help you if I can."

"Okay, well, Doug Christian first. I understand he was Katy Jo Schindler's boyfriend."

"I'm afraid I don't know much about the girls' personal lives. Sorry. This town is small, but not that small."

Sandra's chest tightened. "No problem. What do you know about him? Is he the violent type? Jealous type?"

"You think he would have anything to do with Rufina's case?"

"I've been wondering—do you know his reputation?"

"Never heard anything bad about the guy, but he's been gone from here for a while."

"I don't have to be afraid of him, though, do I? I'm going to meet with him this weekend."

"He a witness?" The tone of his voice rose.

"Possibly. Do I need to be afraid of him?"

"Be sure to meet him in a public place like a restaurant. In the daytime. Then, no worries, but I think the guy is all right."

"BJ says he's a teddy bear."

"Then he probably is. I wouldn't put it past her to check up on all the guys the twins dated. Roy—Commissioner Schindler—would have."

"Okay. Then there's the Rex issue. What the hell's his problem?"

"He's the only son. The baby of the family. Spoiled rotten. Over-indulged. Never did understand how BJ and Roy couldn't see what a punk he is. Roy would bail him out every time he'd get in trouble, starting in juvie court. It was never Rex's fault, always the other guy's."

"That's what I thought. He acts like it, too."

"So he's giving you problems. I can tell by your voice."

"I'm not sure why, yet. Something's going on with him. I knew it wasn't just me—Erma and me—but I wanted to check."

"Well, I'd steer clear of him. Since he grew up with parents—especially his father—covering for him his whole life, he's got this sense of entitlement. From what I heard, he should have been locked up a bunch of times, but he always got off. Never even had to do probation."

Sandra hunched her shoulders and dropped them. Sitting on the bed wasn't conducive to the best posture. "Jared, time for sleep. Great talking to you."

"You, too. Stay in touch. As soon as you get back up here, come to the office. I've had the desk cleaned out for you. I look forward to seeing more of you."

Sandra smiled. That statement certainly had a double meaning. "Me too, so long as you know we're going to be really tied up most of the time."

"I'm flexible. See you soon."

"Goodnight, Jared." Sandra clicked off. She put her cell on Do Not Disturb, turned off the bedside lamp, and slid under the covers, still smiling.

CHAPTER SEVENTEEN

FIFTY-DEGREE WEATHER HUNG over the island the following morning. Though waves washed onto the sand, fog muffled the sound. Everything wore a veil and would leave a kind of grime once the fog cleared off. Dampness permeated clothing making it almost impossible to feel dry.

After she arrived at the office, Sandra stuck her head in Patricia's section. "Hey, Patricia. I'm here but headed upstairs."

Patricia raised a hand but otherwise didn't reply, didn't even look up.

Sandra dumped her things on her desk and climbed up where she found Erma in the small office next to their loft-library, law books spread across the desk. Though they subscribed to online law libraries, since Erma refused to use a computer, they continued to buy law books for her to use. Waste of money, but Erma brought in her share.

Rufina came in from the library. She wore a pair of black slacks and a white blouse with the sleeves rolled up like it was some kind of office uniform. "*Buenos días.*" Her face held a smile and looked more relaxed than Sandra had ever seen it.

Sandra said, "Good morning, y'all."

"We made a hell of a boo-boo," Erma said. "I don't know if you spoke with Patricia when you came in, but we hurt her feelings. You need to apologize when you go back down. I already have."

"What'd I do?" As far as Sandra knew, she had done nothing to offend their secretary.

"Neither of us told Patricia about Rufina's injuries. Patricia was pretty startled this morning when I introduced them."

"Oh, shit. I'm sorry Rufina. Did she say something to you?"

"She said something like 'Oh my Lord, what happened to you?'" Rufina shrugged. "It did not bother me. I've had people staring at me for years."

"But Patricia was embarrassed," Erma said. "Like I said, I apologized. We did tell Mel, right?"

"I'm sure I did." Sandra crossed the room and slipped an arm around Rufina's shoulders, walking her back toward the library. "I'm glad you're not easily offended. We have some tough times ahead of us. Now, Erma must have shown you around downstairs, the kitchen and the bathroom and our offices. You've made yourself comfortable up here?"

"Yes, in the easy chair near the window," Rufina said. "There's good light I can read by. I like to watch the cars going up and down Broadway and the palm trees blowing. So different from Fredericksburg."

Rufina had opened up on the trip down to Galveston. Now she apparently felt safe and more comfortable with them. She was animated and smiling.

"Do you have everything you need?"

"*Sí.* I'm fine."

"Erma treat you well last night?"

"Oh, yes. We had a nice time at her house. Like a slumber party. Do you need me to help with anything?"

Sandra felt good about things as she looked down on the little damaged woman. "No, but if you don't mind, I'd like a few moments alone with Erma. When we get to your testimony—which probably won't be today anyway—I'll give you a holler."

"*Esta bien*." She picked up a book that lay open and face down on the library table and settled into the chair by the window.

Sandra closed the door between the library and the small office where Erma sat thumbing through one of the Southwest Reporters. She dragged up a chair very close to Erma. "Listen, you know what I was thinking? I mean, I'm kinda glad this happened, this bit with Patricia. The whole incident has given me an idea that will help with jury selection."

Erma marked her place and closed the book. "Tell me."

Sandra lowered her voice. She wouldn't want Rufina to hear what they were going to discuss—at least not yet. "Well, I was thinking if we got one or two soft-hearted women on the jury, that might help our cause."

"How're we going to do that?"

Sandra glanced over her shoulder. "If we're diligent, we can position Rufina so no one in the *venire* sees anything but her unscarred profile. She'll keep her face turned away until we tell her. Like, if the judge is one of those who insists on introducing everyone—and even having the defendant stand—we'll tell her to keep her face turned away until we indicate she's to let the potential jurors see her.

"Yeah. Maybe she could wear a scarf."

"What I'm thinking is, you can draw up your jury chart, and you'll be at counsel table where you can watch the *venire*. Then, when I do *voir dire*, I'll re-introduce Rufina and have her stand and turn her face so all the people will see her damaged side at once."

"And I'm supposed to record their reactions—as quickly as possible."

"Right—but just the women's. Most men are never as soft-hearted as women. And then I can *voir dire* them, all of them—men and women—on their reactions—like hey, I saw how you reacted to Rufina. Are you going to be able to set aside your feelings and be fair and impartial to my client in spite of the fact she's been the victim of a fire? We'll be looking for those women who we hope feel guilty because they feel so shocked at seeing her and even more shocked at their own reactions. What do you think?"

Wham. Erma slapped the top of the desk. "Smart thinking. All we need is one to hang up the jury."

Sandra licked her lips and grinned. "I thought you'd like that. Now, I'm going downstairs to apologize to Patricia." Sandra reached the top of the stairs and turned back to Erma. "I only wish we had someone to cover the office during the trial so Patricia could come to Fredericksburg, too."

"She'd enjoy that, but we need her to manage things while we're gone. And you can tell her, too."

Erma was right. Still, someday they'd hire another secretary—make Patricia an official legal assistant with a secretary under her, then she could come to court occasionally if she wanted to.

When she reached the bottom of the stairs, Sandra realized what she'd been thinking. Damn Erma. Somehow, she'd influenced Sandra to forget for a few days about the insurance firm job offer. How did the woman do it? Little did Erma know, though, Sandra was still considering the offer. Still thinking how much simpler life would be if she didn't have to deal with criminal defendants and all their issues.

⚖ ⚖ ⚖

Late that morning, Erma came down to Sandra's desk. "You don't mind that I had Patricia get out a binder and start putting a trial notebook together, I hope."

"Nah. There's no time to squabble over stuff. Did she calendar the trial? Were there any conflicts?"

Erma grimaced. "Only Mel's spring break."

"Yeah. I'm trying to decide what to do." She'd been mulling over the conflict since she'd found out about the trial setting.

157

She and Jack had worked out the custody agreement long ago and generally got along. He wouldn't be the problem. She just didn't want to give up any of her time. Every moment with her daughter was precious.

Erma stood over her. "We do see her almost every day."

"It's not the quality time we'd have if we went someplace together."

"So you'll be pissed if I tell you I told Mel the trial is that week?"

"No. She's got to know." Sandra tapped the space bar on her computer. When it came to life, she pulled up the calendar. Her day was clear except for a new client interview. She would take some time that afternoon to talk to Mel about it. Some private time. She glanced at Erma. "What did she say? Was she disappointed?"

Though she and Jack got along, sometimes he was patronizing. She could hear the conversation between them now. Jack would say something about Sandra having to work and offer to take Mel to Cancun or someplace equally fabulous for spring break to show what a wonderful father he was. And he wouldn't be far from wrong. Except for his attitude.

Erma pulled her sweater across her chest. She wore woolly house shoes in a leopard print. Her long wool skirt almost brushed the top of them. "Chilly in here." She turned up the thermostat.

"You're avoiding my question."

"Since Mel's helping around the office, would it be such a bad idea to take her with us to Fredericksburg over spring break?"

"What? No way. How would that help? I wouldn't have much time to spend with her."

"She could help us a little, search the Internet, run errands, get us fast food for lunch, etcetera, and sometimes be out at the ranch and go riding—I'm sure BJ could arrange one of the hands to take her—and climb that big rock—"

"Enchanted Rock. Yeah, spring would be the best time for that. I remember climbing it in the summer and almost sweating to death. We didn't take enough water and were dying of thirst—"

"Yeah, like that." Erma stood with her hands on her hips. "And all those shops. You can give her your credit card and let her go to town—in a manner of speaking, since the courthouse is at the far end of Main Street."

"You're suggesting I buy her off."

"I wouldn't put it that way." Erma shrugged one shoulder. "Okay, I would put it that way, but why the hell not?"

"I'm not sure she wouldn't be better off with her dad."

Erma sidestepped toward the doorway. "She doesn't think so. She wants to go with us—wants to help us try a case."

Feeling overwhelmed, Sandra didn't have the energy to put up much of a fight. She'd tossed and turned the night before, even as tired as she'd been when she arrived home. "Erma—"

Erma headed back across the hall. "I gave her a choice. You asked what she said. She said she wants to go to Fredericksburg. She said three generations of lawyers . . ."

"Oh, please tell me she didn't start up on that again. I keep telling her she's a high school student and has plenty of time to decide what she wants to do with her life."

"So she has ambitions to be like her mother and grandmother. Is that so bad?"

"We'll talk about it later."

"Aww, let her come with us. It'd be good for the kid."

Sandra pulled her coat together and buttoned it up. "I said, we'll talk about it later. Now I'm going over to the courthouse to talk to one of the assistant DAs and then run some errands. If we have any walk-ins, you can interview them. And don't drink anything. I don't want you breathing bourbon on anyone. Besides, if Rufina sees you drinking at the office, she might lose faith in us." She frowned at Erma.

"I don't know what you're talking about." Erma sat down at her own desk and picked up a pen.

"I'm talking about the pint of Jim Beam you have hidden in your credenza behind the box of business cards and the box of envelopes." Sandra walked into Patricia's office. "*Adios*, Patricia. Text me if anything important comes up."

"Yes, ma'am." Patricia raised her eyebrows to confirm she'd heard the conversation and knew what was going on. She kept an eye on everything. That's what the best legal secretaries did.

☩   ☩   ☩

Erma waited until Sandra drove away before hollering at Patricia. "Did you tell on me, girl?"

"No, ma'am," Patricia hollered back. "But she's not stupid."

Erma walked into Patricia's office. "But she's wrong. The bourbon is Jack Daniels, not Jim Beam. Ha!"

Patricia sat at her computer, her back to Erma, a multicolored knit scarf draped around her neck and shoulders. "You interested in hearing your most recent email from Rex?"

Erma plopped into the chair next to Patricia's desk. "That little fart. What's his problem now?"

"He says, '*Hey, Erma, guess Sandra told you how I helped y'all out.*'"

A chill ran up the back of Erma's neck. "That little son of a bitch. I swear he's bi-polar or something. One minute he's as sweet as honey, the next minute he's trying to sink our defense and gloating about it." Erma pounded Patricia's desk. "Send him back this reply. 'Mrs. Townley to you, young man.'"

Patricia typed the message.

"'And Ms. Salinsky when you're talking about my daughter.'" Erma didn't wait for Patricia to get it all typed out. The little piss ant had gotten on her last nerve. She jumped out of the chair and stomped around Patricia's office. "'Keep out of our case. Quit emailing us, or I'll file a restraining order against you.'"

Patricia's fingers played over the keyboard. "Hit send?"

"Yep. That ought to fix him for a while. I don't know what the hell his problem is." She stopped next to Patricia and leaned over, staring at the computer screen.

Patricia hit send. "Ms. Townley, it wouldn't take much for me to teach you how to send and receive email. I bet you could come up with better responses to people like this Rex person if you'd sit down and write it out yourself."

Erma screwed up her face and shook her head. "Nope. Not me. That's what I pay you for. We're not having this conversation again. I'm not using a computer, either big or little. Let's not talk about it anymore."

Patricia gave an exaggerated sigh.

Erma pressed her shoulder. "I'll be in my office. She strutted down the hall and into her office where she picked up the phone and punched in BJ's number.

"Sandra and Rufina make it back last night with no problems?" BJ asked when she answered.

"BJ, we need a separate place to stay during the trial." Erma sat down in the Queen Anne she kept in one corner and pulled her thick little legs under her. The draft from the hardwood floor was bad at the moment. The cold front that blew in had lasted about five-minutes until the fog took over. Even wearing wool, she still felt the chill from the bottom up.

"My house not good enough for you?" BJ's voice had turned flat.

No doubt Rex had spun a tale for his mother, or else BJ was offended they didn't want to sleep in the house. She could certainly afford to put them up in a hotel for the duration of the trial if she didn't want to give them a cottage. "It's not that." She wasn't about to tattle on Rex—at least not yet. But she didn't want him hanging around them for any reason. And especially not around Mel.

"We need room to spread out. Sandra found us local counsel, so we have access to a library and copier and etcetera, but we're going to need space where we can discuss the case and our trial strategy without being interrupted." What she meant was, where no one could overhear, not only Rex but any members of BJ's household who might think they needed to know what was going on.

"Oh," BJ cleared her throat. "Like a place with a kitchen and a couple of bedrooms?"

"With some privacy. Plus, I think my granddaughter will be coming up for the week, too, if you're all right with that. So it'll be three beds. You don't mind, do you?"

"Well, we did talk about one of the cottages. Is that still an option for you? I have a couple of empty ones. One is two bedrooms with a sofa bed. Full kitchen, of course, but you'd be welcome to eat with us—"

"Uh—"

"If you want to—I know I'm supposed to pay expenses. I'm okay with that. You can eat out every night if you want."

If only she could tell BJ part of the reason was Rex. Did he think all the emails and other annoyances would endear himself to them?

"And I can send one of the girls down to fetch your laundry every few days," BJ said. "Or not, if you don't want."

"Hold on, honey," Erma said. "I'll discuss it with Sandra. She's not here now." She wasn't sure if she was supposed to discuss the exchange of cottages with Rufina yet or ask BJ to agree to a cottage first.

BJ exhaled into the phone.

"Was that a sigh?" Erma asked.

"I guess," BJ said, her voice conveying a sense of resignation. "But don't worry, I'm not going to blubber all over you like I did Sandra."

"Goddamn, that's news to me. When was this?" Erma shifted the phone to her other ear.

"Night before last, I'm embarrassed to say. I've been trying to do the stiff upper lip thing, Erm. But when Sandra looked at me sympathetically, that was all she wrote. I broke down." Her voice wavered. "I don't believe in looking soft, particularly in front of children."

"Don't let it worry you. Didn't you cry all over the phone when you called me and again at the Dairy Queen when we got up there, and I still love you." Erma couldn't believe she said that. The words must have taken on a life of their own, spoken themselves. It wasn't any more her nature to talk like that than it was BJ's. "But never mind."

BJ cleared her throat, again, and breathed heavily. "So when will we see you next?"

"I'm thinking no later than the Wednesday before trial. Hey, you don't happen to know how they handle jury selection, do you? And what about pretrial conference? Does the judge conduct it a week or two before the trial or a day or so or what?"

"You're asking the wro-o-o-ng person."

"Yeah. Yeah. I thought as much. I'm getting antsy with only a month to go. Don't worry about things. We'll keep you posted." She was ready to hang up. "So go ahead and reserve a cottage for us. Ha. Ha."

"Rufina tell Sandra or you anything we didn't already know?"

"BJ, I need to go. And, I'm not sure what I'm free to discuss at this point. So how about you let me get back to you on some things."

"Oh. You take care then, Erma." BJ hung up.

Erma rose to hang up the phone. "So how's the trial notebook coming?" she called to Patricia. She glanced in the direction of the booze. It was close to lunchtime. She'd sort of promised Sandra, and then there was Rufina to consider, so she didn't do anything other than give the credenza a cursory look. But it was going to be a long afternoon.

CHAPTER EIGHTEEN

LATER THAT DAY, Sandra was at her desk, Rufina was up in the library, and Erma was at court, when the front office door rattled as someone opened and closed it.

"It's only me," Mel yelled.

Thankful there were no clients in the office. Sandra called back, "We need to talk. Come on in and grab a chair."

Mel dumped her book bag on the floor and peeled off her leather shirt jacket, dropping it on top of her bag. She did the teenage collapse in one of the client chairs in front of Sandra's desk.

"How was school today? Everything go okay?"

"Same as usual." Mel crossed one starched denim-clad leg over the other. "Did I do something wrong?" Her dark blue polo shirt contrasted with the green in her eyes.

"No, honey. We need to discuss spring break."

"I thought Grandma and I settled that."

A small fire smoldered in Sandra's stomach. Too often Erma interfered with Sandra's parenting. Bad enough Sandra had to deal with Mel's father. Matters were only made worse when Erma got involved. "You know grandma doesn't call the shots where you're concerned."

Mel tensed. "So I'm not going to Fredericksburg with y'all? Why don't you want me to go?"

"Whoa, we're getting ahead of ourselves here. No one said you weren't going. We haven't even established you were going." Sandra tapped her pen on the desk pad. If Erma would stay out of her business with Mel, life would be a lot easier, but when had that ever happened? "I've thought about it and wondered whether I should talk to your dad. He might be happy to have you this spring break, and you could come to me for Easter instead—provided the trial is over by then."

"Why? I don't get it." Mel tossed her head in a way that made Sandra think of herself at fifteen.

"Your dad might want to take you someplace cool, like last year. I had been thinking of some neat places to take you this year, but this trial came up."

"Sandra—Mother—Dad takes me to stuff all the time. I don't need you to do the same thing." She rolled her eyes. "You and Dad don't need to compete for me. I love you both."

"Spoken like a mature person—"

Mel tossed her head. "Well, of course. Who do you think I am? I do have professional people in my life to model after, you know."

"I wasn't trying to buy your love, honey. I just thought—"

"Mom, Grandma said I could help y'all with the trial. A murder trial. How cool is that?"

Sandra laughed. "Real trials aren't like Court TV. Sometimes there are long periods of time waiting around. Preparation time each night—"

"Court TV is boring, but this will be real, Mom. I can't wait."

"You have to understand though, Mel, it's not like you'll get to do much. Take notes, run errands, and etcetera, but that's all. Since you're not an adult, the rules won't allow you to sit at counsel table."

"But I can be in the courtroom with you and Grandma."

The back door of the office slammed. Erma had returned from court. Sandra raised her voice. "Even Erma won't have that active a role. She'll be second-chairing me. I'll do jury selection and all the examination of witnesses, that sort of thing."

"Says who?" Erma's voice came from the kitchen. She stopped in the doorway, one hand clasping her old leather briefcase, the other on her hip. Her coat opened to a black wool suit identical to the one from the day before. Erma had a closet full of outfits very similar to each other. She claimed she had to make fewer decisions that way.

"I'm the one BJ hired. I'm Rufina's lawyer. I control the case." Sandra squared her shoulders, ready to go head-to-head with Erma. She'd made the comment about the active role intentionally so Erma would hear it. Erma still hadn't fully conceded that Sandra was lead counsel. "I thought we got that straight when you dragged me into this."

"There isn't any reason I can't *voir dire* the jury."

"Continuity, Mo—ther."

"Continuity be damned. If I was a young associate, you'd be letting me do more than what I heard you say."

Mel sat on the edge of her chair—her eyes lit up. To Sandra's chagrin, Mel liked witnessing her mother and grandmother argue, finding it funny most of the time. Erma hadn't budged from her position in the doorway.

"First, I ought to leave you down here to mind the office," Sandra said. "But I've agreed to let you accompany me up there and help out." That would get Erma's goat. Both of them knew it took more than one lawyer to successfully defend a murder case. There was always so much to do, so many unexpected events to address. "Second, what is it you're interested in doing? You're going to be jury consultant unless we hire someone."

Erma crossed the room and dropped her briefcase in the chair next to Mel. She pulled off her coat and gloves, stuffing the gloves in her coat pocket. "I'm a better jury selection expert than any of those three hundred dollar an hour whores—uh—consultants."

"Then why would you want to select the jury and me act as the consultant?"

"I'm just saying. I should have some kind of active role." She gathered her things and took them across the hall.

"You can do opening and part of closing—the short part." Sandra'd always intended for Erma to have a role, but she had to maintain a pretense. "What's the matter? You don't want to do any of the argument?"

Erma returned and looked at Sandra cockeyed. Sandra knew the look—Erma's suspicious look. "I'm not going to examine any of the witnesses?" Erma's tone almost sounded hurt, but she was a good enough actress, after decades of trial work, that Sandra didn't know if her tone was real or fake.

"Do we have to decide this now? I'm still trying to figure out if Mel should come with us or not."

Mel jumped up. "Yes!"

Sandra shot her a look. "If you get bored, I won't have time to run you to the airport in San Antonio so you can go home."

"I won't be bored. Mom, it's going to be my first murder trial."

Sandra chuckled, breaking the tension. "Well, as long as you're willing to do the work."

"I am. I am." Mel ran around the desk and threw her arms around her mother. "So give me something to do now, and I'll get right on it."

Sandra drummed her fingers on the desk. "Hmm. All right. Tomorrow I'm meeting with Katy Jo's boyfriend. Find a legal pad and draft some questions for me to use at the interview with him."

Mel nodded. "For us to use at the interview tomorrow. This is my weekend with you."

Sandra glanced from her daughter to Erma. She could leave Mel with Erma, but it wouldn't hurt to take her to the interview. The guy wasn't a suspect. At least not that she knew of. "Yes, us."

"All right!" Mel picked up her things and left for her own desk in the front room. Sandra waited until Mel slid the huge wooden doors closed before addressing Erma.

"How did probate go?" She made some notes on a pad and laid her pen aside.

"The usual. Since I drew the will, there were no problems with it." She rubbed her hands together. "I'm still cold. The wind got to me. Listen, I was thinking, I do want to examine one or two witnesses. I like to keep my hand in, you know?"

"I know. " Guilt about her level of teasing tugged at Sandra. "Of course you're going to do some examinations. I was just giving you a hard time." She shrugged. "At this point, though, we don't know who the state's witnesses are. Holt hasn't responded to the discovery motion."

"It's only been a couple of days."

"Yeah, but since he got the case bumped up, he has to produce now, not later. We're within thirty days of trial. How about getting on the phone and haranguing his office until they send their responses? That would be a big help."

Erma bopped a few steps, a sparkle in her eyes. "That, I would love to do. I still haven't figured out whether the son of a bitch was trying to screw us or what."

"I'm sure he was, but at this point it doesn't matter, since we really want the setting." Sandra turned back to her notes.

"By the way, did I mention I called BJ and got her to give us one of the cottages to stay in? I didn't mention Rufina's cottage though. Where is Rufina, anyway?"

"Upstairs in the library. She said she'd stay out of our way until we need her." Rufina had turned out, so far, to be the ideal client. Kept to herself. Was quiet and undemonstrative in court. Sandra hoped she would remain that way.

"I was happy BJ agreed so readily. I wanted to make sure we didn't stay inside the house, too. I don't want Rex anywhere near Mel."

Sandra's pulse sped up. "That bastard lays one finger on her, and I'll blow his ass from here to kingdom come. In fact, remind me to take my revolver. Just for our protection."

"We could always borrow one of BJ's."

"No. This way nobody will know we have one. I've been thinking, since we don't know who Rufina is afraid of—we should be cautious. When we tell BJ about the cottage switch, we need to be sure she realizes all the windows and doors must have the best locks." The thought of someone lurking around the cottage made her stomach flip. "And Rex is not to know or anyone else who doesn't need to. And Mel is never to be alone on the ranch. I'm not worried about her in town, but I won't have her at risk from whoever is responsible for this mess."

"We're of like mind about that." Erma trod toward her office. "Anyone touches my granddaughter, the ME will have to search the ranch for their body part. Not only will I kill them, I'll distribute their body to the wolves, coyotes, or whatever wild animals inhabit the countryside."

"We're a gruesome pair," Sandra said and wondered whether Patricia could overhear them and what she might think of the conversation.

"Yeah, well, they'll find out how gruesome if they mess with us." Erma went back to her office, the wood floor creaking under her weight, and plopped into her chair.

Sandra drew a line through the note that said, *finalize place to stay*. Below the last item on the list, she wrote, *Clean and oil the .38.*

She called her friend, Ray, to see if he would cover for her while she was in trial. When she was through with the call, she hollered, "Hey, Erma, don't forget to ask Iris to cover probate court for you while we're gone."

"Already did it."

"Hey, Patricia, can you make the plane reservations for Mel, Erma, and Rufina? I'll be driving up a few days early."

Patricia appeared and leaned against the doorjamb. "Why are you hollering, ma'am?"

Sandra shrugged. "Don't feel like getting up."

"Or using the intercom?"

"Or using the intercom. I'm starting to panic. If we could mark some of these things off my list, maybe I'd sleep better. I don't want to be too stressed out when I get there. I want to be at my best against Holt. I sure don't need any brain fog."

"Yes, ma'am, I understand."

"I see you're back in your ma'am mode. Sorry if I offended you."

Patricia tucked her blouse into her skirt and straightened her waistband. She stopped at the doorway. "I've got the trial notebook set up waiting to fill in the sections as you get them ready. I even have a tab for Rex Schindler's emails, so you'll have them with you during trial in case something comes up. Why not give me your list, and I'll see what I can help you with?"

"Thanks, Patricia. You're a doll." Sandra handed over the list.

Patricia scanned it. "I think I can manage most of these things, but I draw the line at cleaning and oiling your .38." She flipped her hair as she departed.

CHAPTER NINETEEN

"I HATE THAT every chain family restaurant has become a sports bar. How are you supposed to hear with all the racket?" Sandra said when she and Mel escaped from the cold, windy weather. They arrived at the Chili's in League City a little after twelve-thirty Saturday afternoon. Strong odors of fried food enveloped them. Sandra winced from the noise of ubiquitous flat-screen televisions blurting sounds from various sporting events. Most of the tables were full of people talking over the TVs. "Just a sec," she told Mel. "I'll see if he's here." She walked past the hostess stand into the restaurant proper, searching for a big red-haired guy. When she didn't see him, she went back to Mel.

"Could we have a table as far away from a television as possible?" Sandra asked the hostess.

"I don't care where we sit," Mel said. "I'd just like a hamburger."

"Do you want fries with that?" Sandra chuckled at her own little joke.

The hostess led them across the room and started walking away when Mel stopped her. "Ma'am, can you put my hamburger order in? Hamburger and fries. And send that red-headed guy over here." She pointed to the front of the restaurant and plopped on a chair, pulling her tunic top down over her leggings. She put her backpack on the chair next to her.

Sandra strained to see past her daughter. A huge thirty-something man stood in the doorway, rather, blocked the doorway. He must have been only a few steps behind them. Sandra hurried over. "You Douglas Christian?" She stood back so she could observe his face. He dwarfed her.

"Yup. You the lawyer?" He wore one of those farmer jackets with a wool collar and held out a hand as large as a catcher's mitt. His blue eyes had tiny green specks in them. He held a gimme cap in one hand.

Sandra looked at his hand and up at his face. "You're not going to hurt me if I shake your hand, are you?"

"No, ma'am." He gripped her fingers for a couple of seconds with a calloused hand.

"Thanks for driving down to meet us. We're on a tight schedule. I sure didn't have time to drive to Dallas to meet you." She beckoned for him to follow her.

"No problem. I had to be in North Houston this week anyway."

"When they reached the table, she hung Mel's backpack on the back of Mel's chair. She sat next to her daughter, on the same side, figuring he'd need a lot of space opposite them. "We haven't ordered yet."

"Except for my hamburger. I'll signal our waitress." Mel waved her hand.

"Well, Douglas, all right if I call you Douglas?" Sandra shrugged out of her coat.

"Doug, ma'am." He draped his jacket over the chair next to him and rested his forearms on the table. "What's this young lady's name?" He nodded at Mel and held out his hand.

Mel shook his hand, looking pleased at being acknowledged. "I'm Melinda Salinsky. Ms. Salinsky is my mother, but I'm her legal assistant."

"More like an assistant to an assistant." Sandra grinned and elbowed Mel lightly on the arm. "Mel works in our law office after school. But, we're not here to talk about my family, Doug. You want to order, and then we can discuss business?"

After the waitress took their order and left their drinks, Doug said, "I understand you want to talk to me about Rufina and Katy Jo?"

"Yes, we do." Sandra sipped from her glass of water. The cold made her shiver.

Mel dug a legal pad out of her backpack and flipped to a page full of questions. "I wrote out a bunch of questions for you we want to go over."

Sandra took the legal pad. "Thanks, Mel." To Doug, Sandra said, "We have your complete name and address courtesy of BJ, but that's about it. So first, I guess, is some background. How long have you been acquainted with the Schindler family and that sort of thing."? Sandra hoped he'd launch into a narrative, revealing something useful.

"Yes, ma'am, well, around Fredericksburg, everybody pretty much knows everybody else. At least they did when I was coming up. A lot more people live there now, like ten thousand or something. And more private schools. A few more churches."

Sandra nodded and put a finger to her lips when Mel looked like she wanted to interrupt.

"Before my time, of course, some people didn't necessarily know others because their families didn't let them associate with each other. I'm not just talking about Mexicans, either."

The waitress delivered Mel's burger. The aroma of beef was almost overwhelming. "Be back with y'all's orders in a few."

"If y'all don't mind, I'm going to go ahead and eat." Mel squirted ketchup over the fries and on the inside of her hamburger and took a huge bite.

"Looks good," Doug said.

"You want some fries?" Mel indicated the pile of fries on her plate.

He shook his head. "I can wait. So, a long time ago, the Catholics and the Protestants didn't get along."

"I saw they each have their own cemetery, one on one end of town and one on the other."

"Yeah, but that wasn't really going on when I was little. As far as I know, they'd quit hating each other. So, we mostly all went to school together, at least high school."

Mel had bit into her burger. She set it down and swallowed. "So you knew Katy Jo and Kathy Lynn in high school?" She glanced at Sandra and mouthed, *it just popped out.*

Doug grimaced when Mel said the twins' names. "Yeah, I did. And middle school. And elementary school." He drew a deep breath, his eyes cast down at the table.

"So most of your life?" Sandra asked.

He nodded and took a sizable swallow from the cup of coffee the waitress had brought. His shoulders drooped, but a moment later he straightened up.

Sandra and Mel exchanged glances. Mel's face screwed up like she was afraid of what he might say.

"Ahem. Doug, you understand we're trying to help Rufina, don't you?"

"Yes, ma'am. Mrs. S—Mrs. Schindler—she explained it to me."

"You think Rufina did it?" Sandra watched his face but saw no indication of anger or hatred in his eyes.

"No, ma'am. That little lady couldn't hurt those girls. She was like their other mother."

"We don't think so either. I'm glad we're in agreement." If he would say that on the witness stand, Rufina's bacon might be saved. "So y'all went to school together all the way up to graduation from high school. I guess you went to their house and vice versa?"

"Yes, ma'am. Kathy Lynn was my first girlfriend."

"Wait a minute. I thought you were Katy Jo's uh—boyfriend?"

"Kathy Lynn was my girlfriend in first grade. I remember once when we were supposed to be napping on our mats, she scooted over and kissed me on the cheek." A smile spread across his face, revealing deep lines. "She got in all kinds of trouble."

"At the time of the uh—uh—event, though, the shooting, it was Katy Jo?"

"Yes, ma'am."

"Sandra—call me Sandra."

Yes, uh…Kathy Lynn and I were never really boyfriend and girlfriend. Except in first grade."

Sandra nodded and glanced at Mel. Mel might be a teenager, but she was a lot closer in age to those goings-on than Sandra. Sandra could remember several boyfriends Mel once had—each lasting about a week. Now that she thought about it, Mel hadn't talked about any boys lately. That would be a subject for another time.

"So you're well-acquainted with the family. I take it y'all were in and out of each other's houses on and off for years."

"Yep, but our families are ranchers, so it's not like we lived real close." He peered over Sandra's shoulder.

The waitress arrived and distributed their plates. "Be back with refills for the coffee."

"You played football, right?" Sandra asked as she put her napkin on her lap.

"Yes, ma—Sandra."

Sandra glanced at the notepad. She'd come to the end of the preliminary questions. Now for some hard ones. "When did you and Katy Jo become a couple?"

Doug twisted his cap and cleared his throat. He glanced down and back up at Sandra and set his cap on the chair next to him. He pressed his lips together before taking a deep breath. "This last time, since college."

"I take it by your answer you'd dated before."

"We dated in ninth grade—if you could call it that back then—only for a couple of weeks. We went to a school dance together. Then in the summer before eleventh grade. That was longer but ended before school started. I did take her to the homecoming dance when we were seniors—when Kathy Lynn was crowned homecoming queen." His jaw tightened.

"Very interesting." She didn't know how that would relate to the murder, so she didn't follow it up, just noted Kathy Lynn was the homecoming queen and wondered whether that was in some way significant.

"So then y'all both went to Baylor and got together there?"

"Yes, ma'am, as sophomores. After my injury when I couldn't play football anymore, I thought she'd dump me, but she wasn't like that. If it had been Kathy Lynn, she might have at the time, but not Katy Jo."

Mel chewed away, but her eyes cut over to Sandra's. Sandra was sure she and Mel were thinking the same thing. From what they'd heard from Erma, and now Doug, about the surviving twin, the wrong one got offed.

"Do you know of any reason why someone would want to kill Katy Jo?"

"No, ma'am. None. K—Katy Jo was—the—the sweetest girl," he whispered.

Pity fluttered in Sandra's stomach. Poor guy. Being forced to talk about it had to be difficult. "But not Kathy Lynn?"

"No, ma'am. Not Rex, either. They both had a streak." He stared deep into her eyes, only breaking off when he stuffed a slider into his mouth.

"A streak?"

He chewed and swallowed. "Guess you could say a wild streak. Or a—a streak of thinking they could do anything they wanted." His deep stare struck her to the core. Was it hopefulness on her part, or was he trying to send her a message without coming right out and saying it? He probably didn't trust her, but surely BJ had given her the seal of approval.

Sandra drizzled dressing on her salad and took a bite. She waited until he'd wolfed down another mini burger before she spoke again.

"Are you willing to testify in Rufina's trial?"

"Yeah, well Mr. H, he already asked me to." His eyebrows hiked up, and his forehead wrinkled.

Heartburn attacked Sandra. She bit her lip and glanced at Mel. Mel might not get what was going on. Sandra wished she didn't.

"When you say Mr. H, you're referring to—"

"The district attorney. He was my next-door neighbor when I was growing up before he moved to Kerrville."

God, she hoped Holt wouldn't accuse her of witness tampering. It would be like him, the prick, even though she had the right to interview witnesses.

"So Doug," Sandra gave him her sweetest smile, "why did the DA ask you to be a witness for the State?"

"Well, not exactly for the State."

"If he calls you as a witness, you're his witness. He's the district attorney. Ergo, you're a witness for the State."

He nodded and breathed heavily. "Well, ma'am—"

"Stop with the ma'am stuff, all right?"

He ducked his head. "I'm sorry if I offended you in any way."

"Okay. Please no ma'aming me anymore, all right? Can you tell me what you're going to say?"

"Well, Miz Salinsky—"

"Sandra. Sandra is fine unless we're in the courtroom."

"Well, yes, ma—Sandra. I'm trying to tell you what you want to hear. I'm going to talk about how I found the gun used to commit the murder."

The burn in Sandra's chest burst into flames. That was not what she wanted to hear. "You found the gun?"

"Yes, ma—Sandra. I thought you knew."

CHAPTER TWENTY

"I ALMOST FELL out of my chair." Sandra said into the setup on her dashboard. She and Mel had left the restaurant and were heading home, but they couldn't wait to tell Erma about Doug. Mel sat shotgun. "Mel, too. She almost dropped her hamburger. We were both speechless for about thirty seconds until Mel started slurping from her soda." She winked at her daughter.

"Goddamn," Erma said. "I can't believe nobody told us before now he was the one who found the murder weapon."

"Sure glad I didn't find out during his testimony." Sandra maneuvered into the center lane of southbound I-45.

Erma drew a loud, audible breath. "Where are y'all now?"

"Are you smoking? Did you inhale?"

"No, I'm not smoking again, but are you driving?" Erma asked. "Are you actually talking to me while driving my granddaughter down the highway?"

"Don't change the subject. I recognize that breath."

"Change the subject? I asked you where you were, and you answered with a question. Who changed the subject? Besides, no matter how hard I try, I can't get any satisfaction from these fake cigarettes."

Sandra laughed. "The ones with the little fan-like thing in them? Didn't you say they're stupid?"

"They are, but at least I can pretend. It feels similar in my hand and when I put it up to my mouth. There's no nicotine. So are you talking and driving and trying to kill my granddaughter?"

"I'm speaking at the dashboard." Sandra glanced at her daughter who stared at the traffic in front of them, the muscle in her jaw flexing.

"Still and all, Patricia did some research. When you drive and talk on that thing, you suffer from what they call inattention blindness. You need to hang up and watch where you're going."

Mel leaned forward to speak. "I need both of you to quit doing sh—stuff that is hazardous to our health. I'm terminating this call, Grandma. If it's not a fake cigarette, please put it out, or I'm calling your doctor." She punched a button, disconnecting the phone call.

"What do you think you're doing?"

"Just what I said. You and Grandma—you both act like your shoe size sometimes."

Sandra choked back a chuckle. She tousled her daughter's hair. "All right. All right."

Mel shrugged off Sandra's hand. "No reason you and I can't discuss what Doug said, is there?"

"For fifteen, sometimes you seem like you're old enough to be an associate."

"I think of myself as a junior associate," Mel said pulling a fake grin. She snapped her fingers and rocked in her seat to a tune only she could hear.

Mel's dancing in her seat was more of what Sandra expected. "Where are your notes?"

Mel unbuckled her seat belt and reached into the backseat for her backpack.

"I wish you'd use a roller bag. You're going to have arthritis in your back and shoulders before you're thirty. Buckle up again."

"Give kids another reason to pick on me? No—way."

Mel was, admittedly, a little nerdy. Not that Sandra cared. She loved her daughter. She didn't care whether Mel played tuba in the band or joined the tennis team or tried out for cheerleader. Whatever the kid wanted to do was all right with her.

Mel had chosen to become a little nerd or geek or whatever they called them these days. Since she'd started working at the law office, she dressed like she thought a lawyer should, way more formal than most kids. It had cost her. She'd shared with Sandra and Erma the jeers and the sneers from the other kids, but claimed she wasn't bothered. Of course, they knew she was. When Sandra suggested Mel modify her behavior and mode of dress, she refused, saying it was their problem, not hers. Sandra wanted to go to the principal and file a bullying complaint, but Mel begged her not to, saying she'd handle it.

Erma wanted to send one of her old criminal clients to pay a visit on the worst of the bullies, but Mel laughed. She thought Erma was joking.

Now, after putting her seatbelt back on, Mel pulled out the legal pad on which she'd made notes and dropped the backpack on the floor between her feet. "Ready." She beamed at Sandra, reminding her of when Mel was a young girl and had done something she'd been especially proud of, like crossing the stage to receive her perfect attendance certificate.

If they hadn't been in the car, Sandra would have reached over and hugged her. "Tell me what you think he said before he choked up."

Mel sighed. "'The gun was lying right there—right beside the path to the cottage where we' something something 'that used to be Rufina's.'"

Sandra scratched her lip. They never did find out what the "something something" was. She'd been embarrassed to see a man choke up and almost bawl into his sliders. What kind of witness was he going to make if he couldn't hold himself together? Not that she cared at this point, since he was going to be Holt's witness.

"He was going to the main house to find out where Katy Jo was and 'practically tripped over it.'" She flipped to the next page. "He thought how weird it was someone would leave a gun there. He was using the flashlight on his phone to light his way to the house."

"He's right. Why would any kind of weapon be on a sidewalk or path to a house? We need to find out more about the path. Paved? Simply worn-down grass from being walked over so much? Lined by bushes? I didn't pay attention when I went from the house to Rufina's to find out why she had locked herself inside."

"I could do that when we get up there. Go and check out stuff like that."

"We'll see. Our position is going to be someone planted the forty-five, figuring it would be found, since it would be in plain sight in the daytime."

"You think that's what happened?"

"Yup. I shore do, honey child."

Mel grinned. "You crack me up sometimes, Mom."

"What?"

"Talking like that. You sound like you just came from East Texas."

"There's only a few things I remember about my daddy, but his way of talking stuck with me. Of course, I reserve the vernacular for people I know well."

"Of course. Anyway—"

"So what else should we be focusing on that he said?"

"He picked up the gun and carried it into the house to ask Mrs. S about it."

"And smeared any fingerprints there would have been, we hope."

"He was carrying it into the kitchen when he heard the screams coming from Mrs. S."

"So he says."

"Mom, you don't think he's a suspect, do you? Just because he found the gun?"

"He says he found it. He could have shot Katy Jo and been heading out of the house when he heard the screams coming from BJ and decided to turn around and go back in and pretend he found the gun."

"Tsk-tsk. I liked him."

"I liked him, too, honey, but that doesn't mean he's not the killer."

"Awww—so you think maybe he and Katy Jo had a fight, and she ran in to tell her mother about it, and he followed and got the forty-five out of wherever it was kept and went looking for her and killed her?"

"That's certainly one theory of the case I intend to present to the jury."

"What? You think he murdered Katy Jo? You really think he did it? Why would he come talk to us if he had killed her?"

"Mel, I don't have to think he did it to argue that."

"Won't he look bad to everybody in town?"

Sandra snorted. "Bless your heart. I keep forgetting this is your first case."

"I don't understand what you mean."

"Think about it. What's our job in this case?"

"For Rufina to be found not guilty."

"Right. You know what burden of proof is, right?"

"Beyond a reasonable doubt. The prosecutor has to prove her guilty beyond a reasonable doubt."

"So if I argue Douglas had means, motive, and opportunity, how will the prosecutor's case be affected?"

"Oh—ohhhh—means—he got the gun." She clapped her hands. "Motive—he was mad at Katy Jo for something. Opportunity—he was in the house, and she was in BJ's room. I get it. Like if you argue he could have killed Katy Jo, somebody on the jury might have doubts about Rufina killing her."

Mel was a quick study. A warm feeling for her daughter wrapped itself around Sandra's heart, though she found it sad Mel was learning some of the facts of life so young. "Exactly. All I have to do is create doubt in one juror's mind to get a hung jury."

"You're going for a hung jury?"

"No. I'll take it, if I can't get anything else, but I'm going for not guilty. We have a long way to go before we've prepared our case, but I'd say Doug got us off to a good start."

"Wow, Mom. That's so cool the way your brain works."

"Thank you, li'l darlin'."

"But don't you care if you smear Doug's name?"

"I'm not paid to worry about Doug. My job is to get Rufina set free."

Mel stared out her window.

"That bothers you, I know. It's a hard lesson to learn." And one of the reasons Sandra tried to discourage Mel from becoming an attorney. In so many other lines of work, she wouldn't witness so much of the seamy side of life.

Mel didn't look at her.

"I'm going to tell you a little story about Erma from when I was young."

Mel glanced at her and back out the window, her body rigid.

"One afternoon when I was probably younger than you are now, I was at Erma's office after school. We lived above the office when I was little and moved to a nice house later, right?"

"Yeah." Mel nodded but still didn't look at her.

"Well, she had this man sitting in her office with her. I heard them talking. I was in the kitchen making a peanut butter sandwich when two cars full of deputy sheriffs showed up. They banged on the back door and the front door. The secretary let them in, and they burst right into Erma's office and arrested the man sitting at her desk."

"Can they do that?" Mel finally looked at her.

"They did, so I guess they could."

"What did Grandma do?"

"Erma didn't do anything. She merely stood and watched them cuff him and drag him away."

"I don't understand."

"Wait, I'm not through. So me: 'Mom, they just came inside your office and took your client away. Aren't you mad?'"

"Erma: 'No, I'm not mad. He's not my client. He hasn't hired me.'"

"What?" Mel turned sideways in her seat. "What did she mean?"

"Here's the rest. About an hour later, a woman came in with a huge wad of cash and hired Erma to defend the man. As soon as the woman left, Erma said, 'Now I'm mad! They can't do that to my client.'"

Mel laughed. "Now I get it. Though isn't that kind of cold-blooded?"

Sandra laughed, too. "You're learning. It's a cold, cruel world out there, trite as that might sound."

"Yeah. Ugly sometimes." She shook her head and rested her head against the window. Neither of them spoke for a few minutes as they approached the Mitchell Causeway Bridge to Galveston Island.

"Mom? I'm wondering something."

"What, sweetie?"

"Is Doug's having the gun the only thing we have to defend Rufina on?"

"So far. I'm still working on my theory of the case. I do think someone framed her for the murder, but we have to figure out why. Who else had means, motive, and opportunity?"

CHAPTER TWENTY-ONE

C CRE-STATE YOUR NAME for the record." In their role-playing, Erma was acting as Mr. Holt. They had arranged their law library furniture, as best they could, to resemble a courtroom with chairs for each court participant. They had drawn the drapes and put up two LED track light bars. Erma sat at one end of the long, dark oak table. Rufina sat in the faux witness stand.

"I already told my attorney, Ms. Salinsky, when she asked me. Rosalinda Rufina Mendez Lopez Barboza. I go by Rufina Barboza. Barboza was my husband's last name." Rufina sat prim and proper with her hands folded in her lap and looked Erma in the eye.

"All right, stop." Sandra scooted to Rufina and crouched down. "Good eye contact with Mr. Holt, but you can't cop an attitude and expect the jury to like you. The jurors' empathy is one of the most important things in this case."

"What did I say?" Rufina arched her back, her undamaged eye flared.

"'I already told my attorney, Ms. Salinsky, when she asked me....'" Erma said, trying to be patient. Patience had never been one of her strong suits. The last few days, having Rufina living with her, had tested Erma. Rufina couldn't have been a better guest—making her bed, cleaning up after herself, even cooking for the two of them. Erma liked her solitude, though. She liked not having to be polite to anyone for hours at a time. She liked talking to herself, doing whatever struck her, and hanging out in her underwear if she wanted to.

"How you spoke sounds defiant, even sarcastic." Staying down at Rufina's eye level, Sandra elaborated. "We will, by then, have established you as much as we can as a regular Jane. We've been over this. This is tough on you, but we have to overcome their difficulty at even looking at you. We plan to do that on direct. Holt won't be happy. He'll try to make the jurors dislike you, so we must be ready when he does. Don't help the DA."

"All the tricks I observed in court as a clerk have gone out of my head now that I'm sitting up here." Rufina covered her mouth with her hands.

"That's very common." Erma understood. She had once been a witness herself. "That's why we practice. Let's move on."

Sandra went back to her place.

Mel watched from the faux judge's chair, her eyes following the conversation, but she didn't say anything.

"So what would your name be if you still lived in Mexico?" Not looking at Rufina, Erma pretended to write on her legal pad.

Rufina glanced from Erma to Sandra and back. "If I still lived in Mexico? I never lived in Mexico, Mr. Holt."

"You're a Mexican national, aren't you? A Mexican citizen?"

"I have dual citizenship, both U.S. and Mexican citizenship. My mama and my papa are from Mexico, so I applied to get citizenship there as well as here."

"Your parents, were they here illegally?"

"No, sir." Rufina pressed her lips together.

"Don't physically react to Holt's provocations. He probably will ask that question, but you, and we, have to conceal our feelings." Erma tapped her pen on the table and clicked it and stared at the legal pad as if she were Holt deciding what to ask next. "So you're not at this time an illegal alien, *Señora* Barboza?"

"Surely he won't be that stupid." Sandra started pacing. "Surely he won't phrase it that way."

"He's an asshole. He's going to appeal to the prejudices of the voters of Fredericksburg. Even if none of them is racist, and I'd be mighty surprised if that were the case, he wants to upset Rufina. Did you see the way her mouth tightened? I guarantee you Holt wouldn't have missed that."

Sandra nodded. "I saw it. Rufina, honey. It's hard, but you gotta be like a turtle and let stuff roll off your back."

"I didn't even realize what I did. Exactly what did I do?"

Mel waved her hand. "Your lips got really tight around your teeth." She looked at each of the women and shrugged like she wasn't sure she should have said anything.

"The other thing is the trick question. He's going to try to hold you to that, so at least during his cross, the jurors will think you were undocumented at one time." Sandra pointed in Rufina's direction. "Things like that can be cleaned up on re-direct, but in the meantime, they remain in the jury's mind."

"Like 'When did you stop beating your wife?'" Rufina asked.

Sandra laughed. "Exactly. And Erma phrased it very well. 'So you're not at this time an illegal alien?' All you can say is yes or no. Even with a no answer, the jury might wonder whether you were at one time an undocumented immigrant."

"I understand." Rufina squared her shoulders. "Some things are coming back to me. I'm glad we're doing this. What I need to do is get in an answer different from what he's implying before he can object."

"Right." Erma said. "He's experienced, so that won't be easy. He's a real son of a bitch and sharp—all the things a DA ought to be. But we're defending you, so we don't like those traits."

Sandra went back to her chair and sat down. "I could go over your citizenship status on direct, but it's irrelevant, so I hate to raise the question in the jurors' minds. I'll have to give it some thought."

"Let me go to the next question, or else let's take a break." Erma licked her lips. Her mouth was dry.

"We'll have a break in a little while. We've barely started." Sandra stood again. "I think at this time, I'll ask for a bench conference. Your Honor, may I approach the bench?"

"You may." Mel grinned and made her posture more rigid.

Sandra approached, and Erma walked up beside her. "Your Honor, I object to Mr. Holt's question due to its being phrased in a prejudicial manner."

Erma coughed and made her voice deeper. "Why I don't know what she means, Judge. It's a perfectly legitimate question."

"What exactly is it about the question you object to, Miss Salinsky?" Mel frowned.

"The way he called her *Señora* Barboza," Sandra said. "He's trying to appeal to the prejudices of the jury by pointing out through innuendo she's Latina. It's no secret, Judge, but you can see where this line of questioning is aimed, though, can't you?"

"Mr. Holt, I will ask you to speak only English in this courtroom."

"Ha! Excellent response, Mel." Erma chuckled and did a little shuffle from one foot to the other, like a dancing elf. "They haven't told us who the judge is going to be, but some good old boy might say that. In other words, Mr. Holt, be more subtle."

As Holt again, Erma lowered her voice. "As long as the same applies to the defendant."

"Well, counsel, she is Latina. I'll excuse her if a word now and then slips out in Spanish. You, on the other hand...well, you know what you were doing."

Erma nodded at Mel like she would a real judge. They went back to their positions.

"Okay, Mrs. Barboza, where were you born?" Erma continued her questioning as Holt.

"Here in Fredericksburg. On the Schindler ranch. A midwife delivered me."

"I think you testified on direct examination that you lived on the ranch until you graduated from high school?"

"I graduated from Fredericksburg High School, got a job with the District Clerk's Office of Mason County, married my high school *novio*—sweetheart. We rented a *casita* on South Milam Street for a short period and moved back on the ranch, where my husband was a hand."

"You knew BJ Schindler in high school?"

"Yes, of course. Consuela, my great aunt, worked for Billie J—Mrs. Schindler's—mother. My father worked as a hand on the ranch. After Billie J and Roy married, they combined Roy's family ranch and Billie J's family ranch. When Consuela retired, my mother became the ranch *señora*."

"By *señora*, you mean—"

"Housekeeper." Rufina's eyes cut over to Sandra as if to ask if it was all right to interrupt Holt. "The same job I hold with Billie J—Mrs. Schindler—now."

"Wait a sec. Let's not get ahead of ourselves," Erma, as Holt, said. "How long did your mother work as housekeeper?"

"For a long time. Then a few years ago, when my father's knees got so bad, they had saved some money, so my mother and father retired and moved to *San Miguel de Allende*, Mexico."

"You're getting ahead of me again here."

"I'm sorry, Mr. Holt." Sporting a small smile, Rufina ducked her head.

"Did your parents move back to Mexico before or after the fire?"

"Objection. Assuming facts not in evidence." Sandra stood again.

Erma jumped up. "Ms. Salinsky asked about that on direct."

Sandra laughed. "Just trying to keep the prosecutor on his toes."

"Objection to sidebar, Judge." Erma was enjoying their rep-artee as DA and defense lawyer.

Mel's eyes grew wide. "Overruled?"

"Thank you, Your Honor." Erma sat back in her chair.

Sandra winked at Mel and sat down again.

"Well, let's talk about the fire, shall we?" Erma clicked a ballpoint pen like Holt had done in the bail reduction hearing. "You hated Katy Jo ever since she set the fire that burned down your house and killed your husband and caused you to be badly scarred, right?"

Rufina kept her eyes on Erma. "No, sir. I didn't hate Katy Jo. I forgave her a long time ago."

Erma stood but stayed next to her chair and asked the next question. "She burned down your house and killed your hus-band. How could you not hate her?"

"Sir, I love those children like they are my own. I don't hate them. Any of them."

Erma peered over her glasses at the pretend jury box and shook her head, like she couldn't believe her ears. "You love Mrs. Schindler's children? All of her children?"

"...Yes..."

"You can't hesitate, Rufina." Sandra moved to where Erma stood, staying behind her. "He'll make something of it. I don't know if you were thinking of one of the children you dislike more than the others or what—wouldn't surprise me if you were thinking of Rex—or even Katy Jo if you did hate her for burning down your house and killing your husband—"

"No. I don't hate any of them." Rufina stared at the two law-yers, her face drawn up, her hands gripping the arms of her chair. "It's just Rex has been unpleasant to me in the last few years."

"And we have no idea what that's about," Erma said. "But the time to find out is not in the middle of a trial. So don't hesitate or Holt will jump on it and make mincemeat out of you."

"We'll talk more about Rex." Sandra went back to Rufina and laid a hand on her shoulder. "Right now, Rufina, don't hesitate. Don't worry. We got this."

Rufina nodded. "May I have a drink of water? My mouth is so dry."

"Sure, in a minute." Sandra raised her eyebrows in Erma's direction.

From her conversations with Rufina and what had come out during their trial prep, Erma realized Rufina was hiding something. Sandra and she had discussed it and intended to discover it and soon. She waved Sandra back and assumed her Holt persona. "So you love Mrs. Schindler's children. All of her children?"

"Yes, sir. All of them. Even when they played tricks on me, like all little children do." She wet her lips. "I only wished I had some of my own, but I never did."

"I like that," Sandra said. "Be sure to say something like that. Get the jury, especially the women, to sympathize with you."

"It's true." Rufina stared down into her lap.

"So, Mrs. Barboza, you didn't hate Katy Jo. Why'd you shoot her?"

Rufina's head jerked up. "Sandra, aren't you going to object?"

Sandra shrugged. "Can't. No grounds. Asking a direct question like that is what Holt will do, and you need to be ready."

"I did not shoot her, sir." Rufina's eyes held steady. She remained still.

"Were you aiming for Mrs. Schindler?"

They all knew BJ had not been in the room when the shot was fired. This was another tricky question that Rufina had to be careful about.

"I wasn't aiming for anyone, Mr. Holt. I wasn't in Mrs. Schindler's bedroom that night. I wasn't even in the house."

"Good answer," Sandra said. "Too bad you can't extrapolate on that and say you weren't in town, in the State, or even in the country."

Erma pointed her pen at Sandra. "Ha. Ha. Very funny, but we don't have time for humor." She looked back at Rufina, being Holt again. "If you weren't in Mrs. Schindler's bedroom, where were you?"

"In my own bedroom. In my cottage, sir."

"A cottage similar to the one that was burned down?"

"Yes, sir."

"There had been a dinner party the night of the murder, correct?"

"Yes, Mr. Holt. A small dinner for the family, and Douglas Christian, and Mr. Elgin Burgess after the big dinner for all the workers."

"Mr. Burgess is who? A friend of the family?"

"He was a friend of Mr. Schindler's and now Mrs. Schindler's."

"Did you serve the meal?"

Rufina's eyebrow lowered very slightly. "No, sir. Two girls, who worked in the kitchen, served. I supervised, and when everything looked like it was going okay, I went home. I'm sure they served the guests and ate their own meals in the kitchen and left as usual."

"You don't take your meals there?" Erma cocked her head like she thought Holt would do.

"Sometimes."

"Not that night?"

"No, sir."

"Can anyone vouch for you, Mrs. Barboza? Can anyone come in here and testify about where you were during that dinner party and afterwards?"

Rufina's eyes shifted from Erma to Sandra and back to Erma. Any fool could see she didn't want to answer.

Sandra had moved over near the window. "You can't cover for Doug and Katy Jo, Rufina. Doug confirmed what you already told me about him and Katy Jo using the second bedroom in your cottage as a meeting place."

Rufina hesitated. "But BJ doesn't know. I promised I would never tell her."

"You won't be telling her. Anyway, Katy Jo is dead, so it doesn't matter if she was sleeping with her boyfriend without benefit of marriage, for Christ's sake." Erma threw her pen down.

"Her mother will think ill of her." Rufina rubbed her lips together and squinted at Erma.

"Screw that, Rufina," Erma said. "Your freedom—the rest of your life—is at stake." There was more to it, something more that Rufina wasn't saying. Erma tried to catch Sandra's eye. They should probably discuss it again before they accused their client of hiding something. "Just tell the jury Doug was in your cottage, spending the night in your second bedroom, at the time of the shooting. Isn't that true?"

Rufina became wide-eyed, like a trapped animal. "A drink of water, please? My mouth is so dry."

Rufina was avoiding something for sure. Erma nodded. "I understand, mine is too. Go ahead." After Rufina left the room, Sandra took the trial notebook and perched on the edge of the table next to where Erma sat. "Mel, why don't you go downstairs to the kitchen and turn off the coffee pot. Smells like it's burning."

"If you don't want me to hear what you're going to talk about, say so." Mel jogged to the door.

"Put some cookies out on a plate, too." Erma imagined the taste of dark chocolate and a black coffee to go with it. "Some of those Patricia baked yesterday, not those store-bought ones your mother got." Erma didn't even glance at Sandra for a reaction. She pushed back in her chair, more than ready for a break herself.

"This is the scenario as I understand it." Sandra laid the binder on the table. She opened it to the tab that said Rufina and pointed to a couple of sentences. "Rufina says she was in her cottage. She was not part of the dinner party."

"Right." Erma stood and stretched.

Sandra flipped to a tab that said Katy Jo. "After dinner and dessert, Katy Jo was supposed to be in her own room, and Doug supposedly had left, but in reality, Doug and Katy Jo were in the second bedroom at Rufina's." She turned to the next tab. Kathy Lynn. "Kathy Lynn was supposedly in her bedroom."

"I hear you. Supposedly. You don't have to show me each tab. I'm aware of where everyone was, supposedly. Rex had gone to his room. Elgin had gone home."

"That left BJ in her room, undressed and ready for bed. She said she had read for a few minutes when Katy Jo came into her bedroom and asked could she talk to her. BJ and Katy Jo only had a few minutes together, supposedly, when BJ went to the restroom. While she was gone, someone came in and shot Katy Jo."

Erma crossed her arms and leaned against the table. "Definitely something is out of whack."

"If I didn't think it was one-hundred percent unlikely that BJ left the room to set up Katy Jo, I'd be suspicious of her being out of the room."

"I can guaran-damn-tee you there was no setup." Erma went to the rear of the library and picked up a marker, writing names on the white board. "Besides who knew Katy Jo was going to be in there? Except Doug."

"And he loved her. So if it wasn't someone who wasn't at the dinner party—like a ranch hand—we have to figure out what was really going on and which of the others committed the murder and why."

"Well, not really, but it would be helpful to know, so we can point the finger at one of them." Erma drew lines from the different characters to each other and wrote where they were.

"That's what I meant." Sandra chewed on the end of her pen. "Are we missing someone?"

"So far, no one has given us any reason to believe someone outside the family—and employees—came into the house that night. When we were first up there, the night you absented yourself," Erma said, giving Sandra a drawn-together-eyebrow look, "the dinner I had with the same crew—minus Kathy Lynn, Katy Jo, and Doug—was pretty civilized, but there was an undertone." Erma put red question marks next to each person's name on the board.

"You have no idea what was up with that? That undertone?" Erma shook her head. "Don't have a clue."

"Let's not forget Carlos, Rufina's brother. He's angry with her. Maybe he returned," Sandra said. "Do we even know where he lives? Would he have had the opportunity if he lived nearby?"

"I think on the ranch. So he could have, but unlikely." Erma wrote his name on the board. "Anyway, if everyone had left like they've said, wouldn't the alarm have been set? Could Carlos know the code?"

Rufina's brother could have been out-of-control angry. As much as she didn't like Rex, Erma didn't want him to have been behind the murder. BJ had enough to deal with already. Erma would rather Carlos—or anyone else—be the killer.

"Anybody could know the code," Sandra said. "People have a way of being careless about things like that when familiar people are around. However, we have no reason to believe any of the other employees had a bone to pick with Katy Jo or any members of the family."

"Well, I know one goddamned thing, we need to get to the bottom of this and quick. If it wasn't Rufina, and we know it wasn't, then Kathy Lynn, Rex, Doug, Elgin Burgess, and possibly Carlos is a murderer." Erma emphasized each name with a slash of red.

"Or, someone no one has mentioned or has forgotten about, or has been ruled out by whomever knows about them. The million-dollar question is, who wanted Katy Jo dead?"

Erma shook her head. "I can't imagine."

"BJ could have been the target."

"Shit." Erma said. "I can't stand to think of that. I can't believe any of them would have a motive to murder my sweet friend."

"We'll work on that, but for our purposes, our job is to figure out which one is the weakest link. Which one of those four, or five, people should we focus on to interject reasonable doubt?"

"Well, we have Doug and the gun, so that's a start."

The toilet flushed and the water faucet began running in the bathroom. Sandra lowered her voice. "The other thing we need to do is find out what Rufina is hiding. I intend to find out that today."

After the break, after Erma had her coffee and cookies, she put Rufina back on their make-shift witness stand to continue grilling her. Rufina was their client, and they were going to do their jobs in spite of her secretiveness. Erma assumed Holt's persona again, down to stroking her jacket lapels like she'd seen Holt do at the arraignment. "Now, Mrs. Barboza, we were talking about where you were at the time of the shooting. You say you weren't the shooter, and you say you were in your cottage. Were you alone?"

Rufina squirmed. She fidgeted with her hands. Her eyes met Erma's, then Sandra's, then Mel's. Something was definitely going on with her.

Erma waited to see if Sandra thought they should send Mel out of the room in the unlikely event something salacious came up.

"Don't worry, Grandma, I know all about sex—if it is about sex." Mel lowered her voice, "Or should I say, 'Don't worry, Mr. Holt.'" She grinned as if to dare either of them to question that statement.

"At fifteen, I'm not surprised." Things were much looser now than when Erma had first started practicing law. She felt a twinge in her heart for Sandra, having to raise a daughter in current times.

"Go ahead, Rufina, answer the question." Sandra's eyes bored into Rufina's.

"I don't want to get anyone in trouble." Rufina's eyes continued darting around.

"By that statement, to whom do you refer?" Erma had never been a patient person and now her patience was running thin. She had a problem with clients who weren't as forthcoming as she thought they should be.

"Can we do this kind-of off the record?" Rufina wore a hopeful expression.

Sandra's face screwed up. "All of this is off the record. Attorney-client privilege." She approached Rufina. "So what haven't you told us?"

Rufina ran her hands up and down on the arms of the chair. "I wouldn't want the real district attorney to find out."

Erma joined them at the faux witness stand. "What don't you want him to know?"

"I haven't told anyone this. Not even Billie J."

"Spill." Erma said, trying not to sound angry. "The whole story." Her back aching, she pulled a chair over. She didn't want Sandra to know how she was feeling. Now was not the time to get into a fuss about her health. She focused on Rufina. She couldn't begin to imagine what Rufina had been hiding.

Mel scooted close and shrugged like I'm-part-of-this-too.

Sandra leaned against the library table.

"I have a—a friend." Rufina smiled a bit, pleased with herself but embarrassed to admit she'd been concealing something. At least that's how Erma took it.

"By friend, you mean—"

"Boyfriend—man friend."

"Goddamn." Erma laughed. "At your age?"

"I'm no older than you, *Señora* Townley." Rufina tilted her head at Erma.

"Erma, not Mrs. Townley. I've told you—but never mind. I'm just so surprised." Erma realized what she sounded like, that between Rufina's disfiguring scars and her age, no one would want her. None of them, of course, would say so.

"I know what you are thinking, but not everyone judges me by how I look." She straightened up and smoothed her blouse around her.

Heat flushed Erma's face like she'd been slapped. "I apologize, Rufina. You're a very nice person." Ashamed, Erma glanced at her daughter and granddaughter. "We all know that."

"What's his name?" Sandra leaned over the library table, her pen and notepad before her.

"Efrain. Efrain Guillermo Montes."

Erma tried not to think about the last time she, herself, had been with a man. "So Efrain was with you in the cottage after the dinner?"

"He's usually with me every night except when he plays poker with his *amigos*, or I'm doing something with Billie J."

"Damn," Erma said. A pang of envy niggled at her. "You lucky—"

Rufina laughed so hard she began choking and covered her mouth.

Erma cleared her throat. "Let's get back to business." She made note of the man's name on her own legal pad. "You said even BJ doesn't know about him?"

"He's a hand on the ranch. She might not like it if she knew. She's a lot more conservative than she lets on. Like with Douglas and Katy Jo."

Erma had visions of Rufina and Efrain doing the deed in one bedroom and Doug and Katy Jo doing it at the same time in the other bedroom. She could understand why BJ might be uncomfortable.

"I'm confused." Sandra began pacing at the foot of the table. "Your brother thinks you're a lesbian, having an affair with BJ."

Rufina's face screwed up. "My brother wouldn't approve either."

"So you let him think you're a lesbian?" Sandra stopped and stared at Rufina. "And Rex. Rex has been spreading that rumor. Where did he get that idea?"

"I don't know. Billie J and I, we spend a lot of time together. We travel together. Rex never liked that." She picked at her skirt, twisting some of the fabric into a knot.

"I thought Rex had a job and lived in San Antonio. Why the hell would he care whether you and his mother went on a trip together?" Erma asked.

"Rex is jealous. He has always wanted to be the center of his mother's attention, even if he doesn't live at home most of the time. When he comes to the house, he can be demanding."

"Was he jealous of the girls, too?" Sandra started pacing again.

"*Sí, sí, sí.* When the girls were younger and Billie J would take them on shopping trips to Houston or Dallas, he hated that. She'd better bring him something when she came home."

Erma crossed her arms and stared at Rufina. So much to think about. She was damn sure glad she and Sandra had put this little session together. This was so much more than she'd expected.

"I wonder where Rex really was at the time of the shooting," Sandra said.

"He and Elgin were the last to go to bed, supposedly." Erma referred to her notes. "Rather, he walked Elgin out after they said their good nights, Elgin left, and Rex went to bed." She took a sip of coffee. Ugh. Cold and bitter.

"I wonder, since Elgin is trying to court BJ, whether Rex told Elgin this lesbian stuff," Sandra said.

"Why? Are you suspecting Elgin now?" Rufina asked.

Sandra threw her hands up. "Hell, I don't know. Kathy Lynn, Doug, Elgin, Rex, and BJ were all there for dinner that night." She took a spin around the room. "I suspect everybody. If I didn't find it so hard to believe a man would kill his sister, Rex would be my number one suspect, don't you think so, Erma? But if he wanted to kill his sister, he's had years to do the deed. What would precipitate his killing her that particular night?"

"Heaven only knows." Erma had spread her legs out in front of her. She put one ankle over the other, thinking it might ease the pain in her lower back. She would have liked a short nap, but they were on a tight schedule.

"Back to your boyfriend, Efrain." Sandra had begun to act like the prosecutor she had been. She stopped in front of Rufina. "Where has he been all this time?"

"When all this happened, I told him to run, to stay away. I didn't want people knowing about him."

"You realize he's your alibi."

Rufina nodded. "I understand, but he can't be. The district attorney cannot know about him."

"Why is that?" Annoyance gnawed at Erma. She wished she'd known this earlier.

"He's been waiting for his papers. He went back to Mexico, like they told him to do. Supposed to stay for four years, but that's a long time, so he snuck back in. Immigration can't find out he's here. He's illegal, and if he gets caught, they'll send him back. He won't ever get his green card."

"Holy shit."

"If he gets up on the witness stand to give you an alibi," Sandra said, "Holt will ask him his status. Same as he will imply you aren't here legally. We can't allow Efrain to lie. We can't let him perjure himself."

"That's why I didn't tell anyone about him." Rufina wore a pouty expression.

"If you have no alibi, you could go to prison for life . . . or worse," Erma said. "Would Efrain want that for you?"

"I don't think Efrain knows what trouble I'm in. I'm not sure he even knows I was arrested for killing Katy Jo."

"Why's that?"

"Because I haven't heard from him. I told him to leave. I told him not to contact me or anyone on the ranch. He and I both knew the first person they'd blame for anything that went wrong would be a Mexican—an illegal Mexican—if they could get their hands on one." A single tear rolled down from her mangled eye. "Well, they couldn't, so they got me."

No one spoke for several moments. Sandra held her lower lip between her teeth like she was stopping herself from saying something. Mel twisted her hair in her fingers.

Erma drummed on the table. "I guess we need to find out if Efrain would be willing to give up the possibility of a green card in order to save your life."

Rufina cast her eyes down again as she so often did, which got Erma to wondering if Rufina had always been so demure or only since she'd been charged with murder. Or, maybe since the fire? Or, could her demeanor be an act? "So where can we find him?"

Rufina didn't answer.

"Come on, Rufina," Sandra said, her tone like she was reprimanding a child. "I know what you're thinking, but at least give the man a chance to make the decision himself."

"He may have gone to *San Miguel de Allende*, to be near my mother and father, but he can't testify."

"How can we get in touch with him? You need to give us the contact information for your parents."

"Efrain, he's not a young man. It's not just about me. He has family here. He wants to spend his last years with his family—and to die here." She crossed her arms.

Erma wanted to conk Rufina on the head. Knock some sense into her. Instead, she sighed long and loud and dragged her chair closer to the table. "Enough for now. You think about it. You think about whether this man you obviously care about should be treated with respect, should be allowed to make his own decisions."

"We'll discuss this another time," Sandra said. "We have other issues to cover today." She slumped into her own chair.

Mel waved in the air, like a student in a classroom.

"What, Mel?" Erma's posture reflected Sandra's.

"I was thinking, I mean, if we're through talking about Rufina's boyfriend. I was thinking about something. Can we go back? Are we sure no one except Doug knew Katy Jo went to see her mother?" Mel was bouncing around like she was being goosed. "Won't Mr. Holt say since Katy Jo and Doug were at Rufina's cottage that Rufina was the only other person who knew besides Doug? Or, could Katy Jo have told someone else earlier that she would be talking to her mother about her and Doug that night?"

Erma and Sandra looked at each other. Good question. But who?

CHAPTER TWENTY-TWO

A FEW WEEKS later, Sandra was on the phone with Mel's father when Erma crossed the hall and perched in one of the client chairs. She set a glass of water on Sandra's desk and popped a mint into her mouth.

"You listening? Sandra?" Jack asked.

"Yes, Jack, I'm sure Rufina's okay with that. Mel has been a great help to us, and Rufina has taken a liking to her." She cradled the telephone in the crook of her neck while she stacked files that had been scattered on her desk.

"But what will she do while you're in trial?" His voice held a patronizing tone she'd grown to recognize, and abhor, when they'd been married.

She adopted the same tone. "Well, let's see. She'll run errands for us, not only going for coffee, but if we need something filed with the clerk whose office is across from the courtroom, she can take those documents there and come back with our file-stamped copies. She can do research on the Internet." Sandra picked up a ballpoint and twirled it in her fingers.

"Does she want to be stuck doing stuff like that for a whole week?" He sounded incredulous.

"She told me she did. Didn't y'all have a conversation about it?" Sandra rolled her eyes.

"Well, yes, but I find it unbelievable a teenager would want to spend her spring break working like—"

"Because you offered to take her on a cruise? Honestly, Jack, I did ask her if she wouldn't rather go on a trip with you."

"I know you did. I just don't understand it." His voice held a tone of disbelief that reminded her of the way prosecutors sounded when cross-examining a defendant.

"What you don't understand, and frankly I don't either, is she's becoming a little advocate, a little lawyer." She glanced at Erma who tapped her watch. "She's been around when I've bitched about being a lawyer. She's heard me talk of going into a different line of work. But she's adamant she's going to be a criminal defense lawyer like Erma and me when she grows up."

He cleared his throat. "No offense, but I'll never understand."

"Me, neither. Listen, I'm on a tight schedule. I need to head to Gillespie County after lunch. So thanks for agreeing to take the three of them to the airport on Sunday. I appreciate it."

"No problem. And if you have to send Mel home for any reason, put her on a plane and call me, and I'll be at Hobby Airport to pick her up."

"Take care, Jack." Sandra disconnected. She knew he wasn't going on a cruise unless Mel would go, but why be argumentative about it?

"Was he being an asshole?" Erma sat on the edge of her chair like she was ready to spring into action.

"Not this time. We've been getting along so well lately, it's scary." She started stuffing legal pads and pens and other office paraphernalia into an ancient, brown leather briefcase the size of a small suitcase. "He doesn't particularly like it that Mel wants to grow up to be an attorney like you and me. I don't either. Maybe she'll change her mind if I move over to the insurance firm."

"Don't start that shit again, Sandra." Erma leaped up. "I'll be damned if I'll let you go work for those bloodsuckers."

"Anyhow, he'll take y'all to Hobby on Sunday afternoon, and I'll pick y'all up in San Antonio. *No problemo.* So did you win our argument with Rufina or not?"

"We were talking about you going to work for that—"

"No. We were not. You're trying to talk about it, and I don't have time now to argue with you. I haven't definitely made up my mind, but I will by the end of Rufina's trial."

Erma looked like she was ready to explode, her face growing as red as a strawberry. She opened her mouth, but no words came out.

"So what happened with Rufina? Did she cave?" Sandra put her laptop in its carrying case and the case in a roller bag.

Erma sat back down. The red in her face abated a bit. "Should I feel guilty for browbeating a client more than usual?"

"She agreed?"

"*Sí.*" Erma grinned. "I had to promise to find Efrain the best immigration lawyer in Texas if he has trouble with his status."

Sandra slapped her desk. "That makes my day. I think we can win this thing if BJ can find someone to drive down to Mexico and somehow bring him back." Sandra grabbed up her phone to call BJ.

"I called BJ, if that's what you're doing. I just got off the phone. Shit, she can talk."

Sandra set her phone back down. "What'd she say?"

"She's a basket case. Asked how Rufina was doing. Was she sleeping? Was she eating? Was Rufina a nervous wreck? Hell, BJ's the nervous wreck. Rufina is about the calmest, most controlled person I've ever met."

"No, what'd she say about Efrain? About sending someone down to Mexico?"

"Well, here's a surprise. She said pretty much nothing goes on around the ranch that she doesn't know about and that includes Rufina and Efrain—and Efrain's status." She gave Sandra a sideways grin. "And I bet she knew about the kids, too, but never said anything."

"I wouldn't be at all surprised. Something like that would be hard to conceal. She does, after all, own and run the ranch. Her job is to know what's happening."

"Anyway, she's going to send one of the *legal* men to see if he can locate Efrain."

"I don't even want to know how Efrain will get across the border. I just hope we won't reach our side of the case until they return." Sandra slid some file folders into the briefcase. "I called the judge's office to find out if Rufina needs to be there for pretrial. The coordinator said no, but Rufina does have to be there for jury selection."

"She ought to be, anyway. She needs to look each juror in the eye until it hurts."

"Patricia booked her on the same flight as you and Mel. You don't mind her being here for another weekend, do you? I don't want to have her on the ranch until we have to."

Erma shook her head. "She's no problem. In fact, she's been cooking breakfast for me. How do you like them apples?"

"I'd like to bite into a juicy apple right about now. I'm hungry."

"Very funny."

"Listen, when I arrive, I'm going straight to Rufina's cottage, which will now be ours, and dumping my stuff. Afterward, I'll inspect the one BJ set aside for Rufina. Rufina's belongings should have been moved and put away by then. BJ promised she'd have the women Rufina is closest to move everything, on the QT. And I'm going to check to make sure there are several locks on each door as well as locks on the windows."

Patricia walked in, two fingers gripping a smallish, gray, triangular-shaped leather bag by one of its corners. "I think this is yours, Sandra. A man with a punched-in nose brought it in, saying it's cleaned and oiled and ready for use."

"That would be Cliff. Set it here on my desk. I'm sure it's not loaded so it can't hurt you."

Patricia set the bag on a corner of Sandra's desk, a good distance from the edge. "I don't know why you think you need that thing."

"What about the trial notebook? Is it ready?"

"Oh, yes ma'am." Patricia did an about-face and marched back out of Sandra's office.

"Think Rufina needs a weapon in her cottage?" Erma asked.

"She might need one," Sandra said, raising her eyebrows, "but she's not getting one. She'd be violating her bail conditions. I can see Holt somehow hearing she has a weapon and sending some deputies to arrest her. I don't want deputies bringing her to court every day and standing around in the courtroom, do you?"

"Hell no. We don't want anything to jeopardize Rufina's freedom."

"By the way, you did tell BJ to make sure no one, including Rex and Kathy Lynn, knows where Rufina will be staying during the trial?"

"Yep, I don't care if they're her kids or what, I'm as suspicious of everyone as you are."

Patricia returned and heaved the trial notebook into Sandra's arms. Sandra thumbed through the tabs. "Well done. Thanks so much."

"I'm glad you approve. I spent a lot of time on it." She turned up one of her long sleeves that had fallen down.

"We know you did," Erma said. "We appreciate you, though we don't say it often."

"Thank you, ma'am." Patricia's face broke into a wide smile. "I'll go back to my desk if there's nothing else."

"Patricia, if you want, you can take tomorrow off," Sandra said. "I won't be here, and Erma's other work can wait 'til Monday."

Patricia glanced from one to the other of them. "I don't think so. Something might come up, and what would you do without me, Miz Townley? You can't even turn on the computer."

Erma sputtered for a moment.

"But I'll save that day until something comes along and I need it."

Sandra gave Patricia a thumbs-up. "You're a gem. You don't have to do that. We'll always let you do what you need to do."

Patricia's eyes crinkled when she smiled. "I know." She beamed and went back to her office.

"I wish we could take her with us," Erma said. "We could use her for any emergency motions we need to file. We could stash her in that man's office."

"Jared. His name is Jared Longley, and I told you his sister will help us out if we need something I can't pound out in the evenings after court. We need Patricia here, but someday, let's take her to court, so she can see us in action."

"You mean me, right? You're probably not going to be here."

"Let's not discuss that now." A series of quiet musical notes came from Sandra's desktop computer. She checked her emails. "Rex, again."

"What does that annoying little bugger want now?" Erma walked around to stand over Sandra's shoulder.

Sandra opened the email. The first thing that popped up was a picture of a syringe. Below that: *I hear the district attorney is going for the needle. Just want to keep you informed of what I learn. Rex*

Erma leaned in, squinting at the screen. "What the hell?"

Sandra moved back to let Erma read. "I thought he had a job in San Antonio. Doesn't he ever work?"

"I'm starting to think he enjoys annoying us. Sweet one minute, irritating the next."

"Well, this time he's misinformed. In spite of Holt's threats, he's never gotten a cap murder indictment out of the Grand Jury."

Erma circled back around the desk and sat down. "Does he think we're so stupid we don't know what Rufina's charged with?"

"He's just getting his jollies with his continuing emails. I've started wondering whether he knows Holt as well as he'd like us to believe."

"Are you sure Holt didn't file something at the last minute?"

"Of course he didn't, why would he? He can't make a capital murder case. Besides, it's too late. And tomorrow at pretrial, I'm going to ask the judge to give the lesser included charge of manslaughter."

"Which he'll never do. It's either murder or nothing. I hate for you to do that since we don't want the case to go to the jury." Erma hiked one leg over the other.

"Just for insurance. I have to ask." Sandra's cell phone rang. The screen read Gillespie County. "Sandra Salinsky."

"District Attorney Holt, here. How are you this fine spring morning, Mrs. Salinsky?"

Sandra ignored the Mrs., which she knew he used to gall her. "Packing up my desk, Mr. Hold."

"Holt."

"Oh, yes, sorry. Yeah, packing up, getting ready to leave this afternoon. And how are you doing? Ready for combat?"

Holt's chuckle didn't sound sincere.

"The reason I'm calling is to ask whether you've considered my offer of life imprisonment."

Sandra mouthed what he said to Erma. "Yes, certainly we considered it. My client is innocent and doesn't want to plead."

"I'm afraid I'm taking it off the table then. We're going for the death penalty."

"Ha. Ha. Ha. Mr. Holt, very funny." She mouthed the words death penalty to Erma whose face started turning red again. Or was it closer to burgundy?

"The death penalty is no laughing matter, Mrs. Salinsky. Do you hear me laughing?"

A slow burn began in her stomach. She studied the ceiling. No way of knowing what was going on or who he might be entertaining in his office. "Mr. Holt, you and I both know twenty-four hours' notice is not adequate under Texas law of the intent to seek the death penalty, even if you were able to get an indictment for capital murder. Do you think I'm stupid?"

Silence greeted her question, followed by some heavy breathing. Sandra began to wonder whether Rex had talked with Holt, and that's where Rex got the idea Holt was going for lethal injection.

"Okay, so I was joking. Bad joke."

"What the fuck, Holt?" She'd like to reach through the phone and punch him square in the nose.

Erma pumped a fist in the air.

"But I'm not joking about taking life off the table. If you don't accept life right this minute, we're going for the full ninety-nine years and $10,000 fine."

"Well, hey pal, if you think you can get it, go for it." Sandra clicked off, sorry her fist couldn't be transported to him.

CHAPTER TWENTY-THREE

S ANDRA NODDED AT the judge, a pale, middle-aged, al-
most-bald man named David Danforth, whom she had not
met before pretrial. She approached the space in front of the
jury *venire,* who filled wooden benches from the first row behind
the bar all the way to the back of the courtroom. She wore her
lucky suit—the one she'd received the most guilty verdicts in as
a prosecutor and the most not guilty verdicts in as a defense attorney—a navy-blue, lined jacket and skirt with a cream blouse.
Knowing she looked good helped bolster her confidence at
being an out-of-town attorney facing a group of people about
whom she knew little.

Dressed in a black pin-striped suit, Mr. Holt was striking
with his dark-framed glasses, piercing hazel eyes, lock of hair
hanging above one eye, and well-trimmed beard. He'd just finished his *voir dire.* After explaining the definition of first-degree
murder, he'd spent most of his allotted time making sure no
one on the panel knew the defendant, as he called Rufina. The
defendant this. The defendant that. And, of course, he asked
whether anyone knew the defendant's attorneys, Sandra or
Erma. The likelihood of that was slim, but prosecutors seldom

took chances. He'd been able to exclude a few jurors who knew BJ, and who stated they couldn't be impartial.

Holt had tried to lay out his case-in-chief for the panel, but Sandra objected loud and long, only reining herself in when he questioned them about whether they could convict a woman of murder. Could they give ninety-years to a woman? He pressed them on circumstantial evidence. Could they convict on circumstantial evidence if the State had no more than that? Could they convict if the State showed there were means, motive, and opportunity?

Now, it was her turn. Her eyes ran across the predominately white faces. "Good morning, ladies and gentlemen. Since the parties in this case have already been introduced, let me just say I appreciate your showing up to perform your service. Without you, Mrs. Rufina Barboza, my client, wouldn't be able to have her day in court. Now then, juror number one, Mr. Schultz, would you describe what you see when you look at Mrs. Barboza?"

Rufina, who'd worn a scarf around her head and kept only her profile visible to the jury panel as much as possible, removed the scarf and turned, so they could see her full face. Her long, gray-streaked black hair was knotted at the back of her head, revealing scarring all the way into her scalp. She wore a long-sleeved, white blouse with a collar open at the neck, showing scars down to the first button, and a short string of pearls, both of which contrasted with her dark skin. Her black pencil skirt fell to her ankles, just above black flats. She stood when Sandra indicated, thereby emphasizing Sandra's height and her own tiny stature. Part of the plan.

Juror number one, a short, thin man with a crew-cut, winced. Sandra focused on him, but with her peripheral vision, she saw juror number two's face scrunch up. Tears filled the woman's eyes.

Erma and Mel took furious notes, Erma, from the counsel table, Mel, from a chair the judge had allowed them to put almost behind the clerk's box. At pretrial, Sandra and Holt had a brief skirmish over a minor's being allowed in front of the bar.

The judge hadn't seen the harm in it, so they'd won a small battle at least. Sandra needed Mel's impressions of the panel. Erma could only look at so many people at one time.

After a pause of several moments, Sandra again asked, "What do you see?"

A muscle pulsed in the man's jaw. He squirmed and sat up straighter. "A very dark, little Mexican woman with a terribly scarred face."

Sandra liked that answer, especially the 'little'. She turned to juror number two. "And ma'am," she read the woman's name from the jury list, "Ms. Coffey, please describe what you see."

Sandra continued that line of questioning all the way to the last person in the pool. Her intention had been to make sure the potential jurors saw how small Rufina was, as well as to see whether any of them shied away from looking at her.

"Now, raise your hand if you think Mrs. Rufina Barboza is guilty of the crime with which she is charged, the crime the prosecutor already told you about." Sandra's eyes met those of each person. No hands went up.

"That's right. Rufina's been charged with a crime, but she has not been found guilty. Any of you have a problem with that?"

The panel shook their heads.

"Let the record reflect the panel as a group shook their heads no. Juror number three, Mr. Shineberger, what is an indictment?"

Mr. Shineberger, who was a head taller than everyone in his row, wore a dark blue suit. On the jury list, his occupation was listed as bank vice-president. He frowned at Sandra, his black eyebrows drawing together. Bankers were notoriously conservative, so here she had a conservative man in a conservative profession in a conservative town. She didn't want him.

He scrutinized her body a moment too long for her taste. He appeared to be at least sixty. "An indictment says a Grand Jury has decided there's probable cause to have the person stand trial for a crime."

Sandra cocked her head. "You've served on a Grand Jury, haven't you?"

He nodded and gave her a fake smile.

"You didn't serve on the Grand Jury that indicted my client, did you?" She thought she was making a small joke.

"Yes, ma'am." Something akin to a smirk danced around his mouth.

Tiny shock waves shot up Sandra's arms. What the hell? She turned to the judge. "May we approach the bench?"

"You certainly may," the judge said.

"Mr. Shineberger, if you'll accompany us for a word with the judge, please?" She opened the swinging door that separated the potential jurors from the lawyers, so he could walk through.

When they reached sidebar, Sandra said, "Judge, move to strike Mr. Shineberger for cause." She fought with herself to keep her hands from her hips. How had someone who had served on the Grand Jury ended up on the *venire*?

Mr. Holt said, "Your Honor, I have no idea how this happened. I have no objection."

Judge Danforth said, "Mr. Shineberger, you're excused. See the clerk across the hall if you need a jury slip. Thank you for your time."

"Thank you, Your Honor." Sandra and Erma exchanged astonished looks as Sandra wove in-between the counsel tables until she was back in place.

Sandra drew a deep breath and let it out, hoping the jurors couldn't read the tension she felt, the questions in her mind about the case being rigged, her imagination running wild. "Did any of the rest of you serve on the Grand Jury that heard Mrs. Rufina Barboza's case?" Silence met her question. "I take it by your silence, the answer is no."

Mr. Holt's head was down as if he were studying the names on his copy of the jury list.

Sandra made eye contact with several of the jurors at the back of the panel. The top sheet of her list of potential jurors had squares drawn and people's names filled in with their numbers on the jury panel. She crossed out Mr. Shineberger's name and flipped to the second page, to the first box, the first alternate. "Mr. Linebarger, you've moved up." His name was too close to Mr. Shineberger's. Bergers, Bargers, all descendants of the original German settlers. What was she to do? Try not to stereotype them, she told herself.

⚕   ⚕   ⚕

When the *venire* had entered the courtroom that morning, Erma almost swallowed her tongue. She hadn't seen such a jury panel, very white and middle-aged, since her early days of practicing law. Being the suspicious sort, she wondered whether someone could have intentionally put brown people at the back, so far back they'd never have a chance to serve on the jury. As soon as they were seated, Sandra filed for a jury shuffle to try to get some color up front, so they might be able to seat one or two people who resembled their client—at least get a few within spitting distance. Judge Danforth had grudgingly granted her motion.

Even with the jury shuffle and careful strikes, the twelve who were seated didn't look all that promising. After a thin little white man, came an old German woman who spoke with an accent. Erma had noted her tear-filled eyes and had taken that as a good sign. Why hadn't Holt struck her? Did he know something they didn't? The third juror, a Latino male who Sandra and Erma thought for sure Holt would strike, could possibly lean their way. Unfortunately, the potential juror's cell phone stayed glued to his ear during every break indicating he had other matters on his mind he thought more important than murder. The next was a rancher who smelled earthy and wore muddy cowboy boots, jeans, a snap-up shirt, and carried his hat in his hands.

Holt wore a shit-eating grin when the clerk called each name, right up to the last one—a real, live, black person seated in the

215

number twelve chair. Erma had seen the woman but hadn't caught her name, hadn't thought the strikes would go so far back. She found her on the list. The thought that a minority woman would have some empathy for Rufina instilled hope in Erma's heart. All they needed was one vote to hang up the jury.

After a ten-minute break during which the judge excused the remainder of the panel, the jurors filed back into the jury box. Mel sat on the first wooden bench behind Sandra and Erma. BJ couldn't be in the courtroom, because she was a witness. The judge read several pages of instructions to the jury and then asked Rufina to stand. Sandra stood with her.

"How do you plead to the allegations in the indictment? Guilty or not guilty?"

Her arms at her sides, her chin up, Rufina turned toward the jury. "Not guilty."

After announcements of ready, the judge crossed his arms and said, "Mr. Holt, you may begin."

Holt circled around his table, the one closest to the jury, and laid several sheets of paper on one corner. "Good morning, again, ladies and gentlemen. Right off the bat I want to thank you for your jury service. As the judge told you in preliminary instructions, we expect this case to last about a week. He also explained the order in which we present our cases. As attorney for the State, for the people, I have the burden of proof. I must prove to you that the defendant—" he pointed at Rufina "—is guilty beyond a reasonable doubt. We discussed that in *voir dire*, so you all have a pretty good idea of what it means, right? And that is exactly what I will do." He paused and looked at each juror.

"What we have here is a simple case of revenge or, in legal terms, retaliation. The defendant," he turned and pointed at Rufina again, "after years and years of holding in her anger, shot and killed the young woman who was responsible for burning down the defendant's house and killing the defendant's husband. That's it, plain and simple."

Sandra and Erma watched the jurors for their reactions and made notes. Several jurors' eyes flickered when Holt said "shot and killed" and again when he said "killing the defendant's husband," but otherwise they all remained deadpan.

He continued. "It's my job to prove this to you. The facts are plain. On the night of the murder, the Widow Schindler had entertained at her home. All three of her children were present as well as a couple of friends of the family. The defendant, the housekeeper, supposedly went to her cottage after supervising the preparation of the evening meal. After dinner, when everyone had retired for the evening, the defendant—if she did go to her residence—returned to the Schindler home with the intention of shooting Katy Jo Schindler. However, the decedent, Katy Jo Schindler, wasn't in her room. Instead, Katy Jo had gone into her mother's room to talk with her mother. Mrs. Schindler got out of bed and went into the bathroom. At that time, the defendant ran into the bedroom and shot Katy Jo and ran away.

"The defendant ran to her cottage, which is only a short distance from the main house. In her haste, she dropped the gun alongside the path. She then undressed quickly and got into her own bed. By the time the police arrived, everyone, including the defendant, had gathered in the house, most of them still dressed in their bedclothes."

Rufina, who had, for the most part, ignored the pad and pen Sandra had provided to her for the purpose of making notes, picked up the pen and began writing as Holt continued his statement.

"We intend to prove the defendant had means, motive, and opportunity. The means was the Schindler gun cabinet full of guns that the defendant had access to. As housekeeper, she had access to the keys to everything in the house. She supervised the cleaning of the house, including the gun cabinet."

Rufina glanced at Sandra and mouthed the word, "No." She wrote more. "BJ had keys to gun cabinets."

"As for motive, the defendant had plenty. She hated Katy Jo for setting the fire that killed Mr. Barboza. Not only was her husband killed, but the defendant was horribly scarred as you have seen. We intend to show you that over the years the anger at Katy Jo built up and built up until, on the eve of Katy Jo's engagement to a nice young man who you will hear from, the defendant could no longer contain her fury. She couldn't stand the idea that Katy Jo would live the good life while she, the defendant, would live out her life as a widow and a servant.

"Lastly, opportunity. Katy Jo was at the ranch for a family dinner party. The defendant got a gun from the gun cabinet, intending to kill Katy Jo in Katy Jo's bedroom, but before she could accomplish that feat, Katy Jo went into Mrs. Schindler's room. Not wanting to lose the opportunity, the defendant followed Katy Jo, and shot her to death as soon as Mrs. Schindler left the room."

Holt continued in that vein for a few minutes more and sat down.

The judge said, "Ms. Salinsky, do you wish to make your opening statement now or wait until you present your side of the case?"

Erma snorted under her breath. The judge was required to ask that ludicrous question. For the defense to wait to make an opening statement left the jury with nothing to think about over the course of the trial except the prosecution's theory of the case. A defense attorney would generally have to be an idiot to wait.

"I'll make my opening now, Your Honor." Sandra walked across the courtroom to stand before the jury.

"Ladies and gentlemen of the jury, I, too, wish to thank you for your time and attention. If it weren't for you showing up to serve, Mrs. Rufina Barboza would never get her day in court. Her name would never be cleared. And so, the defense extends our utmost appreciation to you.

"You all promised in jury selection to keep an open mind. The way this works is the prosecution has the burden of proof. He," she pointed at Holt, "gets the first and last word. As Mrs. Barboza sits here now, she is innocent of all charges against her. She's innocent until proven guilty."

A hinge squeaked at the back of the courtroom. BJ stuck her head inside the door. She held one finger up. Erma shook her head, and BJ let the door fall closed. Erma glanced at the judge, but he didn't seem to notice. Was he even awake? His eyes were closed.

Sandra continued, "As I was saying, Mrs. Barboza may not be found guilty until the prosecutor has met his burden—beyond a reasonable doubt. That's what you should be thinking about as the trial proceeds. Does the evidence as presented to you show you there is no reasonable doubt as to Mrs. Barboza's guilt?

"The prosecutor spoke with you about circumstantial evidence during *voir dire*. You've heard his opening and, unless he has a truckload of evidence, circumstantial evidence is all he has and not much of it. Hold him to his burden. If he cannot prove Mrs. Barboza had means, as he says he can, that would be reasonable doubt. If he cannot prove motive, that she was overcome with anger after all these years have passed since the fire, that would be reasonable doubt. And if he cannot prove opportunity, that she was somehow standing outside BJ Schindler's bedroom with a gun waiting to make her move and no one saw her, that is reasonable doubt. I think you'll find during this trial that the prosecution's case is filled with holes of doubt. Again, thank you for your attention." Sandra stood a moment more, staring into the jurors' faces and took her seat.

The judge, who had been leaning as far back as the chair would go, brought his chair to an upright position. "The court will be in recess until nine o'clock tomorrow morning. Be sure to wear your badges at all times. Meet in the jury room, which the bailiff will familiarize you with now. Remain there until the bailiff comes to bring you to court. Remember you are not to discuss this case with each other or anyone at any time until the case is sent to you for your deliberations. To do so could cause a mistrial and then all of our time would have been wasted. Please be here on time. I want to move this case along."

The participants at each table rose as the judge exited the courtroom. The jurors, accompanied by a deputy sheriff, filed out.

Rufina said, "Sandra, what Mr. Holt said is not true." She held out the legal pad on which she'd been writing. "I wrote down everything he said and what the real truth is."

Sandra took the pad and glanced at it. "Thanks, Rufina. I'll review this tonight." She clasped her arm. "Don't worry. I'll call you if I have any questions about it. What I want you to do now is go back to your cottage and get some rest. This is going to be a long week for all of us but especially for you."

Erma said, "Rufina, you're an experienced court clerk. You've heard stuff like this before. Remember he's just saying what he intends to prove—which I interpret as *hopes* to prove."

"Don't let him get to you," Sandra added. "He'd love to get under your skin."

Mel stood behind the bar. She beckoned at her mother and Erma. "Did you see Mrs. Schindler stick her head in the door?"

"I'm glad we were only doing opening statements," Sandra said. "Otherwise the judge would have been all over us for that."

"Yeah, like flies on shit," Erma said. "Go out there and find out what she wants, child."

Mel was gone only a few moments when she opened the courtroom door and followed BJ down the aisle. BJ had changed into indigo jeans and a flannel shirt and boots, her short hair standing at attention.

Sandra waited until BJ made it down the aisle, then said, "BJ, don't do that again. You know the judge excluded all witnesses from the courtroom even during opening statements, which is unusual. He didn't say anything this time, but I know you don't want to do anything to jeopardize this case."

Nodding, BJ said, "You told me that. Sorry, but I just wanted you to know something." Her lips formed a huge frown. "My
worker returned from Mexico. He couldn't find Efrain."

CHAPTER TWENTY-FOUR

SANDRA SAT AT the defense table with her laptop open, a burning sensation in her chest. She rubbed her sternum and continued scrolling through case reports. She'd been researching case law for a motion for continuance to be granted after a trial had begun. According to the rules, she was supposed to identify the witness. She didn't want to do that. She'd already prepared the motion that gave Efrain's name, but she didn't want to file it. In fact, she had two motions in front of her, one with Efrain's identity and one without.

She'd left the cottage early, so she could be alone to finish her research and clear her head before court convened. She wasn't used to having no time to herself, no time to manage a little exercise, no time to think. That the three of them were crammed into that little cottage would have been bad enough if they'd been on vacation, but on top of that, the stress of knowing someone's freedom was at stake added pressure.

She'd tried to make Erma understand part of the attraction of the insurance firm was they'd promised she wouldn't have to litigate. If she took that job, Sandra would never be responsible for someone being denied her rights, incarcerated, or executed, again. She'd had it up to her neck with criminal cases. Now, in the minutes before court was called to order, her hands shook, and her foot bounced. She was on the losing side of the motion, but she had to try. Scrolling through case report after case report, she could find nothing.

The courtroom door squeaked. Erma trudged up the aisle and pushed her way through from the gallery, followed by Rufina and Mel. Grunting, Erma dumped her handbag and briefcase down. Rufina sat down on the other side of Erma. Mel perched on the front row.

Holt, followed by one of his assistants, came in and nodded at Sandra. The clerk entered from the side door and eased into her chair. When the door opened again, they all stood as the bailiff led the jurors to the jury box. The court reporter, a man named Matthew Grieger, followed and sat behind his machine.

"All rise for the Honorable David Danforth," the bailiff called.

The judge made short shrift of the distance between the door and the chair behind the bench. He wore a blank expression though his eyes darted from one lawyer to the other.

"Be seated," the judge said. "Ms. Salinsky, the clerk tells me you have a motion to present."

Sandra, who had continued to stand while everyone else sat, held the motion. "Yes, Your Honor. I'd like to present it outside the presence of the jury."

Danforth frowned. "I thought I made it clear before this trial started, I wanted to take up all motions before the jury was seated."

The burn in Sandra's chest grew worse. The judge knew as well as she did that matters came up unexpectedly. He was deliberately chastising her in front of the jury to make her look bad. She bit the inside of her cheek. "You did, Judge. But this was unexpected. I couldn't have anticipated the need for this motion." She used words from the statute, so he would be aware she knew the law. "May it be taken up outside the presence of the jury?"

Frowning, Holt stood at his table, arms dangling by his sides. The ballpoint pen in his hand clicked once, then again. The judge looked at him. Holt didn't say anything. Sandra wished he would, but Holt knew better. The visiting judge might not care if an error was made, but Holt would. Nobody in his right mind wanted to try a case twice.

"Deputy Cortez, kindly escort the jury back outside." The judge's eyes bored through Sandra.

Sandra eyeballed the members of the jury as they filed out. Most of them looked like they were enjoying themselves; no sullen glances yet. The trial had just begun, though. Plenty of time for attitudes to change.

As soon as the door closed behind the jury, the judge turned back. "Now, what is it, Ms. Salinsky?"

She gripped the edge of the table. "Motion for Continuance, Judge."

Erma touched Sandra's wrist—which Sandra took to be a sign of encouragement—but otherwise remained still.

"Not at this late date." Holt glared at her.

"I'll decide that, Mr. Holt." The judge crossed his arms.

Sandra held the Code of Criminal Procedure open to the section pertaining to continuances, her forefinger marking the part she wanted to read. "Judge, if I may quote from Article 29.13 of the Texas Code of Criminal Procedure..."

The judge rolled his eyes.

"For the record, Your Honor." Sandra wet her lips. "'A continuance or postponement may be granted on motion of the State or defendant after the trial has begun, when it is made to appear to the satisfaction of the court by some unexpected occurrence since the trial began, which no reasonable diligence could have anticipated, the applicant is so taken by surprise that a fair trial cannot be had.'"

"I'm sure curious about this unexpected occurrence, Judge." Holt crossed his arms as he stood beside his table.

"In a moment, Mr. Holt." The judge turned his attention back to Sandra. "Anything else you want to put on the record at this point?"

Not ever having tried a case to Judge Danforth, she wasn't sure whether he was setting her up, or trying to be fair. She put the book down, but left it open to the section on trial motions. "No, Your Honor."

"So at this point, kindly inform the court, Mrs. Salinsky, what unexpected occurrence has taken you by surprise?"

Sandra flexed her jaw. She hated to give away any part of her case, even a tiny part—which this wasn't. "I'm not trying to blame it on Mr. Holt, Your Honor. This has nothing to do with him. I wouldn't want you or him to think I'm implying anything by putting forth a motion like this."

Holt's face screwed up and turned pink. The clicking of his pen went nonstop.

The judge leaned forward. "Ms. Salinsky, what are you implying?"

"Oh, I'm not implying anything, Your Honor. I'm simply saying what has happened was totally unexpected. I'm sure Mr. Holt had nothing to do with it."

The judge leaned as far forward as the bench would allow, his eyebrows knitted together. "What is the occurrence you're not blaming Mr. Holt for?" His voice echoed off the back wall.

Sandra stepped back and bumped into her chair. Erma's eyes had grown round. Teeny smile lines had formed at each side of her mouth. Sandra clasped her hands in front of herself as if she were walking forward for communion. She took as deep a breath as she could, her chest tight. "My alibi witness has gone missing."

"Judge!" Holt's legs bumped his chair causing it to crash into the separating wall behind him. "I didn't have a God—a dad gum thing to do with anybody going missing, especially her alleged alibi witness."

Sandra wrinkled her forehead at Holt as she held up her hands. "Judge, I said I was sure Mr. Holt didn't have anything to do with my witness missing, didn't I? I don't know why he's all worked up."

Holt pointed his finger at her. "You—you—"

Judge Danforth banged his fist on the bench. "Mr. Holt, restrain yourself."

Holt snorted like a bull and glared at Sandra who maintained a placid face. She didn't dare glance his way. She stood with the tips of her fingers resting on the written motions she didn't want to file. Anxiety bounced around in her chest.

"When did you ascertain this witness became unavailable, Ms. Salinsky?" The judge eased back in his chair, the expression on his face somewhere between consternation and enjoyment. Not knowing him, his look was hard to interpret.

"Yesterday, Your Honor."

"Yesterday, when, ma'am?"

"Yesterday after you recessed for the day."

"And how did you ascertain this information?"

"I was informed by another person, Judge."

"Would you like to share with me who the other person was?"

"No, sir. At least not without the person's consent."

The judge nodded. "Is that person present in the courtroom?"

"If I may be so bold as to ask," Holt said, "why are we playing twenty questions?"

Judge Danforth shot him a dark look. Holt returned the judge's stare, not backing down. Sandra had to respect him for that.

"Do you have a written motion for continuance, Ms. Salinsky?" The judge sat with his arms crossed.

"You're not going to grant her motion without even giving me a chance to argue against it, Judge." Holt's tone was a statement more than a question.

The ancient furnace hanging off the wall clanged but did little to warm the courtroom. Sandra crossed her arms in an effort to increase her body heat. The calendar might reflect spring, but the weather in the Texas hills didn't. The nights were cold, and the insides of the old courthouse never reached what she thought of as a habitable temperature.

"Mr. Holt," the judge said, "the last time I checked, I was the judge and you, the lawyer. Don't tell me what I am or am not going to do."

"I just meant—"

"I know what you meant. I'm asking to be presented with the motion. I haven't said whether I'll grant it. You have a problem with that?"

Holt stared at the tops of his shoes. "No, Your Honor. So long as she has a copy for me as well."

"I sure do, Mr. Holt," Sandra said. "Let me hand the original to the judge first." She carried the original to the judge. Back at her table, she pulled out a copy and held it across the aisle to Holt.

"Judge," Holt said after perusing it for a moment. "What kind of game is she playing? She doesn't identify her witness or where he lives."

The judge's eyes flitted from the paper in his hands to Sandra and back again. Sandra and Erma exchanged glances. They both knew the motion wouldn't fly, but at least the judge and Holt didn't appear to be such good buddies anymore.

"Ms. Salinsky, I'm quite sure you're acquainted with the rules."

"For the record, Your Honor," Mr. Holt said, "I object to the motion for the following reasons in addition to the fact she hasn't identified her witness: no due diligence is shown in procuring his presence at trial—not even a subpoena issued—no facts she expects to prove through the witness." He tapped his finger on the paper. "All we have is her statement that the unknown person is an alibi witness. And she doesn't even allege the motion is not made for delay." Holt held his copy in the air by two fingers.

"Ms. Salinsky, I'm sure you know better than to file such a motion." A muscle twitched next to the judge's left eye.

Sandra stared down at counsel table. She and Erma had agreed if they got any indication the judge would grant a motion if one that fulfilled all the legal requirements were to be presented, they would file the second motion. Unless and until they got that indication, they didn't want to let Holt learn Efrain's name or what he would testify to.

Holt would take Efrain's identification and run it through every database in existence. If he couldn't find anything, he'd guess Efrain was in the country illegally. If Efrain turned up later and came to the courthouse, as soon as Holt was aware of his whereabouts, Holt would have him picked up. They were in a lose-lose situation.

On the other hand, if the judge granted the motion for continuance—the second one—they would have more time to build a better defense for Rufina and possibly would never need Efrain. And there was always the chance his immigration papers would come through.

"Your Honor," Sandra said and laid her copy on her counsel table, "I'm at a loss for words. The way Article 29.06 is written, it places the defense in a delicate position."

"Judge," Holt said, "with discovery, they know our case so it's only fair we know theirs. Since Texas law doesn't require the defense to provide us with the names and addresses of witnesses upon whom they will rely, this rule is only fair. Not to require her to give us that information is giving her a free ride."

"Judge, we haven't asked for a continuance before. We've been put to trial real fast. This is our first such motion."

"True, Judge, but Ms. Salinsky wanted a quick trial date. She asked for a speedy trial date. Now that she's been given what she asked for, she's complaining."

"When I asked the coordinator to move the date up, I didn't know my witness would disappear." Hell, she had no knowledge at the time that such a witness existed.

"Ms. Salinsky, you must have had some indication your alleged witness wouldn't appear before this trial started." The judge's eyes were pinpoints, his voice approaching snide.

There it was. Sandra looked at Erma who nodded. The judge's words and tone had given them a clear indication he'd deny any motion they filed. Sandra put her shoulders back. A pain in her chest had begun creeping up the left side of her neck and into her jaw. "Judge, I withdraw my motion. We're ready to proceed to trial."

Holt threw his copy down and dropped into his chair. The judge offered the original back to Sandra who approached the bench to retrieve it. He had not asked the clerk to file-mark the motion, so it wasn't part of the record.

"What was that all about?" Rufina whispered to Erma so loud Sandra heard her.

Erma shielded her face with her hand. "I'll explain during the recess."

Moments later, the bailiff opened the door and said, "All rise for the jury."

They stood again. The members of the jury returned to the courtroom and entered the jury box.

The pain moved into Sandra's teeth. She flexed the muscles in her jaw, but the pain didn't subside. She breathed deeply. When she tried to take a second deep breath, she could only draw in a shallow one. She rubbed her sternum. "Erma, pour me a glass of water."

Erma did so from the pitcher standing in the center of the counsel table and handed it to Sandra, who took a swallow. "What's wrong?"

Sandra shook her head and took a short breath. She leaned on one hand. "I'll be all right in a minute."

"You don't look so good, girl." Erma moved her chair closer to Sandra. "Are you in some kind of pain?"

Sandra nodded and sat down. The jury wasn't quite seated, but she couldn't stand any longer. The pain felt like a dark mass inside of her, growing larger and darker.

Erma jumped to her feet. "Your Honor. Someone needs to call 911. I think Ms. Salinsky is having a heart attack!"

⚰ ⚰ ⚰

"What can I do?" Erma stood over her daughter, her hands flapping.

Sandra's face contorted in pain. Her jaw clenched, the muscles visibly throbbing. She rubbed her chest with the heel of her hand. Her attempts to breathe were loud and labored. She sat with her head hanging forward.

"Does she need some more water?" Matthew, the court reporter, stood on the other side of the table. "I can fetch some more water."

If they were focused at all, Sandra's half-closed eyes were on Erma's, but Erma suspected Sandra wasn't seeing much, rather just feeling the pain.

"Yes, water. Anything." Erma yelled, "Has anyone called 911? You do use 911 in this county, don't you?"

"I did, ma'am," Deputy Cortez called from across the room. He stood back from the jury box where the jurors were filing out again.

Erma hadn't heard the judge give an instruction for the jury to exit the courtroom. Her attention had been focused solely on Sandra. Holt stood at counsel table, hands on hips, his lips in a derisive curl.

Sandra had shifted forward and now hung over her knees. Her breathing continued to be labored. Erma squatted. "Child, what can I do? Where does it hurt?"

Sandra shook her head. Her hair came loose from the clip that had been holding it off her neck. The clip fell to the floor with a clatter and skittered under the table.

Mel leaned over the bar, so far forward she could have fallen face first on the floor. "Mom! What's wrong?"

In a hushed tone, Erma said, "Let's wait for the EMTs."

Sandra shook her head again. "Give me a moment. I'll be all right."

"I don't think so." Erma held Sandra's hand, mentally imploring the EMTs to hurry. The minutes crawled past. Everyone left in the courtroom appeared frozen in place.

"Make way!" The hall door burst open and two men rushed inside with a gurney between them, running up the aisle with it. "Excuse me, ma'am." The first one made a sweeping gesture at Erma. She backed away, giving them plenty of room.

"I'll be okay." Sandra's voice was raspy. She raised her head and looked at the first young man.

"We'll be the judge of that." The second one wrapped a cuff around her arm and pulled out a stethoscope. "Don't move."

"Don't worry." Sandra spoke in a whispery voice.

"Don't talk, either." The first EMT's hand encircled her wrist, his fingers on her pulse.

Erma hurried around to Mel who stood with tears streaming down her face. She put her arm around the girl and sat down on the first bench. "It's going to be all right." She stroked Mel's hair.

Holt still stood next to his chair, rooted to the floor. The judge had left the bench. The court reporter stood next to his machine. He held a cup of water in one hand. The bailiff had returned, his body in front of the door leading the jury room. Everyone watched the EMTs.

A few moments later, the second EMT whispered to the first one. The first one whispered back. Both nodded. The first one said, "Can you stand, ma'am?"

"Sandra Salinsky," she uttered. "I'll be fine if you can give me a few minutes."

"No, ma'am, Miz Salinsky," the first one said. The second one lowered the gurney. "You're to lie down on this gurney. We have to take you to the hospital."

Sandra groaned. "I don't need to go to the hospital."

"Just lie down. We'll let the hospital decide what to do with you."

Sandra continued to rub a place on her chest as they wheeled her away. Mel and Erma followed them into the hall to the elevator. Erma had never seen Sandra like that. The worst Erma'd seen Sandra in adulthood was the depression, the funk she'd been in ever since the Parker murder case and Stuart, and that wasn't any physical ailment, just in her head.

"As soon as the judge declares a mistrial, I'll be over there," Erma told Sandra. "Son, where is the hospital around here?"

The elevator dinged and opened. The two men wheeled Sandra inside. Mel held on to her mother's foot for a moment.

"Hard to miss," the second one said. "On the Kerrville Highway, kind of opposite the high school."

Erma took Mel by the arm and moved back. That would be easy enough to find. She stood there until the door closed, then turned on her heel to find Mr. Holt leaning against the courtroom doorjamb. He wore a sneer a foot wide. "You're not going to get away with it."

"You go on back into the courtroom and sit near Rufina." Erma prodded Mel and straightened the peplum on her jacket. When Mel had gone inside, Erma said, "What are you talking about?" She attempted to walk around him and into the courtroom. She didn't want a verbal scuffle with the district attorney.

"Her histrionics aren't going to get you that continuance." He had one hand in his pants pocket, jingling his change. The other gripped his hip.

Erma pivoted and walked up to Holt, jabbing her forefinger at his chest. He might be a head taller, but she wasn't going to let him bully her. "I don't know what you may have heard about us, if anything, but understand this, mister. My daughter would never engage in histrionics for a continuance." Her face and hands had grown warm.

"Not going to work." He smirked. "Not going to work."

He sounded like a little boy in a schoolyard. She glared up at him. "This is no trick. It's real. I have a history of heart problems. I only hope she didn't inherit heart trouble from me."

A tall, muscular, fair-haired man, with a sheaf of papers in one hand, charged up the staircase. Dressed in a dark brown suit with a bolo tie at the neck and shiny black leather boots, he sprinted around them to the courtroom door and flung it open. Sticking his head in, he called out, "Ricardo, where's Ms. Salinsky?"

Erma couldn't hear the bailiff's reply. Who was that man, and what did he want? He let the door fall shut and started for the clerk's office. "I'm her mother. You're looking for Sandra? I'm her mother."

The man stopped. He towered over her as much as Holt did, not an unusual occurrence. "You're Mrs. Townley?" He shook her hand. "I'm Jared Longley. Did something happen to Sandra? They said downstairs in the tax office that a woman lawyer collapsed in the courtroom."

"She didn't exactly collapse," Erma said. So he was the man whose law office Sandra had been using as a home base? Not bad.

Holt snorted. Erma shot him a look that, had it been a bullet, would have killed him.

"Well, where is she?" Jared shifted from foot-to-foot like he was about to start a race.

"The EMTs took her to the hospital to have her checked out. At least that's what I understood."

"EMTs?" He rubbed the back of his neck. "Then it must be serious."

Erma rested her hand on his forearm. "I only hope it wasn't a heart attack. I had one about a year or so ago. I'm hoping whatever ails her will go away."

Holt snickered and took a step back.

"Shut the fuck up, Mr. Holt." Erma's face radiated heat. "I don't appreciate your insinuation."

"Now, wait a minute," Holt said. "You're an officer of the court. You can't—"

Erma ignored him, giving her full attention to Mr. Longley, who, though his eyebrows were raised, didn't get involved in the exchange.

Jared said, "Mrs. Townley, I'm going to the hospital. You want to ride along?" He held his hand out like he'd take her arm and escort an old woman down the stairs.

She shook her head. "Can't. My granddaughter is still in the courtroom. And Rufina, our client."

"Of course. I know about Rufina," he said. "I guess you can't leave if the trial's started."

Erma expected Holt to make some smart-ass remark, but he kept quiet. She turned her attention back to Jared Longley. "Yes, well, I have business to take up with the judge. Would you do me the kindness of calling me if you can find out how she is? As soon as I get free, I'll drive over there with my granddaughter." She handed him a card out of her pocket.

"It would be my pleasure, Mrs. Townley. Nice meeting you." He nodded and took the stairs down two at a time.

"Mrs. Townley?" Holt held his chin high. There was a tightness around his eyes. "Are you ready to go see the judge?"

Erma had a bad feeling about his desire to get right back in front of the judge, but it couldn't be helped. She had no prepared motions—no written motions—but she'd been practicing law over thirty years. If she couldn't wing an argument for a mistrial at this stage of the game, she had no business practicing law.

Holt held the courtroom door open and waved his hand. Erma walked inside and found Mel, leaning against the wall, wiping her eyes with her sleeve. The girl had probably heard everything that'd been said. Erma slipped her arm around Mel's waist and walked with her toward the benches. Rufina stared from where she sat at the end of the counsel table. "It'll be fine," Erma mouthed. Rufina's ruddy complexion was several shades lighter. She clasped her hands in front of her.

"Ricardo, would you tell the judge we're ready?" Holt asked.

They took their places, Erma standing at the chair Sandra had occupied. As she thought about what she would argue to the judge, her mouth dried up like an old peach pit. The cup of water the court reporter had brought for Sandra sat on the wooden parapet that surrounded the jury box.

"Matthew, would you mind?" Erma asked, indicating the cup.

The court reporter brought it to her, and Erma slurped it down, setting the cup on the counsel table. The judge returned before the bailiff had a chance to ask everyone to rise. The few people who were there were already standing, including BJ, who had just come in.

Judge Danforth, a red file under one arm, entered, his black robe billowing. As soon as he seated himself, his eyes went to Erma. "Mrs. Townley, how is Mrs. Salinsky?" His eyes darted to Mr. Holt's face and back to Erma's.

"Ahem. We'll find out in a little while, Judge. They took her to the hospital. And I want to talk to you about that—what I wish to make a motion about. I'm sure Mr. Holt would agree that being as how my daughter—Sandra—Ms. Salinsky had some kind of attack right here in the courtroom in front of you, the jury, and God, and everybody, I'm sure he wouldn't want this jury to be biased in favor of the defense on account of the physical ailment of the defense attorney. So I want to say, the facts being what they are and all, I'll be glad to join in a Motion for a Mistrial."

Holt's mouth gaped open.

The judge practically threw himself backward in his chair and made every attempt to hide a grin. "What do you have to say, Mr. Holt? Are you ready to move for a mistrial?"

Holt shut his mouth, swallowed, and opened it again. "Your Honor, not only is the State not moving for a mistrial, the State is ready to proceed."

Erma feigned the most surprise she could muster. The son of a bitch wasn't going to give their side an inch, not a centimeter. She rested her hand on her chest. "Why, Your Honor, it's gratifying to see Mr. Holt has so much faith in the citizens of Gillespie County. In that case, may I ask Your Honor whether if I move for a mistrial without his joinder, whether Your Honor would entertain such a motion?"

The judge, still looking amused, cocked his head. "You may certainly move for a mistrial, Mrs. Townley, but I can tell you the court is not inclined to grant it."

"Uh huh. I understand, but I must move for a mistrial to protect my client's rights."

"Denied."

"Judge, technically I haven't made the motion you just denied." Erma had been in enough courtrooms to know the judge's look said make it and move on. She cleared her throat. "Your Honor, in light of the first chair in this jury trial coming down with some kind of ailment that appeared to be a heart attack in front of the jury, the defense hereby moves for a mistrial."

"Denied. If you want to file something handwritten for the record, I'll sign it later."

"Yes, Judge. Now, here's the thing. I would like to go to the hospital to see what's going on with my daughter."

"I can understand that." The judge nodded.

"If in fact she's had some kind of serious attack, I would like to be by her side. As would her daughter, who is sitting behind me."

"I can understand that, as well." Judge Danforth wrote something.

"Judge," Mr. Holt said, "we're in some kind of dilemma here. While I'm not willing to move for a mistrial, I was looking forward to trying this case against Mrs. Salinsky, not Mrs. Townley."

Erma rested her knuckles on the table in front of her. If Sandra could hear the two men tossing around Mrs. when they referenced her, she'd have a cow. Now, what was Holt up to?

"Are you saying you're in agreement with the earlier Motion for Continuance?" the judge asked.

"No. I'm not saying that at all, Judge. I want to go forward with this case. The defendant needs to be locked up before she has a chance to harm someone else."

"What?" Erma cried. "Are you seriously asking that my client's bail be revoked because the first chair defense lawyer was taken to the hospital?"

Judge Danforth appeared as confused as Erma felt. "Here's the deal, Judge." She glanced at Rufina. Rufina was all crossed arms and legs, wrapped up in herself. "If you can give us the afternoon, a continuance for the afternoon, so we can do a couple of things, we can be ready to go forward with this trial in the morning."

"Who is we, Judge?" Holt asked, his hands in his pockets, his legs spread.

Erma pointed back at Mel. "This young lady is our part-time legal assistant, Your Honor. While she can't second-chair this case—she doesn't have a law license—"

"Law license?" Holt stamped his foot. "That little girl doesn't have a high school diploma. What does Mrs. Townley mean she's a legal assistant?"

"I only mean I want her to sit up here at counsel table with me, Judge. I need someone to help me, and Mel has been around for the whole of this case and works half a day in our office and knows a little about organization."

"I don't know what she's up to, Judge, but what I was trying to say is I don't want to try this case against Mrs. Townley. I'm ready to make another offer to Mrs. Barboza and if she'll accept it, we can all go home. Otherwise, I'm not sure how to proceed."

Erma felt like she had her head in a cloud—a dark, stormy cloud, swirling around with strong winds. Another offer? Yeah, right.

Judge Danforth said, "Step over to defense table and make your offer, Mr. Holt. And Mrs. Townley I strongly advise you to urge your client to take it."

Holt glanced twice at the judge in quick succession. The muscles in his jaws flexed as he stood for a moment studying the floor.

Rufina was still wrapped up in a ball and wouldn't meet her eyes. Holt stepped across the aisle and tugged on Erma's arm. He pulled her away from the counsel table to the bar on his side of the courtroom where Mel and BJ couldn't hear what was being said. "Here's the deal, take your choice," he said. There was no evidence of a smile, no glint in his eye. He was as somber as a corpse. "Number one, she pleads guilty to murder and goes to the jury for punishment. Number two, she pleads guilty and takes fifty years."

Erma's stomach lurched. He had to be kidding. What kind of offers were those? He was out of his fucking mind, and if they hadn't been inside the courtroom, she would have told him so. She straightened up and asked the judge, "May I have a short recess, so I can discuss these offers with my client?"

Judge Danforth's mouth was fixed in a grim line. "The jury is going to be tired of waiting. Five minutes." The judge stepped off the bench.

Erma refrained from making a sarcastic comment even under her breath where Holt could hear her. Holt exited the courtroom, leaving her with Rufina. "I don't know about you, Rufina, but I have to pee."

Rufina unwrapped herself. "What did he say?"

"Two ridiculous offers."

"What were they?" BJ asked, causing Erma to flinch. She'd forgotten BJ was in the courtroom.

"Do you mind if BJ hears this, Rufina?"

Rufina walked to where BJ was behind the bar. The four women let out a collective sigh. "No, I don't mind. I don't understand what Mr. Holt's problem is, but I don't mind talking about it with BJ here."

Mel stepped closer to the other women. The bailiff had left the courtroom, so they were alone. Erma pulled them even closer. "Fifty years or go to the jury on punishment."

Rufina shook her head. *"Que demonios?"*

"Crazy, right? I wouldn't even let you take a better offer," Erma said. "Not when there's still hope. We haven't seen their case yet."

"Well let's hurry down to the bathroom," BJ said.

"I'm going to press for at least this afternoon off even if he won't give us several days." Erma touched Bj's arm. "BJ, you originally called for me to represent Rufina. I guess you're going to get your wish."

Rufina said, "That's okay with me. I only hope my case is not what caused Sandra to have a heart attack."

"Don't start feeling guilty over it. We don't even know it was a heart attack. Come on. We'd better hurry." They walked out of the courtroom together. BJ had her arm around Rufina. Mel held her cell phone in her hand and tapped something into it.

When they returned, the players were all in position. The judge was on the bench, and Holt stood at his table. The bailiff stood in front of the door leading to the jury room, and the court reporter sat behind his stenotype machine as though ready to take down Rufina's plea. At least that's what it looked like to Erma.

"You're late," the judge said, as the women walked up the aisle.

Erma said, "Sorry, Your Honor, we needed to use the necessary room. Since we didn't know if the jury was milling about, we had to go downstairs."

"What—ever," the judge said. "What did you decide?"

The four women took their places, BJ sitting next to Mel.

Rufina sat up at the table with a confident demeanor instead of all wrapped up like she was a babe in swaddling clothes. She nodded at Erma.

"Your Honor, for the record, Mr. Holt offered a plea of guilty and fifty years or a plea of guilty and my client would go to the jury on punishment. Mrs. Rufina Barboza rejects both of the offers of the District Attorney."

The judge let out a huff of air. "Is that correct, Mrs. Barboza?"

Rufina stood. "Yes, that is correct, Judge." Her eyes were on the court reporter as she said it. The court reporter was writing. Rufina sat back down.

"I'm only assigned to this court for two weeks, and we're in the second week. Enough of this nonsense. Bring the jury in, Deputy Cortez." The judge addressed Mr. Holt. "Call your first witness."

"But Judge," Erma said, her heart thumping. She didn't know how to express her surprise and disgust at the way they were being treated. The bailiff stopped in the doorway. Holt stood still. Erma flexed her fingers as she stood there, not wanting to be seen with clenched fists. "We'd like a continuance until tomorrow, so we can go to the hospital, and, also, you haven't said if Mel can assist me."

"Motion for Continuance denied. She can assist you. Bailiff, bring the jury in. And Mr. Holt, I hope you have a witness in the hall. We need to put some testimony on the record today." The judge pushed off from the bench, his chair bumping the wall behind him, and crossed his arms, daring either attorney to make one more argument.

CHAPTER TWENTY-FIVE

"THE STATE CALLS Deputy Oskar Bumgarner." Holt sat down and picked up his pen. He murmured something to the young assistant next to him.

The bailiff opened the side door and called, "Oskar Bumgarner." Erma peered over her shoulder as a bulky, middle-aged, white man in a tan regulation sheriff's uniform entered the courtroom behind the bailiff. He approached the witness stand and raised his right hand. The judge swore him in, and the man took a seat. Rufina was grim-faced. Mel wrote something on a yellow legal pad. BJ had left the courtroom as soon as the judge denied the motion.

"State your name for the record." Holt proceeded to establish Bumgarner as an employee of the Gillespie County Sheriff's Department. He'd worked as a deputy for nine years. Lived in the county. First on the scene at BJ's house on the night of the shooting. "Now, Deputy Bumgarner, approximately what time did you arrive at the premises of Mrs. Schindler?"

"Approximately 12:30 a.m., sir." The deputy rested his arms on the counter, his mouth too close to the microphone, his voice reverberating.

"What did you observe when you arrived?"

"Well, sir, several cars and trucks were parked out front." He peeked at the jury. "One man stood outside the front door. It was cold, being December and all. The rest of the people was inside the house."

"The rest of the people being who?"

"Mrs. Billie Jo Schindler and her daughter. Kathy Lynn is her name. I'd met Mrs. Schindler before but not her daughters."

"Where was her son, Rex?"

"Yeah, well, Rex was the man standing outside waiting for me to arrive."

"Who else was present at that time?"

"A Douglas Christian." Bumgarner rocked back and forth in the witness chair. "He was the boyfriend of one of the twins. I recognized him right away from when he used to play football."

"Anyone else?"

"Yes, the defendant."

"By defendant, are you referring to Rufina Barboza?"

"Yes, sir." He pointed at Rufina. "She's sitting at the end of the table."

Holt looked where the deputy pointed, like he didn't realize Rufina sat there. "For the record, would you describe an item of clothing she's wearing?"

"Sure. Long brown skirt and matching jacket."

"Did you know Mrs. Barboza at the time of the event in question?"

"No, sir. Never had met her before, though I'd heard of her."

Erma didn't know what he'd allegedly heard, and she wasn't going to ask. She'd let the testimony develop, wait for the moment when Holt tried to pull something. He probably wanted her to ask the deputy what he'd heard, but Holt would have to ask that question because no way Erma would fall into that trap.

"So what happened when you arrived, Deputy?" Oozing confidence, Holt sat back in his chair, his legs stretched out in front of him.

"Rex, he came up to the car as soon as I got out and said someone had killed his sister."

"What did you do?"

"I ran for the house. He yelled after me, saying when he called 911, he also asked for an ambulance. I rushed inside and found the other people clustered between the front door and the kitchen, which is off to the side."

"Then what happened?"

"I told the mother to take me to the decedent. I told her Rex said his sister was dead, but was she sure? She was crying a lot, but said she thought so. She hurried to the back of the house—the house is huge, let me tell you, and I followed."

"And you found what?"

The deputy glanced at the judge and the jury. "A woman, a young woman, coated in blood, lying in a king-sized bed. I had no doubt she was dead."

"Because . . ."

"Her eyes were open wide and fixed, and there was a hole in her."

Holt and his assistant turned to the jury to emphasize the testimony. The jurors' faces were impassive, even the women's. Erma fingered her copy of the deputy's report and pretended to read it.

"What did you do then?"

"Well, I did eyeball her up close to be sure she wasn't breathing and then ushered the mother out of the room. Poor lady was losing it. So we went to the kitchen where everyone was. It's not far from the front door."

"Everyone was in there? Everyone?"

"Not Rex. I guess he was still outside."

"Can you describe the demeanor of the people in the kitchen?"

"The mother, Mrs. Schindler, and her surviving daughter stood with their arms around each other, crying most of the time. It took forever for them to be able to talk. Doug Christian stood close to them. He had been crying. I could tell by his face.

Rufina Barboza, the defendant, leaned against the kitchen cabinets, bent over, holding her stomach."

"What did you do then?"

"I radioed for assistance and for the justice of the peace and called the sheriff at home. Being as how the decedent was the daughter of a former county commissioner, I thought the sheriff would want to know right away. I wrote down everyone's names and addresses. After a few more minutes, the EMTs showed up, and I told them she was dead. They went back there—to the bedroom. Then my shift supervisor, a detective, and the sheriff showed up."

"Did you leave at that time?"

"After I spoke to my superiors, they told me to go back out on patrol."

"So you left?"

"Yes, sir."

"Did you later make a written report?"

"Yes, sir."

Holt stood. "Pass the witness."

"Proceed Mrs. Townley." The judge's face was expressionless.

Erma studied the deputy's face for a moment. "Deputy Bumgarner, my name is Erma Townley. I'm representing Mrs. Barboza in this case." She sat down and flipped to a page Mel had handed her from the trial notebook.

"Yes, ma'am, nice to meet you."

"Now, Deputy, you say when you arrived, Rex Schindler stood outside the house?"

"Yes, ma'am. The porch light was on. As I drove up, he was pacing up and down."

"What was he wearing?"

"What was he wearing?"

"Yes. Do you remember what he was wearing?"

The deputy paused for a moment and gazed up at the ceiling. "A buff-colored leather jacket, a turtleneck shirt—black, I believe, black pants, and black leather boots."

"Thank you. You have amazing powers of recollection."

His face crinkled with pleasure. "That's what they say."

"How close to Rex did you get, sir?"

"How close did I get?"

"Yes, sir. Were you close to him when he spoke to you? When he told you his sister had been killed?"

"Pretty close, for a moment."

"Did you notice anything unusual about him?"

"Did I notice anything unusual about him?"

"Yes, sir. Deputy Bumgarner, let me ask you this—do you suffer from a hearing loss?"

"Do I—" He winced. "Oh, no ma'am. I know what you're getting at. I don't know why I do that. I just do."

"You mean why you repeat everything the defense attorney asks you?"

He took a deep breath, his eyes darted around the room, and he let the breath out. "Yes, ma'am. I apologize. It's a bad habit of mine."

Erma cocked an eyebrow. A bad habit he didn't apply to prosecutors. "So let's go back to my question. Was there anything unusual about Rex Schindler?"

"Unusual like what?"

"Like the smell of alcohol? Were his eyes bloodshot? Did he stagger or stumble? What was his demeanor?"

"Oooh. Well—" he got right up on the microphone again "—he did smell like a distillery."

A small twitter came from someone in the jury box.

"Could you tell what it was? Did it have a distinct aroma?"

"No, but not bourbon."

"And his demeanor? He staggered a bit, didn't he? And weren't his eyes bloodshot?"

Holt jumped to his feet. "Objection. Compound question."

"One at a time, Mrs. Townley. One question at a time." The judge crossed his arms, his face deadpan.

Erma stood and ducked her head. "Yes, Your Honor." To the deputy, she said, "He was staggering, right?"

"A little. I'd say just a little."

"His eyes were bloodshot, too, right?"

"Yes, ma'am, I had enough light to see that, but just about every time I run into Rex around town, his eyes are bloodshot."

A couple of chuckles came from the jury.

"All right, Deputy," the judge said. "That'll be enough of that."

The deputy rocked back in his chair and nodded. "Yes, Judge."

Erma sat down. "Let's go back inside the house. Talk about the other folks for a bit. An aroma of alcohol on anyone else's breath?"

"Mrs. Schindler smelled like toothpaste, but it could have been toothpaste mixed with the smell of wine."

"Nobody else?"

"No, ma'am, not like Rex, anyway. I did get close enough to smell them."

"Okay. Can you tell me how the people in the house were dressed?"

"How they...Mrs. Schindler wore a nightgown and a bathrobe. The nightgown had blood on it."

Erma had not heard of that. She'd have to talk with BJ and find out what else she hadn't talked about.

"What did the surviving twin have on?"

His eyes roved around the courtroom, as he stalled for time to think over what he would say. "Sweater and jeans."

"Sweater and jeans," Erma repeated for the benefit of the jury. "And Mr. Christian?"

"Jeans and a western-style shirt, you know what I mean, plaid with snaps. And boots."

"What did Kathy Lynn have on her feet?"

"Running shoes. Pink." He wore a satisfied smile.

"My client, Mrs. Barboza, what was she wearing?"

The deputy squinted at Rufina. "Her hair was in a long braid, and she wore a bathrobe over a nightgown. Oh, and on her feet, some Crocs. The ones without the holes in them. Beige colored over white socks."

"Thank you, Deputy. Now, was a Mr. Elgin Burgess anywhere around? Mr. Burgess had been at the house for dinner earlier, did you see him anywhere?"

"Objection, Your Honor." Smoke practically spiraled out of Holt's ears. "She's testifying."

"Sustained." The judge frowned at Erma. "Rephrase your question."

"Elgin Burgess, he owns a spread next to Mrs. Schindler's, did you see him anywhere on the night of the murder?"

Holt jumped up again. "Judge, she's doing it again."

"Mrs. Townley, approach the bench. You, too, Mr. Holt."

Pasting on her most innocent face, Erma walked to the front of the courtroom. She had to stand on tiptoes to be able to speak over the top of the bench.

The judge whispered, "Mrs. T, you're a seasoned trial lawyer. I know it and you know it. Mr. Holt knows it, too. I'm sure you know every trick in the book and then some."

Erma tried to look indifferent, though she wanted to smile. He was giving her a dressing down, a flattering dressing down.

"I'm warning you, Mrs. T, if you persist in this kind of behavior, you're subject to sanctions."

"But Judge—"

The judge shook his head. "I don't want to hear any excuses."

"Yes, Your Honor."

Holt smirked in her direction as they returned to their tables. Erma said, "Deputy—"

"No, ma'am. I didn't see no one else. I've given y'all the names of everyone who was there."

"Thank you, sir. Now let me ask you this, no one else besides Mrs. Schindler had blood on their clothes, did they?"

"No ma'am."

"My client, Mrs. Barboza, did not have blood on her anywhere, did she?"

"I said no."

"How big would you say Mrs. Barboza is, Deputy?" She turned to Rufina. "Rufina, please stand."

The deputy took a moment to look Rufina over. "About five feet tall and a hundred plus pounds. Not real big."

Erma motioned for Rufina to sit again. "Are you familiar with guns, Deputy Bumgarner?"

"Yes, ma'am. Somewhat."

"What about a .45 caliber?"

"Yes, ma'am." He nodded. "Some makes."

"How much would you say a .45 caliber pistol weighs, Deputy?"

"Objection, relevance."

Holt was trying to get her goat. "The relevance will become apparent, Judge, in a moment."

"Overruled. You may answer, Deputy."

"Depending on who makes the gun, it can weigh anywhere between two and three-fourths pounds to almost six pounds."

"Kinda heavy for a woman, wouldn't you say?"

He's eyes flashed. "Some women."

"The larger the woman, the easier it would be for her to handle a whole lot of gun like that, right?"

"You could say that."

"But would you say that?"

"Yes, ma'am."

"Did you determine whether the bedroom was dark at the time of the shooting?"

"It was kind of dark when Mrs. Schindler took me in. The door to the bathroom was open and light came from that and a small bedside lamp."

"Did she turn on the overhead light for you?"

"She didn't need to. I could see the young lady was deceased."

"But did she?"

"No, ma'am."

"You could see the hole in the decedent's chest without the overhead light, couldn't you?"

"Well, there was blood everwhere. I mean a lot of blood on her."

"So that's a no?"

"I saw where it was. Where the wound was."

"The wound was smack dab in the middle of her chest, wasn't it, Deputy?"

"Yes, ma'am, I believe it was."

"One last question before I let you go. What was the dead woman wearing?"

He sat for a moment, his eyes searching the room like the answer would be written on one of the walls. "A bathrobe over a nightgown, what I saw of it."

"And on her feet?"

"I don't believe I could see her feet, Mrs. Townley, they was under the covers."

"Oh, I just remembered something, Mr. Bumgarner. You did see a .45 caliber pistol lying on the bar in the kitchen, did you not?"

Deputy Bumgarner sat up straight in his chair. He looked at the judge and then at Holt, as if asking for help. He pointedly did not look at the jury or the bailiff. Finally, his eyes met Erma's. "No, I did not, ma'am."

Erma let a beat go by. "Thank you, Deputy Bumgarner. Pass the witness."

CHAPTER TWENTY-SIX

"CALL YOUR NEXT witness, Mr. Holt." The judge's eyes swept the courtroom from Sam Holt all the way around to the jury box. He leaned back, his arms crossed.

"Get ready," Erma said to Mel, who sat at the counsel table with her. "I don't know who he'll call next." If she couldn't have Sandra, at least she had Mel who had been keeping up pretty well. Erma prayed Sandra would be all right. They'd check on her later, but for now, they had a case to try.

Mel flipped through the binder. "You want me to pull the section on the next witness as soon as he says his name?"

Erma elbowed Mel. "Yep. You're getting good at this."

Holt stood at his table." Sheriff Ed Krichman."

Mel clicked open the rings and took out what they had on the sheriff, handing the pages to Erma. Erma glanced at Rufina, who appeared to have homesteaded the end of the table, and winked.

Rufina had said she preferred to see everything going on in the courtroom, including who peered through the doors. She wouldn't sit with her back to the gallery. She held a pen, ready to take her own notes on the legal pad she'd been provided.

The sheriff, a huge man dressed in full tan uniform except for the gray Stetson he held under his arm, trod down the aisle and nodded at Holt. He passed through the bar and stepped up into the witness stand. After the judge swore him in, the sheriff sat down and twisted the microphone until it was right below his mouth. He had yet to give Erma even a cursory glance. He was seventy, if he was a day, with salt-and-pepper hair and a gray-white lock combed back from his forehead. Deep lines etched his weathered face.

Holt took several minutes to establish not only who the witness was—that he'd been Sheriff of Gillespie County for nearly thirty years—but to qualify him as an expert in weapons and ballistics and as a crime scene investigator. After the preliminaries were out of the way, Holt ascertained whether Krichman had responded to a call at the Schindler ranch. Preening for the jury, Holt continued, "Sheriff, did you find any weapons at the ranch?"

"Yes, I did." Krichman's elbows rested on the counter. Thick-fingered paws encircled the base of the microphone, his mouth, an inch away. His words, crisp and clear, proved he was an experienced witness.

"Would you tell the judge and jury where you found a weapon or weapons?"

The sheriff turned toward the jury. "In the Schindler den."

"Describe for the jury what you found in the way of weapons."

"I don't want to sound flippant, but the den was virtually a small arsenal of guns, knives, and rounds—bullets."

"To get right to the point, let me ask you this. Prior to entering the den, did you have a chance to see the decedent's body?"

"Yes I did."

"Did you examine her in any way?"

The sheriff coughed. "No. Clearly, she was deceased. She had a decent-sized bullet wound in her chest, and blood was everywhere."

"So is it safe to assume the weapon used was a gun? In other words, no evidence a knife had been used on the decedent?"

"Definitely a gun. No evidence of a knife."

"Then, Sheriff, let's go back to the den. Aside from the knives and bullets, what did you find in this 'small arsenal'?"

"Let's see. Mind if I refer to my notes?"

Holt cut his eyes at Erma, the skin stretched tight across his face in a pained look. She knew he hated to say yes, because once the sheriff referred to his notes, she would get to see them if she wanted. Erma gave him a Cheshire-cat grin.

"You need them to refresh your memory?" The muscles in his jaw flexed, which they often did.

"Like I said, it was a small arsenal. I inventoried the weapons myself—made a list for our records, partly to protect my boys. I had the missus sign off on it, agreeing to my inventory." For just a moment, his eyes took in Erma.

Erma leaned over to Mel and whispered, "Get me our copy of the inventory, honey. It's under a separate tab."

"The missus you're referring to is Mrs. Schindler?" Holt asked.

"Yes, sir. The son, Rex, wanted to be in there with me. He wanted to read the inventory. He wanted to be the one who signed off on it, claiming some of the guns were his, but they were in Mrs. Schindler's house, so as far as I was concerned, they were hers. Possession being nine-tenths of the law and all." He made eye contact with Erma again before shifting his eyes back to Holt.

His deep, vibrant voice had already resonated with Erma, but his steadfast indigo blue eyes nailed it. Something about him struck a chord deep in her, like she'd known him in another life. She shook off the feeling, stared down at her copy of the gun inventory, and wondered whether his notes would reflect anything different, anything useful to the defense.

"May I approach the witness, Your Honor?" Mr. Holt asked.

"You may."

Did the sheriff's glances mean something? Or was he just relaxed enough by that point in his testimony to venture out of his safe zone and survey the courtroom?

"I hand you what's been marked as State's Exhibit One for identification, Sheriff. Do you recognize it?"

"This is the typed-up version. What I was talking about—what I did was write down everything on my notepad and my secretary typed it up—my handwriting is not very good, but she's been with me long enough she can read and understand what I give her."

Holt shook the papers in front of the sheriff. "I get it, but we're talking about the pages I have in my hand. Do you recognize this document?"

"Yes, I do."

"What is it?"

Erma listened as Holt went through the requirements of proving up a document for it to be admitted into evidence. Holt showed her the typed list before offering it into evidence. "No objection."

"Now, Sheriff, I refer you to State's Exhibit One. Tell the jury how many rifles were in the Schindler den."

"Twenty-two, including a couple of antiques—a Winchester 1873 from the nineteenth century, a real beauty—"

"Sheriff," Holt said, "we all know you're a lover of guns and rifles and other weapons, but for the purposes of this trial, please just answer my questions."

"Objection." Erma rose. "We all don't know that. I don't know that. Only that he's an expert on them."

"Rephrase, Mr. Holt."

Holt gave Erma a go-to-hell look. "Sheriff, please listen to my questions and answer them as briefly and succinctly as possible."

"Sorry, Mr. Holt." Again the sheriff glanced at Erma. His eyes flickered past hers and back to Holt.

When Erma turned around, no one was at the door or window. She glanced at Rufina, who shrugged. Two old men sat about midway in the gallery, one on each side of the aisle, and an old woman perched on the edge of the back bench, looking like she was stopping by to rest her feet. Typical court watchers.

"Now, Sheriff," Holt leaned back and draped one arm over the back of his chair, so he was almost facing the jury, "tell the jury how the weapons were stored."

"They were all in locked gun cabinets. The rifles in tall cabinets with glass in them, but you could see them, and several gun safes."

"Describe the room for the jury, please."

"Wall-to-wall gun cabinets and gun safes with a large—very large—oak desk sitting plumb in the center."

"And a desk chair?"

"A desk chair and a green leather easy chair. Nothing much on the desk except a desk pad and a calendar and a light—one of those fluorescent ones with a magnifier in it."

"What, if anything, was unusual about the room?"

"Not a thing. I've been in there a number of times in the past. When Commissioner Schindler was still alive—when he was still a county commissioner—he had some of us officials over from time-to-time for drinks and a little supper. I saw nothing out of the ordinary after the murder."

While the sheriff testified, Holt's face screwed up. The sheriff wouldn't keep his answers short. Erma knew Holt wanted to tell him to shut the hell up, but he couldn't do that, at least until the judge called a recess.

The judge wore a long-suffering expression, his forehead resting on his palm. He appeared to be the type who expected the lawyers to control their witnesses and, if they couldn't, he wasn't going to do their job. His glance at Holt was a hard one, his jaw muscle flexing.

"Sheriff, if you'd answer what my questions call for, I promise to get you down from the witness stand as soon as possible." Through clenched teeth, Holt smiled at his witness.

"Yes, sir."

"So the room, the den, appeared to be dedicated to guns. A gun room in other words."

"Yes, sir."

The sheriff's eyes wandered to the jury, looking them over for a few moments. Erma followed his eyes, wanting to detect any apparent connection.

"Did any of the rifles or guns appear to—strike that. Were all the cabinets locked?"

"Yes, sir, they were."

"And the gun safes. Were they all locked?"

"Yes, sir. Locked up as tight as a—"

"Thank you, Sheriff. Did you unlock each one and examine their contents?"

"Yes, sir, I did. Mrs. Schindler stayed in the room—even in her agitated or what I guess you would call her grieving state—she was present the whole time."

"Did Mrs. Schindler say if they had their own inventory of the guns?"

"Later, Mr. Holt. I didn't ask her that night, but my investigator went back later, and she gave him copies of the insurance policies covering the weapons and the itemized list provided to the insurance firm."

"Back to the night of the murder, Sheriff. You unlocked the cabinets and safes and examined the contents?"

"Yes, sir. Mrs. Schindler gave me the keys. I inventoried each and every cabinet and safe."

"Did it appear that any weapons were missing from the cabinets and safes? Any racks not filled, any spaces that might have the outline of a gun in the dust? Any indication of a missing gun?"

"Objection." Erma stood. She was sure getting her exercise. "More than one question, Judge." She plopped back down.

"Sustained. Mr. Holt, we're on a tight schedule, but please—"

"Sorry, Judge."

Erma didn't care if he asked ten questions at once. She'd objected because the Q and A was starting to go too smoothly. She wanted to break up any intimacy developing between them.

Holt clicked his pen and straightened the papers in front of himself. "So did it appear that anything was missing, Sheriff?"

"No, sir. It did not."

"Did Mrs. Schindler indicate she thought everything was in order?"

Erma could have objected again, but she let it go. BJ would testify later.

"Yes, sir. She said everything looked fine to her."

"Now, Sheriff, did you find any weapons in the rest of the house? Other than common kitchen knives and the like?"

"Yes, sir, I did."

"Please tell the jury what you found and where in the house you found it, if you'd be so kind."

The sheriff turned in his chair to face the jury. "Well, there was a .38 revolver in Mrs. Schindler's night table, top drawer. And, oddly enough, when I entered the house and walked into the kitchen where everyone was gathered, a .45 was lying smack dab in the middle of the kitchen counter."

Erma had been wondering whether and when they were going to get to that.

"Did you question anyone about this .45?"

"Yes, I did. I asked the group standing in the kitchen why a gun was lying on the kitchen counter."

"Did anyone answer you?"

"Yes. Douglas Christian said he found it on the path outside. The path leading to the defendant's cottage."

Holt let that statement sink in before he proceeded to his next question. "Sheriff, what kind of gun was it? I mean, the model?"

"Smith and Wesson m1917 .45 caliber revolver."

"May I approach the witness again, Judge?"

"Yes, Mr. Holt."

Holt circled around to the front of his table, reached inside a soft-sided brown leather briefcase and came out with a pistol, which looked to Erma like something out of a cowboy and Indian movie. The gun barrel was long, the whole gun looking like it was a foot in length. Though Sandra had seen it when she'd been in Fredericksburg earlier, Erma hadn't had a chance to examine it herself.

"Sheriff, I hand you what's been marked for identification as State's Exhibit Two. Do you recognize it?"

"Yes. It's the revolver I found in Mrs. Schindler's kitchen."

Erma had been expecting the proffer. She sat back and assumed an air of someone who had no concern for what was transpiring in the courtroom, thumbing through some paperwork and making some notes. She murmured to Mel, "Pretend I'm saying something important to you and nod your head vigorously."

Mel put on a serious face and nodded like crazy.

Holt stepped over to Erma and showed her the gun. Erma gave it a once over and stood, "No objection, Judge." She sat back down and continued to pretend nothing of importance was going on while Holt placed the gun into evidence, and the sheriff talked about it.

"Sheriff, tell the jury what you did when you found the gun on the kitchen counter."

Sheriff Krichman cleared his throat. "Well, I'd forgotten my gloves, so I went back out to my patrol car and retrieved a pair."

"Excuse me, Sheriff, but tell the jury what kind of gloves you're talking about."

"Latex gloves. You may have seen them on television, worn at crime scenes. So I pulled them on and picked up the gun by the grip and placed it in a paper bag. I then took the weapon to my patrol car and locked it in the trunk." His eyes roved around the room, stopping for a moment on Erma's face.

Adrenaline spiked through her, and Erma shivered.

"What did you do before you put it in the bag, if anything?"

"I sniffed the gun barrel."

"What did you smell?"

"The weapon had been fired."

Holt frowned. "You mean, you smelled cordite, right?"

The sheriff cocked his head. "Cordite hasn't been used in about sixty years."

Holt's face grew crimson. "But you could tell the gun had been fired?"

"Yes, sir, Mr. Holt."

"So what did you do?"

"I put the gun in the paper bag and took it out to my car."

Mr. Holt stood. "Pass the witness, Judge."

"We'll take a five-minute recess. And only five-minutes." The judge cut his eyes at Erma in a don't-be-late expression.

⚖ ⚖ ⚖

When they returned, Erma remained standing. "May I proceed, Judge?"

"Yes, you may."

She closed one eye and tilted her head. "Sheriff Krichman, have we met before?" She pretended to be ready to write. When he cast his indigo blue eyes on her, a rush of energy struck her chest.

"No, ma'am, we sure haven't. I would have remembered."

She leaned over her legal pad and hoped her face hadn't turned as pink as the prosecutor's had a few moments earlier. "I wondered, because—"

Holt jumped to his feet, his ballpoint pen clicking. "Objection, Your Honor. Is that a question or is this a private conversation between my witness and the defense attorney?"

Erma stood again. "I was getting to a question, Judge."

"All right, you two." Judge Danforth's eyebrows drew together. "Let's move on."

"Sheriff, I take it by your direct testimony State's Exhibit Two is alleged to be the murder weapon?"

"Yes, ma'am, it is."

"Sheriff, you said Rex Schindler wanted to be in the room while you inventoried the guns and, well, let's see—" She referred to her notes. "You stated, 'He wanted to be in there with me, and he wanted to read the inventory, and he wanted to be the one who signed off on it.' Isn't that your testimony?"

"Yes, ma'am, that's what I said, all right." He swiveled in the witness chair, turning more toward her.

"Did you form an opinion on why Rex Schindler wanted to be in the den with you?"

"Objection." Holt only rose half out of his chair. He must be tired to getting his own exercise. "Calls for a conclusion on the part of the witness."

The sheriff looked at Holt and then the judge and didn't answer.

"Sustained."

Erma hoped Mel was taking in any notable expressions on the part of the jury. "Well, then, let me ask you this, Sheriff Krichman. You did exclude him from the room while you conducted your inventory, didn't you?"

"Absolutely, ma'am."

"Rex didn't leave the room willingly, did he?"

"He protested, but I didn't have to physically throw him out if that's what you mean."

"I didn't mean anything," Erma said.

"Objection."

"What is the nature of your objection?"

"Uh. Uh. Sidebar comment?"

The judge frowned. "Overruled."

Erma refrained from smiling. All the years she'd played poker with lawyers and judges worked to her advantage. Perhaps Mr. Holt would figure her out before the trial was over. Perhaps not. "Let's go over this inventory for a few minutes, Sheriff.

You said there was a sh—a load of guns in the den, and I see by this inventory you were correct."

"Is that a question, Judge?" Mr. Holt again.

"Ask your question, Mrs. Townley." The judge rolled his neck from side to side and shrugged, like his muscles were stiff.

"Yes, Your Honor," Erma said. "Sheriff, there were a lot of small guns in the den, correct?"

"Yes, ma'am."

"Derringers, smaller pistols—more lightweight weapons?"

"Yes, ma'am."

"In fact, you came across a pink gun, correct?"

"Correct. Several pink guns and one baby blue."

"Would you say those guns were generally smaller and easier to handle than the Smith and Wesson m1917 .45 caliber revolver?"

"Usually pink guns are guns for the ladies, ma'am."

"So yes?"

He cleared his throat again. "Yes, ma'am. Smaller and easier to handle most of the time. Some are large and weigh more."

"We'll get to weight in a moment. Ladies don't generally have the same strength in their hands as men, do they?"

"Some do; most don't. Unless they workout or train with weapons like female deputies and other female police officers."

She couldn't ask for a more cooperative witness. Holt, chewing on the end of his pen, could have been an over-ripe melon about to burst. Erma turned to Mel, "Quick, give me my research on the gun." She stood. "May we have a moment, Judge?"

Judge Danforth nodded while maintaining his long-suffering demeanor, his lips compressed.

Mel thumbed through the trial notebook and extracted some pages. When she closed it, the clack of the three binder rings echoed through the courtroom.

"Get me the photographs of the den, too, honey," Erma murmured. "Then take your phone and go call the hospital. Check on your mom."

While Mel combed through their box in search of the file containing the pictures, Erma laid the pages of research on the table. "Now, Sheriff, the weapon that has been placed into evidence was the gun Indiana Jones in Raiders of the Lost Ark—"

"Objection!" Holt jumped about a foot off the ground.

Erma stood, all wide-eyed innocence.

The judge sighed. "What is your objection this time, Mr. Holt?"

"I don't know what Indiana Jones has to do with this murder case—irrelevant, I guess, Judge."

"Your Honor," Erma said, "I'm trying to give a little background about this weapon to the jury."

"Mrs. Townley, I don't see how the history of this gun has any relevance. Sustained."

"Thank you, Your Honor." Erma sat down. "Sheriff, the m1917 revolver, was a gun the U.S. Military in World War One and also in World War Two used, correct?"

"Same objection, Judge."

"Same ruling." The judge glared over his glasses.

"Thank you, Your Honor," Erma said, knowing most judges didn't like to be thanked. It could confuse the jury about whether the ruling was favorable or not. "Sheriff, tell me this: The m1917 revolver would typically be described as a man's gun rather than a woman's gun, correct?"

Mr. Holt got half-way to his feet and sat back down again, his jaw muscles rigid.

"You could say that. It's a mighty big weapon for a woman to carry around."

Erma looked at her notes again. "In fact, the gun is over ten inches long, isn't it?"

"Yes, ma'am, the entire weapon is about ten point eight inches long." He returned Erma's studied stare. "The barrel is five and a half inches long. Sometimes the weapon is modified to make the barrel shorter, but this gun is in its original condition. Mint condition for its age, I might add."

Erma restrained herself from doing a little jig. The sheriff couldn't be more helpful. "Isn't it true this gun weighs over two pounds?"

"Yes, ma'am. About two and a quarter pounds."

"Would you say it's a heavy gun for most women to carry around?" She intentionally repeated the Sheriff's words.

"Well, like I said earlier, some women are stronger than others, especially if they work out or are built like a—"

"Thank you, Sheriff. Are you acquainted with the defendant Rufina Barboza?"

The sheriff stared at Rufina for a moment. "Yes."

"How did that come about?"

"She worked in the Mason County District Clerk's office for many years. I would occasionally run across her at their courthouse when I had to go up there for something, when I was a deputy, and then as sheriff."

"How would you describe her? Strike that. Let me back up a minute to the time you entered the house." She hinted at a smile and lifted one eyebrow. "I understand the kitchen was practically overflowing with people, right?"

"Well, I don't know if I'd say overflowing, but there were a number of people standing around in the kitchen."

"Rufina Barboza was one of them, right?"

The sheriff nodded. "Yes, she was."

"Would you tell the jury what Mrs. Barboza was wearing?"

"What she was wearing?" He studied the ceiling for a moment. "A bathrobe over a nightgown, and tan shoes, Crocs."

"Did the bathrobe have pockets in it?"

"Objection," Holt said. "Relevance."

"Mrs. Townley, are you fixing to show relevance any time soon?" the judge asked.

Erma stood to answer. "Yes, Your Honor. In a moment."

"Overruled."

"Sheriff, you may answer." Erma sat again. She'd be tired of all the standing up and sitting down if adrenaline wasn't rushing through her body. "The question was 'Did the bathrobe have pockets?'"

His eyes searched the ceiling again. Erma refrained from glancing up. Funny how so many people did that when they were testifying. She kept her eyes on the sheriff.

"I believe so," he said.

"I beg your pardon, Sheriff, but can you answer more affirmatively?"

"I do remember her leaning against the kitchen counter with her hands tucked into her pockets."

"Thank you. How big were the pockets?"

"Large enough for her hands to fit in."

"Now, I'll ask you to describe Mrs. Barboza for the jury."

"Objection," Mr. Holt said. "I don't see how the defendant's appearance enters into it. Irrelevant. Besides, the jury can see what she looks like for themselves."

Erma stood again. "It's very relevant to our defense of Mrs. Barboza, Judge. The record cannot see her." She wanted Holt to think she was protecting the record, and that was indeed part of it but not all.

"Overruled," the judge said. "Sheriff, you may answer."

Sheriff Krichman looked at Rufina. "Could she stand up?"

Erma motioned to Rufina to stand. Rufina rose and stepped away from the table.

"Yes, I'm correct in my recollection of her. She didn't stand much taller than the counter in the clerk's office. She's a very small—I guess you could say—petite woman, about five feet in height and my guess would be she weighs about a hundred pounds."

"Go on, Sheriff," Erma said.

"She's a dark-complected Latina with black and gray hair—long but up in a bun thing today, dark eyes, and part of her face and one hand badly scarred, most likely burn scars."

"Describe her hands please, I mean, can you compare the size of her hands to anything?"

"Hmmm." He scrutinized the courtroom and the witness stand. "I don't really see anything—maybe a three-by-five card or a bit longer than five inches. Quite small compared to a man's. At least an average man's."

"Thank you, Sheriff." Erma made some quick notes they'd be able to use in final argument. A three-by-five card was a great comparison and something that could be held up in front of a jury. She motioned to Rufina to sit down.

Erma watched the sheriff. She didn't need to look at Holt to know he was wondering what she was up to. She could almost hear his teeth grinding. "Going back to the night of the incident, Sheriff, and back into the kitchen, can you remember anything about the size of the pockets on Mrs. Barboza's dressing gown?"

He cocked his head. "Not much larger than her hands, maybe just a little. I didn't pay close attention."

Erma kept her eyes on him. "Well, could a ten-inch-long revolver be hidden in her bathrobe pocket, or would it have been noticeable?"

He stifled a laugh, his hand slapping the counter. A huge hand, Erma noted, one she wouldn't mind seeing more of, or feeling, either. She mentally shook herself and refocused.

"Well, ma'am, I certainly would have noticed if a big gun was sticking out of one of those little pockets. It probably would have stuck out three or four inches, at least."

"Objection, speculation," Holt said.

"Sustained," the judge said. "Jurors, disregard the very last statement."

"May I approach the witness, Your Honor?" Erma asked.

"Yes, you may.".

Erma wanted to move closer to the sheriff, to get a whiff of him. She stood and straightened her skirt and jacket before ambling up to the witness stand, wishing now she'd varied her wardrobe from the black skirt-suits she'd been wearing since her friend's funeral the year before. She held out a photograph. "I show you what's been marked for identification as Defendant's Exhibit One. Would you tell the jury what this is?"

"A photograph."

Erma kept the picture within his view. "You didn't take the photo, did you, Sheriff?"

"No, ma'am."

"What does the photograph show?"

"One of the gun cabinets in the Schindler home."

"Does it truly and accurately depict what that particular gun cabinet was like and contained on the night in question?"

"Yes, ma'am."

Erma ran through the rest of the requirements to prove the photograph was admissible. She followed up by showing the photograph to Mr. Holt who glanced at it and flicked his fingers as if to say it wasn't worth his attention. Erma offered the picture into evidence.

"No objection." Holt didn't stand or look up.

"It's admitted."

"Thank you, Your Honor." Back over to the sheriff, Erma leaned close when tendering the picture to him. She chastised herself for acknowledging an attraction to the man in the midst of a trial, but she couldn't help how she felt.

"Sheriff, I draw your attention to the gun cabinet. Do you see the weapons we discussed a few minutes ago?"

"You mean the pink ones?"

"Yes, sir."

"Yes, ma'am. All the pink guns were kept together in that cabinet."

"Any of them ten inches in length?"

"No, ma'am."

"In fact, they're considerably smaller than the Smith and Wesson .45 that has been put into evidence today, correct?"

"Considerably."

"Judge, may I tender this photograph to the jury?"

"Hand it to the bailiff, Mrs. Townley, and retake your seat."

"Yes, sir. Thank you." Erma handed the photograph to the Deputy Cortez who passed it to the first juror.

She walked back to her table and sat down, pausing to give at least some of the jurors time to look over the picture. Where was Mel? The call shouldn't have taken long. "Sheriff, the prosecutor has qualified you as a firearms expert, correct?"

"Yes, ma'am, Mrs. Townley."

"So I take it you're familiar with a wide array of firearms from handguns to rifles, revolvers, semiautomatic weapons—"

"Yes, yes, yes."

"You've fired many weapons? You've trained with them? Trained others on them?"

"Affirmative."

"Would you step down from the jury box and demonstrate for the jury the proper stance someone should assume when firing a revolver such as the m1917 Smith and Wesson .45 at someone across a room?"

"Judge." Mr. Holt leaped up.

"What now, Mr. Holt?" The judge cupped his ear toward Holt like he was hard of hearing and straining for the answer.

"I don't think it's a proper line of questioning."

"Overruled. Go ahead, Sheriff."

The Sheriff eased out of the jury box and took a position between the counsel tables and the bench. He spread his legs apart and crouched down a little.

"And the proper grip, Sheriff. Would you demonstrate the proper way for a person to hold a revolver?"

"You want me to show you with the .45 over there?"

"Oh, no, sir. Just like you'd show a newbie who has never held a gun—before you actually let him hold one in his hand."

The sheriff put his hands together and demonstrated how a gun should be held with both hands. "This is the proper way to hold a revolver, but a semiautomatic would be held differently.

"We're only concerned with the revolver today. So the proper way is to hold it with both hands?"

"Yes, the support hand stabilizes the gun and makes the shooter more accurate. I do teach them, however, to get comfortable using one hand—even their non-dominant hands—in case they should be disabled."

"You may retake the witness stand, Sheriff. Thank you."

Erma made like she was taking a few notes, but she needed a moment to calm herself. Mel should have been back. She took a deep breath and let it out slowly. She hoped Sandra was going to be okay.

"So, Sheriff, is it safe to say there is a lot to learn about handling and shooting a firearm?"

"Yes, ma'am. Most people could probably pick one up and shoot it but suffer the consequences of improper handling."

"So suffice it to say most people would not shoot a gun one-handed like in the movies all the time—like we saw Indiana Jones do in Raiders of the Lost Ark and his other movies—and if they did, their shot would not be accurate?"

"Objection, Judge," Holt said. "You've already ruled on this."

"Approach the bench."

As soon as Erma got within the judge's earshot, she whispered, "Your Honor, I've laid a foundation for this question. I'm simply trying to demonstrate for the jury what they have seen on television and in the movies is not realistic. It takes training to shoot a gun accurately and the use of both hands in most instances."

Holt began to talk, but the judge shut him down. "I'll allow it." As they went back to their tables, the judge announced, "Objection overruled."

"Yes, Mrs. Townley." The Sheriff's face was not quite as stony as it had been earlier. "I agree with you there. Most people would not fire a gun one-handed or if they did, it would not be accurate."

"Sheriff, would the length of the barrel make any difference in accuracy?" She wanted to deflect what she thought would be the prosecution's comeback.

"Yes, a longer barrel is usually more accurate."

"Especially from a great distance?"

"Um—usually. Depends on the gun—the reliability of the gun."

"Which a shooter wouldn't know about unless he was familiar with the gun?"

"Correct."

"I have a few more questions, Sheriff. The five-and-a-half-inch barrel of the m1917 Smith and Wesson .45 caliber revolver would make that gun more accurate as opposed to a small, snub nose revolver or one of those pink guns shown in Defense Exhibit One?"

"Again, generally speaking, yes, but some long-barreled guns do have accuracy problems. The shooter really should be acquainted with the gun."

Erma stared down at the table, her fingers covering her mouth as she went over in her mind how she wanted to ask her last few questions for maximum impact.

"Sheriff, I read somewhere—"

"Objection, defense counsel is testifying."

"Sustained."

She chewed on the inside of her cheek. "Isn't it true if the grip of the gun is too large for a person's hand, that too will affect accuracy?"

"I'd say if the grip of the gun is too big for a person's hand, it could affect several things, accuracy being one of them. You want a proper gun grip on a proper size gun and your support hand in its proper place to stabilize the handgun and make the shooter more accurate. It's hard to get that if the gun—therefore the gun grip—is too large."

His testimony was like a classroom instructor's, exactly what Erma wanted from him. Holt had called the sheriff as his witness, but Erma was confident she'd turned him into her own.

"Sheriff, given your decades of experience and training, in your expert opinion, would the grip of the m1917 Smith and Wesson .45 caliber revolver fit properly in the hand of Rufina Barboza?"

Holt sprang up, his neck and face ripe tomato red. "Your Honor—"

His face deadpan, the judge held up his palm toward Holt. "He's your expert, Mr. Holt. Now, sit down. Court reporter, read back the question."

The reporter, Matthew Grieger, pulled out a length of narrow paper from his machine and read the question.

The sheriff shook his head. "Properly in her little hand? Not hardly. She'd be able to shoot it, all right, but—"

Clicking his pen like nobody's business, Holt jumped up again. "Objection, non-responsive."

Not waiting for a ruling, Erma asked, "And if she had no training in the use of firearms and were to pick up that gun and shoot it at a target in the dark, how accurate do you think—"

He shook his head. "I'd have a hard time seeing how it could be accurate."

Erma stood. "Pass the witness."

As Erma sat again, Mel plopped into the chair next to her. "Sorry I took so long. Mom wanted to know what was going on with the testimony. She's getting out tonight!"

CHAPTER TWENTY-SEVEN

ONCE SANDRA'S PAIN subsided, a different slow burn grew inside of her, one that arose from being stuck in the hospital for most of the day. She hadn't been able to dissuade the EMTs from taking her to the ER. Now, hours later, she sat on the side of the gurney and fumed. She felt like she was incarcerated. She wanted to return to the courthouse. Could the medical staff be any slower? The black institutional clock on the wall ticked her life away. She'd actually seen one of the hands move.

Mel had called and said Erma had things under control, the case was going smoothly. Mel was having fun seeing her grandmother best the prosecutor. Her last words were something like, "Grandma is getting down with the case."

Which made Sandra think of her insistence that Erma take it easier since her heart attack. To relieve Erma's stress, Sandra had started doing all the litigation, both civil and criminal. Erma was left with office probate work and only minor court appearances. Erma had been happy enough. Hadn't she? She hadn't missed trials, longed for them like a lost lover. Had she? Surely Erma had felt the weight of litigation lifted from her shoulders, had enjoyed working shorter days and fewer weekends.

When Sandra paid attention to someone other than herself, which she knew she needed to do more of, she had to admit there had been less spring in Erma's step since Sandra had taken over. Erma could still be cantankerous. That hadn't changed. More and more though, Erma had complained she was bored by most estate cases. Rarely was probate litigated, and Sandra was doing all the litigation anyway. Erma missed that part of their law practice—the preparation, the trial, the adrenaline rush. In an estate case, the main party was dead. There was no reason for Erma to hurry to work each day. No one really needed her.

Since BJ had hired them, Erma had perked up. The sparkle had returned to her eyes. She had bustled around the office, often thinking aloud, brainstorming with Patricia and Sandra. When Mel came in from school, Erma had bounced ideas off Mel. She'd explained the reasoning behind a lot of what they were doing in their preparations.

The news from Mel was good on how the trial was going. Erma and Mel were getting along fine without Sandra. They would be fine without her if she left the law practice. The decision to leave or stay was hers and hers alone. Of course, it always had been, but now more than ever she realized she needed to search her heart. They'd be all right without her. What did she want?

Hell, what she wanted was more of the same. If she decided not to take the job, she'd have to admit it to Erma and listen to Erma when she said I-told-you-so. But being back in the saddle, so to speak, had caused Sandra to rethink her life, again. Maybe it was shaking off the depression and the humiliation of the Stuart situation. Or maybe, whether she admitted it publicly or not, she liked criminal defense work. Or was it the prospect of fighting for the underdog, fending off powerful forces that threatened an injustice?

Sandra had been relegating those thoughts to the back of her mind while she focused on the murder case. She'd more or less laid out a plan, but Rufina's case had interrupted that plan.

Life had interrupted her plan. She recognized how much she valued the past few weeks with her mother, her daughter, and even Patricia. She didn't think she wanted to give that up. This non-heart attack had given her a few minutes to articulate to herself what the thoughts swirling around in her head were. She had been about to make a more serious mistake than the Stuart thing, by abandoning her life in Galveston. So, she'd made that admission to herself now, but before she said anything aloud, she'd sleep on it. Could be she was simply tired and annoyed at being stuck in the hospital.

What the hell was taking so long? Where was everyone?

She swung her legs back and forth and listened for any noise that indicated her jailers might be coming to release her. No voices, no footsteps, just general hospital clamoring and the odor of disinfectant. She jumped down from the bed and put her head out from behind the curtain. The people who had attended her were nowhere to be seen. She rubbed her arms. Hospitals were always cold. They should make long-sleeved, wool hospital gowns. She eye-balled the plastic chair near the gurney, where her clothes were folded in a pile. Might as well dress while she waited.

The clock ticked. Erma probably was having the time of her life. She'd been raring to go ever since the day BJ had called, even when Sandra refused to take Rufina's case. She was back to her old self. Sandra had suspected all along that Erma had manipulated her into resigning from the DA's office, so they could practice law together. Then the heart attack. Things had changed. Then Erma's friend Phillip had been murdered. Things had changed again. Now they might change a third time, change for the better.

A conversation outside the curtained area grew closer. When the curtain was slung back, the resident who'd been taking care of her walked in with a nurse's aide.

"All right," the resident said, "you're released, Ms. Salinsky. When you return to Galveston, you need to make an appointment with your primary care physician about your esophageal spasms, particularly if you have them often. I'm sure you don't want another debilitating incident like you suffered today."

"If the EMTs had just let me talk, I would have told them what was happening."

"Look, I realize you're angry at having been here most of the day but think of this as a wake-up call. Incidents like the one you had are often a result of stress, of a person's lifestyle. Maybe you're due for some changes."

Exactly what Sandra thought, the concept of working for an insurance firm, bloodsuckers as Erma called them, had created the wrong kind of stress, had brought the spasms on, not Rufina's trial.

"With the tests we ran, at least you know your heart is in good shape. You have any questions?"

"I need to go back to the courthouse. Do y'all have taxis here?"

The aide accompanying the resident handed a clipboard to Sandra and pointed out where she was to sign. "Your friend is outside waiting for you."

"Good luck." The resident patted her back.

Sandra signed where the woman told her. "Thank you, Doc. I apologize for being so difficult."

She approached the ER lobby in search of her "friend." She hardly knew anyone in the Hill Country. Maybe BJ? She spotted Jared, with his briefcase on his lap, his head bent over some documents. A warm feeling forced her face into a smile.

"Nice of you to come." She was thankful he was there even though it could be interpreted as implying more intimacy in their relationship. God, was that what it was?

He pushed his briefcase aside and stood and kissed her on the cheek. "I was here earlier, but they wouldn't let me see you."

"You didn't have to return." How did she get into a relationship with a man who lived five hours away, six if she stopped for lunch?

"Someone needed to drive you. I'm a lot better than our limited taxi service."

"Well, thank you. I guess I would have had to wait for Erma to come, or walk. Walking very far in these shoes can be difficult." They both looked down at her four-inch heels, which she only wore when in jury trials.

"Where do you want to go?"

Her stomach growled.

"You haven't had anything to eat since breakfast, have you?" Jared loaded his papers into his satchel.

She shook her head. "I guess I shouldn't be thinking about food after this morning's experience, but I can't help it. I do like to eat."

"I've noticed." His smile wasn't mean.

"Do you have dinner plans?"

"Nope," he said. "No plans for later in the evening, either. Come on. Walk this way." He held his briefcase in one hand and touched her lightly on the back with the other, guiding her toward the exit. His aftershave gave off a light peppermint-piney scent, a relief after a day of hospital smells.

"If you don't mind an early dinner, I'll let you take me wherever would be a good place. But no dessert." Their eyes met.

"No problem. I understand. I've seen the paperwork spread out in my office. You must still have prep work to do for the next witnesses." He held the hospital door for her. "That's me over there. The blue Chevy pickup."

Sandra raised her eyebrows. A pickup truck? She wasn't real surprised. He did, after all, live in the country. "May I use your cell when we get to your truck? I need to see where they are in the trial." She drew a deep breath as they walked through the parking lot. The lack of antiseptic smell was a welcome change. "Depending on what's going on, would it be all right if Erma, Mel, and Rufina joined us? Or, should I tell them to meet us back at your office after dinner."

"Whatever you want. I don't have anything else scheduled today."

"You're too good to be true." She didn't know why he liked her, with all the other women in the world, but for now, she was glad he did.

When they were inside the truck, he handed her the phone and drove out of the lot. Mel answered on the first ring.

"Mel, Mom. They released me from the hospital."

"Yea! I'm so happy they let you out. I told Grandma they were going to. So you're okay?"

"I'm fine, just some stomach spasms, so no worries. I guess you're not in court or you wouldn't be answering."

"The judge just let us go. He said he was adjourning early, because he had a lot of other stuff on his calendar."

Sandra glanced at her watch. Four o'clock was the judge's idea of early? "Jared's taking me to eat. Ask Grandma if y'all can join us for an early dinner. Rufina, too, if she wants to come."

"Rufina went back to the ranch with BJ. Grandma and I were going to walk around downtown a little. I wanted to look in the shops, but I'd rather eat at a restaurant with you. Grandma heard what you were saying. She said we can meet y'all."

Jared told her where they were going, and Sandra relayed it to Mel. "Bring my purse and cell phone, please. See you in a bit."

Sandra handed the phone back to Jared. She admired his profile. He was one good-looking son of a bitch. Strong jaw. Slightly reddish stubble. Dark blond hair.

"What are you looking at?"

"You, fella." Now wasn't the time to discuss "them," so she steered the conversation away. "Do you have any idea what went on in court today?"

"Only a little." He cut through some side streets. "I called Annie in the clerk's office. The sheriff testified for most of the afternoon."

She would have liked to cross-examine the sheriff. "I've been thinking of taking a job at an insurance firm." Why did she spit that out after the soul-searching she'd just done? For feedback? Too late to take it back.

He maneuvered his truck out on the highway and through the traffic in front of the high school. Sandra didn't know where they were going. She had to trust him. He didn't respond. "Aren't you going to say anything?"

His jaw flexed. "I think it's kind of cool you practice law with your mother. Not too many people get to do that."

"Yeah. I guess not." She stared straight ahead, the oak trees on the side of the road in her peripheral vision. The two-lane road was busy with pickups of kids—mostly high school boys— driving too fast.

"You don't get along with your mother?" He kept one hand on the steering wheel, and the other rested on the console between them.

Why had she started this conversation? He turned left off the road onto a smaller two-lane, not-quite-dirt road. They came to a large parking lot beside a replica of a log cabin with a wide porch. The strong wind moved empty rocking chairs forward and back like they were occupied by ghosts. Milk cans filled with flowers sat out front. Jared parked and cut the engine.

He laid an arm across the steering wheel, his other hand stayed on the console close to her arm. "I might be wrong, but Erma appears to be happy with things the way they are. The little I saw, she was giving Sam Holt hell and enjoying it." He stroked her forearm with one finger.

"It's me, not her." His touch went further than the surface of her skin. She unsnapped her seat belt and turned in the seat. "I've been questioning whether criminal law is for me."

"From what I've been told, you're good at it. Something happen to make you want out?"

How much should she confide in this man? Was he interested in what she was saying? She still hadn't figured out why he was

276

attracted to her at all, except she was someone new and different from the women in that small town. She could tell him what she had been thinking of doing with her future and get an outsider's perspective. Their eyes met. His were greener than the last time she'd focused on them. He stared at her, solemn faced.

"I always thought I was a good judge of character." She watched for a reaction. "When I was in the DA's office, I was pretty good at understanding where the defense attorneys were coming from and predicting how they'd proceed with their cases."

His forehead drew up in a studied look, his eyes on her eyes.

"Well, turns out I wasn't so good at it in my personal life." She ran the side of her forefinger back and forth over her lips.

Jared didn't say anything. His eyes roved over her face as she spoke.

She was uncomfortable with the scrutiny. "Are you sure you want to hear this?"

He nodded. "Very much so."

Her stomach growled again. Where were Erma and Mel? She hoped they hadn't gotten lost. He continued to stare at her as if to say, get-on-with-it. "Well, I was in a relationship with an attorney in a civil practice. His name was Stuart. Wait, I told you I've been married twice, didn't I?"

"Yes. Mel is from your first marriage?"

"Yeah, she lives with her father and step-mother most of the time. I have liberal visitation rights. She works with us after school and gets credit in a program they have at the high school."

He smiled on one side of his mouth. "You're getting off topic."

Sandra hunched her shoulders. "I guess I'm nervous. I don't normally spill my guts to anyone."

"No close girlfriends?"

She shook her head. "Nope. I've always been kind of a loner."

"You're stalling."

She shrugged. "Well, so Stuart and I were going hot and heavy. In fact, I thought he wanted to move our relationship to the next level. He said he did. I wasn't sure I did."

"So you're not with him anymore? What happened?"

"Umm—I was so not a good judge of character." She looked out the window, knowing she was being evasive, but still not comfortable telling Jared all the sordid details. Erma pulled into the parking lot and took the space closest to the restaurant entrance. Saved.

Jared glanced where she was looking and grasped her arm. "Sandra—"

She faced him again. "Turned out he had a secret life. Some people say everyone does, that everyone keeps secrets from their partner. I never believed that. I thought if some things weren't shared, they didn't amount to much." Shaking her head, she said, "Well, stupid me, I believe it now. Stuart turned out to be a different man than I thought he was. A very different man with a completely secret life. Not in a good way, either."

Jared leaned toward her. "I'm so sorry."

"I've thought and thought about what happened. I was depressed for a long while and though I've pulled out of that, I've concluded I'm not a good judge of character. I've been thinking I need to take myself out of any position where I'd have to rely on my judgment. I never want to make a mistake like that again."

"And you think that means giving up the practice of law, or at least litigation?"

"Well, I did." Mel and Erma had gotten out of the car and were walking toward the restaurant. Jared's eyes followed hers.

Sandra said, "I've given myself until the end of this trial to make a final decision about what I'm going to do." She wasn't ready to say she'd pretty much made up her mind to stay, still wanting to see if she felt the same when she woke up tomorrow. She yanked on the door handle. "You never know. Something might turn up to convince me I'm wrong."

Jared gave her arm a squeeze and reached for his own door handle. "You're right. You never know."

CHAPTER TWENTY-EIGHT

L ATE THE FOLLOWING morning, Holt said, "The state calls BJ Schindler." He wore another pinstripe suit and a smirk from hell.

"What the heck?" Sandra whispered to Erma, toning down her rhetoric since Mel, who was on the first row of benches behind them, could overhear most of what they said. "Did she tell you she was going to testify? I thought she was going to Mexico to find what's-his-face." Sandra was first chair again, so she sat next to the aisle, closest to Holt. She wanted to reach over and smack that expression off his face.

"She didn't say anything." Erma spoke in a hushed tone. "When we left this morning, she was fixing to go find Efrain. Wait a minute, is BJ on their witness list?" Erma flipped through the trial notebook and took out the State's response to their discovery motion. She paged through it. "I don't see her name."

Sandra sprang to her feet. "Judge, I object to this witness."

The jurors perked up. The morning had been slow, with a state's expert testifying about the wound and the autopsy. On cross, Sandra had made short shrift of him. Nothing to be gained from a lengthy cross-examination of some witnesses.

"Approach the bench." The judge beckoned them to come around to the side farthest from the jury.

Matthew picked up his machine and preceded them. Once Matt was in place, the judge rolled his chair to the edge of the steps leading up to the platform and hunkered down so the jury couldn't hear the conversation. "What's the nature of your objection, Mrs. Salinsky?"

Sandra cringed at his calling her Mrs. again. "Mrs. Schindler is not on the State's witness list."

With raised eyebrows, he regarded Holt. "Response, Mr. Holt?"

Holt, a pen clenched in one fist and a manila folder in the other, cleared his throat. "That's true, Judge. She is, however, present at the courthouse every day and hanging out with the defense. They excluded her from the courtroom, when they invoked the rule against witnesses being in the courtroom during testimony, so I figured they were going to call her."

"Judge, you know that doesn't mean he can call her without listing her. He can't rely on what we might do." Sandra clenched her fists behind her back.

"I was going to file an amended witness list earlier, but this trial has been moving so rapidly my office couldn't prepare it in time." Holt opened the folder, revealing some legal documents. "I have the amended list here and would like to file it with the court now."

The judge took some stapled pages from Holt, who also handed a copy to Sandra.

Before she'd even grasped it, Sandra said, "What? No, Judge. He can't do this. If he wants to cross-examine Mrs. Schindler after we put her on, if we call her as a witness, he's certainly welcome to do so, but he can't call her as a witness and then file the motion."

"You do intend to call her, Mrs. Salinsky?" Judge Danforth gave her the stink eye.

Sandra's head throbbed like it would explode. What was that about? Holt was the one who wasn't abiding by the rules. "We're considering it."

"Then no harm, no foul," the judge said.

"No, Judge. I'm not sure who I'll call until all the State's witnesses have testified, until we've seen all the evidence. We might not call anyone." She'd like to rip the copy Holt had given her to shreds and throw it in their faces.

The judge's deep frown made her feel like a three-time loser waiting to be sentenced. "I'm going to allow it." He pushed back in his chair, rolling to the center of the platform.

Flames of anger licked at Sandra. What the hell? Was he treating their side of the case unfairly because he was a jerk, because she was an out-of-town lawyer, or because he thought a little Mexican woman didn't deserve a fair trial? She huffed and strode back to her place, tossing the motion on the table.

Holt just about two-stepped back to his side of the room.

"Objection overruled," the judge said. "Mrs. Schindler may testify." He picked up a pen and wrote something before leaning back in his chair.

When BJ arrived at the front of the courtroom, her face held a help-me expression, but there was nothing they could do. They hadn't prepared her, but BJ was a mature woman who should be able to hold her own.

Erma whispered. "Can't say I've never seen such favoritism, but it's been a while. Probably payback for the sheriff being as friendly as he was."

"Unbelievable," Sandra muttered under her breath, hoping the ruling didn't reflect the judge's personal attitude toward minority defendants.

BJ took the oath and sat down, still looking their way in apparent confusion.

"You may proceed, Mr. Holt."

"Hello, Mrs. Schindler. I'm Samuel Holt, the duly elected district attorney for this judicial district, which includes
Gillespie County."

"I'm well aware of who you are." BJ held her handbag in her
lap as though she were afraid someone might snatch it.

"Ma'am, you were the mother of Katy Jo Schindler, were
you not?"

BJ bit her lip and nodded, her face crinkling up like she was
about to burst into tears.

"Ma'am, I need you to answer out loud for the record."

"Yes."

"Would you describe for the jury the events on the night
she died?"

BJ, who wore a jacket over a button-down shirt, fiddled with
the shirt collar, her hand trembling. "We were having dinner at
my home."

Erma murmured, "She's way more nervous than I thought
she'd be. If we'd had just a few more months before trial, she'd
have had more time to deal with her grief."

Sandra put her finger to her lips.

"When you say we, who are you speaking of?" Holt asked.

"The girls—"

"Katy Jo had a twin sister, correct? An identical twin?"

"Yes. The girls, Katy Jo's boyfriend, Doug, my son, Rex..."

"That would be Roy Schindler the Third, correct?"

BJ's expression had changed, her jaw set. "If you'll quit interrupting me, I'll tell you who was present."

Holt's cheeks sprouted roses. "Yes, ma'am. Continue."

"So Katy Jo, Kathy Lynn, Doug, Rex, Elgin Burgess—the
man who owns the ranch next over from mine," she said,
shooting daggers at Holt as if daring him to interrupt her again,
"and me."

"And the defendant?" Holt pointed to Rufina.

"No."

"No? What do you mean?" He reared back as though surprised, the look on his face full of wide-eyed, fake disbelief. "Let me ask you this, Mrs. Schindler. You and the defendant have known each other for a long time, am I right?"

"Yes."

"How long?"

"About fifty or so years."

"She lives on your ranch?"

"Yes."

"Does she live in the house with you?"

"No, she does not."

"Did she?"

"Did she what?"

"Did the defendant ever live in the house with you?"

"No, she did not."

"Didn't she live in the house with you after her house burned to the ground?"

"She stayed with me for a while after she was released from the hospital, but she didn't live with me."

"Mrs. Schindler, you were subpoenaed to be here today, were you not?"

"Just this morning." She turned to the judge. "Shouldn't I have been given more notice, Judge? I would have had time to rearrange my schedule for the day."

Judge Danforth shrugged but otherwise didn't respond.

Erma spoke behind her hand, "Son of a bitch."

Holt tapped his pen on the legal pad in front of him. "So you didn't come here voluntarily."

"Correct."

"What is your relationship with the defendant?"

"She's my best friend."

Sandra watched the members of the jury. When the last answer came, there were tells on the faces of a couple of them. Nothing too obvious, just little movements of surprise. One of them, who'd been rocking back in his chair, sat up straight.

"Yet, she wasn't invited to the dinner party."

"Do you invite all your friends to every event you have at your house, Mr. Holt?"

Holt stood. "Objection. Non-responsive." Without waiting for the judge to speak, Holt said, "Was she invited to the dinner party that night at your house? Yes or no."

"No."

"Why not?"

"It was a family get together."

"If she's been your best friend for nigh on fifty years, isn't she like a member of the family?"

"She is to me."

"Not to your children?"

"Not to all of them."

"Which ones?"

"Which ones what?"

Holt stood again. "Judge, would you instruct the witness to answer the questions?"

The judge said, "Mrs. Schindler, listen to the questions asked by Mr. Holt and answer them to the best of your ability."

BJ didn't say anything. She stared at Holt.

"Which members of your family didn't consider Rufina to be part of the family?"

"You'd have to ask them."

Holt blew out a breath and shook his head. He stood again. "Judge—"

The judge rolled his chair closer to the witness box. "Mrs. Schindler, this will go a lot faster if you'd be so kind as to answer the questions."

BJ's eyebrows drew together, and she nodded.

"Mrs. Schindler, let's look at the relationship of the defendant with each of your children. Rex doesn't like her, isn't that correct?"

"He blows hot and cold."

"Kathy Lynn doesn't like her, isn't that correct?"

BJ shook her head. "I don't know about that."

"You don't? Well, she's not particularly friendly to her, is she?"

"She's always been on-again, off-again. Way more friendly than not over the years, I'd say."

"And Katy Jo?"

"Katy Jo loved Rufina."

"The defendant didn't love Katy Jo, though, and that's why she killed her, isn't that right?"

"Your Honor," Sandra yelled before she could get to her feet. "I object!"

"What is your objection, Mrs. Salinsky?"

"Uh, uh, calls for a conclusion on the part of the witness."

"Overruled."

Sandra stamped her foot.

The judge gave her one of his darker looks. At least he realized she was there.

"Be careful, my girl." Erma gave her a warning glance.

Sandra rubbed her hand over her chest. Judges like Danforth gave her heartburn, but it wasn't another esophageal spasm. She knew the difference.

"You may answer," Holt told BJ.

BJ looked at Sandra again as though at a loss for words. Sandra wanted to help her, but there was nothing she could do.

"Rufina loves all my children, and she most definitely did not—"

"Thank you, Mrs. Schindler. And the reason she didn't like Katy Jo was Katy Jo was the one who set the fire that burned down the defendant's home, killed the defendant's husband, and inflicted severe burns with horrible scars that would last the defendant a lifetime." Holt drew a deep breath. "Isn't that true?"

"Absolutely not." BJ's voice echoed off the walls like she had spoken into a megaphone.

"Which part of that is not true?"

"Rufina loves—loved Katy Jo."

"So the other part is true. Katy Jo set the fire?"

"I've never been one-hundred percent convinced of that."

"Isn't it true Katy Jo confessed to setting the fire?"

BJ looked about as miserable as anyone could. "Yes, but—"

"Wasn't she sent to the Texas Youth Commission for a year and then on juvenile parole when she got out? I mean, she had to plead guilty in court, didn't she? Had to admit she'd done it?"

"I never thought she did it. I still don't."

"The fact remains she was adjudicated a delinquent child and sent to TYC for setting the fire, correct?"

"Yes." BJ wailed and grabbed a handful of tissues from the box next to the microphone, covering her face with them.

Erma began to rise, but Sandra grabbed her arm, preventing Erma from doing anything that might further jeopardize their position. Rufina had her head bowed. Behind them, Mel sniffed. BJ's sobs could be heard over the murmurings of the jurors. Sandra stood and said, "Judge, I think now would be a good time to take the morning break."

Judge Danforth nodded with a look of relief. "I agree." He turned to the jurors and instructed them to take fifteen-minutes and not to discuss the case with anyone or each other.

As soon as the room emptied, Erma hurried to BJ. "Come on, honey bunch." Erma slipped an arm across BJ's shoulders.

BJ, head-hanging, stepped down from the witness stand and let Erma walk her to counsel table, where BJ sat down. Rufina rolled her chair around and sat knee-to-knee with BJ, taking her hands in her own and squeezing them.

"It's *bueno*, Billie J. Look at me." Rufina put her head close, almost forcing BJ to open her eyes. "We know Katy Jo was a good girl." She shook BJ's arm. "Look at me," she said again. "I'm not crying, and I'm on trial for murder."

A small smile appeared on BJ's lips. "This is no time to kid around."

"We knew this would come out, didn't we?" Rufina asked. "Even if we never believed it."

Sandra stood over them, listening to every word. No one could doubt the two women were the closest of friends. Rufina had never believed the allegations against Katy Jo, and BJ didn't believe the allegations against Rufina. Mel handed BJ a glass of water and dropped a packet of tissues in her lap on top of her purse. Erma gripped the back of BJ's chair, smoke practically streaming from her ears.

"You don't hate—didn't hate Katy Jo," BJ said. "You never hated anyone."

Erma took a step back. "Except maybe the fucking prosecutor."

Mel raised her eyebrows but didn't say anything.

Rufina shook her head. "He's just doing his job."

BJ mopped her eyes. "I didn't know testifying would be so hard. I thought I could just tell what I knew." Tears continued to flow down her face.

Erma put her hand on BJ's shoulder. "I sure was surprised to see you this morning. Thought you were running down to Mexico."

"I was on my way out the door when a deputy showed up with a subpoena. I literally had one foot outside the door, getting ready to lock it." BJ blotted her nose. "He followed me all the way here like he thought I might not come."

Sandra crouched down. "You're going to be all right but be prepared for Holt to be just as hard on you the rest of the morning when court reconvenes."

BJ smeared her mascara with the damp tissues. "I—I just need to go downstairs to the restroom and fix my face. I feel better now." She touched Rufina's arm. "I'm sorry, Rufina. I hope I'm not making a mess of things."

Erma said, "Rufina, you understand we were going to open our defense with BJ's testimony—let her talk about you and her and how close you've always been since high school before we got into the case?"

Rufina nodded and took BJ's hand. "Do the best you can when you get back up there, Billie J." She stepped in front of BJ and dipped her head down until she could catch her eye. "We'll get through this."

Sandra felt the urge to give in to tears herself but swallowed the lump in her throat. "Let's go downstairs and take advantage of this break before our fifteen-minutes expire." She ushered them toward the courtroom exit. She wanted a few minutes to give BJ a pep talk before Holt resumed his questioning.

A bit past the fifteen-minute deadline, the five women entered the courtroom. The judge, the prosecutor, the bailiff, and the court reporter, all men, were in place and watched them walk up the aisle. The court reporter and the bailiff turned away, taking their respective places, but the judge and prosecutor, who were already in place, frowned and stared.

Sandra waited for the judge to remark on their being a minute or two late, but he hovered over the counter, his eyes scrutinizing them, his arms crossed, and said nothing.

They took their seats, Erma turning to BJ first and saying, "Show them some spunk, *amiga*."

BJ walked to the witness stand and stood next to it.

"You may retake the stand, Mrs. Schindler." The judge's tone and demeanor had softened. "Have you pulled yourself together?"

A muscle in BJ's jaw flexed. She set her purse on the floor and squared her shoulders. "Yes, I have."

The bailiff brought the jurors back into court and the trial continued.

"Now, where were we, Mrs. Schindler?" Holt made like he was studying his notes. "Oh, yes. We were talking about the decedent, Katy Jo, having burned down the defendant's house and being adjudicated for it. Correct?"

BJ squared her shoulders. "Yep, Mr. Holt. That's what you were asking about, all right. I'm sure you have my daughter's records right in front of you in case you need any more information, even though the file is supposed to be sealed."

Erma muttered. "That's my girl."

Holt's assistant pushed a file folder next to his legal pad. Holt cleared his throat again. "Let's go back to the dinner the night of your daughter's murder, all right?"

BJ didn't say anything.

"Besides your twin daughters, the other attendees were your son, Katy Jo's boyfriend, and Elgin Burgess. Correct?"

"Yes. Six of us."

"Did you cook the dinner, ma'am?"

"No, I did not."

"Who cooked the dinner?"

"Two of the women who work for me prepared the meal under Rufina's supervision, if that's what you're getting at."

"So the defendant was at your house when dinner was being prepared and served, and yet she wasn't invited to sit down and break bread with the family."

"That's right."

He shook his head like he was confused. "Wait, wait, wait. Let's back up. The defendant works for you?"

"Yes. Rufina works for me."

Sandra couldn't tell from Holt's face what he knew. Surely their investigation had revealed everything there was to know about Rufina.

"What is the nature of her employment?"

"She's the ranch housekeeper, which includes supervision of the household staff."

Holt rubbed his hands together like he was warming up for the kill. Sandra was familiar with that action, having seen it in court many times. Now, she hadn't a clue about where he was going with the current line of questioning.

"How many people do you have in your household staff?" Holt asked.

Sandra got to her feet. "Objection, relevance."

Holt stood, but the judge was faster. "Overruled."

"So how many people work in your household, Mrs. Schindler?"

"In the household? Four women including Rufina."

"What do the four women do each day?"

Sandra stood again. "Isn't this getting a little off topic, Judge? Really, what relevance could the duties of the household staff have to whether or not my client, Mrs. Rufina Barboza, committed the act in question?"

The judge's gaze went to Holt.

"I'll move along, Judge."

The judge failed to rule or say anything. That kind of thing always annoyed Sandra. "Are you going to rule on my objection, Judge?" She wanted to make sure the record reflected every single thing that transpired in the courtroom, to preserve it for appeal.

The judge's eyes flitted to Sandra's face and back to whatever was on the counter in front of him. For all she knew, it was a crossword puzzle. "Sustained."

"Mrs. Schindler, let me ask you this. Those four household staff, do they all live on the ranch?"

"Yes, they do."

"Where do they live on the ranch?"

"Well, you already know Rufina has a cottage near my house. Her cottage has always been the housekeeper's cottage. The other women live in smaller cottages in various locations around the ranch."

"So no one lives in the house with you?"

"None of the staff, no."

Holt nodded and checked something off on his legal pad. He muttered something to the assistant sitting second chair. "So each evening, the staff goes home to their cottages?"

"If they're through with their duties. If I entertain, they stay until I don't need them anymore."

"So on the night of Katy Jo's murder, when did the staff leave?"

"After serving dinner."

"They didn't stay to clean up?"

"They clean up in the morning."

"The defendant left as well?"

"After dinner was prepared, I believe."

"Don't you think it was offensive to the defendant to have to go home when everyone else was sitting down to dinner? I mean, couldn't you have asked her to sit down with the rest of y'all?"

"I could have, but I didn't." BJ's eyes went to Rufina who was biting her lower lip.

"Why not?" Before BJ could answer, Holt modified his question. "Why didn't you ask the defendant to have dinner with the family?"

"She has a life, Mr. Holt. Every one of them has a life outside of working for me."

The jurors were like spectators at a tennis match, their eyes, if not their heads, bouncing from lawyer to witness and witness to lawyer.

"What do you mean, ma'am?"

BJ's face screwed up, and she shrugged like she thought he was a dimwit. "They have husbands. They have children. They have other things to do besides work in my house."

Erma whispered into Sandra's ear. "That's telling the dumb ass." Sandra reined in a snort.

Holt scribbled some more. "The others may have all that, but what does the defendant have?"

"Well, for one thing, Mr. Holt, that night Rufina had a date who was waiting for her in her cottage."

There was a small pull at the side of Holt's mouth and his eyes flared. He scooted toward his assistant and said something, clicking his pen many times in quick succession. The assistant thumbed through pieces of paper.

Rufina covered her mouth with her hands, her eyes wide, apparently surprised at BJ's testimony.

"Stop that," Erma said in a fierce whisper to Rufina. "Hands down. Sit up straight."

Holt wrote something and leaned far back in his chair. He crossed his right leg over his left, his elbows propping him up on the arm rests. "You expect this court—this jury—to believe the defendant had a—a boyfriend waiting for her on the night of the murder?" His tone spoke volumes.

"Is that so hard to believe, Mr. Holt? Rufina is a lovely person." BJ winked at Rufina where the jury couldn't see it.

Holt tapped his pen on his lips. "Was he waiting for her to get off work? Waiting in the cottage?"

"I'm not one hundred percent sure he was there when she left my house, but he was supposed to be meeting her."

"Did anyone see him?"

"I have no idea."

Sandra and Erma exchanged glances. Doug would have seen him, but Doug wasn't supposed to be in Rufina's cottage. Had Doug told anyone Efrain was in Rufina's cottage? Rex couldn't have known, or he would have told Holt, but Holt appeared surprised by that bit of information.

Holt made a few more marks on his legal pad. "What, pray tell, is this alleged boyfriend's name?"

BJ's face blanched. Her eyes met Sandra's in a plea for help. Sandra made a barely perceptible shake of her head. If BJ didn't tell Holt or said she didn't know, no one would believe a boyfriend existed, which would blow at least part of their defense. If she did tell Holt, he would immediately have his office check out Efrain. They wouldn't be able to find anything since Efrain had no U.S. or Texas criminal history and wasn't in the country legally. That would open up further examination as to his existence.

BJ clasped her hands in front of her mouth. "Efrain Montes."

"I didn't hear you, Mrs. Schindler," Holt said. "Take your hands from in front of your face."

BJ pulled her hands down and cast her eyes at Rufina again. "Efrain Montes."

The expression on Holt's face was nothing if not startled, like he thought BJ wouldn't know the boyfriend's name. "Tell the members of the jury where Mr. Montes lives."

"I have no idea."

"You have no idea?"

Sandra hoped the jury disliked Holt's demeanor as much as she did. She hoped they didn't appreciate his sarcastic questions and comments and immature behavior. Furthermore, she hoped his behavior would adversely affect at least one of the jurors, make him or her focus even more on reasonable doubt than he or she otherwise would have. Her eyes roved over their faces and came to rest on the black woman who was juror number twelve. The woman made brief eye contact, sending a tiny jolt of hope through Sandra. Could the juror feel a connection with the defense side of the case?

BJ said, her mouth way too close to the microphone, "That's what I said, Mr. Holt. Efrain is Rufina's boyfriend, not mine. Why should I know where he lives?"

"Has she introduced you to this alleged boyfriend?" Holt asked in a skeptical tone.

"No."

"Well, if the defendant is your best friend like you say she is, why wouldn't she have introduced you to her boyfriend?"

"You'll have to ask her." BJ let her shoulders drop and crossed her arms.

Erma said, "Huh," slightly louder than a whisper. The judge's eyes flickered at her, and she shrugged one shoulder. Sidling over to Sandra, she whispered, "He asked the wrong question."

Holt stood. "At this time, Your Honor, I'd like to reserve the rest of my questioning for cross-examination."

From her experience in the Galveston DA's office, Sandra knew Holt was buying time, so he could conduct a criminal background check on Efrain. In fact, she was sure he'd run as thorough a check on Efrain as possible to see if the man truly existed.

"Any questions at this time, Mrs. Salinsky?"

"No, Your Honor. I reserve my questions for direct examination, should I choose to call Mrs. Schindler as a witness."

"Court will be in recess for lunch until one-thirty this afternoon." The judge left the bench and went into chambers.

Sandra put her knuckles to her mouth to hide the smile she couldn't quite conceal. Holt couldn't ask Rufina a damn thing unless she testified. And he wouldn't be able to cross-examine BJ later, if they never put her back on the witness stand.

CHAPTER TWENTY-NINE

A FTER LUNCH, WHEN court reconvened, Holt said, "The state calls Adrian Wegner."

Following the ER doctor's advice, Sandra had eaten only a small salad and had agreed to let Erma cross-examine the fingerprint expert. This time, Erma sat in the aisle chair across from Holt. Sandra flipped to the trial notebook pages containing documents the State had produced in response to the Motion for Discovery.

Holt took the witness though preliminary questions, establishing him as an expert, then dove right in. "You're the resident fingerprint guru in this area, are you not, Mr. Wegner?"

Wegner, a short, wiry man of about fifty with bulging eyes like a cow, tented his fingers, his elbows on the counter in front of him. "You could say that, Mr. Holt."

"You've testified in court before?"

Erma hopped up. "Judge, I think Mr. Holt covered this when he established Mr. Wegner as an expert."

"Sustained. Move along, Mr. Holt."

Erma sat back down. Sandra met Holt's eyes behind Erma's back. She could swear laser beams were flying across the aisle.

"Sir, you said you're a forensic fingerprint expert?"

"Correct. Also known as a latent print examiner."

"As a fingerprint expert, you were called by the sheriff to examine fingerprints on State's Exhibit Two, the weapon used to kill the decedent, correct?"

"Yes, sir. My job is to consult on fingerprint identification, examine items for fingerprints, analyze fingerprints, compare fingerprints, and make an identification, if possible, among other things."

Sandra and Erma exchanged glances. This guy was one of those who couldn't answer with a simple yes or no.

"You did that in this case, Mr. Wegner?"

"Yes, sir, I did, and found three fingerprints. Two of them were smudged beyond usefulness. I did find a partial fingerprint, though, on State's Exhibit Two."

"Did anyone give you an impression to compare the partial fingerprint with?"

"Yes, sir. The sheriff's office provided me with the fingerprints of a Mrs. Rufina Barboza."

"Tell the ladies and gentlemen of the jury what you found, Mr. Wegner."

"The partial print comes from Rufina Barboza."

Sandra held Erma's forearm to stop her from jumping up. Erma's usual style was to interrupt as much as possible in the hope of confusing the jury. Sandra thought a more direct approach would be better. She and Erma had discussed it, and Erma had agreed. Erma shook off Sandra's hand.

Holt let several seconds go by. The judge's tapping of his pen on the counter sounded like a woodpecker striking a tree. Voices from out in the hall came through the walls. The heating unit kicked on with a rattle, smelling like something burnt. Sandra scooted over in her chair and laid her hand on Rufina's arm. Rufina put her hand on top of Sandra's, her lips hinting at a smile. She had been and remained the most composed of any of them, as though she had complete faith in her defense team.

Holt shifted in his chair. "Thank you, Mr. Wegner. Now let's break down what you found. Tell the jury what you were looking for and what you discovered in your comparison of the two prints."

"Objection." Erma sprang from her chair. "Calls for a narrative."

"Sustained," Judge Danforth said. "Mr. Holt, proceed in question-and-answer format."

Holt's mouth turned down. "What were you looking for in comparing the two prints?" He gave Erma a sideways look, as if he was afraid she'd object again. "Strike that. Judge, may I approach the witness."

"You may," the judge said, looking bored.

Holt placed the gun on the counter in front of the witness. "First, where was the identified fingerprint found on State's Exhibit Two?"

"On the trigger guard." He held up the gun and pointed to the trigger guard like no one on the jury would know what that was.

"Did you find prints anywhere else?"

"Just those two smudges I already mentioned, but otherwise, it had been wiped clean."

"Objection," Erma said, rising about halfway out of her chair. "Calls for a conclusion on the part of the witness."

Holt stood. "Judge, if he didn't find fingerprints anywhere on the weapon except the trigger guard, someone would have had to wipe it clean. Obviously, someone would've had to handle it in the past, or it would never have arrived at the premises."

"Unless the person who fired the gun on the night in question wore gloves." Erma stood with her hands on her hips.

"You attorneys approach the bench." The muscles in the judge's jaws flexed. When all four lawyers arrived at sidebar, the judge gave them a sour look. "Y'all aren't going to do this throughout the rest of the trial. If you have an issue like this to discuss, approach the bench. I'm not going to have arguments like this in front of the jury."

Both Erma and Holt nodded. "Yes, Your Honor."

Erma shrugged on her way back to the table. So did Sandra, hoping the jury would get the impression the sidebar conference was of no importance. At least the judge didn't side with Holt.

"For the record, objection sustained."

Continuing his white-knuckled grip on his pen, Holt perched on the edge of his chair. His jaw muscles flexed like the judge's had a minute earlier. "Which finger matched the print?"

"The trigger finger of her right hand."

"So now tell the jury what you were looking for when examining—when comparing the prints." Holt leaned back and put a tiny smile on his lips, as though confident his witness would do right by him.

"Well, sir," Wegner said, puffing out his chest, "what we look for are points. Matching points."

"By that you mean places on both prints that appear to be the same?"

"Yes, sir, more or less. Points of similarity. Matching ridge characteristics." He liked using buzzwords.

"What did you find in this instance?"

"Well, sir, I was able to identify eight matching points."

"What you're saying, sir," Holt said, "is in that partial print alone you were able to match eight points of similarity between it and the full print the sheriff's office took from the defendant and conclude the prints were one and the same. Correct?"

"Yes, sir," Mr. Wegner said, dusting the arm of his jacket as if to remove something.

"Ahem. Pass the witness, Your Honor." Holt inclined his head at Erma.

Erma was halfway to her feet when the judge said to proceed. "There are no universal standards of matching points. True, Mr. Wegner?"

"Yes, ma'am, that is true." He pursed his lips and sneaked a glance at Holt.

"In fact, the FBI has said there should be no minimum standard. Right?"

His eyes went to Erma and back to Holt. "Yes, ma'am."

"The same is true in the United Kingdom, specifically England, am I right?" Erma held her pen with both hands like she was about to break it into two even pieces.

Wegner nodded.

"Answer for the record, sir," the judge said.

"Oh, sorry. Yes, correct."

"In other countries, there are set standards," Erma again.

"Yes."

"In Australia, they have a minimum standard of twelve matching points. In France and Italy, the standard is sixteen, correct?"

"Yes. In this country, examiners have varying standards ranging from eight to sixteen points."

"But no set standard."

"No, no set standard."

"So each examiner establishes his or her own standard."

"Yes, true."

"Your standard is eight?"

"Well, in a partial print—"

"So what we have here is your subjective opinion that the fingerprints match?"

"Yes, ma'am."

"There is no objective test."

"No, ma'am."

"In other words, another examiner might have a minimum standard of ten points, or twelve points, or sixteen points, right? Another examiner's subjective opinion might be contrary to yours, correct?"

Wegner's eyes shifted to Holt and back. "Well, yes, ma'am."

"Pass the witness." Erma tossed her pen on the table and stared down at the legal pad in front of her.

"Re-direct, Mr. Holt?" the judge asked.

"Yes, Your Honor." Holt leaned as far toward the witness as the table would allow. "Mr. Wegner, your conclusion the fingerprint belonged to the defendant was based on your identifying eight points of similarity. Tell the jury why you're confident your opinion is correct."

Wegner turned toward the jury. "If a partial print contains eight points, one can only assume a full print would contain ten, twelve, or even sixteen points of similarity."

"Objection." Erma drew herself up to her full height. "The witness is drawing a conclusion."

"Sit down, Mrs. Townley." The judge's arms were crossed. "The witness has qualified as an expert and is permitted to draw a conclusion."

"Pass the witness."

"Anything more, Mrs. Townley?"

"Just a couple more, Judge." Erma folded her hands in front of her. Her smile didn't quite reach her eyes. "Sir, with that reasoning, couldn't it also be true that even though there are eight points of similarity, if you had the whole print where there was the possibility of ten, twelve, sixteen, or more points of similarity and no other points of similarity were found, a conclusion could be drawn that the partial print is not the print of my client, Rufina Barboza?"

The judge held his chin in the palm of his hand and covered his mouth. Sandra couldn't tell if he was hiding a smile or a frown. Holt stood up and sat down and clicked his pen like mad. Erma maintained her pose.

"Well, Mr. Wegner? Do I need to repeat myself?" Her question sounded like the end of it should've been, *you moron.*

Sandra risked a peek at the jurors. Several of them quickly hid their smiles.

"No, ma'am."

"No, ma'am, I don't need to repeat the question or no, ma'am, a conclusion couldn't be drawn."

"A conclusion could be drawn," Wegner said, his shoulders slumped when he looked Holt's way.

"A conclusion could be drawn that the print was not Mrs. Barboza's?" Erma's loud voice bounced off the walls.

"Yes, ma'am."

"One more question, sir, and I'll be through with you. You did say the partial print was found on the trigger guard, not the trigger, correct?"

Wegner coughed into his hand. "Yes, ma'am. That's what I said."

Erma whispered to Sandra, "Can you think of anything else?"

Sandra shook her head. If Holt's witnesses couldn't do any better than Wegner, the defense might have a real shot at an acquittal. Across the aisle, Holt's rigid posture and blanched profile indicated his awareness of the case's problems.

"Pass the witness, Judge."

CHAPTER THIRTY

❝I'M THINKING WE shouldn't let Rufina testify." Later that night after they'd returned to the cottage, Erma had changed to an ankle length, heavy cotton dress and thick socks. She rocked back and forth in an overstuffed glider, her feet propped on a footstool.

Sandra, wearing a dark red chenille bathrobe and flip-flops, sipped wine and paced around the little living room. She hoped the wine would help her fall asleep, though she would probably get slightly inebriated and lie in bed staring at the ceiling in the dark, thinking about what the next day might bring.

She moved a curtain aside. The sun had set. Mel had gone horseback riding with the son of a couple who worked on the ranch. Their cottage was nearest to Rufina's, the one Erma and Sandra were using during the trial. He'd taken Mel riding once before, and she'd come back in one piece, so Sandra let her go again.

"It's gotten dark. Mel should have been back a while ago." Sandra moved to another window, but the scenery didn't change. She shouldn't worry. BJ had assured them Mel was safe with Diego. "You think that kid is crushing on Mel?"

"Maybe, but don't worry about it. We won't be here much longer."

"I saw the way he looked at her." That's all Sandra would need, to get home and have her ex-husband, Jack, call and complain that Mel was pining over some kid in Fredericksburg. He'd make innuendos about Mel working for them after school and about what might happen the next time she wanted to take Mel someplace for any length of time. If she went to work for the insurance firm, though, he'd most likely find something else to complain about.

"Not to change the subject back to what I was talking about, Rufina's trial, but we do continue tomorrow," Erma said.

"I heard what you said about Rufina not testifying. I've been trying to look at it from the jury's point of view."

"Well, of course."

Sandra plopped down on the sofa and bounced up again like the sofa was a trampoline. "Number one, if we don't put Rufina on, they'll wonder whether she's guilty, of course, but number two, they won't have a sense of who she is." Sandra traipsed into the kitchen and refilled her wine glass. She raised her voice. "I don't care what anyone says, she's scary-looking. We don't see her scars like we once did because we know her well by now, but the jury doesn't. Some people will feel sorry for her, but others will be repulsed, whether we want to admit it or not.

"I once had a friend, a black friend, who ran for office," Erma said, turning in the rocker to watch Sandra. "His campaign photo was stern-looking, mean-looking some might say. I told him he needed a smiling face in his campaign photos, that white people are scared of black people, and he needed to give them the impression he was no one to be afraid of."

Sandra returned to the living room. "Your point being?"

"Well, he didn't agree. He liked the serious-looking picture, thought it made him appear dignified." Erma rocked hard in the chair, like she'd just been injected with a shot of energy. "Long story short, he lost the election. I still think more white people would have voted for him if they hadn't been afraid he'd get into office and do something to them."

"Yeah, I think you're right, whether anyone would admit it or not. So you think we should put Rufina on?"

"I don't know. I don't think Holt's proven their case."

"I think there's reasonable doubt."

"You're damn right there is, but does the jury think so?" Erma shuffled into the kitchen. She took a highball glass from the same cabinet as the wine glasses. "Don't say a word," she said over her shoulder in a loud voice. "I'm only having one drink. Not like you, who has been having more than one every night, even though I'm sure the doctor told you to cut back."

Sandra ignored that jab. She'd had esophageal spasms over the years, and they were never related to drinking wine. "Next you'll light up a cigarette."

"No. I keep telling you I've given them up for good."

"I'm shocked you haven't started again. Proud of you." For years, she'd been battling Erma to quit, especially after her heart attack. Could what she said be true? That remained to be seen.

Erma gave her a sidelong glance and uncapped the bottle she'd taken from a shelf.

"Here's what I think, Erma. We should discuss it with Rufina first and wait to make our decision after our motion for instructed verdict of acquittal gets shot down."

"Rufina wants to testify." Erma poured two fingers of bourbon.

"I know she does. Every client wants to testify, so what else is new? I'm inclined to let her, though."

"We woodshedded her pretty good before we came up here."

"I just don't know what Holt'll do to her." Sandra started to pour herself another glass of wine and realized her glass was still full.

"Oh, he'll do his best to put her in her grave." Erma leaned against the counter and sipped the bourbon, closing her eyes as though she could taste it better that way.

Sandra put the bottle of wine back in the refrigerator. "No question of that." She took a swallow from her glass. "Holt is almost through with his case," she said. "I'm thinking tomorrow he'll put Doug Christian on, and then maybe Kathy Lynn and Rex and Elgin to talk about the get together the night Katy Jo was killed. That shouldn't take very long."

"God knows what Rex will say. And Kathy Lynn, too. I wish she hadn't been avoiding us."

"I just thought of something." Sandra whacked her forehead with the heel of her hand. "I wonder if Doug can alibi Rufina."

"How's that?"

"If he was with Katy Jo here, in this cottage, before she went in to see her mother, and if Efrain was here with Rufina—"

"I don't see how Rufina could have hid Efrain from Doug and Katy Jo." Erma's voice filled with excitement. "They all had to use the same entrances and exits, and this place isn't all that big."

"No lie. I never thought to ask him that."

"Hell, we were unaware of Efrain when you and Mel interviewed Doug."

"I need to dig through my notes and see if I can find his cell number, so I can talk to him tonight." Sandra was heading for her bedroom when there was a noise at the front of the cottage. Mel must have returned. She pivoted so she could open the front door.

Mel came in and slammed the door. "Someone was following me."

"Goddamnit!" Erma jogged to the bedroom.

"Are you all right?" Sandra took Mel in her arms.

"I was so scared. I heard footsteps behind me."

Erma rushed out of the bedroom and bolted to the door, flinging it open, the revolver in her hand.

"Where are you going?" Sandra hollered.

"I'm going to kill the son of a bitch," Erma yelled over her shoulder. She darted out into the dark, still in her socks.

"Come back here," Sandra hurried to the doorway, dragging Mel with her, but Erma was out of sight. "Your grandmother is crazy sometimes," she said. "I'm sure whoever he was is long gone."

Mel stood behind her, shielding herself. "Are you going after her?"

"No. I'm staying with you. Besides, she can shoot better than I can." She stuck her head out, didn't see anything, and pushed the door closed. "Why were you alone?"

"I—I was walking back here after we put up the horses."

"Diego was supposed to bring you back to the main house first and then put up the horses."

Mel gave Sandra a helpless look. "I know, but it was still early, so I told him I'd help take off their saddles and all."

Sandra hooked her arm around Mel. Kids. "So you were walking back here alone, I guess, in the dark."

"It wasn't dark when I started out. I wanted to stop by Rufina's and see her for a few minutes before I came home."

"You didn't tell Diego which cottage Rufina was staying in, did you?" Erma asked.

Mel shook her head. "I know it's a secret. I just told him I'd walk back to the house, that it was okay."

Anger circulated in Sandra's body. She had made sure Diego understood he was to escort Mel back to the ranch house safely. "So then what happened?"

"I did go to Rufina's for a little while. We sat in her kitchen, and she gave me some pecan cookies she'd baked. She told me some stories about how life was on the ranch when she was little, when her parents worked here, but it was pretty dark when I left."

"You couldn't have called?" Sandra asked. "Did you have your cell with you?"

"Yes, Mom, but you know it doesn't always work out here, and, anyway, I thought I'd be all right. Her cottage isn't very far."

Erma came back in and slammed the door behind her. "I didn't see anyone."

"Put that thing up." Sandra nodded at the gun.

"I'm glad I didn't find him. I'd have shot the mo-fo." She stopped next to them and pulled some leaves from her socks.

"No one is going to hurt my granddaughter." She wrapped an arm around Mel's shoulders.

"I wonder if whoever it was thought she was Rufina." Sandra looked from one to the other. "When she got under the porch light, he could see she wasn't."

Mel held her hands palms up. "I'm sitting right here. The 'she' is me."

Sandra hugged Mel. "I know, honey."

"She is small like Rufina—well, not exactly like Rufina, but small. If it had been you, Sandra, he would have known you weren't Rufina," Erma said. "So whoever it was, he doesn't know Rufina's not living here. He, if it was a he, only knows this is Rufina's cottage."

"Just about everyone who lives and/or works on the ranch would know this is her cottage," Sandra said. "Actually, I'd be surprised if everyone hasn't already figured out she's not living here now. We've been coming and going every day."

"I'm going to check all the locks on the windows and doors." Erma held the thirty-eight down by her side. "And put the gun back."

When they were alone, Sandra cupped Mel's cheeks. "Is there anything else you want to tell me? Did anything happen you don't want to talk about in front of Grandma, something more than being followed?"

"No, Mom." Mel studied Sandra's face. "What? Oh no, Mom. No. I get what you mean, but no, nothing else. I'm okay."

Relieved, Sandra hugged Mel again.

"I'm sorry, really. I should have had Diego take me to BJ's."

"You need to understand when I give instructions, I'm looking out for your safety, not trying to make life difficult."

"I—I really do know that." Her lip trembled. "I'm going to take a shower and put on my pajamas. I want to wash off the feeling of someone's eyes on my neck."

A lump formed in Sandra's throat. "If you need me, I'm right here." When Mel left the room, Sandra trod back into the kitchen and dumped out her wine. She wanted to be ready if something else happened. Shivers ran circles on her body, and she took great gulps of air. She could have lost Mel.

CHAPTER THIRTY-ONE

L ATE THE NEXT morning, during the recess, Sandra exited a stall in the ladies' room and found Erma waiting for
her. "Hey, what did the sheriff say?" Sandra turned on the faucet to wash her hands.

"He asked me if I saw anyone when I ran outside." Erma
leaned against the wall. "Then he asked me if Mel could describe
whoever followed her. Did she smell him? Was there any noise
when he walked, like his gait was off? How tall was he?"

Sandra checked in the mirror to make sure her blouse was
smoothed down before she buttoned her jacket. "We didn't
ask her any of those things. I don't think we'd make very good
cops." She brushed at her hair with her fingers.

"With all the cross-exams we've conducted, you'd think
we'd have gotten more information out of her." Erma started
pulling up her long skirt before she closed the stall door behind herself.

"There wasn't all that much to get. I'll wait for you outside."
Sandra had known it would be useless to go to the sheriff, but
Erma had insisted. Earlier, she'd described him and his testimo-
ny to Sandra, so Sandra wasn't really surprised Erma wanted to

see the man again. She could use the excuse of the incident with Mel if she wanted to, but Erma wasn't fooling anybody.

Rufina stood across the hall, her long braid trailing down one shoulder, the scarred side of her face toward the window. The side toward Sandra showed smile-wrinkles around her eyes, a rounded cheek, knobby nose, and pert lips, or what passed for lips.

Judging from an eight-by-ten photograph BJ had shown Sandra of the two of them with their arms around each other when they were teenagers, Rufina had been quite attractive in her youth. A twinge of sadness struck Sandra. "What're you thinking about?"

Rufina sighed. "How much I love spring."

"I bet it's beautiful up here once the flowers and trees start to bloom," Sandra said. "You ready to go back in? Our time's almost up."

Sandra stood aside and let Rufina go up the stairs. They always used the downstairs restroom, far away from the jurors and clerks. "I'll be right behind you as soon as I have another word with Erma."

Erma came out of the restroom. "How'd the direct on Doug go? Holt score any points with the jury?"

Sandra beckoned for Erma to precede her up the stairs as well. "He basically testified to the same thing he told Mel and me when we had lunch with him. The jury didn't like it that he found the gun on the path to Rufina's cottage. You should have seen their faces."

"Hmm. No surprise there. Have you done your cross?"

"Nope. Fixing to now."

"Not much to ask him." Erma was breathing hard. She held on to the railing.

"I have a few things up my sleeve." Sandra stopped. "Mom, you going to make it?" Erma looked grayer than she had at the beginning of the trial. The stress was wearing on her—both of them had been sleeping restlessly every night, especially the night before.

"Don't hassle me. I'm just a little tired." She halted for a moment on the landing. "I don't suppose you were able to talk to Doug before testimony began this morning. I wish I could have been there." She continued trudging upward. "But the trip to the sheriff had to be done." A weak smile crossed her lips.

"I spotted Doug before the judge called the court to order, but he was practically pinned down by one of Holt's assistants."

"Damn." Erma swung the courtroom door open.

Rufina sat at the end of the counsel table, her folded hands resting on the legal pad. Doug Christian was at the prosecutor's table with Holt. The slow burn that was with Sandra every day of the trial, sizzled. Witnesses should not be sitting at the table of either attorney.

Sandra stepped over to Holt's table. "Mr. Christian, you may retake the witness stand for my cross-examination."

Doug Christian stood.

Holt rose to his full height and faced-off with Sandra. "You don't tell him what to do."

"You are so wrong to do this, Holt. I can't believe you get away with this behavior with the local attorneys. Mr. Christian, please step out from behind the counsel table before the jury comes back."

"Yes, ma'am." He shrugged one shoulder and walked to the witness stand, not stepping up and sitting down.

"Thank you." In Holt's direction, Sandra mouthed *You're a jerk.* She dropped into her chair a moment before the judge entered.

The bailiff brought in the jury.

Erma sat to Sandra's right, the trial notebook open to the section with Doug Christian's name on it. "Do you need anything out of here?"

"Nope."

"What is this 'nope' stuff?"

"I'm in a mood."

The judge said, "Mrs. Salinsky, are you ready with your cross-examination?"

Sandra stood. "Yes, Your Honor."

Doug Christian sat in the witness box and turned slightly toward Sandra.

Holt clicked his ballpoint pen two times and whispered something to the assistant beside him.

"Mr. Christian, we've met, correct?"

"Yes, ma'am. Back in Galveston County."

"And obviously I was present this morning when you testified on direct examination."

"Yes, ma'am." His red hair shone in the fluorescent light. Wearing a long-sleeved red and blue plaid shirt and slacks, Doug could have been from anywhere, of any background. He presented well as a witness.

"I have a question about the gun, Mr. Christian. You testified you found the gun on the path leading to Mrs. Barboza's cottage, correct?"

"Yes, ma'am. Lying there bigger'n—"

"So what did you do with the gun after you found it? Did you immediately turn it over to the deputy when he came in?"

Christian shifted in his chair. "No, ma'am."

"Why not? Where was the gun when the deputy arrived?"

"In my jacket pocket."

"Your jacket pocket. So you were wearing a winter jacket? The weather was still quite cool, correct?"

Holt got up. "Judge, she's not letting him answer the questions."

"Mrs. Salinsky..." The judge raised his eyebrows.

"Sorry, Your Honor. Mr. Christian, can you answer my last question?"

"Yes. I wore a winter jacket because it was cold outside."

"You previously testified you and Katy Jo had been at Rufina's cottage, that Katy Jo hadn't returned from the house, and you went to find out where she was. You put your jacket on when you left Rufina's cottage?"

"Yes, I did."

"Okay, so you didn't give the gun to the deputy, correct?"

"Right. Everyone was so upset, crying and all. I forgot the gun was in my pocket."

"You forgot that big gun was in your pocket?" Sandra's eyes cut away to the jury. The majority of them looked spellbound.

"Yes, ma'am, but I remembered later."

"Later being when?"

"When the sheriff came—well before the sheriff came, really—I put my hands in my pockets and realized the gun was in one of them, so I laid it on the kitchen counter."

For several seconds, Sandra held her hands in front of her mouth in an attitude of prayer. She wanted the jury to have a few minutes to think about the business with the gun. "Let's move on. Other than what you've revealed, did you testify to anything different this morning from what you told me at our meeting in Galveston County?"

Holt stared down at his legal pad, his pen poised in his hand. "No, ma'am."

"Are you positive, Mr. Christian?" His forehead wrinkled, his brows drawing together. "I'm pretty sure."

"Pretty sure but not one hundred percent sure?"

"Well—"

"So you're not certain?"

Holt jumped up. "Objection. She needs to let him answer the question, Judge."

Sandra held her arms out, palms up, like What-is-this-Judge?

"Overruled. This is cross, Mr. Holt."

"I'm not trying to confuse you, Mr. Christian. Really, I'm not. I want to be sure the story you told this morning was the same story you told me when we met in League City."

"Objection!" Holt jumped up again. "That was not a story, Judge. It was his sworn testimony."

"All right, then," Sandra said before the judge could rule. "Your testimony here today was the exact same statement you gave me earlier this year. Is that what you want the jury to believe?"

"Judge!" Holt got halfway up again.

"Approach the bench, counselors." Judge Danforth turned his head away from the jury and grimaced.

Sandra fisted her hands. "Yes, Your Honor."

"What is your objection, Mr. Holt?" The judge's breath smelled minty.

"She's making it sound like my witness isn't telling the truth." He cut his eyes at her. The ballpoint in his hand clicked several times.

"*His* witness, Your Honor? Anyway, I'm not sure what exactly Mr. Holt is objecting to, are you?"

"I don't like the way you're phrasing your questions." Holt clicked his pen like nobody's business.

"Your Honor, is Mr. Holt allowed to tell me how to examine a witness? How to try my case?"

"She knows what I mean, Judge."

The judge focused on Holt. "Just what is your objection, Mr. Holt? I haven't yet heard a proper objection from you."

Holt's cheeks blew up like they were filled with bubble gum. "My objection...badgering the witness!" His eyes flared. The pen clicked on.

The judge turned his attention to Sandra, eyes round, a twitch at the side of his mouth. "Don't badger the witness, Mrs. Salinsky. Now both of you go back to your tables and behave yourselves."

Sandra did an about-face. She gave Erma and Rufina a half-smile.

"For the record," the judge said, "the objection to badgering the witness is sustained."

"So, Mr. Christian, your position is that you have testified here today to the exact same thing you stated to me when I interviewed you, correct?"

Holt's chair scraped across the floor. Sandra shook her head. He was really going to hate what was coming up.

Christian nodded. "Yes."

"You've testified that you and the decedent were staying in my client's cottage."

"Yes, ma'am."

"You and she often stayed together at Mrs. Barboza's cottage, because Mrs. Schindler didn't approve of premarital sex?"

"Yes, ma'am. Mrs. S is old-fashioned, so Katy Jo had persuaded Rufina—Mrs. Barboza—a long time ago to let us meet there when I was in town." His face had become blotched and red.

"Behind Mrs. Schindler's back."

He licked his lips. "We planned to be married. We just didn't want to wait until we got married. You know…"

"But you weren't married, and you were sleeping with the decedent behind her mother's back."

Standing up, Mr. Holt said, "Asked and answered."

"Sustained." The judge arched an eyebrow at Sandra.

"So sometime in the past, Katy Jo had somehow persuaded Rufina Barboza, Mrs. Schindler's best friend, to let y'all stay in the second bedroom at her cottage and keep it a secret from Mrs. Schindler."

"You have to understand. Mrs. Barboza was Mrs. Schindler's best friend, yes, but Rufina loved Katy Jo and would do anything for her."

"Thank you, Mr. Christian." Sandra let his testimony sink in while she turned to a blank page and wrote down his exact words, 'Rufina loved Katy Jo and would do anything for her.' She stole a glance at Holt who sat with crossed arms. She could almost hear his teeth gnashing.

"Mrs. Salinsky, are you through with your questioning?" The judge peered over his glasses.

"Not quite yet, Judge. Only a few more." She turned her attention back to Doug Christian. "And your testimony is, the night she was killed, Katy Jo went to tell her mother that y'all wanted to get engaged, to ask for her approval?"

"Yes, ma'am."

"That's the sum of your testimony under oath today, is that right?"

Holt stood up. "Your Honor—"

"Strike that," Sandra said to the court reporter. "So, Mr. Christian, is it your testimony today that you did not tell me there was a Latino male staying with my client at her cottage on the night of the murder?"

Holt, who had never sat back down, said again, "Objection."

The judge shook his head. "Now what, Mr. Holt?"

"Assuming facts..." Holt paused like he was rethinking the nature of his objection. He shot a look at Sandra and back at the judge and at the witness and back at the judge again. "Withdrawn." He sat down.

Doug Christian hovered over the microphone. "I don't understand your question." His voice bounced off the walls.

"You didn't tell me Rufina had a man staying with her that night?"

Holt stiffened in his chair. His pen clicking, getting on Sandra's last nerve, but she enjoyed knowing he was racking his brain to come up with a valid objection. The real question became whether he'd risk asking about the Latino male on redirect. It was a tricky situation for him that made Sandra feel good for giving him some of his own back. No matter how Doug responded, the idea would be permanently lodged in the jury's mind.

"I didn't tell you a man was staying with Mrs. Barboza at the same time Katy Jo and I were staying at Mrs. Barboza's?"

"Correct."

"No, ma'am. I didn't tell you that." He glanced at Holt and then at the jury.

"You're sure?"

Holt jumped up a third time. "Asked and answered, Judge. She's badgering him again."

Sandra made her eyes wide and innocent. "Just one more question, Judge, before I pass the witness back. Mr. Christian, did you know where Mrs. Schindler kept the keys to the gun cabinets?"

Doug wrapped his hands around the microphone. "Yes, ma'am. Almost everybody did."

"Pass the witness."

The judge looked at Holt. "Redirect?"

With a mouth formed into a grim line, Holt shook his head, his eyes cutting Sandra to ribbons.

CHAPTER THIRTY-TWO

"STATE CALLS ELGIN Burgess."

A shiver of surprise ran through Erma. Though Burgess was on Holt's witness list, she and Sandra had figured Holt would call Rex and rest the State's case that afternoon.

All through lunch, Sandra and she discussed whether they should put Rufina on the stand if the judge made them go forward right away. Rufina had watched and listened and hadn't said much. She'd said since they were the lawyers, she'd leave the decision about whether she'd testify to them. Rufina's trust made Erma feel like shit, but she'd taken on the case or rather, practically forced Sandra to take the case. Now Erma had to take responsibility for it.

Erma rested on her elbows. Her stomach stirred with consternation. "I can't figure out what the hell he thinks he's going to prove through Elgin. Just bolstering his case, maybe."

"I'd give you the section in the notebook about Elgin, but what do we have, mostly blank pages?"

"A brief history of his relationship with BJ." Erma snickered under her breath. "Or what BJ described as his trying to have a relationship with her."

The door to the hall opened and in walked Elgin. Instead of the plaid long-sleeved shirt, jeans, and dirty boots he usually wore, he was dressed in a cowboy suit. He wore a buff-colored jacket and matching pants, brown buttoned-up vest over a white shirt, leather belt, bolo tie, and Lucchese ostrich boots. He carried a tan Stetson. Inclining his head at Holt, he held out his hat in a kind of salute to the defense table.

Erma whispered, "His goddamned belt buckle is bigger than a cow pie."

"Looks like a rancher businessman—or someone going to a wedding," Sandra whispered back.

"Well, hell," Erma replied, "he is the former. Guess we're going to hear what's up with him now." She flashed her eyebrows up and down at Rufina, who shrugged.

After he was sworn in, he settled down on the witness stand, overflowing it with his large frame, like the sheriff had. Holt began the questioning by asking Elgin's name and address. He then launched into the night of the murder.

"You had dinner at the Schindler home on the night of Katy Jo Schindler's demise, correct?" Holt asked.

"Yes, sir. I often dine at Mrs. Schindler's home."

"Who all was there, Mr. Burgess?"

"Well, sir, Mrs. Schindler, of course, both her twin daughters, her boy Rex, and me."

"What about Doug Christian?"

Elgin shook his head. "Oh, yeah. I forgot, sir." He glanced at Erma and Sandra.

Holt held his chin in the air. "Let me ask you this. Was the defendant there at the dinner?"

Elgin stiffened, and his eyes cut over to Rufina. He moved closer to the microphone. "No, she was not—not at the dinner itself."

"You did see her that night?"

"Saw her in the kitchen. She was overseeing the two Mexican girls who were fixing the food, and she helped serve."

"Did she speak to you, or you, to her?"

"No, sir. I caught her looking my way a few times. I was facing the kitchen door."

Holt shot a look at Rufina. "You do know her, right?"

"Yep, I know her. She's Mrs. Schindler's maid."

Erma ducked her head in Sandra's direction. "Racist pig."

Holt said, "You mean her housekeeper."

"Yeah. Yeah. Her *señora*. That's what they call them in Mexico. Same thing, to me."

"She supervises the women who work for Mrs. Schindler and runs the house, doesn't she?"

"Well, yeah, yes. I guess that makes her the housekeeper."

"Moving on. What, if any, relationship do you or have you had with the defendant?"

"Nothing. No relationship. I never took a shine to her. She don't like me either, as far as I can tell. Never been friendly to me."

"No reason she should be, is there?"

"No, sir. She was my friend's employee, that's all."

"By friend, you mean Mrs. Schindler, right?"

Elgin cleared his throat. He turned to the jury, so his expression was partially concealed. Some of the jurors smiled at him. The son of a gun wanted to make sure they understood his implication. Erma started to whisper an expletive to Sandra again but decided against it in case the judge overheard. Her fingers itched to get ahold of him. She could hardly wait until her turn came to question him.

"Yeah. Yes," Elgin responded. "The Widow Schindler."

Erma clenched her fists. She didn't like Elgin and what he was implying. She knew if BJ were there, she wouldn't either. On cross-examination, Erma would have to explore that, so the jury would understand more clearly what was in Elgin's mind.

"Back to the night of the murder. You were at dinner with the Schindler family. I assume the ladies in the kitchen served the meal—then what happened?"

"I didn't see them after that. Well, the two younger Mexican women. The defendant stuck around for a while and then disappeared."

"What was the defendant's demeanor?" Holt shot another look at Rufina.

"I'd have to say she appeared angry. Hard to say with that face."

Erma drew a sharp breath. Sandra gripped Erma's arm. Rufina wore a poker face.

Holt's jaw was working. "Did she do anything to make you think she was angry?"

"Just the way she walked. Rigid. Her eyes unfriendly."

"Who do you think she was angry with?"

Erma stood. "Objection. Calls for speculation."

The judge, who had been almost reclining in his chair, bounced to an upright position. "Sustained."

Holt said, "Did she do or say anything to indicate who she was angry with?"

"Well, sir, it was the way she was acting. She looked at me like she could kill me."

"Objection—"

"Sustained," the judge spoke before Erma could complete her objection.

What was up with Elgin? Besides being a racist and a sexist, he sounded like he hated Rufina. But why?

"Let me ask you this," Holt said. "Without interpreting what her expressions looked like to you, did she do anything else you thought inappropriate?"

Elgin shifted around in the witness chair. "Well, I hate to say it, but she was making goo-goo eyes at Mrs. Schindler during the same time period as she gave me the look I already described."

Erma leaned over to Sandra and whispered, "You think he's heard the rumors BJ and Rufina were lovers?" Rufina looked as brittle as a slice of burned toast. The poor woman's demeanor had to be a response to Elgin's testimony.

Sandra said behind her hand, "There's some subtext in what he says and, hell, in this whole sorry situation. You'll have to find out more on cross."

Holt had paused and was looking in their direction, probably to give the goo-goo eye statement time to sink in. He could, however, hope the jury would watch her and Sandra and wonder why they were conversing. Erma elbowed Sandra and straightened up.

"'Goo-goo eyes'?" Holt said. "What do you mean by that?"

"Hell—I mean, heck, everybody knows Rufina—the defendant—worships the ground Mrs. Schindler walks on. I think she's jealous because Mrs. Schindler and I are courting."

Erma's whole body tensed. She wrote on her legal pad in huge letters. *WHAT THE HELL?* Her hands shook. If only BJ hadn't left town to find Rufina's boyfriend.

"Calm down," Sandra hissed.

Erma scribbled again, "Just figured out Holt's alternate theory of the case. He's implying Rufina intended to shoot BJ out of jealousy and shot Katy Jo instead." She pushed the pad in front of Sandra. Sandra glanced at it and pushed it back.

While writing the note, Erma had missed the next question.

Elgin said, "Yes, sir, I've been seeing Mrs. Schindler for months now, and Rufina, I mean the defendant, hasn't liked it one bit."

Holt leaned back in his chair and exhaled audibly. "She didn't stay long after the meal was served, and she didn't have dinner with the rest of y'all?"

"No, she did not."

"Sir, do you recall where everyone went after the dinner was over?"

"I think to bed. Rex walked me to my truck and said he was going to bed." Burgess stroked his chin. "Everyone else had scattered. BJ and the twins cleared the table and took the dirty dishes to the kitchen for the maids to clean the next day."

"Before you left, did you see anyone lingering around outside?"

"No, sir. Rex had went back inside as I started up my vehicle. No one else was around. Of course, it was dark, but the porch light was on."

Holt rose. "Pass the witness."

Erma stood. "Judge, do you think we could have a little break? I drank a lot of tea during lunch, if you know what I mean."

A couple of the jurors snickered.

"Take ten-minutes." Giving a vulture look at everyone in turn, the judge added, "And don't be late." He swept off the bench like a bird in flight.

The bailiff escorted the jury out of the courtroom.

"Rufina, you gotta go?" Erma snatched up her purse.

Rufina shook her head. She had wrapped herself up in her shawl. Erma suspected Rufina suffered from the chill of fear.

"Good, stay there. You, too, Mel. You can go anytime. Come on, Sandra, we've gotta talk." She grabbed Sandra's arm. As soon as they were in the hall, out of hearing range of the other court participants, Erma said, "So what the hell do you think Holt's doing?"

Sandra rested a hand on the wall above Erma's head. "I think he's laying out every conceivable theory of the case and going to let the jury choose the one they like the most."

"How in the hell are we supposed to defend against that?"

"The best we can. We'll refute every argument he puts forth. We have to be prepared since at final argument, he gets to open and close. We have to guess what his closing will be, but we're smart girls, Mom."

"I don't know what you're grinning about."

"I don't either. I feel like shit. The stress is getting to me. I'm worried about Mel. And my face is breaking out." She touched a red bump on her chin. "I'm too old to have pimples."

"Oh, for Christ's sake. At least you can get laid to relieve your stress. What's an old dame like me supposed to do?"

"Is the sheriff married?"

Erma shoved at Sandra's arm. She walked across to the water fountain and took a drink. "I don't have to go to the restroom. I needed a minute. Imagine that ass Elgin implying Rufina meant to kill BJ out of jealousy. What a crock."

Sandra said, "Go get him."

Erma shot Sandra a fake smile before returning to the court-room. She would do whatever she could to show what a jerk Elgin Burgess was. She swung open the door. Rufina sat stone-faced like a skinny Buddha. Elgin stood at attention next to the witness stand. No one else had returned. Erma scooted around the prosecution table to Elgin and peered up into his face. She didn't say anything, just looked up at him like a sergeant would do a soldier in a line up.

The door to the jury room creaked, so she went back to her table. She grinned at Rufina. "Hang in there, my friend."

After everyone was seated, Erma asked, "May I proceed, Your Honor?" When the judge nodded at her, she said, "Mr. Burgess, I'm Erma Townley, one of the defense lawyers for Rufina Barboza."

"I know who you are." He spoke in a monotone, looking like he was focusing on a spot on the wall in the back of the court-room. Holt had probably told him to do that.

"We've met, right?"

"Yes, we've met several times."

"On the night of the incident for which we are in court, you and Rex Schindler were drinking mezcal, weren't you?" Since the two of them had been drinking mezcal the night she'd had dinner with them, odds were they had been on the night of the murder.

His head jerked so hard he could have gotten a whiplash. He didn't answer.

"Some people think drinking mezcal prolongs one's sex life." Erma didn't watch the jury to gauge their response. She hated grandstanding lawyers. "Is that what you thought? That you were going to get lucky with BJ—Mrs. Schindler that night?"

"Objection," Holt yelped, leaping up. "She's testifying. She's not allowed to testify, Judge."

"Sustained," the judge said.

Erma gave Holt her best pitying expression. What a crybaby.

"Putting aside your thoughts about your sex life, Mr. Burgess, you never answered my first question. You were drinking mezcal the night of Katy Jo's murder, correct?"

Holt's pen clicked twice.

Burgess's eyes flickered in the direction of the judge. "Yes, but by suppertime, we'd moved on to wine."

"How much mezcal had you imbibed by supper?"

"A couple of shots." He still wouldn't look at her.

"A couple. So two? Two shots?"

"More or less."

"Well was it more? How many shots exactly?"

"Well...uh...four."

Erma squared her shoulders. "Ahhhh, was it four? You remember you had four shots of mezcal? And mezcal is in the tequila family, am I not correct?"

The ballpoint pen clicked. "She's asking more than one question, Judge." Holt rose partway to his feet.

"Sustained."

"Was it four or not, Mr. Burgess?"

"Yes, it was four shots, Mrs. Townley." He frowned.

"Four shots of Mezcal. And it's made from the agave plant, like tequila is, right?"

He nodded.

"Answer for the record, Mr. Burgess," Judge Danforth said.

"Yes, made from the agave plant like tequila." His face had grown granite hard.

"When you say shots, Mr. Burgess, do you mean like from shot glasses? Shot glasses like bartenders use? Or water glasses? Or those special little tinted glasses from Mexico?"

Holt's head rolled around on his neck, and he sprang to his feet again. "Judge—"

The judge grimaced. "Mrs. Townley, you know better than that. Stick to one question at a time."

"I was trying to save the court time, Your Honor." She turned her attention back on the witness. "Mr. Burgess, describe the kind of glass you and Rex Schindler were tossing shots out of." Not correct English, but the best she could do and most likely more to Burgess's understanding.

Burgess's eyes darted back and forth between Holt and the jury. He pursed his lips. "American bartender-type shot glasses."

Erma folded her hands in front of her. "All right. Y'all were drinking mezcal and then wine with dinner. What kind of wine?"

"What difference does it make?" Burgess's tone was sharp.

"I'll ask the questions, Mr. Burgess. If you're unaware of the type of wine, say so."

"It was red, okay?"

"What'd y'all have to eat with the red wine? Was it steak?" Erma saw out of the corner of her eye that Holt held his head in his hands. He stared down at his table like he was long-suffering.

"Yes, steak. You want me to tell you the precise cut?" He folded his arms across his chest.

Someone on the jury tittered. The judge's dark look wasn't wasted on Burgess, who squirmed.

Holt's pen clicked several times.

"So you and Rex Schindler, BJ Schindler's son, had been doing mezcal and then wine for a couple of hours that night?"

"Yes—well maybe an hour and a half."

"Were y'all in the living room? The den? The den is where the liquor is kept, am I not correct? Not the den with the guns, but a separate den, right?"

"Yes, you're correct. We were sitting around the other den."

"Where was BJ Schindler?"

"In and out. Same with the girls."

"When you say the girls, you mean the twins or the kitchen help?"

"The twins."

"Rufina was in the kitchen with the two young women who prepared dinner."

"I assume so."

"What about Doug Christian?"

Burgess's head jerked again. He raised an eyebrow. "I don't remember Doug Christian being there. Maybe he was."

Erma doodled on her legal pad. Sandra bumped Erma's leg under the table and shoved her legal pad under Erma's nose. *How come he doesn't remember Doug being there?* Erma nodded. "The twins—they were identical, right?"

"Yes."

"Could you tell them apart?"

"Nope—no. Not many people could, as I understand it, except their mother."

"Not even Rex?"

"I don't think so. Not always. He told me when they were young, the girls would play tricks on him. He wasn't always sure which one to tell on."

Several scenarios were playing out in Erma's mind. She wasn't quite ready to put it all together, wasn't quite sure where Elgin Burgess fit into the picture, but she was quite sure he was involved with the killing somehow, along with Rex. She couldn't prove it, of course. But that wasn't her job. Her job was to create reasonable doubt.

"Mrs. Townley," the judge said in an ear-splitting voice. "Are you through with your examination?"

She'd let her mind wander a bit too long. "Sorry, Judge." She made a few quick notes before her thoughts became too jumbled and confused and the ideas that had come to her disappeared. "Now, Mr. Burgess, would you describe the Schindler twins to the jury, please?"

Holt jumped up, his pen clicking continuously. "I don't think that's necessary, Your Honor. The surviving twin is on my witness list—"

"Are you going to call her?" Erma also got to her feet.

Holt looked from the judge to Erma to the judge again. "Strike that objection."

"You may answer," the judge said to Burgess.

"Blond, blue-eyed."

"Petite?" Erma asked.

"I guess you could say that."

Erma wanted to walk up to the witness stand and slap the shit out of him. Not that she wasn't used to witnesses on cross being difficult, but she didn't like Elgin anyway, and his attitude made everything more annoying. "Do you say that? That they are—were—petite?"

"Yes, if you mean small, short and small-boned, yes."

"Like Rufina?"

Someone gasped, and it didn't come from the defense table.

"Mrs. Barboza is almost black, so no, they weren't like her."

"For the record, Mr. Burgess, my client is very small, isn't she, in spite of being 'almost black' as you say?"

"Yes she is." He picked a tissue from the cube in front of him and dabbed his forehead with it.

Sandra snorted. "That's one for argument."

Erma noted his words. "All right. Let's go back to your direct testimony."

Elgin straightened, his eyes searching the courtroom as if for an escape hatch.

"How long would you say you and Mrs. Schindler have been courting?" Erma had to struggle to keep a normal tone of voice.

"Oh, heck, 'bout a year or more I would say."

"So for a year or more, you've been going over to the Schindler home to see Mrs. Schindler?"

"Every chance I got." His mouth formed a smug smile.

"How often would that be?"

"Once or twice a week, at least."

"She would invite you over?"

"Rex would ask me for drinks if he was home from San Antonio."

"Would Mrs. Schindler invite you the rest of the time?"

"Well, ma'am, sometimes I would just happen to be there, like for business or something."

That caught Erma's attention. Business? What business did they have in common? And what was the something? She wasn't about to ask. "When you were there for 'business or something,' she would ask you to stay for dinner?"

He nodded. "Right."

"For a year or more."

"That's what I said."

"That's a lot of steak dinners."

Some of the jurors laughed.

Holt sprang up. "Objection!"

Erma ignored Holt, as did the judge. "In the last year or more, how many times did you take Mrs. Schindler out for a steak dinner, or for that matter, any kind of dinner, or to any event?"

Elgin shifted in the chair. "We never went out. She never would go out with me." He turned to the jury. "Always had an excuse."

"In the last year or more, you've never slept with the Widow Schindler, have you?"

"Judge!" Holt almost knocked over his chair as he scrambled to his feet.

The judge had perked up during Erma's cross. From the expression on his face, almost a smile, he looked like he was enjoying himself. "What, Mr. Holt?"

Holt stood for a moment, his pen now tapping on the table, his eyes averted. "Nothing." He sat back down.

"You may answer, Mr. Burgess," the judge said, still leaning toward him. "Do you want the question repeated?"

Erma almost laughed out loud. The judge was toying with Elgin. Everyone in the courtroom knew what the question was.

"No." Burgess shook his head at Erma. "No to repeating the question, and no, I haven't ever slept with Mrs. Schindler."

"Have the two of you necked or whatever the kids call it today? Made out?"

He shook his head. "No." He glowered, his lips stretching across his teeth.

"Have you ever even kissed?" Erma raised her eyebrows in an expression she hoped showed doubt.

"I kissed her, yes." He rolled his shoulders back and turned toward the jury.

"Did she kiss you back?"

His slump was noticeable. "To be perfectly honest, no."

Erma loved it when witnesses said *to be perfectly honest,* like they haven't been honest before. She took a moment so it would appear she was reviewing her notes before eyeballing the jury. Everyone must be getting tired, but the judge didn't seem inclined to take another break. She mouthed at Sandra and Rufina, "Any questions?" They shook their heads. She had one more line of questioning, only a question or two, and she'd be finished.

"Why do you think that is, Mr. Burgess? Why do you think Mrs. Schindler didn't respond to your advances?" Erma knew the answer. Because he was an asshole. But she'd like to hear his version.

Elgin tilted his head to one side and shook it. "I don't know, to tell you the truth. We've known each other for years. I was friends with her late husband. I thought I was making progress with her."

There it was again. *To be perfectly honest. To tell you the truth.* But now was not the time to hassle him over it. "You implied that my client, Rufina Barboza, feels the same way about BJ Schindler as you do, correct?"

He sat silent.

"Are you trying to tell this jury BJ Schindler must have reciprocated the feelings you say Rufina Barboza has for her? That otherwise she would have welcomed your advances?"

He shrugged. "Well, I don't know. Maybe."

"In other words, you're saying you think Rufina Barboza and BJ Schindler were lesbian lovers, correct?"

Holt breathed out like a deflating balloon. He rolled back in his chair, hitting the bar behind him. Erma ignored him, her eyes on Elgin Burgess. The ruddiness had drained from Elgin's face.

"I didn't say that," he said, his voice hoarse.

"You implied it. You implied it when you said Rufina made 'goo-goo' eyes at BJ, and if BJ didn't reciprocate your feelings, it must have been because she had feelings for Rufina. Isn't that what you meant to imply?"

His lips twitched, but he didn't answer. Erma let the silence linger. To her right, Sandra bore down on a legal pad, writing fast and furiously.

When the silence had gone on long enough, Erma asked, "Who told you BJ Schindler and Rufina Barboza were lovers?"

Burgess had crossed his arms. He clamped his lips shut. His cheeks puffed out, his face almost white except for his red, veiny nose.

After a minute that felt like an hour, Erma asked, "Judge, would you be so kind as to instruct the witness to answer?"

The judge rolled his chair to the bar separating the bench from the witness chair. "Mr. Burgess—"

"Rex," Burgess said, his voice faint. Then louder, "Rex Schindler."

CHAPTER THIRTY-THREE

AT JARED'S OFFICE after the judge recessed the trial for the evening, Erma said, "I always thought that son of a bitch, Rex, was somehow the root cause of all this mess." She sat at the conference table, a short bourbon in front of her.

"Yeah. Me, too." With her shoes off, Sandra was massaging her toes through her tights. Her feet would be a lot better off if she'd ignore the current fashion in ladies' shoes. "He's been nothing but trouble."

"If BJ had known how much trouble he would be, I wonder whether she would have considered an abortion." Erma took a gulp from her glass and wiped her chin where some bourbon had missed her mouth.

Sandra straightened up. Her mother could be harsh. "Speaking of BJ, I just remembered. I received a text from her. Want to hear what she says?"

"When'd you get that?"

"During your cross. I forgot about it." Sandra read from her phone, "'Can't call, lousy cell service. Found Efrain. Heading back now.'"

"Does she say when she'll return?"

"No, but she says, '14 hours to border from San Miguel. Then have to drive there.'"

"Shit. She say where she was texting from?" Erma hung over the table.

Sandra shook her head. "No, that's it."

"We're running out of time. Holt's gonna run out of witnesses. He's got to rest his case soon."

"I can probably drag out Rex's testimony for at least a full day. Can't think who else Holt will call, in spite of all those names on his witness list." Sandra sipped from a glass of white wine.

Jared stuck his head in the room. His tie was askew, the collar of his pale blue shirt unbuttoned. "You ladies up for some dinner in a little while?" His eyes roved over Sandra's body, meeting her eyes with a smile full of promise and a cocked eyebrow.

Sandra pushed thoughts of a possible liaison from her mind. "What did I tell you, Jared?" She made a pretend mean face, knowing he understood she meant his once-over.

Erma coughed. "I wouldn't object to something meaty, like duck or quail or a big piece of—"

"Not beef," Sandra said. "I don't want to think of anyone eating beef for a long time."

"What's that about?" Jared stepped inside the room and rested a hand on the back of a chair.

"Elgin Burgess mooching steaks off BJ." Erma shook her head. "Freeloader."

Jared looked from one woman to the other. "Wish I had time to sit in on the testimony. I'm missing all the fun."

"If you only knew," Sandra said. "I'll tell you about it sometime."

"In the future?" His face lit up with a huge, telling smile.

She didn't respond and avoided his eyes.

Erma shook her head. "Okay, you two, we have more talking to do about what tomorrow might bring, and I really do want to eat."

"You always want to eat," Sandra said.

"I'll be back for y'all in about thirty-minutes," Jared said. "There are some things waiting for me on my desk anyway." He closed the door as he left.

"Wish I could have what I'm assuming you're going to have." Erma chuckled and took another slug of bourbon.

"Ha. Ha." Her mother knew her better than she'd like. Sandra poised a finger over her phone. "Should we text something back? Ask her when she thinks she'll arrive?"

"Yeah, do that. I'm going to walk a cramp out of my foot."

"You're going to ask Laura to give you a refill, and right now I don't care."

Erma rubbed the arch of her foot as if to show Sandra there really was a cramp and then went to find Laura.

Sandra texted BJ and reclined in her chair, studying the top shelf of law books. Some of them were antique, old with gold lettering. She closed her eyes, enjoying the momentary peace. She'd had little quiet in the past days and weeks and months since they'd taken Rufina's case.

Though the trial wasn't far from her mind, thoughts of Jared dominated. She was tempted to accept his offer—his implied offer. She could use a night with him. He'd proved to be a more than considerate lover. Anticipating his touch, the warmth of his caresses on her body, she shivered. Did she dare spend the night with him when Mel was with them? What would her daughter think? At fifteen, Mel understood what went on between women and men. Would she think less of her if she knew her mother was having sex outside of marriage?

"What're you doing?" Erma asked. "You're not sleeping, are you?"

"I wasn't asleep. Just enjoying the feeling of the inside of my eyelids on my eyeballs."

"Sometimes you're weird, Sandra." Erma clapped her refilled glass down on the conference table. "I think we should take Jared up on dinner. I called Rufina. The girl who picked Mel and her up has gotten them safely back to her cottage. She's going to stay with them until after dinner. After we eat, I can take the car back to the ranch." She stood beside the chair she had previously been sitting in, rising up on her toes and lowering herself, then repeating.

"What are you doing?"

"Trying to rid my foot of that cramp. So, you can go with Jared, get laid, and he can bring you home. I'll tell Mel y'all went out for an after-dinner delight."

"Erma!"

"I meant to say after dinner drinks." She swallowed from her bourbon.

"Drink more water and less booze. You think it would be terrible of me not to see my daughter until tomorrow at breakfast?"

"If I thought it was terrible, I wouldn't be suggesting it."

Sandra covered her mouth with her hands. Putting thoughts of Mel aside, she wanted to be with Jared, but she didn't want to lead him on. Their relationship had no future, not with her in Galveston and him in Fredericksburg. She'd never leave the Galveston area while Erma was alive, even after Mel went off to college. Those two were her only family.

Jared's family was in Fredericksburg, and his real estate work didn't take him out of town, as far as she could tell. Even if she wanted things to develop between them, long distance relationships rarely lasted. Still, she'd like to spend some time with him. They hadn't been together in a while, though it seemed like forever.

Sandra's phone emitted two musical notes, a signal she'd received a text. "Gotta be from BJ."

Erma perked up. "What's she say?"

"'Hope to arrive with Efrain the day after tomorrow late.'"

"That's good news."

Sandra said, "It's only good news if I can keep Rex talking for a day or a day and a half or however long it'll be until she gets here. I'm going to tell her to hurry." She texted back.

"There's Kathy Lynn, too, don't forget."

"Holt's not going to call her. You can count on it. I don't know what's behind his hesitancy, but I feel certain she won't be testifying." Sandra sat up. "He probably had as hard a time pinning her down as we did."

Erma rubbed her lips. "We still have Rufina. We can start with Rufina instead of taking her last, and when BJ and Efrain show up, we can put them on."

"If we decide to call Rufina, that's the only way we can proceed. The thing is, Judge Danforth said we only have until the end of this week. We're running out of time."

"He's full of shit. His assignment may have given him a set number of days, but he can't rush us. He can't make us do anything. This is a murder trial, and anything he does like that will be reversible error."

Sandra nodded throughout Erma's statement. What she said was true, but pushy judges sometimes influenced jurors. She hoped it wouldn't come to that. She didn't want the jury to think the judge had an opinion on the case—that he favored the prosecution, for instance.

CHAPTER THIRTY-FOUR

THE NEXT MORNING, they took Mel with them so she could watch Rex's testimony. They arrived back in the courtroom to find Holt and a young lawyer huddled near the empty jury box. Holt nodded at them. The defense team took their usual places, with Sandra in the lead counsel chair.

When the judge came in, Holt and his associate scurried to their table. The associate remained standing next to Holt, a cell phone in her hand. She looked ready to run. While the jury filed in, Sandra let her mind wander. The evening with Jared had been great, just what she'd needed, even if it was in the middle of a trial. The more time she spent with him, the more she thought she'd like to try to make a long-distance relationship work.

Erma interrupted her reverie. "Hey, something's up."

"Call your next witness, Mr. Holt."

"Roy Schindler the Third, also known as Rex Schindler."

Erma watched the door. Sandra watched Holt. He didn't indicate by his body language he was expecting anyone to enter, not looking in the direction of the door. A minute passed. Another two minutes. Three, a long time to wait for a witness.

The judge's quiet tapping of a pen on his desk pad sounded like a loud thumping.

"Mr. Holt?"

"Yes, Your Honor?"

"Where is your witness?"

Holt shook his head. "I don't know, sir. He said he'd be here early, at eight-thirty, but no one has seen him."

"Approach the bench." When all four attorneys were within spitting distance, the judge whispered, "I trust you've phoned his home number?"

"All he has is a cell phone. We've called it continuously for the last hour."

The judge looked at Sandra. Sandra looked at Erma. "Was he at BJ's last night?"

Erma shook her head. "No sign of him. Just us girls."

The judge asked Holt, "When's the last time you saw him?"

"Last evening."

The judge lifted his head. "Deputy Cortez, accompany the jurors back to the jury room." He flicked his fingers at the attorneys. "Y'all go back to your tables."

After the jurors left, the judge said, "You have another witness you can call, Mr. Holt?"

Holt licked his lips. He said something to his associate. He tossed a pen from hand to hand and chewed on the inside of his cheek.

"Mr. Holt, I asked you a question." The judge's face was like a dark cloud.

Holt asked, "May we have a short recess, Judge?"

"Thirty-minutes. If you don't have a witness here to testify in thirty-minutes, you'll have to rest your case. I warned both of you at pretrial that I will not wait on witnesses." The judge's chair banged against the back wall when he vacated it.

Holt's face reflected the fear in Sandra's gut—an airy adrenaline rush, alarm sweeping over her like a wave.

"Holy shit." Erma's eyes had grown as round as fifty-cent pieces. "What are we going to do?"

Sandra's hands shook. Holt conferred in harsh tones with his associate, who had misery written all over her face. Erma grabbed Sandra's elbow.

"I heard you." Sandra jerked away. "We have less than thirty-minutes to decide if Rufina will testify or not."

"Regardless," Erma hissed, "BJ and Efrain will never make it here in time."

"Let's get out of here." Sandra took her purse and pushed through the swinging door that separated them from the gallery. She beckoned at Rufina and Mel. "You, too."

"What the hell could be up with Rex?" Erma asked as the four of them traipsed to the end of the hall, out of anyone's earshot.

"No clue," Sandra said. "If he doesn't show up, he'd better be dead, because if he's not, Holt's going to kill him." If Rex failed to appear, Holt would rest his case, making it show time for the defense. Sandra's heart thumped. Nut-cutting time.

Rufina leaned against the windowsill with her arms around herself, dark brown eyes darting back and forth between the lawyers. Mel had the same stance, except she stared toward the floor. Erma muttered under her breath.

Sandra stood with hands on her hips, like she was about to lecture a class. "This is how I see it. Our case consists of Rufina," she nodded as she gave Rufina a hint of a smile, "BJ, Efrain, and possibly Kathy Lynn, if we could find her to testify."

"Kathy Lynn has made herself as scarce as Rex has today," Erma said.

"Just about," Sandra said. "BJ and Efrain are on their way from Mexico. I have no idea if she can get him past the border. I don't even know what mode of transportation she took down there." If BJ didn't hide Efrain in her vehicle, how would he come over? Did BJ have access to whatever legal documents he needed? She hadn't told them how she would go about getting him across, just that she would. If Border Patrol caught her smuggling him, she'd be in real trouble.

"She took that giant car," Mel said. "The one with the ginormous trunk." Her eyes went from her mother to her grandmother. "What? One of the maids told me."

"The Chrysler 300." Rufina ran her hands up and down her skirt. "It's Billie J's favorite car."

"How come I haven't seen it?" Erma's eyebrows drew together.

"Doesn't matter," Sandra said. "Let's focus on the trial."

"She doesn't drive it much since Roy died," Rufina said. "She keeps it closed up in the garage."

Sandra's fingers tingled. She kept flexing them. She needed to shake off her nervousness. "I hope it's not so fancy that Border Patrol will want to check it out, but that's not my immediate problem." She eyed each one of them and frowned. If she lost Rufina's case, she would be letting them down, but Rufina most of all, of course.

"Unless we put you on the witness stand, Rufina, and drag out your testimony, and unless Holt crosses you until the cows come home, there still isn't enough time for them to make the drive." Sandra began pacing.

Erma frowned at Rufina. "We all thought she'd have more time."

"If they're fourteen hours away in San Miguel, they could make it to the border in one day," Rufina said.

"They probably would spend the night somewhere," Sandra said. "She didn't know—we didn't know—we'd need him so soon. Figuring one day to the border and across it, and a second day to drive up to Fredericksburg...we can't count on them making it."

"So what alternatives are there?" Erma had been picking at her cuticles, a bad habit Sandra hadn't seen her engage in for a long time.

"If Rex doesn't show in the next few minutes and Holt comes in and rests the State's case, we'll have to call a witness or rest our case." Sandra waited for a reaction from Rufina.

"I know how it works, Sandra." Rufina's voice was barely audible. Her hands went to her mouth.

"I know you do. I'm thinking out loud, that's all." She patted Rufina's arm.

Rufina's lips were pressed together so tightly they turned pale pink.

"There's still Kathy Lynn," Erma said.

"The mysterious Kathy Lynn who has acted like she's afraid of us," Sandra said.

"I could testify," Rufina said. "I want to."

Thunder rumbled in the distance.

"If we put you on and your testimony doesn't last long enough for BJ and Efrain to arrive, we'll have to rest—unless Kathy Lynn makes a surprise appearance."

Erma said, "But if we call Rufina to the stand, we'll open the door to Holt putting on rebuttal witnesses. Rex might show up by that time. God only knows what that little bastard would say."

"Of course the judge is supposed to restrict rebuttal to evidence that rebuts our case," Sandra said.

"Like that would happen." Erma began pacing, too. "I don't think the judge thinks the rules apply to him—or Samuel Holt. He might let Holt ask Rex anything he wants."

Sandra's esophagus burned with a repeat of breakfast. She had hardly tasted the food the first time and didn't want to taste it a second.

"But," Sandra said, "if Rex's testimony takes long enough, BJ and Efrain might show up by the time we reach re-rebuttal. And Kathy Lynn could still come. Speaking of which, Mel, I'll give you her cell number, and you can call her. She won't recognize it. Maybe she'll pick up."

"Yeah, okay." Mel grinned like she was happy to have a role to play.

Erma stopped in front of Sandra. "One, would BJ and Efrain's testimony be enough to overcome whatever damage Rex's testimony does? Two, what do we do if the judge restricts our re-rebuttal even if he doesn't restrict Holt's rebuttal?"

"Appeal."

"Appeal?" The pitch of Rufina's voice was as high as the ceiling.

Sandra clasped Rufina's arm again. "I hope it won't come to that. Anyway, this is only one scenario. We have to weigh all the possibilities. If you testify, Rufina, and the jury doesn't like you for some reason, we'll have a real problem."

Mel put her arm around Rufina. "Why wouldn't they like her? She's so nice."

Rufina smiled up at her. "You're so sweet, *mi amiguita*."

Sandra stood at the window, the scene outside benign. A small town with blooming trees and flowers. Fluffy clouds overhead turned voluminous and dark in the distance. Inside, a hostile environment. An impatient judge. A testy prosecutor. A jury with who-knows-what on their minds. The question for her, the defense attorney, boiled down to whether or not she should put Rufina on the witness stand, something she'd been debating almost from the time she took the case. Although it was true all she needed was one juror to hang up the jury, could she risk all twelve of them not liking Rufina or not believing her testimony?

Holt was itching to cross-examine Rufina. Sandra had been a prosecutor long enough to know what was going through his mind. If she were him, she'd be dying for Rufina to take the stand, too. In spite of Rufina's years of working in the District Clerk's Office, being around trials and seeing what attorneys did to witnesses, Rufina would never hold up. She was too sweet, too passive. Holt would make mincemeat out of her. Could they risk his twisting her words around until she was so confused she'd be tricked into agreeing with some premise Holt put out there and realize too late what she'd said?

"So it comes down to: do we think Holt has put on enough evidence to convict Rufina?" Sandra folded her hands like she was going to pray and held them in front of her mouth.

"No," Rufina said. "It's whether the jury thinks there's enough evidence to convict me."

Back in their chairs, except for Mel who had gone to call Kathy Lynn, again, they all stood when the judge entered. The jurors filed in, as quiet as actors in a slow-motion silent film. Thunder from the north grew louder, nearer. Once the jurors were seated, the judge said, "Mr. Holt, call your next witness."

All eyes turned to the door to the courtroom. Holt shook his head and said, "State rests, Your Honor."

Sandra's stomach turned over. "Judge, defense has a motion to file with the court." Sandra pulled a prepared motion from the stack of papers on the defense table.

The judge held out his hand. Sandra gave the judge the original and a copy to Holt, before picking up a copy for herself.

"Bailiff, escort the jurors from the courtroom." The judge wore a deadpan face.

The jurors rose, some of them muttering. They filed out. The deputy closed the door, standing in front of it with his arms crossed.

"Motion for Directed Verdict of Acquittal," the judge read. "You may proceed, Miss Salinsky."

Sandra noticed the Miss before her name. She launched into her argument that the judge must grant her motion since no reasonable jury could reach a verdict of guilty. All nervousness had left her for the moment. Rarely did a judge grant such a motion, but every defense attorney had to file and argue one.

When she was through, Holt stood. "May I, Your Honor?"

"There's no need, Mr. Holt. The motion's overruled." He inclined his head at the bailiff and started to speak.

"Your Honor, the defense has another motion." Sandra felt a little weak-kneed as she picked up the next motion.

"What is it now?" Annoyance was written across his face.

"Motion for Continuance." Sandra handed the papers to the judge.

Holt stood so fast the wheels in his chair spun. "I object."

On her way back to the defense table, Sandra handed a copy to Holt. "Judge Danforth, if Mr. Holt's presentation of his case had been better organized, this wouldn't be necessary."

"I really object to that," Holt said.

The judge glanced at the motion. "What are your grounds for a continuance, counsel?"

"Judge, we were expecting the prosecutor to call more witnesses from his witness list. We thought his case would last at least another day."

"Your Honor," Holt said, "this is ridiculous. She must not have prepared very well if she has to use that tired old excuse. She should have been ready to proceed whenever the State finished its case."

The judge's eyes could have cut Holt to ribbons. "Once again, Mr. Holt, you're trying to usurp my role in this courtroom. I will do the lecturing and the chastising around here, not you."

Holt clenched his teeth and didn't say anything.

"Now, Miss Salinsky, how long are you asking for? I'm assigned for this week, and the week is coming to an end. Can you give me any good reason why I should grant your continuance?"

Was he really considering granting her motion? Sandra held out some hope. "Judge, we only need about a day and a half." That would take them through the rest of that day and one more day and give BJ and Efrain enough time to arrive by the following morning. Sandra held up her hand toward the judge as if to say, hear-me-out. "I know what you're going to say. That puts us into the weekend, but Your Honor, couldn't you call and ask the Administrative Judge to extend your assignment for another week? At least a part of next week?"

"I doubt he'd be inclined to grant that, Miss Salinsky." The judge hovered over the bench, over her motion, like a bird of prey.

"This is a murder case, Your Honor. I would think the Administrative Judge would allow more time for a case of this severity."

"Even if I was of a mind to make such a request, madam, what possible reason could you have to persuade me?"

"Unavailability of a witness." Sandra fisted her hands behind her back.

"You used that one already," the judge said, like she'd said the dog ate her homework.

"Two witnesses, actually. Mrs. Schindler isn't available." Sandra drew the deepest breath possible and dove right in. "She's gone to find our alibi witness."

Holt jumped up again. "That's b—" He stopped when the judge glared at him.

"They're two days away," the judge stated with flat affect.

"Yes, sir."

Thunder boomed so loudly Sandra flinched. Lightning flashed outside the windows, illuminating the courtroom.

The judge arched back in his chair. He tented his fingers. His eyes traveled to Holt and back to Erma, who sat near Rufina at the end of the table. After a moment, his eyes fixed on Sandra's. He pulled himself up to the bench again, sitting very stiff and straight. "Motion denied. Call your first witness."

Rain splashed against the windows. Sandra's heart constricted, and her head dropped to her chest. She had only seconds to make her decision. After a moment, she glanced to her right at Rufina and Erma. The door opened at the back of the courtroom. Mel entered. She shook her head. Sandra closed her eyes for a moment and turned back to the judge. "Defense rests."

CHAPTER THIRTY-FIVE

“MAY IT PLEASE the Court.” Holt nodded to the judge as he approached the podium. “Ladies and gentlemen of the jury, we've now come to the most important part of our case.”

Erma whispered to Sandra, “I wonder how much of his time Holt'll stand on his soapbox.”

“He'll probably split it twenty-forty.” Sandra held her pen ready to make notes. “I would.”

Holt gripped a copy of the charge. “This charge and all the physical evidence will be sent to the jury room with you, with the exception of the murder weapon. I know you will follow the judge's instructions and read the whole charge aloud, before your deliberations begin.”

Jittery, Sandra doodled on her legal pad, trying to remain still.

“I want to talk about burden of proof for a moment.” Holt launched into the language contained in the charge. “As I'm sure you know, the State of Texas, represented here today by me, your duly elected District Attorney of Gillespie County, always has the burden of proof in a criminal case. In criminal law, the burden of proof is always beyond a reasonable doubt. Because the burden of proof is so onerous—”

"Objection!" Sandra said at the same instant she jumped to her feet. "He's not allowed to characterize—"

"You'll have your turn, Mrs. Salinsky." The judge gave her a simpering smile. "Overruled."

Heat rushed to her face. So this was how it would be? Holt's argument would be out of bounds, and the judge would allow it, the final act in a trial where the judge clearly favored the State, where Rufina didn't stand a chance. Fists clenched at her sides, Sandra sat down, but stayed on the edge of her chair. The judge might favor the prosecution, but Sandra would object for the record and for the benefit of the jury every step of the way. She hoped the jurors would notice the way the judge was treating the defense.

Holt's monotone continued. Sandra knew her focus was wandering, but she couldn't help but think about the fact this could have been her last trial, ever. She'd made up her mind to continue to practice law with Erma but as yet hadn't told Erma or Mel. There would be time for that later. Holt's toneless voice was like a bee buzzing outside the window. Erma nudged Sandra. Sandra refocused her eyes on his back.

"So, what any good police officer, investigator, or prosecutor does, when evaluating whether a suspect is likely the perpetrator in a case, is look at means, motive, and opportunity. That's what my staff and I did in this defendant's case." Holt turned to the defense side of the room and pointed at Rufina. "This defendant had all those."

The side door to the courtroom squeaked open. A young woman Sandra recognized from pretrial as being an employee of the prosecutor's office entered and sat on the first bench, right behind the counsel table. Holt shot her a look, his brow furled. She made the ASL sign for talk.

Sandra leaned over to Erma. "Did you see that?"

Erma said, "Something's going on, important enough for her to risk his wrath by distracting him during closing."

Holt continued, not missing a beat. "One, the defendant had the means. She had access to the gun cabinet keys. Two, motive. The rancher's daughter burned down the defendant's house, causing the defendant's husband to die, and scarring the defendant for life. Third and last, opportunity. Who had more free access to the house, to movement about the house without raising suspicion, than the defendant, Rufina Barboza, the alleged best friend of—"

Sandra leaped up, intending to assert her objection as fast as she could. "Objection, Your Honor. Mischaracterization of the evidence by use of the word *alleged*. There's no question but that Rufina and BJ Schindler have been best friends since high school."

As soon as Sandra stood, the judge scrambled to an upright position. He'd been leaning so far back in his chair, his head almost touched the wall. He didn't have time to cut her off, to rule in the middle of her objection. "Sustained."

"Okay, then. Best friend of the rancher." Holt peered over his shoulder at Sandra as if to say, *satisfied?*

Sandra sat down and muttered to Erma, "At least that woke me and the judge up."

"Ladies and Gentlemen, since the State has the burden of proof, we have the choice of presenting our argument all at one time or dividing our time to do our closing in two parts, before and after the defense. I have chosen the latter. This concludes my remarks for now. I'll speak to you in a few minutes." Holt picked up the paper he'd carried to the podium and returned to the State's table.

Sandra approached the podium and drew a breath to steady herself. "May it please the Court." As she was about to begin, Holt interrupted.

"Your Honor, may we approach the bench?"

"What the—" Sandra spun toward the judge. Holt had loped to the bench. Erma followed Holt. Holt's associate brought up the rear.

"What is it?" The judge turned off his microphone.

Erma, being a head shorter than the others, strained to hear the conversation.

Holt said, "Rex Schindler's upended truck was found this morning on the shoulder of Highway 16, on the road to Kerrville."

"Whoa." Erma stepped back.

Sandra didn't know if that was in response to Holt's statement or his strong aftershave, which threatened to throw her to the ground.

"A woman spotted the truck and called the sheriff. She found Rex in the tall grass alongside the overgrown ditch."

"He's dead?" Sandra exchanged glances with the judge, who seemed more interested in the turn of events than he had in Holt's argument. His face livened up, eyes sparkling. His cheeks bloomed. He most likely wondered the same thing she did. What, if anything, did Rex's accident mean?

"I need an immediate recess," Holt said. "He's not dead, not yet. I need to go to the hospital and talk to him."

"I'd like to go, too, and hear his deathbed confession," Erma said.

Sandra stepped back on Erma's toes. Erma jerked her foot out from under Sandra's.

Neither of the men responded to Erma's statement, didn't even look her way.

"So you're asking for what, a continuance?" Sandra couldn't help sneering. The judge might give Holt a continuance even though he'd denied hers.

Holt shot her an if-looks-could-kill glance. "Judge, I don't know what to make of this, but I don't see how we can continue until Rex Schindler's condition is ascertained. If you would be so kind as to now call the Administrative Judge for a twenty-four-hour continuance, at least to start, that would give me time to find out if he's going to live and whether his truck flipping over had anything to do with this case."

"Well, we know Rufina Barboza had nothing to do with it anyway." Sandra crossed her arms. She sure as hell wasn't going to let him try to implicate Rufina.

"I don't know anything at this point," Holt said. "If his condition is not too bad, I'll file a motion to reopen, Judge, and put him on the stand."

Over her dead body, Sandra thought. But, on the other hand, BJ might show up by then with Efrain. What was good for the goose...

"Are you going to oppose such a motion?" The judge's eyes flickered from Sandra to Erma.

Sandra licked her lips, wishing she had more than a moment to think it over. "I don't want to have to try this case twice. I suppose I wouldn't object if he's not in real bad shape and can testify soon, but if this thing is going to drag out a couple of weeks, I think you'd have to declare a mistrial."

"Umph." The judge gritted his teeth, his jaw muscles flexing. He rolled back his chair. "Jurors, this is highly unusual, but we'll be in recess until tomorrow morning at nine. Do not discuss anything you've heard or seen today with anyone or each other. Please be prompt when you return."

☩   ☩   ☩

Erma headed to the ladies' room, saying she'd meet them at the car. The others walked downstairs. At the door to the courthouse, Mel said, "Rufina and I don't want to go to the hospital. The rain's stopped, so we're going to Main Street to the shops and for something to eat."

"Rufina, is that what you want to do? You don't want to go to the hospital?"

"I don't think it would look right." She held her purse in front of her, over her stomach, like a package she was taking to mail. "Do you?"

"If you wouldn't mind going with Mel, I'd appreciate it. Spring break is almost over, and she's going to return to Galveston even if we have to remain here through part of next week. Don't know when she'll ever get back up this way."

"Aww, Mom! I thought I could stay for the whole trial. I wanted you to write me a note, so I'd be excused from classes."

"You have a ticket to fly out of San Antonio on Saturday, so enjoy Fredericksburg while you can."

Mel threw her hands up. "A real assistant would be here through the whole trial."

"I like spending time with Mel, so Main Street *es bueno*. Rex wouldn't want me at the hospital anyway." Rufina held a hand in front of her mouth, as though she was afraid to speak her piece aloud, and said, "And I'm a little tired of Rex's *comportamiento estúpido*."

Sandra said, "That means—"

"I take Spanish." Mel held her chin in the air. "Come on, Rufina." She spun around, her little skirt flapping around her legs, and hooked her arm in Rufina's.

"We can call the ranch and ask someone to come pick us up when we're ready to go home." Rufina held on to Mel's arm. They could be two girlfriends up to no good.

"You have money?" Sandra called after them.

Mel glanced back, her eyes catlike. "Dad gave me a credit card."

Sandra pushed through the back door into the unseasonably warm day. She clicked her key fob to start her Volvo as soon as she got within range so the air conditioning would cool it down some. Even though Fredericksburg was situated in the Hill Country, the weather was as unpredictable as Galveston's. The temperature was probably at least twenty degrees warmer than it had been the day before.

Erma caught up with her. "Where're the girls?"

"They didn't want to go," Sandra said as they reached the car. "Went to eat and do some shopping." She fanned her face with her hand.

When she opened the car door, thankfully the air whooshing out was only warm, not brutally hot. Sandra removed her jacket, throwing it into the backseat. She rolled up her long sleeves.

"What the hell is up with this town?" Erma threw her purse in, followed by her own suit jacket. "I thought spring was supposed to be mild up here."

"Climate change?" Sandra eye-balled the parking lot for Holt's maroon Silverado, which wasn't there. "We need to get going."

Perspiration plastered hair to Erma's temples. "Shit, it's hot." She buckled her seat belt.

"They said it was a heat wave. At least the humidity is way lower up here, and the rain cooled things down a little." Sandra pointed the car toward the hospital. She jerked a couple of tissues from the package on the console and tossed them at Erma. "Blot." She pulled out two more and blotted her own forehead, temples, and neck. "You bring any summery clothes or just those black suits you've been wearing since Phillip died?"

"Hell no. You? Or just—"

"Hell no." Sandra eased onto Highway 16. "We'll possibly have a few minutes to buy some lightweight clothes this afternoon, depending on how Rex is. Something cotton would be good."

"The little shit," Erma said. "I bet he was driving ninety-to-nothing like he was a high-schooler and just as stupid."

"For BJ's sake, I hope he'll be okay." Sandra cast her eyes at Erma. "I mean, he's a jerk and the world would be better off without him, but he is her son."

"Yeah. And I hope it was an accident."

"You think it could be otherwise?" Sandra had wondered that herself but was going to wait until she heard the facts surrounding the incident before she allowed herself to voice any suspicions. "Let's see if we can get a copy of the police report."

"And the medical report." Erma shifted around on the leather seat. "I wonder if he was drinking or doing drugs."

"I wonder if he was alone. Have you noticed he's always alone when he comes to BJ's?"

"He's such a little asshole, no one wants to be with him," Erma said. "He was engaged once, and the girl broke it off."

"I think you're right," Sandra said. In only a few minutes, they arrived at the hospital. "I'm not putting my jacket back on." She turned the ignition off and grabbed her wallet and cell phone and tucked her purse under the car seat.

"Me, neither, and I wish I hadn't worn pantyhose. They're glued to my skin." Erma hefted herself out of the car.

"You're going to have a heat stroke someday. It's okay these days not to wear hosiery." Sandra locked the car and came around to Erma's side. "Are you wearing a girdle, too?"

"It chafes me if I don't have pantyhose underneath." She straightened her shoulders and untucked her blouse. "I'm making a concession here."

"Oh my God," Sandra said. "I'm serious. Even if you weighed fifty pounds less, you shouldn't be wearing a girdle and pantyhose at your age—hell, at any age in Texas, most anytime of the year."

"All right now." Erma strutted to the front door. "Don't start on me."

Sandra followed, shaking her head. When they returned to Galveston, she'd call Erma's doctor and discuss it. She didn't want her mother having a heatstroke on top of the heart attack.

When the elevator door opened, Holt stepped off.

"You leaving? Didn't you just get here?" Sandra asked.

"He's in a coma."

Sandra and Erma backed away from the elevator.

"How bad is he? I mean, how badly was he hurt?" Sandra stretched an arm around Erma's shoulders. Rex had been a little jerk, yes, but Erma had known him since he was a toddler. She must have some feelings for him.

Holt glanced toward the hospital entrance a couple of times as though he was eager to get away. "They're going to finish working up the doctor's notes and give me a copy. I'll give you one, too."

Erma said, "Yes, but how bad? Has anyone notified his mother? Or his sister?"

Holt swallowed. "I didn't ask about notification of next of kin. As far as his injuries, his head injury is the most serious, though, as I understand it, he has internal injuries and some broken bones." He towered over them, especially Erma. His sleeves were rolled up to his elbows, his tie loosened, the top shirt button undone. His cheeks were flushed, and a sweaty lock of hair hung over his forehead. If he'd left the courthouse right away and driven straight to the hospital, he should have cooled down at least a little.

"You need to drink some water," Sandra said to Holt. "My guess is you haven't had much water today. I think you're overheated."

Erma looked at her like she was out of her mind.

"I'm okay." He ran his fingers through his hair.

"No, really, go into the charity shop and buy a bottle of water and guzzle it before you go back outside. I bet you're overheated as well as overwhelmed."

He wore surprise in the form of drawn up eyebrows and a crooked smile. "I think that's the nicest thing you've ever said to me. You sound like my mother."

"Ha!" Sandra took a step back. "I think that was supposed to be a compliment, but I know what someone overheated looks like when I see them. Go in there and get some water."

"Yes, ma'am." Holt saluted her and crab-walked toward the shop. His gait was slow, not normal for him.

Erma pulled away from Sandra. "What's with you?"

"I wouldn't wish a stroke on anyone. He's not exactly my worst enemy, just my opponent." She stood there until he exited with the water, opening the bottle and swallowing half of it. He nodded at them before turning toward the door.

Sandra pulled on Erma's sleeve. "Let's go find out what we can for ourselves."

⚖ ⚖ ⚖

Erma walked right to the nurses' station in the ICU. "I'm the lawyer for the Schindler family. Rex Schindler's mother is out of town. I need to see him."

For once, Erma felt tall. The woman sitting at the computer looked like if she stood, she'd be about the same size as a first grader. She glanced at Erma and back at the computer and back at Erma, as if deciding which was more important.

Erma held her fists on her hips, legs spread apart. If she'd had a gun, she'd be in the perfect position to fire it. Instead, she fired her finger in the woman's face. "I said, I need to talk to Mr. Schindler." She hated to call the little punk "Mister," but maybe that would get the woman's attention.

Finally, the woman rolled her chair until she was right across from Erma but below Erma's eye level. "I've been updating his chart. What did you say your name is?"

"Erma Townley, Esquiress."

Sandra, who Erma could feel standing almost smack dab behind her, cleared her throat. Or maybe Sandra was muffling laughter. Erma tried the same trick Sandra had pulled on her, stepping back on her foot, but Sandra was too fast for her.

"Well, ma'am, Miz Townley, you may go back there but only you."

Erma pointed down the hall toward the closed double doors. "He's back there?"

"I'll buzz you in."

Sandra said, "Where's the waiting room? I'll park myself in there."

"Round the corner to the left." A buzzer sounded.

Erma hustled through the doors before the nurse, or what-ever her role was, pulled her finger off the button. Both doors

356

opened wide and began closing again behind her. More than a whiff of antiseptic air swirled around—and something else not pleasing to the nose. She hastened to another counter where more hospital personnel gathered. "Rex Schindler?"

"All the way to the end." A woman indicated the direction but never looked up.

"Well, all right then." Maybe flipping your truck and almost dying was pretty routine in the Hill Country. Erma dodged gurneys, tall white laundry bins, and a mop and broom that leaned against the wall, until beside one doorway she found Rex's name.

Next to the door to the room was a huge square window with the curtains standing open. Rex lay on an elevated bed. Tubes and wires and monitors and beeping noises surrounded him. She probably shouldn't go inside. Since she didn't want to, it was not a problem. She'd always been able to deal better with murder and mayhem than with injuries, which was why she'd practiced criminal law and referred out her personal injury cases, one of the many things she and Sandra had in common.

Anyone could have been in that bed. White bandages held by one of those stretchy tape things encased his head, which looked as huge as a pumpkin. The only features she could make out were one swollen eye, nostrils, and a hole where his mouth was supposed to be. None of it boded well. A sheet covered him, but one leg in a cast extended out. The opposite arm, also in a cast, lay by his side.

Erma crossed her arms and stared at the inert body. Images of him as a toddler flashed through her mind. He'd been a cute little thing even though he'd been a terror, one of those brats who bit and kicked and screamed bloody murder.

Bloody murder. Could this have been an attempt at murder, another murder in the Schindler family? Or had Rex been driving crazy on the two-lane road between Fredericksburg and Kerrville? If she recalled correctly, at least one kid died on that road every year or so.

She knew better than to ask about his condition, what with confidentiality laws, but it didn't take much to see what his situation was. Rex lay in the bed like he was dead. The beeping sounds were constant. One machine showed a consistent squiggle, until it didn't.

Loud beeps burst out. People ran in her direction, hollering to each other. Erma stood to the side of the window as hospital personnel crowded into the room, two of them pushing a crash cart. They didn't take the time to draw the curtains. She could see everything as it happened, but not Rex, with so many people surrounding him.

BJ burst through the doors at the end of the hall. "Erma!" She grabbed Erma's elbow. She screamed something unintelligible and slapped her palms and forehead on the window, peering inside. Her breathing came fast. She choked and coughed. Erma pulled her from the window and took her in her arms and let her sob into her shoulder. The loud and long beeps kept coming from the room at almost the same rhythm as BJ's heart.

Rex might be a real ass, but he was her good friend's son. Erma had trouble holding back her own tears, though she didn't believe in making a spectacle of herself. She tried to think of something else, anything else, while BJ wrapped her arms tighter.

"I'm so—so scared," BJ said in a muffled voice.

Erma hugged her back. "Of course you are, darlin'." She couldn't do anything except be there for BJ.

They stood for what seemed an interminable period of time, Erma looking around BJ into the room, trying to figure out what was going on, and BJ continuing to soak Erma's blouse with tears.

Sandra showed up carrying their purses, her lips pressed together in a grim line. The door to the room stood open. Sandra put her head inside for a few moments before mouthing to Erma, "It doesn't sound good." She held a tissue cube she must have gotten from the waiting room and offered it to Erma.

The voices that had been so loud not very long ago toned down, down, until finally they were no more. One voice rang out, a death knell. "Let's call it."

BJ crushed Erma to her and wailed, "No-o-o-o."

Other voices started up again, not loud but businesslike. Still others were muted. The machine noises ceased. The staff wandered out of the room, glancing at Erma and BJ, shaking their heads, until only one person lingered next to the sheet-covered body.

After a few minutes, a stocky man in scrubs came out. "One of you his mother?" His name tag indicated he was a physician.

Erma nodded and pointed at the still crying BJ. She whispered in BJ's ear. "Come on, now, honey. The doc wants to speak with you."

Taking the tissues, BJ let go of Erma. She wiped her face and blew her nose several times. Setting her eyes on the man BJ said, "My son...is dead?"

"I'm so sorry. We did everything we could." He put a hand on BJ's shoulder. "His injuries were too extensive."

BJ nodded and sniffed and stared at the man. She ran a tissue across her face.

"Would you like to go inside?" he asked.

When anguish crossed BJ's face, Erma's chest grew tight. "You know you do, honey. See him and hug him while he's still warm, while a little life is left in him, and say goodbye."

BJ nodded at Erma. "Will y'all wait for me?"

"Of course," Sandra said. "We'll be in the waiting room."

The doctor escorted BJ toward the bed. He peeled the sheet back for her. He prodded her closer and said a few words before returning outside. "I told her she can stay as long as she likes," he said to Sandra and Erma.

In the waiting room, Erma sighed as she dropped into one of the cushioned chairs. She took a tissue from the cube and blew her nose. They sat watching each other for a few minutes, before Sandra broke the silence.

"I saw BJ in the hall. She told Efrain to take the car back to the ranch. They drove all night."

Erma crossed her arms and propped her head against the wall behind her. They could drive BJ home when she was ready.

Sandra gave a slight shrug. "I understand you're sad, but I didn't care for him so don't expect me to act like I'm sorry about what happened."

"Ahem. I didn't like him either. I'm just sorry for BJ and Kathy Lynn."

"BJ, yes. I'm not so sure Kathy Lynn will mourn him much." Sandra copied Erma's posture, her eyes never wavering.

Erma watched Sandra. She could tell Sandra had something to say, but either wasn't ready to say it or thought it was not the right time. Erma wasn't going to press her. What she wanted most right then was a stiff drink—a couple of shots of bourbon, and she'd be better able to tackle the world.

"I guess we should call Mel and Rufina."

Erma needed a moment or two alone to grapple with her thoughts and the events of the day. "You go out in the hall and call."

Sandra left. No one else was in the waiting room. Erma closed her eyes and dropped her shoulders and took a couple of deep breaths. She had an idea of what was going on that she wanted to share with Sandra. It might not be the right time, but in the current situation, when would be? She must have drifted off because when she opened her eyes, Sandra was back in the same chair.

"Mel was shocked but not upset. She didn't like him either. I told her we were waiting for BJ, that we'd go to Jared's office afterward, so I can knock out a Motion to Reopen. Then we would go home."

"I'm in agreement. So, I want to run something past you."

Sandra perked up. "I was fixing to say the same thing. About the case, if you think this is a good time."

"What better time will there be? Here's what I'm thinking." Her chest tightened with anticipation. "If Rex wasn't acting like a stupid ass and driving too fast and or recklessly, I think someone helped the accident along." Sandra didn't look a bit surprised, which didn't come as a shock. Sandra was, after all, her daughter.

"I think someone helped the accident along whether or not Rex was acting like his usual self." Sandra wore a smirk.

"So we're in agreement."

"I think we are. Now the question is, who?" Sandra rubbed her hands together.

"A lot of people work at the ranch. Any number of them could have had a grudge against him." Erma got up and began walking around the room.

"I'm sure many of them do."

"Assuming—God I hate that word—Rex's accident was related to this trial. That would narrow it down quite a bit. I don't think it was anyone kin to Rufina, for instance. Like her brother." Erma stopped in front of Sandra. "For all his interest initially, he's been AWOL since the trial started."

Sandra rotated her shoulders and tilted her head to each side. "I can go with that. Carlos is a little intense, but I don't think he has a real motive. At least for taking out Rex. He's still on my short list for Katy Jo."

"And I don't think it was—"

BJ appeared in the doorway. She held onto the wall like she was close to falling. Erma hurried to her, took her by the elbow, and helped her to a chair. They'd have to continue their discussion later.

CHAPTER THIRTY-SIX

THE NEXT MORNING, through a tumultuous downpour, the defense team paraded back to the courthouse. Sandra, Erma, and Mel rode in the first car, BJ and Rufina rode in BJ's car, and Efrain followed in one of the trucks from the ranch.

Each of them sheltering under an umbrella, the five women slogged through the standing water in the parking lot, the warm wind-driven rain soaking the lower half of their bodies and clothing. Efrain parked a block away and remained in the truck, safely out of the prosecutor's attention. If he wouldn't be needed, he'd return to the ranch.

They straggled into the ladies' room and dried off with paper towels before going to the courtroom. The judge was already on the bench. Holt slouched in his chair, leaning over and whispering to the same young attorney who had been in and out throughout the trial. No more than a moment after Sandra laid her things down, the judge said, "For the record, Mrs. Salinsky, my clerk informed me Mr. Rex Schindler passed away yesterday evening."

BJ winced and slumped onto the first bench behind counsel table. When Sandra turned around, Mel had put an arm around BJ.

Erma and Rufina shed their raincoats and draped them over the corner of the bar with their umbrellas. Sandra's eyes landed on a document lying on their table.

"Yes, Your Honor, that's correct."

The judge held up some papers. "I have a Motion in Limine filed by Mr. Holt this morning. He's requested a hearing before the jury is brought back in for the conclusion of final arguments. Do you want to peruse the motion for a minute?"

Though chilled from the rain and wind, and standing in still-wet shoes, Sandra pushed down the heat rushing through her body during the judge's speech. She refrained from looking at Holt. What a weird time to file such a motion. She could only imagine what ambush the motion contained. What else would Holt want to limit other than any reference to Rex's death?

She handed her coat and umbrella to Erma, who handed them off to Rufina. Sandra dropped into her chair to read the motion. Erma started to say something, but Sandra held up a finger, silencing her.

When she reached the end of the motion, Sandra said, "Get our own motion." She stood at her chair. "I'm ready, Judge." She still didn't look at Holt. She wanted to step across the aisle and knock his legs out from under him, so she thought it best to keep her attention on the judge.

"You may proceed, Mr. Holt."

Matthew, the court reporter, who'd been browsing on his cell phone, poised to take notes.

"Judge, as you're aware, Mr. Schindler passed away yesterday after being in an accident on the Kerrville Highway. After you recessed to enable us to go to the hospital and check on his condition—"

"What does this have to do with the Motion in Limine?" Sandra held a ballpoint pen in her hand behind her back and clicked the plunger in and out in rapid succession like Holt had done all throughout the trial. Erma tapped her arm and handed up their motion.

"If she'd let me finish, Judge."

The judge cast his eyes at her. "Go ahead, Mr. Holt."

"Well, anyway, I went to where he was, and he was in critical condition in the ICU. When I returned downstairs to depart, the defense lawyers were just arriving with the intention of checking on Mr. Schindler themselves. When I last saw them, they were entering the elevator."

Sandra shifted her feet. Her toes were wet, and as cold and clammy as her hands. She put her pen and his motion down and rubbed her hands together. Although spring had definitely come outside, the courtroom was still icy cold.

Holt continued arguing his motion. "Now, of course I have no way of knowing what transpired between the decedent and the defense before he passed on, but on the off chance he regained consciousness, I'd like Your Honor to prohibit them from telling the jury anything Schindler may have said."

"You mean like a deathbed confession?" Sandra winked at Erma. That remark would annoy Holt. "When, exactly, would I be able to impart his last words to the jury?"

Judge Danforth dipped his head and looked at them over his glasses. "Certainly anything the decedent said would be objectionable during final arguments, Mr. Holt. I think it goes without saying Mrs. Salinsky knows that."

"Of course I do, Judge."

"In an abundance of caution, and no insult intended to you or your m—Mrs. Townley, I will grant Mr. Holt's Motion in Limine."

"Thank you, Judge," Holt said, "but there is a second part to my motion on the next page. I'd like the court to prohibit the defense from mentioning he—meaning Mr. Schindler—died."

BJ made a noise similar to a hiccup. Erma rolled back in her chair to the bar separating them and reached over to take BJ's hand. Rufina had been staring down into her lap and continued to do so. Sandra gave Holt her best are-you-kidding-me look.

"That request is granted also," Judge Danforth said. "Anything else?" He made a show of glancing at the clock on the far wall.

"Yes, Your Honor," Sandra said. "The defense has a motion we'd like to file with the court. May I approach the bench?" After the judge nodded, Sandra handed him a copy and then one to Holt on the way back to her table. "May I proceed?"

The judge inclined his head, his eyebrows drawn together. There was no doubt he'd been tired of the case almost as soon as it had started. Sandra didn't know why some judges insisted on sitting by assignment after they retired.

"Your Honor, in the interim between the beginning of Mr. Holt's final argument and last night, Mrs. Schindler located Mrs. Barboza's alibi witness and brought him back to Fredericksburg."

Holt had stood also and was snorting as loud as a mad horse.

"Since final arguments have not concluded and, in fact, I barely began before being interrupted by news of Rex Schindler's accident, the defense humbly moves the court to reopen and allow the defense to put on our case."

"Judge—"

"I'm not through," Sandra said. "I just paused to get my breath."

Holt crossed his arms.

"Additionally, we have Mrs. BJ Schindler, who was not available when the time came to put on our defense. So we'd have two witnesses, Judge, and only two. Mrs. Schindler, whom I know Mr. Holt had wanted to cross-examine again based on his statement earlier in the trial, and the alibi witness." Sandra stopped for a moment to get another breath. The courtroom was so quiet, the clock's ticking sounded abnormally loud. "That's all, Judge, only two. We pray, in the interest of justice, you grant our Motion to Reopen."

Holt looked like he was going into cardiac arrest. His hand went to his chest. "May I respond, Your Honor?" His voice bounced off the walls.

The judge cleared his throat. He ducked his head, looking down at the motion on the counter in front of him. He peered over his glasses, from Sandra to Holt, to Erma and Rufina, and finally, at BJ. "Ordinarily I'd allow you to respond, Mr. Holt, but in this case, it's not necessary. Motion denied."

Sandra's heart fell to the floor. She didn't need to hear the rest of what he said. In fact, anger overcame her so quickly she was incapable of hearing what else he said, only that the bailiff was to bring in the jury.

Before she stood to begin her final argument, Sandra drew a deep breath. As she rose, she said to Erma, "I'm going with my theory of the case."

"What?" Erma grabbed Sandra's arm. "You can't. I'm not even sure what that is."

Sandra pulled her arm away. She whispered over her shoulder as she spun to the side to get up, "Don't worry." She thought she knew what had really happened the night of the murder and was hopeful by the time arguments were over, the jurors would agree.

She straightened the cotton jacket she'd found in a shop on Main Street, buttoning the waist button. The print jacket had dark pink and yellow flowers. The skirt and blouse were a solid fuchsia, a color that went well with her dark hair. Her peep-toe pumps matched the skirt and blouse. She'd liked them when she bought them but now wished for warmer, closed-toe shoes.

"May it please the Court." Sandra walked to the podium one last time. She gave the judge and Holt cursory nods because it was customary, not because she had any respect for them. She'd swallowed her anger by then, convinced winning the case was her best revenge.

"Ladies and gentlemen, thank you for your patience this week. In all trials, matters arise that cause delays. Sometimes the judge and the attorneys have to put their heads together to resolve an issue. Often the best thing to do is send you to stretch your legs. This was one of those times, and I appreciate your forbearance."

The judge had confined the lawyers to a small space behind the podium, out of meanness, Sandra thought, advising them if they moved from that area, he'd dress them down in front of the jury. She felt constrained by the restriction, like the judge had pinned her elbows to her sides. Her way was to speak with her body, her arms and hands, and move around more than a bit.

She drew a deep breath and made eye contact with each juror on the front row. "This case is styled 'The State of Texas versus Rufina Barboza,' which only means someone in authority has chosen to proceed against Mrs. Barboza. Mr. Holt, in this case, is that someone. He has the sole discretion to prosecute or not regardless of whether there has been an indictment handed down by a Grand Jury. In this case, Mr. Holt chose to prosecute the Widow Barboza solely based on circumstantial evidence."

Sandra switched her focus to the people on the back row. "In the charge, which you will take back to the jury room to read over before you begin deliberating, circumstantial evidence and direct evidence are defined." Her greatest desire was to stand up there and tell them the case was bullshit brought because the now-deceased Rex Schindler had convinced his buddy, the prosecutor, to bring it, for what real reason, she didn't know. "I implore you to study those legal definitions. Now, on the night in question, after heavy drinking by several guests—"

"Objection," Holt said from behind her. "Mischaracterization of the evidence."

Sandra faced the judge. "What do you call it, Your Honor, when people gulp at least four shots of mezcal and top it off with wine? I call it heavy drinking."

The judge raised an eyebrow. "Overruled, Mr. Holt. You may continue, Mrs. Salinsky."

"On the night in question, after dinner and numerous drinks, supposedly everyone either went home or to their rooms or cottages. The two women who worked under Mrs. Barboza left shortly after serving dinner. Doug Christian testified Katy Jo went to Rufina's cottage where the couple was staying over-night. Kathy Lynn and BJ went to their rooms. Well, BJ did.

"We don't know where Kathy Lynn went." Though she didn't suspect Kathy Lynn of killing her twin, Sandra's job was to instill reasonable doubt in the minds of the jury. She'd wait a moment more and let the unknown whereabouts of Kathy Lynn sink in.

She swallowed from a small bottle of water she'd taken up to the podium. As she did so, she glanced at the gallery to her right. Along with some courthouse regulars she'd seen during the tri-al, Jared sat on the back row. She appreciated his coming. She hadn't decided what to do about him but was glad to see him.

"Kathy Lynn aside, supposedly Rex Schindler walked Elgin Burgess to his car and went to his own room." She made eye contact with the one juror they hoped was on their side. The woman didn't drop her eyes. Eye contact was usually a good sign. "That accounts for everyone at the dinner. Except, did Rex Schindler truly go to his room? We've heard no evidence about that."

Sandra glanced down at her notes while her words sank in. She was sure the jury could see the holes in the State's case. "We don't know if Rex really did walk Elgin Burgess to his car, as Mr. Burgess testified, or if Elgin Burgess really did leave. He could have started his engine, waited for Rex to go into the house, and turned off the ignition. He could have gone back inside him-self. The home has several entrances. There's been no testimony about the security system."

"Objection, Your Honor," Holt said. "She's testifying."

"Sustained."

Without missing a beat, Sandra said, "Nobody said if Mr. Burgess had a key to the Schindler home. No one asked him, and no one said. No one testified about the security system and whether Burgess knew the code.

"Not long after everyone supposedly went to their rooms or left the premises, BJ Schindler was in the master bedroom bathroom, which is on the other side of the wall from the king-sized bed. Katy Jo had doubled back and climbed into bed with her mother, like she had when she was a little girl and wanted to discuss something. The lights were off, the bedroom dark. From the doorway the killer couldn't tell who was in the bed."

The jurors, several of whom were on the edge of their seats, wore doom-and-gloom expressions, all eyes on Sandra, just the way she liked them.

"Someone—someone no one saw—opened the door and fired." Sandra thrust her forefinger up. "Bang!"

Several jurors jerked.

"He didn't drop the gun, no, he made a quick exit before Mrs. Schindler came out of the bathroom and before anyone else could run to the master bedroom and catch him." She stepped back from the podium, released a deep breath, and stepped forward again. All eyes were still on her.

"Ladies and gentlemen, there were no eyewitnesses to this shooting. Doug Christian allegedly discovered the weapon on the path to Mrs. Barboza's cottage. No eyewitnesses told us who put it on the path, who may have thrown it or dropped it accidentally and not stopped to pick it up. Any one of the unaccounted-for people could have been responsible for positioning the gun outside the cottage, if, in fact, that's where Doug Christian came across it."

Acid was making inroads in Sandra's stomach. She took another sip of water.

"When law enforcement arrived at Mrs. Schindler's home, the family had gathered in the kitchen, and, when I say family, I'm including Rufina Barboza. Elgin Burgess was nowhere to be seen. Doug Christian had taken the gun inside but kept it in his pocket at first.

"Mrs. Barboza was in her nightgown and a bathrobe. The state is asking you to believe she took the gun with her to her cottage sometime before the shooting, returned to the house to do the shooting, ran back to her cottage, changed into her nightclothes and returned to the house again. If she had dropped the gun on the path to her cottage, wouldn't she have stopped to pick it up and gotten rid of it?

"Further, the State is asking you to conclude that Rufina Barboza, this little lady at the table behind me," Sandra pointed at Rufina, "somehow, sometime received handgun training enabling her, in spite of her disability—her scarred hand and arm—to shoot into a dark room and hit her target. The state's position stretches the limits of credulity."

One good thing about standing behind a barrier, at least she could wipe off her hands. They had grown sweaty, in spite of the cold. She flexed her fingers, stiff from gripping the podium.

"Though it's difficult to discuss someone's disability or injuries, today is one of those times when it must be mentioned. You could not have failed to see the massive scarring covering one side of this lady's body. The scarring extends to her limbs, her hand. You've heard testimony that not only would it be difficult for such a small woman to handle the weapon in question, but she would need to have strength and flexibility in her hands to do so. No logical person would have chosen a huge, heavy handgun..."

She chanced walking to the small table where the exhibits sat and picked up the gun, holding it with both hands like it was a heavy burden. The judge didn't say anything. His admonition must not apply to the space between the lectern and the exhibit table.

" ...when a smaller one, easier for her to use, was available."

She put the gun back and pointed to Rufina. "Mr. Holt argued this lady could have gotten keys to the gun cabinet. He said having keys to the gun cabinet gave her one of the three factors authorities look at in a criminal case. Like he told you, those three are means, motive, and opportunity. He claims she had means. She did. She had access to the keys, but so did everyone else in the family, or at least everyone knew where Mrs. Schindler kept the keys.

"Think about this for a moment. If Mrs. Barboza had the means on the night in question, she'd had the means ever since she found out where the keys were—ever since her best friend, Mrs. Schindler, asked her to take over the role as *señora*. Why, of all the nights in all the years she's had access to the keys, would she have chosen that particular night to take what Mr. Holt has said was her revenge? She wouldn't, and she didn't. She's had plenty of chances over the years to plan the demise of Katy Jo Schindler. Would any idiot have chosen that night when so many people were in and around the Schindler home? The answer to that question is yes. But Rufina Barboza was not that idiot. The idiot was someone else, possibly someone who'd had too much to drink."

Holt's chair clattered against the bar behind Sandra. "Your Honor, I object."

"What is it now, Mr. Holt?"

"She's..." he stopped as if realizing he didn't have an objection.

Sandra shook her head like *you-poor-man*. "All right." She shrugged one shoulder. "It could have been anyone, not just one of the—the people who had drunk too much mezcal and wine.

"Back to the issue of the gun, let's scrutinize this occasion a little closer. How logical is it to think a disabled woman would choose a heavy weapon, which was difficult for her to handle, when there was a relatively light one—one of those pink guns you heard about—just a cabinet away.

"But, what man with access to the cabinet keys—or who knew where Mrs. Schindler kept the keys—wouldn't want to feel that historic weapon, the Smith and Wesson m1917 .45 caliber revolver in the palm of his hand?

"Since we're talking about means, what about the second part of the trinity? Motive. One might say Mrs. Barboza had a motive to kill Katy Jo at the time of the fire—say after her husband's funeral or after her hospitalization, that is, if she were a vengeful person. But she was not and is not. She was and still is full of love for the Schindler family. She was a second mother to Katy Jo. Mrs. Barboza would never kill a young woman who was like a daughter to her.

"Mr. Holt said Mrs. Barboza had carried hatred in her heart for years. I'm asking you to think about all the possible times over the years she could have carried out an ill intent. Mr. Holt's argument makes no sense, particularly in light of the fact Katy Jo and her boyfriend spent many nights in Mrs. Barboza's cottage." Sandra caught BJ in the corner of her eye. Now, BJ had her arm around Mel, squeezing her tight against her. Mel pressed her trembling lips together.

"We don't know who else might have had a reason to kill Katy Jo Schindler. We didn't hear from—"

"Objection!" Holt jumped to his feet again. "May we approach the bench?"

The judge nodded. Holt shot Sandra an if-looks-could-kill glance as he strode up. Sandra put on a simpering smile. What she had said was objectionable. The rules didn't allow her to comment on what someone who did not testify would have said, but heck, she'd be remiss not to try.

Judge Danforth cupped his hand beside his mouth. "You know better, Mrs. Salinsky."

The hairs on her arms rose as she anticipated his next words.

"Do it again, and I'll sanction you, and you won't like it."

Holt straightened his shoulders and shot his cuffs.

"Yes, sir," Sandra said. "I apologize for my slip." For the benefit of the jury, she nodded with exaggerated sincerity.

"Continue your argument." Judge Danforth's smile was as phony as hers. "And let me advise you if you see any of the jurors' eyes rolling up in their heads, it's time to stop and take your seat."

Could he be more patronizing? She calmed herself as she walked back to the podium. The jurors hadn't appeared restless yet. In fact, they looked enthralled. The judge was the one who was restless, eager to get home, no doubt.

"Sustained," the judge's voice rang out.

Holt plopped into his chair, banging against the bar again, and held up his palms as though it was an accident.

"Now, where were we?" Sandra flipped through several pieces of paper. "The question is, who else had a motive to kill Katy Jo? Any number of people—not limited to those at dinner. For the sake of argument, though, there were four people unaccounted for: the decedent's twin sister, the decedent's boyfriend, the decedent's brother, and the man who wanted their mother."

Sandra longed to be closer to the jury. Once she returned to Galveston, back to her office, she was going to research whether a judge could restrict a lawyer from moving about during final arguments. The rule in Texas during witness examination, to stand or sit at one's chair, generally was hard and fast, but she couldn't recall a restriction on movement during argument except for touching or laying papers on the bar separating the lawyers from the jurors.

"The room in which Katy Jo died was the master bedroom, the room where Mr. and Mrs. Schindler had slept during their married life. The room was not Katy Jo's room. How could anyone have known BJ Schindler was not in her bed? How could the shooter have known his target was not BJ Schindler?" She inclined her head at BJ. "He couldn't." In spite of having practiced those words, a shiver ran down Sandra's spine. She imagined BJ felt one, too. Most of the people in the courtroom stared at BJ, and not surreptitiously.

"If you think about it, we're not sure who the target was. If it wasn't Katy Jo, then who would want to shoot Mrs. Schindler? Not Rufina, her best friend. Her other daughter? I think not. What about the two unaccounted-for men—her intoxicated son and her intoxicated, spurned, want-to-be lover, who said he thought Mrs. Barboza was a lesbian?"

Sandra made eye contact with a few jurors again.

"Lastly, I want to talk about the fingerprints. Only one partial, the State's expert testified, could have belonged to Rufina Barboza. Even if you believe the expert, what does that mean?

373

She cleaned and supervised the cleaning of the guns. Wouldn't it have been more surprising if no fingerprints were on the gun? Clearly, the real perpetrator wore some kind of gloves, or wiped off the gun as best he could before dropping it or throwing it on the cottage path."

Sandra took a deep breath and glanced at her mother, who had clasped her hands and rested them on the table, at Rufina, who finally held her head up, at Mel, who perched on the bench behind the bar as if she were about to spring, and at BJ, whose head hung down to her chest. Sandra's eyes met Jared's. He wore a wide grin like he was reading her mind and knew what she would say next. The other people, the onlookers, wore poker faces undoubtedly formed from years of having observed arguments and having been told not to dare flinch inside the courtroom.

"If that's all Mr. Holt has against my client, Mrs. Rufina Barboza, I say to you, members of the jury of Gillespie County, you must acquit and set her free."

CHAPTER THIRTY-SEVEN

AFTER SANDRA SAT down, after Holt finished his closing, and after the judge sent out the jury, Erma rolled her
chair up next to Sandra's. "What the hell is the matter with
you?" She breathed hard into Sandra's ear. "You could at least
have told me this morning what you planned to say."

"Back off." Sandra pushed her mother away a couple of
inches. "The jury's out, so you don't have to get so close."

"Couldn't you have said what you were going to do on the
way into town?" With the pout she wore, Erma looked like an
oversized baby. "Do I have to remind you I'm second chair?"

Sandra kneaded the knot in her stomach. She should have
talked with Erma about what she planned to argue but hadn't
wanted a protracted discussion. Once she'd decided, there was
no way she would have changed her mind. "I won't lie to you. I
just wasn't going to let you persuade me not to do it."

"Well, it hurt my feelings." Erma turned her head away and
crossed her arms. "I felt like you didn't trust me."

"How about I let you be lead counsel next time?" Sandra
pressed her lips together.

Erma jerked in her chair and spun back around. "What?
Very funny. You've made it clear this is your last case."

Sandra clasped her hands across her middle. Waiting for a verdict always caused stomach upset. "A girl's got a right to change her mind. At least, that's what you've always told me."

Erma cocked her head like a chicken in a farmyard, eyeballing Sandra. "You mean you're not headed off to work for the enemy?"

"Uh-uh." Sandra bit the inside of her cheek to stop herself from smiling.

Erma rolled her chair closer. "You really changed your mind?"

"I never decided for sure that I would. I was just thinking about it."

Erma removed her glasses and wiped her eyes with a tissue. "What made the pendulum swing back?"

"Don't get all sappy about it." She reduced her voice to a whisper. "Sitting in this trial, seeing Holt trying to make a case out of nothing. Watching him persecute Rufina. I don't know whether Rex convinced him somehow to do it, or if he's prejudiced against Latinos." She drew a breath. "When I first decided to go to law school, I wanted to help people, not corporations, not insurance companies. People like Rufina."

Erma dabbed at her face again. "I'm so relieved."

Sandra couldn't stop herself from rolling her eyes. "All right. Let's huddle up." She wheeled her chair around facing BJ and Mel on the front row behind them. "Rufina, come over here with the rest of us. Mom, scooch over."

When they were all together, close enough that Holt, who stood with an associate near the empty jury box, was out of range, Sandra asked, "So what do y'all think they're going to do?"

Rufina took Sandra's hand, giving it a strong squeeze. "Not guilty. Your argument, it was *muy bueno. Gracias.*"

A chill ran up Sandra's neck and out the back of her arms.

"Not guilty." BJ's eyebrows drew together, belying her confidence.

"Not guilty." Mel smiled about the sweetest smile Sandra had seen on her daughter's face since Mel had become a teenager.

"That makes it unanimous." Erma wore a shit-eating grin.

"I hope y'all are right. My stomach is roiling. I can hardly stop my hands from shaking. I'm just not sure." She eyed each of them. They all appeared more confident than she did. "How long's it been since they've been out?"

Mel clicked on her cell phone. "Ten minutes."

"Crap," Erma said. "Feels like ten hours."

"Always does," Sandra said. "So, y'all don't think Holt swayed them in his closing when he reiterated his previous points and tried to come up with a story for where Rex and Elgin Burgess were at the time of the shooting?"

All four shook their heads.

"Do you think I raised reasonable doubt when I suggested the gun might not have been found where Doug said it was?"

Mel said, "I thought you were going to point the finger at Doug more than you did."

"Thought it might be overkill." Sandra focused on Mel. "I'm hoping the jury will come up with that themselves and wonder about him, too."

Mel rubbed her hands on her pants. "I think you pointed out lots of holes."

"Thanks, honey." Sandra hooked her arm around Mel's neck and pulled her close.

"I hate to say this, with him being an old friend of the family," BJ said, "but I think they'll definitely wonder about Elgin. I sure do." A squeak in the back of the courtroom drew their attention from the discussion. Kathy Lynn stood in the doorway. "What the—" BJ rushed toward her daughter.

"Where in the hell has that girl been?" Erma rose to her feet.

Sandra stopped her from following BJ. "We'll find out once BJ is through with her."

The door in front of them opened, and the bailiff came in. "All Rise." Matthew, the court reporter, hurried inside and took his seat.

"What the hell?" Erma rolled her chair back to the table, urging Rufina to do the same. Holt and his associate sidestepped to the prosecution table.

Before the judge had even seated himself, he said, "We have our first note."

"Oh, shit," Erma said.

Sandra elbowed her. "Keep your voice down."

"That can't be good."

"You don't even know what it says yet." Sandra met the judge's eyes and forced a weak smile.

"You ready, Matthew?" Judge Danforth asked. The court reporter nodded. The judge read, "'We would like to hear Douglas Christian's testimony again.' The note's dated and has the time and the signature of the presiding juror." He picked up a pen. "What say you Mr. Holt?"

"Could you ask them to be more specific? I don't want to spend the rest of the day listening to testimony redux."

"I agree with that, Your Honor," Sandra said.

The judge wrote something and handed the note back to Deputy Cortez. "I'll be in chambers." He stepped off the bench.

The bailiff exited. Holt and his associate dropped into chairs. The court reporter picked up his machine and carried it around to the witness stand, where he positioned himself in front of the microphone. Erma pulled on Sandra's sleeve until they stood in the farthest corner from Holt. "I'm not sure if that's good for us or not."

Sandra glanced at the back door. She wanted to talk to Kathy Lynn. She grimaced at Mel. "We'll find out in a minute." She leaned against the bar and watched the door to the jury deliberation area, crossing her arms and cupping her elbows with shaking hands.

Rufina got out of her chair and walked the few steps to where they stood. "Do we think that's good or not?"

Erma laid a hand on Rufina's shoulder. "Hard to tell."

"But Douglas didn't say anything bad." Rufina's face was scrunched up as if the fluorescent lights hurt her eyes.

"Only that he found the gun on the path to your house."

"And he didn't say he saw Efrain at your cottage," Sandra said.

"I don't think anyone asked him that," Rufina said. "I don't remember if he saw him or not."

Sandra and Erma exchanged glances. Sandra frowned at that misstep. Nobody's perfect, she thought, hoping that little error wouldn't prove to be monumental.

The bailiff came in again and announced the judge.

They all stood. The judge entered. "Bring 'em in."

The attorneys and Rufina sat down after the jury did.

"Mr. Presiding Juror, you've narrowed down what y'all want the court reporter to read back?"

"Yes, sir. The part about him finding the gun."

Matthew said, "I have it right here, Judge. "The judge nodded, and the court reporter began.

"Douglas Christian: 'I was going to the main house to find out what Mrs. S had said to Katy Jo after Katy Jo told her about us. I practically tripped over the gun. It was weird someone would drop a gun in plain sight—well plain sight if it was daylight. I was using the flashlight on my cell phone to see my way to the house.'

Mr. Holt: 'What did you do when you found the gun?'

Mr. Christian: 'I picked it up and carried it into the house to ask Mrs. S what a gun—'specially this gun, which was one of Mr. S's collector guns—was doing lying on the ground between buildings. As I went into the kitchen, I heard screams, so I ran to the back of the house.'" Matthew glanced over his shoulder. "You want me to go on?" The judge nodded.

"Mr. Holt: 'Were you wearing gloves when you picked up the weapon?'

"Answer: 'No.'

'Pass the witness.'"

"You can stop there," the judge said. "Jurors, is that what you wanted?"

The presiding juror stood. "Yes, Your Honor."

"Bailiff, escort them back to the jury room." The judge swept back through his chambers' door.

After the jurors had gone, the women all collapsed back into their chairs.

Erma said to Rufina. "Don't even ask, because I have no idea what that means."

Rufina raised her eyebrows at Sandra. Sandra shook her head.

The door opened at the back of the courtroom. BJ stood framed in the doorway with Kathy Lynn behind her. She beckoned to them. Erma said, "You go. I'll stay here in case something else happens."

Sandra hurried to the back. "Hey, Kathy Lynn." She tried to keep the ire out of her voice. "We were hoping you'd come earlier in the trial. Much earlier." Kathy Lynn's eyes wouldn't meet Sandra's.

BJ said, "She has something to tell you." She frowned at her daughter and corrected herself. "A lot to tell you. I'm not sure what all, but I think we need to find out."

Sandra's stomach couldn't churn more than it already was. "God, I wish this courthouse had a conference room for the lawyers. We're lucky it's turned out to be a pretty spring day. Y'all go out the first-floor door and meet me behind the courthouse. I'll be right out." She returned to retrieve her phone and told Erma to call her if the jury reached a verdict. Outside, a mild breeze blew from the north, the crisp air fresh, not recycled like inside. BJ and Kathy Lynn sat on a bench under a huge oak tree. As far as Sandra could see, no one would be in a position to overhear. Cars drove up Main Street. A few people strolled by on the sidewalk, but they were way out of ear shot. Sandra perched next to Kathy Lynn, with BJ on the other side. "While I'm thinking about, BJ, did anyone tell Efrain to go back to the ranch?"

BJ said, "I texted him earlier."

"Okay, now what's this all about?"

Kathy Lynn turned sideways, facing Sandra, her back to her mother. She rotated her hands in her lap, as though washing them. "All right, well, where do I begin?" Her sky-blue eyes met Sandra's.

Sandra waited, watching Kathy Lynn's face, knowing the young woman wanted to talk, or she wouldn't have shown up. BJ, who had blood-shot, teary eyes, prodded Kathy Lynn's shoulder.

"You can start from today and work backward," Sandra said.

Kathy Lynn reached behind her and laid her hand on her mother's knee. "Well, I wouldn't be here now if Rex hadn't died."

Sandra slapped her leg. She knew it. Rex was the key to everything. The muscles in BJ's jaw were flexing.

"Rex had stopped you before?" Sandra asked.

"Yeah." She sucked in a breath. "I don't why I'm so nervous, since he's dead. I'm just so used to being afraid."

"Did he threaten you?"

"This whole thing is such a mess—been a horrible mess for years." She peered over her shoulder. "Mama, I know I've never been much of a daughter. I know everyone calls me the evil twin."

BJ started to say something, but Kathy Lynn stopped her. "No, don't say anything. It's true."

Sandra flexed her fingers. Kathy Lynn's face was one big frown.

"Believe it or not," Kathy Lynn said, "I've changed. I've been in counseling." She took her mother's hand. "I have a prescription I've been taking that makes me feel different—better."

"What did you feel like that needed to be different?" Sandra glanced at her cell phone.

"Like I wanted to kill someone."

Sandra shivered.

BJ tensed. "You're not trying to tell me you—"

"I didn't shoot my sister. I know I didn't act like I loved her most of the time, but I did. I used to get so mad that she was so sweet, and I couldn't be like her." Her head went back and forth as she spoke. "So I made myself opposite of her. I can't explain it, but my doc thinks I've been depressed for years."

"How long have you been on medication?" The information was interesting, but if the young woman didn't have anything useful to say, Sandra was going back inside.

Kathy Lynn faced Sandra. "Since Katy Jo died." She bit the edge of a fingernail. "I didn't feel right. I should have been sadder. I should have felt worse than I did." She rubbed her hands together. "I joined a grief group to find out what was wrong with me. One day, I had a serious meltdown, and the leader pulled me aside and told me she thought I should be in individual counseling."

"I'm not trying to be rude or anything, but we have a jury deliberating. I need to go back." Sandra touched Kathy Lynn's hand. "Can you tell me how this ties in with Rex?"

"Yeah, okay. I hope I won't have to go to jail over this."

"Just tell me."

Kathy Lynn turned her head from one to the other of them again. "I had been blackmailing Rex since we were kids."

"What?" BJ cried out.

"I know, Mom. See? I really was a terrible person." Her eyes welled up with tears.

"That's why you were scared of Rex?" The story was a lot more complicated than Sandra had hoped it would be. Impatience gnawed at her. "Why were you blackmailing him?"

"Rex is the one who set the fire—"

"Oh my God." BJ wrapped her arms around herself. "I knew it couldn't have been Katy Jo."

Sandra stood, shaking her head. The bad seed. Two bad seeds, if Kathy Lynn could be counted with Rex.

"He talked Katy Jo into saying she did it. He could be so persuasive. He told her nothing would happen to her because everyone liked her so much, but if he got caught, he'd get into terrible trouble." She rubbed her lips together. "You know how he was always doing things, Mom, how he was always in trouble."

"Why did Katy Jo agree to do it?" Sandra was itching to do something, go for a run, shake off the restless feeling.

"He was our little brother." Kathy Lynn shrugged. "Our baby brother. She loved him."

BJ said, "Katy Jo had always been the one to take care of him when he was little. She used to carry him around before he could walk, scared the hell out of me. I was afraid she'd drop him. She'd pick him up and tote him around the house and feed him, like he was her little baby doll."

"We all spoiled him," Kathy Lynn said.

BJ shook her head. "More than spoiled him. We never disciplined him enough."

Sandra stared at the two Schindler women. That's why he had behaved like he had a sense of entitlement. If only she had been told this before the trial, Rufina's case would've gone differently. "Why did he set fire to Rufina's house?"

BJ started to speak, but her daughter interrupted her. "He never liked Rufina from the time he was a little boy." She turned to her mother. "You know he didn't. She'd try to hug him, and he'd wrestle away from her." To Sandra, she said, "When Rufina's parents moved back to Mexico, and Rufina took over, she let him get away with a lot less than Rufina's mother or Mom and Dad did."

"That's no reason to burn down her house."

"I don't think he thought it through. He wanted her to move to Mexico, too. He got mad when I asked him about it and said he wanted her and her husband out of there. You know how stupid teenage boys are." She sighed. "I guess teenage girls, too."

"So instead of telling your parents the truth, you blackmailed your brother?"

"Uh-huh." She stared down into her lap. "I was going to tell if he didn't do what I wanted. I made him give me part of his allowance. Once he got a job, I made him give me money." Her face had grown pink.

"I'm confused," Sandra said. "Why were you afraid to come to me, to testify about anything you knew about Katy Jo's murder?"

"Rex said he told Mr. Holt that he'd seen Rufina with the gun that night."

So that was why Holt had been so keen on prosecuting Rufina. Rex was going to testify against Rufina. He was going to be the witness who tied up the whole thing, that would make the prosecution's case a slam dunk. Sandra shook her head, trying to clear it. "Had he seen her with the gun?"

"No."

The little shithead. Sandra had known narcissistic people before, and Rex fit right in with them.

"Why did he hate her so much?" BJ asked.

"Mom, you know how prejudiced he was. I always thought part of the reason he didn't like Rufina was because she was Latina, and she was your good friend, and later because every time he saw her, her appearance reminded him of what he'd done."

"How did my children turn out so different from each other?" BJ said to no one in particular.

"This is a mess." Sandra bent down on one knee. "Now tell me, honestly, did Rex kill Katy Jo?"

Kathy Lynn's face screwed up, and she burst out, her hands flying around her, "I don't know."

"And you were scared of him because . . .?"

"Because after I started my medication, I could see more clearly. I finally told him I was going to tell the truth."

"The truth about what he'd told you?"

"About everything. He said if I did, he'd kill me, too."

"Too? Did you take that to mean that he'd killed Katy Jo?"

"Either her or Rufina's husband."

Sandra's head was spinning.

"I need to tell y'all something else." She put her hands over her face for a moment. "The other night I was on the phone with him. I told him I was coming to Fredericksburg to talk to you, Miss Salinsky. He yelled and screamed and hung up on me. Later, after I got dressed, I left Kerrville and was on my way here, and he zoomed up behind me in his truck and bumped the back of my car." She ran her fingers across her lips.

Sandra shook her head. BJ, one hand in Kathy Lynn's, the other at her throat, stared at her, too. A few moments passed. A motorcycle roared down Main, a bird twittered, and the wind blew Sandra's hair across her face. Kathy Lynn drew a deep breath, and her shoulders dropped. She put her other hand over her mother's, glancing from BJ to Sandra.

"My Mustang can take the curves on Highway 16 much better than Rex's pickup."

Sandra's cell phone rang. She glanced at it before answering. Erma was on the other end. "We have a verdict."

CHAPTER THIRTY-EIGHT

SANDRA HURRIED INTO the courtroom as the jurors were filing into the jury box. Except for the judge, all the other court participants were in place.

Mel grabbed Sandra's hand as she swept by her. Sandra gave it a shake. Erma crossed her fingers, her arms resting on the counsel table. Sandra mumbled under her breath, "Pull your hands down, Erma, so no one can see you do that." Rufina sat with her head bowed, her hands in a pose of prayer. Sandra touched her shoulder and whispered, "Rufina, switch chairs with Erma so you'll be standing between us when the verdict is read."

Rufina nodded and shuffled around Erma. Sandra leaned down. "Everything's going to be fine. You'll see."

Holt's cheeks were rounded in a smug expression. His associate entered just as the Deputy Cortez announced the judge. "All rise."

Sandra dropped her arms to her sides. Erma and Rufina stood at the same time. A squeak at the back of the room indicated the door opening. That would be BJ and Kathy Lynn and any onlookers who heard the verdict was about to be returned.

The inside of Sandra's mouth tasted like a dirty nickel. She slowed her breathing. While the judge settled into position, Sandra glanced at the juror's faces. Most of them would not look at her. But, the woman she'd argued to, the woman they'd pinned their hopes on, winked. Did that mean a not guilty verdict?

"Be seated," the judge muttered.

"Did you see that?" Sandra whispered to Rufina and Erma. "Our juror. Did you see her just now?"

They shook their heads. Erma held Rufina's hand. Rufina took a deep breath and shuddered. From behind them, Kathy Lynn said in a low voice, "Good luck, Rufina."

Sandra bit her lip. Her pits were damp, as was the back of her neck. She brushed her hair behind her ears.

"Jurors, I understand you've reached a verdict." The judge's eyebrows drew together. "Is that correct?"

Juror number three, who they'd figured out earlier was the presiding juror, stood. "Yes, Your Honor." He held the charge.

"Tender the charge to the bailiff, if you will." The judge peered over his glasses, his face grim.

The bailiff took the charge and carried it to the judge. The judge flipped to the back page. He looked down at the paper and back up at the jurors. His eyes ran back and forth, across the two rows of jurors. He looked down at the paper again.

Sandra's breath wouldn't come. Her heart raced. She hooked one of Rufina's fingers with one of her own and squeezed.

The judge leaned over and handed the charge to the clerk. The clerk stamped the first and last pages of the charge and wrote something on it. She glanced at the judge.

The judge nodded. "Would the defendant please stand?"

The three women at the defense table stood.

"Would the clerk read the verdict, please?"

The clerk recited the cause number and the style of the case.

Her heart continuing to thump hard, Sandra felt like Rosie the Riveter at work. She gritted her teeth.

The clerk glanced at Mr. Holt. Her eyes swept across the occupants of the defense table. She held the paper out before her. "We, the members of the jury, find the defendant, Rufina Barboza, not guilty."

A cacophony of deep inhalations arose from the defendant's side of the courtroom. Brushing the unintended tear off her cheek, Sandra finally expelled the breath she'd been holding. Rufina threw herself into Sandra's arms and hugged. Mel said in a very soft voice, "Mom. We won." Erma and BJ hugged over the bar.

Sandra released Rufina and peeked across the aisle. Holt looked like rigor mortis had set in. Sandra's eyes skirted to the jury. Several of them had her in their sights. When their eyes met, they smiled. Juror number twelve gave her a thumbs up. Sandra's heart raced again, but this time because her faith in her fellow Texans was restored. She acknowledged the jurors before turning her attention back to her side of the courtroom.

After a few minutes, the judge slapped the counter in front of him. "Settle down. Would either side like to have the jury polled?"

"No, thank you, Judge." Sandra's voice was so loud it echoed.

"No, Your Honor," Holt said in a firm, but quiet voice, his face pale.

The judge recited the required words to adopt the verdict and instructed the jury they were free to discuss or not discuss the verdict. He released Rufina from her bail. Moments later, he rushed away like a man on a mission. The clerk walked over to the jurors, slips of paper in her hands, and told them to exit the courtroom.

Sandra stepped across the aisle and shook Holt's hand, which was customary behavior. "You did as well as could be expected with the evidence you had."

"Congratulations." Holt dropped her hand. "I can't take the time to talk. I'm going to speak to the jurors briefly, and I have some additional business regarding this case to attend to."

Sandra raised her eyebrows.

"Don't worry. It doesn't concern your client."

"Mr. Burgess?"

"Yup. I hate to admit I'm as convinced as you that he was involved." He strode to the courtroom door, before turning back. "Safe travels back to the coast." The young assistant who had been in court the last few days gathered their files.

BJ and Kathy Lynn and Mel and Erma surrounded Rufina in a group hug. Sandra started to join them, but some movement from the back of the courtroom caught her eye. Jared. In a few long strides, he reached her, came past the bar, and wrapped his arms around her.

"Congratulations!"

He smelled like crisp, cool, country air and a bit of mesquite. She let him hold her against him for a few moments. Nothing ever felt so good. Relief overwhelmed her. She hadn't realized until then how much she'd been afraid of letting everyone down.

He released her, brushing his lips across her temple. "You did a great job."

She laid a hand on his chest and peered into his eyes. Still not sure what she was going to do about him, she wanted to relish the time they'd have together before she returned to Galveston, before spring turned into summer with its heat and humidity. "I was so scared. The evidence wasn't there to convict, but still, I was so scared."

Rufina wrapped her arms around Sandra, hugging her again. "I will forever be in your debt, Sandra." She sobbed into Sandra's chest.

Sandra rested her chin on top of Rufina's head, her arms around Rufina's shaking shoulders. "You're fine, Rufina. Everything is okay now."

"I will never forget you." Rufina clutched her tighter.

Sandra hugged her back. "Hey, I'm not disappearing into the night. I imagine I'll be coming to Fredericksburg every once in a while." Her eyes met Jared's. "When I do, I'll come by the ranch. You'll be there, won't you?"

Rufina stepped back and grasped Sandra's hands. "I thought of going to Mexico, to be with my family—my parents—Efrain, but I think I will stay here."

"Good. BJ will want you by her side for the rest of your lives."

"Yes. Billie J and I will keep running the ranch as we have been." Her smile sparkled in the fluorescent light as she let go of Sandra. She glanced at Jared before walking back to the other women.

"Are you and the other ladies planning on having a big cele-bration?" Jared guided her to where the others stood.

"We hadn't planned anything. But now I'm thinking we just might."

"Sandra," Erma said, "BJ is taking us all out to dinner. Afterward, let's pack up and get the heck out of Dodge at the crack of dawn tomorrow."

"I guess that answers your question," Sandra said to Jared. "Is Jared invited, BJ?" If he wasn't, she wasn't going.

"Sure," BJ said. "The whole world is invited." She turned to Rufina. "*Amiga*, call Efrain and ask him to come to the restaurant."

"Where're we going?" Jared slid his arm around Sandra's shoulders. "I'll need to go back to my office first and can meet y'all there later."

"Will's. Where else?" BJ's grin was so enormous, the wrin-kles in her leathery face looked more like pleats.

"Where else?" Sandra poked Jared in the side. "I need to pack up our stuff at your office, too."

"Will's...my favorite place," Jared said. "At least it has been for a while now."

Sandra tried to ignore the warm feeling caressing her insides at his statement. The relationship might not last, but she was going to squeeze every happy moment out of it while she could.

Mel hugged Sandra's neck. "Way to go, Mom. You're the best role model ever." She eyed Jared.

Sandra choked back a sob. She needed to leave before the dam burst. She didn't know why she felt so weepy, but, hell, who could control their feelings twenty-four seven? She kissed Mel on the cheek. "You're the best daughter ever," she whispered into Mel's ear. "By the way, this is Jared. I think you may have heard about him."

Mel nodded and looked sideways at him. "It's your office we've been using, but where have you been?"

"Keeping out of the way." He grinned, the smile wrinkles at the corners of his eyes crinkling. "Great to meet you."

Erma cupped her hands at each side of her mouth. "All right, everybody, let's take this mutual admiration society to the bar at Will's. I'm ready for a drink."

"Erma, call Patricia when you can and tell her about the verdict," Sandra said.

Mel touched Sandra's elbow. "I need to call my dad if I'm riding home with y'all instead of flying out of San Antonio tomorrow."

CHAPTER THIRTY-NINE

HOURS LATER, WHEN Sandra was lying against Jared's bare chest, Jared turned on his side. "So tell me, what do you think actually happened the night someone killed Katy Jo?"

"You're fantastic at post-coital conversation." She muffled a giggle.

He snorted. "Yeah, sorry." He ran his fingers up and down her arm.

She snuggled against him, reaching for his other hand. Soon she'd be gone. She wanted the night to last but knew she needed to go back to the ranch before morning and pack up. Mel needed to get ready for school on Monday. Erma and Sandra needed Sunday to catch up at the office before Monday morning.

"I do have my suspicions about what happened, of course. Pretty much what I implied in argument. You were there."

"For most of it, but not all."

"We'll probably never know for sure, but I believe Rex put Elgin up to it. Why, I'm not one-hundred percent sure. Unless Rex did it himself." Sandra shifted a bit to the side, so they were face-to-face.

Jared, his forehead drawn up almost in a knot, asked, "You think Rex would kill his sister?"

"That's right, I forgot, you don't know what Kathy Lynn told me while the jury was out."

"Something totally unexpected?"

"Enough so if the jury had found Rufina guilty, we would have been able to get a new trial." She sighed. "There may be more than she told, but now it's Mr. Holt's problem, not ours."

"I'm getting more confused by the minute. So who killed Katy Jo? And why?" He raised his eyebrows.

"I'm guessing Elgin." Her eyes met his. "Hold on. Here's what I think, now that I've talked to Kathy Lynn. I think Elgin wanted to marry BJ to combine her ranch with his and have the largest ranch in the Hill Country. I'm also wondering, after Erma's cross of him, whether he had financial problems and that was part of his motivation.

"So that night, Rex, who it turns out was the real culprit in the fire that killed Rufina's husband—"

"No way!"

"Yep, according to Kathy Lynn. Rex never liked Rufina because he was jealous of her relationship with his mother, and because he doesn't like Latinos—Mexicans, if you will." She pulled his arm tightly around her. "He didn't like Rufina bossing him around. He was a spoiled punk with a sense of entitlement. It was one thing for Rufina's parents, who were there before he was born, to look after him and tell him what to do, and another when Rufina took over."

"So he set fire to Rufina's house."

"He may have been showing off for his sisters, but ultimately, it caught fire. The fact that he was responsible for burning down the house, killing Rufina's husband, and scarring Rufina for life weighed heavily on even his blackened soul. He was reminded of it every time he saw her."

Jared rolled over and got out of bed. "How about a glass of wine, and you can finish this story in the kitchen."

Sandra let her eyes walk over his body as he pulled on some boxers. Shame she had to go home. "Coffee, for me. I have to drive back to the ranch."

She went into the bathroom, where she cleaned up. When she came out, she dressed while Jared took his turn. He returned in a navy-blue terrycloth bathrobe. They walked to the kitchen barefoot. Sandra perched on a bar stool while Jared made coffee.

"Go ahead," he said. "I'm listening."

A small ache made itself known in the vicinity of her heart. "So, this is what I think." She licked her lips. "Rex played on Elgin's desire to hook up with BJ, even though he would have interfered every way possible had his mother been interested. Anyway, over time, he convinced Elgin that Rufina and BJ were in a lesbian relationship. On the night of the shooting, he plied Elgin with drinks and convinced him to take a shot at Rufina when she was in BJ's bed. Of course, it was Katy Jo, not Rufina."

"He could have killed his mother." Jared set a cup in front of her and pulled up a bar stool.

"I know. I'm guessing, remember? Anyway, Rex provided the gun as well as the alcohol and you see what happened. With the amount they'd had to drink, it had to be a lucky, or unlucky, shot."

He tugged her bar stool closer to his. "That's nuts."

"Yes, but that's not what was really going on. I mean, that was part of it, but there was more to it. Here is where it gets complicated." She explained to him what Kathy Lynn had told her while the jury was out. "So there were several other possibilities going on as well."

"Like?"

"Like Rex somehow knew Katy Jo had gone in to talk to their mother about her relationship with Doug. In his intoxicated state, he thought she was going to tell BJ everything—about the fire and all. Katy Jo and BJ were really close. Or, he could have seen Katy Jo and thought she was Kathy Lynn going in to tell their mother everything that had gone on since they were kids. Or, Rex could have put Elgin in his truck and sent him home and took the gun and fired the shot himself."

"But you like the first theory?"

"That he set Elgin up to think he was shooting Rufina? Yes. For one thing, why do it yourself when someone else can do your dirty work? So, when it turned out to be Katy Jo, he did some quick reassessing and decided it'd be prime time to frame Rufina for the murder."

"My head is about to burst," Jared said. "TMI."

"Or too much alcohol this evening." She sipped her coffee. "Whatever happened, I'm glad the trial is over and Rufina's free."

Jared smiled at her over his cup. "Me, too. And I have news for you. BJ told me about Efrain. I found him outside the courthouse. He told me his story. I'm going to find him an immigration lawyer, so he can get a green card."

"That'll be hard to do in this climate."

He flashed his eyes, his smile bordering on wicked. "I represent a lot of businesspeople in this area—government officials and people who want homes in the Hill Country and—"

"Okay, I believe you." She slid down from the bar stool. "Between you and BJ, I believe y'all can pull some strings, and I hope you do. Efrain was prepared to jeopardize his future to protect Rufina. He deserves a chance to live in this country."

Jared took her arm. "So you have to leave?"

"I do."

"But you'll come up sometimes?"

"Yes, and you'll come down this summer and visit me, and we can do all kinds of beachy things. I'll take you to hear some wonderful musicians late at night in downtown Galveston—"

He stopped her with a kiss. She was going to miss moments like these. They hadn't had as many as she would have liked. She placed the hand that was coffee-free on the back of his neck and pressed his head to her. When they separated, they stood nose-to-nose, eye-to-eye, and her insides melted. Finally, she stepped back.

"I'm going to get my things and go."

"Am I invited to breakfast at the ranch this morning?"

"No. It'll be hectic out there. Let's say our goodbyes now." She started toward the bedroom for her shoes and jacket.

He followed her. "All right, but I'm not saying goodbye. Just so long for now." He grabbed her from behind and twirled her around and planted another kiss on her mouth.

CHAPTER FORTY

WHEN SANDRA AROSE later that morning, after only a few hours' sleep, she dressed in jeans with a shirt and sneakers. She wanted to take a run, but it was past time to depart. They were already behind schedule. She tossed the rest of her clothes in a bag and went into the kitchen for coffee and breakfast.

Sitting at the bar in the kitchen were Erma, Mel, Kathy Lynn, and Douglas Christian. BJ and Rufina stood near the stove. All of them were fully dressed in various styles of casual clothing and engaged in an animated discussion.

"There's our sleeping beauty," Erma said. "Our princess. No, our heroine."

"Woo hoo!" they yelled.

"Don't give yourself short shrift, Erma." If she'd ever seen a happier collection of faces, Sandra couldn't remember when.

"Hungry, Sandra?" Rufina picked up a plate and stepped over to the stove.

"Starving. I need some coffee first, though." She poured herself a cup and scanned the faces around her. Something was different. Douglas Christian's bar stool stood awfully close to Kathy Lynn's. Was something developing between them?

Everyone laughed. Sandra wanted in on the joke.

"The sheriff called this morning," Erma said. "Ed and Holt went out after the trial and brought in Elgin Burgess for questioning."

Sandra took her coffee to the bar and bumped Mel's hip with her own. "You're young. You can stand."

Mel hopped off the bar stool. "I've heard all this, so I'm going to finish packing. Good morning, Sandra." She pecked her mother on the cheek.

"Don't start that Sandra stuff again, young lady," Sandra said. "The trial is over. You're going back to being a student and a half-day helper in the office. I'm Mom to you."

"All right, Mom." Mel giggled as she bounced away.

"So what did the sheriff allow?" Sandra gulped down a large mouthful of coffee. The warmth trickled down, helping her perk up. She only hoped it would be enough pick-me-up to make her a reliable driver.

Rufina set a plate of scrambled eggs, bacon, sausage, two biscuits, and a dish of honey in front of her. "Mr. Burgess did it." The circumference of her dark eyes, well, one of them, was about as big around as the biscuits. She wiped her hands on her apron and turned back to the stove. "Why did Rex hate me so much?"

BJ put an arm around Rufina's shoulders.

Sandra had guessed right. Rex had convinced Burgess to do the deed. "What else did the sheriff say? Wait a minute." She pointed at Erma. "You said Ed, as in Sheriff Ed Krichman, I presume."

Erma's chin jutted out. "So what if I did?"

"Ed? When did he become Ed?"

"When he called me this morning and asked me to go to breakfast." Erma was primping like a robin in a birdbath.

Sandra shook her head. "Obviously, you didn't go."

"No, told him we were in a hurry to get home this evening before too late but convinced him to clue me in over the phone."

"Uh-huh."

"He's going to come down to Galveston the next time he's got a day off." She gave Sandra a meaningful look accompanied by a wry smile. "We'll have breakfast then. Ha!"

Sandra chuckled. "All right. You can tell me those details on the way home."

BJ said, "Maybe Ed and Jared can ride together."

"Maybe." Sandra dug into her breakfast while Erma and BJ filled her in on what the sheriff had said. Turned out, her guess was right. Elgin was so drunk, he let Rex put the gun in his hand and walk him to the door of BJ's bedroom. Rex opened it, Elgin held the gun out, and fired. An unbelievable shot. Rex hurried him out the front door and shoved him in his truck and told him to take off. Rex must have thrown the gun on the path to Rufina's cottage.

Kathy Lynn added, "I'm pretty sure Rex thought I was in there telling Mama on him. Only he made Elgin think it was Rufina."

Doug slipped an arm around her shoulders. "Who would ever think something like this would happen?"

BJ had come around the bar and stood close to Kathy Lynn, stroking her hair. "It's okay. How could you have known?"

Sandra took small bites so she could swallow and talk. "Kathy Lynn, for the longest time I thought you were Katy Jo and you were pretending to be Kathy Lynn until this was all over."

Kathy Lynn dabbed at her watery eyes. "I would give any-thing if that were true."

Sandra still wasn't sure she'd gotten the whole story, but if something had been left out, she didn't need to know. She had more than done her job. She wanted to go back to Galveston where country folk—who, God love 'em, were all right—were few and far between.

Swallowing a last bite, she stepped off the stool. She shook Doug's hand, stroked Kathy Lynn's back, and kissed BJ and Rufina on the cheek. "Time to go. Y'all come see us sometime."

Mel came from down the hall, dragging their roller bags. "I've got both of ours. I'll go put them in the car."

Erma said, "Mine are already out there." She turned to BJ. "Listen, darlin', if you ever need me again, you know where to find me." They hugged, then Erma hugged Rufina. "*Adios, amiga*." She turned to Doug and Kathy Lynn, "Best of luck to you kids. Come on, Sandra. Let's saddle up."

They walked out of the house together. Sandra got behind the wheel. She'd drive until she was too tired, then switch with Erma. Mel climbed into the back seat. She hung out of the window and waved to everyone. Sandra raced the Volvo's engine. They needed to leave if they wanted to miss Houston rush hour traffic. Maybe while they were driving, she could make Erma understand why it was important to learn how to operate their computer, why she needed to enter the twenty-first century. Maybe she could entice Erma by telling her she'd be able to have private emails with Sheriff Ed...

THANK YOU FOR READING!

If you enjoyed reading *Death of a Rancher's Daughter*, I would appreciate it if you would help others to enjoy this book, too.

Recommend it. Please help others find this book by recommending it to friends, readers' groups, and discussion boards.

Review it. Please tell other readers why you liked this book by reviewing it online wherever you received your copy, on social media, and your website.

If you do write a review, please send me an email at susan@susanpbaker.com so I can thank you with a personal note.

If you would like to be on my mailing list so you can receive news of upcoming events and publications, go to www.susanpbaker.com.

ABOUT THE AUTHOR

Susan P. Baker, a retired Texas District Court Judge, is the award-winning author of nine novels, all with a legal bent. Three are the Mavis Davis Mystery series, featuring an uncensored Houston P.I. and her wacky staff. The other five novels were stand-alones, all but one with female protagonists—lawyers, judges, or litigants caught up in the justice system. The first book in what is now her Lady Lawyer Mystery Series, was *Death of a Prince*, first published in hardcover by Five Star Mysteries in 2005.

Susan has also published two nonfiction books: *Murdered Judges of the 20th Century* and *Heart of Divorce, Advice from a Judge*.

Susan is a member of Texas Authors, Authors Guild, Sisters in Crime, Alliance of Independent Authors, and Galveston Novel and Short Story Writers. She is delighted to be the proud mother of two daughters and grandmother of eight children, ages 10 to 28.

Read more about Susan and sign up for her mailing list for newsletters and other offers at www.susanpbaker.com.

Like her at www.facebook.com/legalwriter

Follow her on Twitter www.twitter.com/Susanpbaker

Instagram: www.instagram.com/suewritesandreads